LOOKING FOR LUCY

JANE E JAMES

For M
God bless...

They buried my body
And they thought I'd gone,
But I am the dance,
And I still go on.

LUCY

My name is Lucy Valentine, and I have been missing for thirty-one days. I can count to 100, and I am eight on my next birthday. When I am not here, I live at Moon Hollow with my mummy and daddy. I know I am not supposed to, but I like Daddy best. He calls me Lulu for short and makes me laugh, which makes Mummy pull a face.

The things I miss most about home are my doll Heidi and my treehouse. I do not go to school like other children, which means I play on my own a lot. I used to feel sad about this, but that only made Mummy cross. She said I was lucky because not everybody got to be home educated like me. I know now that Mummy was wrong. I am not lucky at all.

I was playing in the treehouse the day *it* happened. That is how the miniature china tea set that daddy had bought me got broken, but I was a good girl and did not cry about it until afterwards – not until I realised Heidi had got left behind.

I

Heidi's hair and eyes are brown, like mine. I am the only one in my family with dark hair. Mummy used to bleach it, to make it appear lighter, until Daddy made her stop. They did not talk for a long time after that. Heidi's hair used to be long, but I snipped it off to match my own after Mummy insisted on getting mine cut. "Unkempt" she called my hair, but I still do not know what that means. All I know is I miss Heidi more than my long hair.

I do not like it here. I am made to sit still for hours so I can be drawn, which is hard to do and boring. Some days I cry, but nobody passes me a handkerchief or tells me to be a big girl. There is nothing nice to eat, and no one remembers to brush my hair.

My name is Lucy Valentine, and I have been missing for thirty-one days. I can count to 100, and I am eight on my next birthday. I would very much like to go home now.

1

CINDY

Without telling anyone, I have, as I've been instructed to do, left my life behind to come here. It doesn't matter that my life's already in ruins. It's still my life. Or *was*. Now I'm missing from it, as surely as Lucy Valentine is missing from hers.

Instead of concentrating on my reason for being here, *looking for Lucy*, I'm wondering if my coldhearted mother, Esther, will shed a tear when she realises her only daughter has disappeared. In all honestly I doubt she'll notice. Catching myself in time, I realise I'm doing it again. That Cindy thing. Behaving like a needy brat when I'm a grown woman with a child of my own. I'm only twenty-eight, so I sometimes find it hard to accept I'm already mother to an eight-year-old.

Not much of a mother, I remind myself harshly. On that sobering thought, I approach the imposing metal gates belonging to Moon Hollow and get a familiar feeling. A sense that I've been here before.

I know something about the house's history, having

googled it on the bus journey here. Built as a castle in the sixteenth century, it was later demolished and rebuilt as the manor house it is today. From what I've seen of the surrounding Fenland countryside that they call Hollow Fen, it's depressingly flat, as Cambridgeshire is famous for, consisting mainly of ugly farm cottages that weren't built to be admired. Unlike Moon Hollow, which has a faded grandeur all of its own.

A dilapidated gatehouse, empty of panes of glass and crawling with ivy, guards the main house, and beyond it acres of parkland are dotted with black-and-white horses who never once lift their heads. Lifting the latch to the side gate, I give it a feeble nudge, but it resists as much as I do. Once I walk through it, there's no turning back. Knowing I don't have any choice, I push the gate again, and this time it swings open without a creak or groan. Noises I'd felt certain of hearing. The absence of such sound effects, however, does nothing to lessen my panic.

The creeping sensation that I've been here before persists. I feel it in my bones. In every part of my body. Convinced that the gate could yet slam shut behind me, imprisoning me in the grounds of this spooky old mansion, I'm relieved to hear the reassuring whisper of its latch settling in place. Somebody must've recently oiled those gates, yet everywhere around me suffers from an air of neglect. As if somebody had fallen out of love with the house and left without a backward glance.

That's what I should do. Turn my back on Moon Hollow and the questions that lie in wait behind its ditch-water-grey windows. Questions I've no hope of answering. How on earth can I be expected to find someone else's missing child when all I can think about is my own? I have failed my daughter, Grace, miserably, but because of her, I'll stay and see this thing through. For as long as it takes. For as long as the Valentines need me.

Conjuring up Grace's face, which gives me the courage I lack, I take my first tentative steps on the gravel drive that snakes its way up to the steps at the front of the house. I try to picture Grace's face at least once a day. Sometimes I find it harder than others. How long has it been? Six weeks? It feels more like six months. Six years.

So much for having psychic abilities when I couldn't prevent what happened to my daughter. *I didn't even see that night coming.* People say I got what I deserved, but they're wrong. If that were true, I would be as dead on the outside as I am on the inside. I don't need reminding that I'm a useless mother, a terrible one, but I can't change the past. Nor can I alter the fact that I'm a pretender of the worst kind. Everything from my orange tan to my blond and red dip-dyed hair and scarlet fingernails is false, which means people are right to label me a fake. Hasn't the press already proven that?

I must focus on what *is* important – the people who blackmailed me into coming here. I should look about me, try to take things in. Get a feel for the place. Isn't that what proper psychics do? Isn't that what the Valentines expect of me?

Fuck them, I think. But I'll do as I've been told. For Grace's sake.

To my right there's a creepy cemetery, where untended graves hide amongst creeping thistles. An oak tree throws gloomy shadows over the grass, making shapes that seem to want to hold hands. I don't stray too close to the old bones in the ground, just in case! It must be hell having dead neighbours. Moon Hollow might be a grand old house, but I wouldn't swap it for my tiny two-bed terrace.

I'm not interested in the countryside or wildlife, yet I'm drawn to a swarm of honeybees that cling to the trunk of the oak tree. The bees are crowding around a resting queen, who rules from somewhere inside the mass of moving workers, and a sickly sweet smell fills my nostrils – extracts from whatever flowers the bees last foraged on. But it's the queen's powerful pheromone that catapults me into her world.

As images of orange bodies burst like flash photography across my mind, I become aware of a sense of physical contact with the colony, of antennae tickling my skin. I understand the frustrations of the sterile female workers and the queen's unquestionable dominance over them all. Without wanting to, I see what will happen to the colony in three days' time. Their destruction. Brought about by a masked human administering a cloud of poisonous dust.

Having trespassed into the bees' peaceful world, I leave it feeling responsible for their fate. No matter how much I tell myself that I'm not to blame, that there's nothing I can do, I find I must guiltily drag my eyes from the swarm.

I've never told anyone how often I'm plagued with such visions. They occur a lot more than I let on. It's safer for me not to get involved, because when I do warn someone that something bad is about to happen to them, I end up being blamed for it. Often, people grow to hate me, imagining I have some power or hold over their life. That's why I remain silent. A habit I'm about to break, I realise grimly. Knowing that it's impossible to give people the answers they want, this makes my undertaking at Moon Hollow even more dangerous.

Deciding that I can't put off the dreaded moment any longer, I trudge towards the house, not liking the prickly touch of its shadow on my skin. At the bottom of the concrete steps that lead up to the house, two lions made from stone are waiting to greet me. Coming to a standstill, I tilt back my head and gaze up at the house I fear even before stepping foot inside it. The walls are a cancerous shade of yellow, brightened only by the royal-blue blooms of wisteria that hang like dusty grapevines over the majestic double doors.

So, this is Moon Hollow. The house I'm going to share with strangers. Sensing I'm being watched from one of the windows that look down on the driveway, I feel a sharp, stabbing pain behind my right eye. It's a familiar symptom. One I know well.

Somewhere inside those walls, my blackmailer waits. A woman who, like me, is in danger of losing a child forever. But unlike me, Jane Valentine fears nothing and nobody.

2

JANE

As if they were a pair of identical bookends, John and Jane Valentine stand at either end of the long line of sash windows that peer menacingly down on the drive. Without once gazing at each other, they watch Cindy approach the house, but only Jane notices that *the girl*, as she has come to think of her, has her eyes down as if scared of glancing up. John is oblivious to everything but a pretty face and pert bosom. Cindy certainly impresses in both areas.

On the galleried landing behind Jane is a collection of portraits that feature the same fair-haired, fair-skinned family with uniformly pale, cold eyes. The Valentines' likeness to the people in the portraits is uncanny, but John has the kinder eyes of the two. There is something odd and dated about the couple, as if they live in a different era. Jane has an aristocratic air with mother-of-pearl skin and elegant, swanlike hair. She wears matronly clothes to disguise her womanly curves, while John, in a blazer and open-necked shirt, is handsome in a public-schoolboy way he has never managed to grow out of.

'We cannot possibly have that woman come to live here,' John accuses Jane.

'My mind is quite made up. I will not be persuaded otherwise.' Jane does not turn to look at her husband but continues to press her cheek against the cold stone wall. Nobody looking at her could guess what she is thinking – that she has already seen enough of Cindy Martin to know she was right to hate her from the start.

Jane feels no shame in the fact that she repeatedly stalked Cindy, had in fact blackmailed her into coming to Moon Hollow to help them find Lucy. Cindy's refusal at first had staggered Jane, made her doubt in the godliness of others, but when Cindy, who was not in a fit state of mind at the time, told Jane about her situation with the courts and everything, Jane saw this as an opportunity and selfishly grabbed at it. After promising to help Cindy get her child back from the authorities and offering to act as a guardian by placing the child under her roof, something no one else was prepared to do, Cindy eventually came round to the idea of helping them.

John had complained, of course, and tried to get Jane to stop "this madness" until at last she grew suspicious about his motives. Jane admitted to having doubts too, especially concerning the business of Cindy's child, but she felt she had no choice. Everyone, including the police, had given up on Lucy by that stage. Only a psychic could help them now.

'What if she doesn't help us?' John's voice intrudes on Jane's thoughts, nudging her into the present.

'Then we will send her back to where she came from.'

In the silence that follows, when all they can hear is the faint crunch of Cindy's shoes ploughing through the gravel, Jane looks at John. 'You still think the police will find her, don't you?'

'Don't you? Jesus Christ, Jane. Sometimes you act as if you don't want Lucy found.'

'I want her back just as much as you.' Jane narrows her eyes. 'I've invested almost eight years in her development.'

'Invested! Development!' John laughs bitterly. 'Is this how a distraught mother talks?'

Jane ignores the insult as if John's low opinion of her does not matter. This seems to exasperate him further. Without trying to stop him, Jane watches him storm towards the winding stone staircase that looks down on the three floors below. Before reaching the first step, he pauses, as if he might be preparing to hurl himself down them. Jane knows her husband better than that. He is too much of a coward to do the right thing. When he looks back at her, she notices real fear in his eyes.

'What if she suspects me as the police did?' he asks hesitantly.

'But I told her everything,' Jane insists.

'Not everything.' John wags a finger in her direction. 'You haven't told her everything.'

3

CINDY

I've never been inside a drawing room before – at least that's what I'm told it is – but it's much like a normal living room, really, only grander. The bright sunlight oozing in through the multiple windows stings my eyes, but that doesn't prevent me from noticing the polished piano top, which has a silver-framed photograph of a sad-faced girl on it. *Lucy.*

I can hardly believe I'm here, perched awkwardly on the edge of a chaise longue, facing John and Jane Valentine, who sit apart from each other on a sofa, appraising me. The echo of a ticking clock is the only sound in the room. The silence unnerves me.

Sensing that I'm likely to break the paper-thin china cup and saucer I'm holding in my trembling hands, Jane smiles frostily at me before relieving me of it.

'Would you like to see Lucy's bedroom now?' Jane is curt, straight to the point.

'Not until Grace arrives.' I swallow nervously.

'Can't you start looking now?' John complains.

'That's not what we agreed,' I say to Jane, feeling cornered.

John is on his feet at once, raking a hand through his floppy, boyish hair and rolling his eyes. 'You're a mother yourself. Do you have any idea what we are going through?'

It's my turn to rise. 'I'm only here because I *am* a mother and I *do* know what you're going through, but until you help me get my child back, then I'm sorry, I can't help you find yours.'

There. I said it. I never thought I would have the courage to stand up to the pair of them. Here, amongst these rich, educated people, I'm out of my depth.

'You don't trust us, is that it?' John slouches back on the couch, looking resigned.

He's taking more of a lead than I expected when we all know who's really in charge. I don't understand why Jane isn't saying more. She wasn't this silent when she sought me out and asked, no, *demanded* that I help them.

'If you didn't need my help, there's no way you'd be helping somebody like me,' I say shakily, trying not to sound too judgmental. 'As soon as my daughter arrives, I'll do everything in my power to help you find yours. But not before.'

I watch John shake his head in disgust and then scowl at his wife before lurching to his feet again.

'How do we know you *can* help us?' he growls, pacing up and down the room. Then to Jane he says, 'She might be a fake, for all we know. Like the papers said.'

I feel the tears building. They're never far away. 'I didn't ask to come here,' I tell him. 'I would never have got involved again if it weren't for...' I pause for a moment, unable to meet Jane's cold eyes, and so I plead with her husband instead.

'I'm not a fake. But there are no guarantees. Sometimes I get things wrong, and it can be dangerous. An innocent man died because of me.'

4

Then

Eyes you never want to meet. Bulging beneath papery thin eyelids – hiding a story you never want to hear. A prisoner, hard to age due to the purplish tinge to his skin, is sprawled on the floor next to an iron bed that has been stripped of everything except a stained mattress.

Prisoner 335 does not swing from side to side as you would imagine a suicide victim would. Hanging is impossible in a modern prison facility like this, as there are no high bars to attach anything to. Instead, the rolled-up sheet around his neck has been tied to the end of the bed frame, and he slumps grotesquely on the floor at the end of it, head lolling loosely to one side. He could have stopped any time he wanted to. But chose instead to die.

His last image on earth would have been the shit-stained toilet. Too bad he didn't take a piss before deciding to slowly suffocate himself. He's now wet himself. The stench of urine, along with cannabis, is everywhere. The landings outside are deadly silent. Nobody listens. Nobody cares. Bloated and blue, with milky eyes that can no longer roam where they are not wanted, was this person ever human, you ask yourself? It's easy to convince yourself he's the kind of person you don't know, but he is your son, your husband; he is everywhere. He may live in your street or next door. A friendly neighbour who has already offered to take out your bins or give your daughter a lift home from school.

His face is so distorted he would be unrecognisable to his own family. But he does have one distinguishable feature that will provide the coroner with a positive ID – a tattoo of a large black cross that takes up the length of one vein-stretched arm.

5

CINDY

Now

J ohn and Jane are on their feet, standing close enough to hold hands but somehow resisting that urge as they stare with incredulity at me. I've seen this look enough times to recognise it for what it is. Disgust. Horror. Fear.

'It was all my fault.' Tears spill down my cheeks as I undo my halter-neck top and lift my wild, tangled hair out of the way to expose the burn mark around my neck. I don't explain how it got there because I have no idea. All I know is it appeared there, all by itself, around the same time that Adam Lockwood took his own life. 'I made a mistake. Got the wrong man,' I confess.

I close my eyes, not wanting to see the face of the man I wrongly accused of murder and whose death I'm responsible for. In this self-imposed darkness, my senses come to life. Outside, I hear the rustle of the trees, the hum of the poor bees, and something else, a whisper, a passing promise of a familiar song. I crick my head and focus on the sound. It's a man's voice. Throaty and deep and somehow full of self-righteousness, but I was wrong before. It's not a song but a hymn. A well-known hymn.

"Dance, then, wherever you may be, I am the Lord of the Dance, said he."

The sound disappears when John's less-than-subtle coughing intrudes on the silence. Concentration broken, my eyes flash open, and I can tell by the way Jane is looking at the floor, and not at the mark around my neck, that she's disturbed by my admission. I won't let this stop me. They deserve to know the truth.

'I can still feel him slumped there, gasping for breath, slowly dying, not wanting to save himself, because of me.'

6

I wake up sensing that something isn't right. At first, I've no idea where I am. Then, I remember I'm at Moon Hollow. That I was summoned to this cold and indifferent house by the Valentines to find their daughter. As I recall what I'm here to do, I feel panic rising inside me. There's nothing I can do to stop it. I've woken from one nightmare only to fall into another because there's a shadowy, child-sized shape sitting at the bottom of my bed.

Its head is cricked in my direction, observing me with eyes I can't see. I think I'm incapable of doing anything except feeling fear and shock, but when it extends one arm and its short grubby fingers crawl across the bed towards me, I open my mouth to scream, only nothing comes out.

I hit the switch on the wall, and light suddenly floods the room. It takes another second for me to grasp that the small dark figure is no longer on the bed, but its indentation on the cover remains. Throwing off the tangled bedclothes, I fall clumsily out of bed, desperate to escape in case the ghostly figure reappears.

It occurs to me then that it could be elsewhere in the room. Hiding under the bed! Not daring to look, I hug myself for comfort and stay in the middle of the room, where I feel safest. Gradually, my breathing returns to normal, as does my heart rate. I think it's gone. But what was it? Could it have been Lucy Valentine? Trying to tell me something. Wanting me to know where to find her. Or was it Grace? Haunting me. Wanting me to pay for what I did to her.

After seeing the hopelessly small, lonely figure on the bed, the room seems even bigger than it did last night when Jane first showed it to me. It looks the same, but it feels different.

You hadn't been drinking then, Cindy, my inner voice taunts.

I'm at my most relaxed after having a drink, and usually I'm hit with all kinds of visions when that happens. I'm often left feeling as if I've been involved in a car crash.

Oh God, there's that word. I can't go there yet. I'm not ready.

But could the half bottle of gin I polished off before going to bed really be the reason for me seeing an apparition of a little girl, who might or might not have been Lucy? Right from the start, Jane had insisted I give up drinking while under her roof, and I'd agreed to her terms, *all of them*, knowing I wouldn't stick to any of them. But what Jane doesn't know is that alcohol helps me to see things. Things she may *want* me to see.

While I'm no longer the alcoholic she thinks I am, it's

true that booze doesn't always agree with me. It affects my judgement. Makes me reckless. I know the oblivion I've sought from drink in the past isn't the answer. I've only got to think back to what happened on the night of the accident to know this.

7

Then

The minidress comes too far up my thighs. I try to pull down the hem, but it rolls further up. I swear anybody walking by will be able to see my pants. My fake-tanned limbs have ugly streaks on them, and my stiletto heels are scuffed, not the must-have fashion accessory I thought they were. This makes me wonder how many treats Grace missed out on so I could buy them. It's fitting that my feet should hurt like hell from wearing them.

Nobody knows what I've done. That's why the doctors and nurses are being kind to me. When the truth comes out, they'll want to lynch me. Or worse. The nurse leaning over Grace's hospital bed looked sad when I admitted I had no one to call. I have no doting mother or protective older brother to support me through the worst night of my life. That doesn't mean I don't have a mother or brother; I have both, but not ones I can count on. I could call Dad, of course, but what with Mum and everything, he already has enough on his plate. It wouldn't be fair to burden him with this too.

My eyes are red from crying, and mascara runs down my over-made-up cheeks, but for once I don't care. When I look at the bruising and grazing on Grace's face, I feel such deep shame I want to vomit. But if I get in any more trouble, they'll throw me out of the room again, as they did earlier when I wouldn't, *couldn't* calm down when asked.

Somebody lent me a bobble so I could scrape my unruly hair into a ponytail, and a thin blanket has been thrown over my shoulders, I suspect more to cover my exposed cleavage than anything else. It feels like a cold hug, the sort my mother would give, but only if she had to. I watch the nurse shining a torch into my daughter's once brilliant blue eyes and pray that she'll wake up soon. I dare not ask for more information, because when I do, the nurses shake their heads. The look on their faces puts the fear of God in me.

'Lucy. Lucy.' The nurse is leaning over my daughter's hospital bed. Her long dark ponytail swishes cheerily, but her face is unsmiling. Although pretty, her eyes are serious, and her mouth is drawn into a thin line. The same nurse taps my daughter's lifeless hand. It has a scratch on it that they tell me is unconnected to her other injuries, but I don't know where it came from. *Shouldn't a mother know such things?*

I think about closing my eyes, concentrating hard, willing the knowledge to come to me, but, as always with Grace, it's impossible. I've never been able to read her as I can other people. I put this down to there being some sort of mother-and-daughter blind spot.

'Lucy. Can you hear me, Lucy?' the nurse calls again. I

can tell by the tremor in her voice that my daughter's condition worries her too. Grace, with her doll-like face, cupid's mouth, and yellow hair, has that effect on people. No number of monitors, drips, or oxygen masks can take that away from her. *She's my Grace, not yours*, I think petulantly, feeling jealous of the nurse's proximity to my daughter when I've been banished to a chair in the corner. *Shame I wasn't this possessive about my daughter before*, I can't resist thinking.

Sighing, because nothing is happening, I massage my head, hoping to erase the monster hangover that lives there. I want to curl into a ball and sleep it off, but one more look at Grace's deathly pale face is all the aspirin I need. Belatedly, I twig on to the fact that the nurse has repeatedly got my daughter's name wrong. This pisses me off big-time.

'She's not called Lucy. Her name's Grace.'

The nurse looks at me and frowns.

'That's what I *have* been calling her,' she says, shooting me a puzzled look.

8

Now

I must have known, even then, that I would become involved in the manhunt for Lucy Valentine. Why else would I have imagined the nurse getting my daughter's name wrong? All those weeks ago, Lucy's name kept creeping into my head, like a constant whisper, but I couldn't make sense of it at the time. The last thing I wanted was to be thinking about somebody else's child when my own was in danger, fighting for her life.

'Grace.' I stifle a sob, wishing I could hold her, see her. How could I have ever resented her? My own child. What a fucking idiot I was. I'm so pleased I'm not that person anymore.

Shit. Who am I kidding? The real Cindy is in here somewhere. People don't change. *For fuck's sake, stop beating yourself up.* My kinder self comes to the rescue, but I push her away. Just as I've pushed away anyone who's ever tried to help me.

Fighting back tears, I warn myself to keep my shit together even though I get the feeling that this is a bad room, a bad *house*. It has a vibe to it that I can't shrug off.

Knowing I won't fall back to sleep again, not on that bed, where it's all too easy to imagine somebody sitting on the end of it, I decide that I've no choice but to wait until it's light before I can escape this room. Instinctively guessing that Jane wouldn't want me exploring the house on my own at night, I take an interest in my surroundings for the first time. The blue room, as Jane calls it, is bigger than my whole house.

Each wall is taken up with white fitted wardrobes. As far as I know, they're empty. But, for some reason, I find myself not wanting to open any of them in case I'm wrong. That's why my small suitcase remains unopened at the foot of the bed. I'm surprised Jane didn't send in a maid last night to unpack it for me.

Then I remember that John told me they don't employ any staff. Which means there are fewer people I can ask about Lucy. Parents rarely tell the truth about their children. I know this better than most. So, it would have been useful to have other people to question to get a sense of who Lucy was. It's weird, though, that they don't have any help for a house this size. I wonder who does the cleaning. I can't picture Jane getting her hands dirty.

Cindy.

The whisper of a young woman's voice in a foreign accent I can't place reaches me as one of the wardrobe doors pops silently open.

A cold flow of air wraps itself around me and lingers on my skin like a hand might. I shiver with cold, yet my palms are clammy with sweat. Before I know what I'm doing, my toes point in a direction my gut tells me I shouldn't take.

Cindy.

That voice. That sound.

I feel it entering my body, taking me over until I'm two people. One I know. The other I don't. Not yet. Closing my eyes for a second, I hear an accompanying heavy, laboured breathing and feel the swell of my chest as I take a step forward. Then another. The temptation to follow that voice is so strong I can't fight it. *Don't do it, Cindy,* I tell myself. *Don't go any closer. You know something isn't right here in this room. You've felt it all night. First the child on the bed, and now this.*

The smell of anaesthetic, heavy in the air, weakens me and makes me feel sluggish, as if I can't possibly take another step. It feels like the stuff is pumping around my veins, faster than adrenalin. It makes me want to lie down and go to sleep. Blinking rapidly, I force myself to swing open the wardrobe door. I must know what, *who,* is inside.

I gasp in shock when I see that the wardrobe is empty. This is the last thing I expected, as I could have sworn there was a presence of some kind waiting on the other side of the door. *Perhaps I'm as bad a psychic as everyone says I am.* Then, I notice that it's not quite as empty as I thought. There's a single velvet coat hanger inside, which smells heavily of mothballs. *That explains the anaesthetic smell.* It hangs from a metal rail above my head.

When I push it aside, it taps against the hollow-sounding interior of the wardrobe, revealing a gap in the wood panelling. Groping in the dark, my fingers find the edge of the gap, and when I push against it, it slides open to reveal a hidden door. Beyond it, dusty wooden steps lead up an unlit stairwell.

That's when I see it.

The imprint of a fast-vanishing footstep heading up the stairs.

That's when I hear it.

Cindy.

As I'm about to climb the stairs, the lights in the bedroom flicker, and a door slams shut somewhere in the house. The flush of water along the landing convinces me that either Jane or John is on the move, and that's enough to send me running back to the bed, which suddenly seems a lot less scary than before, and throwing myself on it. Once there, I hide my face in the pillow and keep my eyes shut, ignoring the sharp, stabbing pain behind my eye.

9

JANE

Blowing her nose, Jane frowns at her reflection in the mirrored tiles that take up the length of the bathroom wall, strategically placed so that John can admire his physique before plunging into an ice-cold shower. For once, she does not fret over her husband's propensity for vanity and self-indulgence. She has other fish to fry, as the saying goes. Try as she might, she cannot get the smell of that girl's cheap perfume from her nostrils.

Despite it being a warm night, Jane wears a floor-length dressing gown buttoned up to her throat but still finds herself shivering. This is nothing new. She has suffered from a lack of warmth her entire life. She has lost count of the number of times she has been accused of being cold and hard-hearted, mostly by John. But what does he know? He is just a man when all is said and done. Hardly a step up from a dog in the grand scheme of things.

Does she love him? She is not sure it matters anymore. She certainly does not trust him. Never has. She knows what he gets up to behind her back with other women.

Nothing gets by her. But they will never part. She and John. They are bound together forever.

Earlier, when she had crept out of bed, careful not to disturb him, she had stood looking at him, desperately wanting to bring something heavy crashing down on his head. She wondered what his split-open skull would look like, how much mess there would be.

Not that she ever would do such a thing, mind, but it is not as if he does not deserve it. Part of her wants him to pay for what he has done. To her. To all of them.

When Jane comes back into the bedroom, she is surprised to find John awake. Usually, he does not stir once his head hits the pillow. Jane, on the other hand, spends most nights tossing and turning, haunted by Lucy's face. She resents John's ability to sleep peacefully, especially after what happened. Out of all of them, he is the one who least deserves to rest.

John does not watch her unbutton her dressing gown, nor does he say anything when it drops to the floor, although she is standing naked in front of him. They have been together too long for her body to have any fascination for him. But Jane is not naked for his sake. She would not stoop so low. Despite being susceptible to the cold, she has never been able to sleep unless she is completely nude.

'What are we meant to do about her child?' John asks as Jane slides into the bed beside him, keeping her distance as always, making sure they do not touch.

Jane replies matter-of-factly, 'We will cross that bridge when we come to it.'

10

CINDY

Having woken with the worst hangover and promising myself that I'll never drink again, *not a single bloody drop*, I stare at my red-eyed reflection in the bathroom cabinet mirror and fight back a fresh wave of nausea. I feel as though I'm burning up. My hands are shaking too, as if from a fever. Massaging my queasy tummy, I don't need to be a psychic to know what comes next. When I feel my stomach contract, I get down on my knees, lean over the toilet bowl and throw up the remains of yesterday's chicken nugget meal.

Last night I told myself that the bottle of gin – "mother's ruin" they call it, rather ironically – I'd hidden under my pillow was a one-off. I wasn't going back to my old ways. I just needed a good night's sleep. Difficult enough in this creepy old house, especially after what I saw and heard, or thought I saw and heard in my bedroom. The memory of the child on the bed and the voice calling from up those stairs sends a shiver down my spine even now.

Oh God, here I go again. When I'm done, I flush the

toilet and watch the signs of my relapse wash away. I'm so thirsty I'd lap straight from the toilet bowl if I had to, so I run the taps, which screech in protest before pumping out a dribble of dirty grey water. As I wait for the water to run clear, I notice that the marbled tiles are as bloodshot as my eyes, causing me to groan out loud. I'm not looking my best.

Now that it's morning and light, I can admit to being a tad melodramatic about the whole ghost-on-the-bed, door-opening, strange-woman-calling-up-the-stairs incidents. In a house as old as this, it's probably normal for things to go bump in the night. Despite all my protestations, I was able to go back to sleep in the end.

Thirst getting the better of me, I cup some water into my hands and drink greedily. When I straighten up, I see a reflection in the mirrored cabinet that isn't my own.

A young woman with a purple birthmark running down one side of her cheek is staring at me. Backing away, swallowing fear and bile in equal quantities, I fumble for the door handle behind me, but I'm unable to tear my eyes away from the woman's haunted expression as her eyes lock with mine. Her long black hair hangs lankly around her shoulders, and the shadows under her eyes suggest she has not slept in days, weeks.

Sinking to my knees, I turn my head into the wall. 'Make it go away.' I whimper, groping again for the door handle that simply won't open although I know I didn't lock it behind me.

Seconds pass. White noise. A silence I can't endure. *Nobody could.* I can't hear my own breathing. Yet I know it's coming fast and furious out of my mouth.

I've no choice but to take another look. I must know if

what I saw in the mirror is real. *How can it be real, Cindy?* Praying that the apparition is no longer there – gone forever, with a bit of luck – I approach on tiptoe, terrified of what I might see. When I'm finally brave enough to peer into the glass door, I'm relieved to see my own reflection looking back at me. The woman has vanished. Only I am left behind.

I convince myself that what I saw was due to an overactive imagination, brought on by the half bottle of gin I knocked back last night. *No more drinking for you, Cindy girl. Ever.* But when I see a trickle of blood running out of my nostril, I know the drink isn't to blame. Nosebleeds accompanied by a tingling sensation in the middle of my forehead and a throbbing in my eye mean only one thing. The woman is real. A vision of some kind, yes, but of someone who once lived and who now has a story to tell. A story she wants me to hear.

But who is she?

11

_____

When I come back into the bedroom, I don't take my eyes off the wardrobe in case the door opens again. Even as I sit down at the gilt-edged dressing table, intent on making myself look half decent, *less hungover*, for Jane's sake, I keep looking at the wardrobe over my shoulder. Scraping my hair into a ponytail, I peer at my sick-looking reflection, thinking that I shall never be able to look in a mirror again without expecting to see that poor girl's face.

Raised voices outside startle me, making me jump, and I accidentally knock a perfume bottle off the dressing table and onto the floor. It doesn't break. It simply rolls away out of sight. Dismissing the perfume bottle as unimportant – it was empty anyway – I walk over to one of the open sash windows that overlook a pretty rose garden and peer out. Hanging back out of sight, in case one of the two men should look up and see me, I recognise John straightaway, but not the other man.

Wearing a tweed cap, wax jacket, and Wellington

boots, the stranger has John pinned by the collar. He might be twice John's bulk, but, to his credit, John shows no fear.

'What did you go and bring her here for?' I hear the stranger demand.

'It was Jane's idea,' John replies calmly. 'Of all people, do you think I would want her here?'

It's me they're talking about, I grasp quickly. *They can't possibly be referring to anyone else. That would be too much of a coincidence.* And psychics, even bad ones like me, don't believe in coincidences.

'You can't believe anything she says.' The stranger takes off his cap, revealing a mop of curly brown hair beneath, and screws it up in his hands before putting it back on again.

'Just go along with it for now. For Jane's sake,' John pleads, reaching out to touch the other man's arm; then, seeming to think better of it, he drops it back by his side.

'Don't you mean Lucy's sake?' the man argues before marching away.

I watch John stare after him, then pluck a rose from one of the bushes before scattering its petals on the ground. His shoulders sag. I imagine he'll stay there for some time, gathering his thoughts, but instead he spins around and glares up at the window as if he senses I'm there.

'Shit.' I jump back, hoping I haven't been spotted. I dare not look again in case John is still standing there, waiting to catch me out. Biting my lip, I back away from the window, intent on escaping the room, this house, and gasp out loud when I see that the wardrobe door is open once again and the perfume bottle is back on the table.

B lond heads parked together, almost touching but not quite, Jane and John hover on the galleried landing, whispering. Jane barely registers the fact that Lucy's portrait hangs on the wall behind them. They are so used to seeing it there that it no longer takes them by surprise. Even John's eyes are not softened by it.

'We have to go through with it, John. We have no choice.' Jane can barely keep the impatience from her voice.

'But it's madness, this whole mad-psychic-who-has-had-her-child-taken-away business,' John insists, glancing over his shoulder in case somebody should overhear them. 'Even Hugh is against it.'

'Hugh!' Jane tuts. 'Since when do we care what he thinks?'

'He has as much of a right... He was there that night.'

'Nobody has more of a right than the child's mother. Nobody,' Jane screeches, spit spraying from her top lip onto John's face. He does not attempt to wipe it away nor take a step back from her.

'It won't work, Jane.' John blinks, not once but several times, as if he has trouble seeing her.

The older a woman gets, the more invisible she becomes, Jane concedes bitterly.

'Surely you can see that,' John urges. 'We must stop now before it's too late.'

'Our daughter is missing.' Jane is of a similar height to her husband but appears the taller of the two. 'It is already too late.'

CINDY

I could have sworn I heard voices echoing along the corridor – not that poor girl's voice, anything but that – but when I reach the galleried landing, there's no one there, yet expensive perfume lingers as if somebody had been there a moment ago. According to Jane, there are two main staircases in this house, but this is the only one I've come across so far. I can't imagine the other one being as creepy as this. Its stone walls, creaking floors, and the watchful eyes of the people in the portraits bring me out in goosebumps.

Peering over the balustrade, I see that dozens of concrete steps lead to several different floors below, and I start to think that this house is bigger than I first imagined. Coming from a working-class background, council house and proud, I find it difficult to comprehend that only two people live here in this vast space – forgetting for the moment that there used to be *three.* John and Jane wouldn't have to see each other for days if they didn't want to. And perhaps that suits the Valentines, because I haven't yet witnessed a flicker of warmth between them. After all they've been through, I'd imagined they'd be close.

Hating the thought of having to transverse all those steps in a bid to find Jane, who will no doubt take one look at my bloodshot eyes and guess that I've broken my promise to give up the booze, I turn my attention to the portraits on the walls, starting with the more recent occupants of Moon Hollow – John and Jane, who sit proudly erect in their gilt-edged frame, cold blue eyes trained dutifully on whoever it was that painted them. They look stiff and expressionless, not at all lifelike.

It's only when I come to stand in front of Lucy's portrait that I feel my chest tighten. How different she is to the rest of them. Poor, sad little Lucy. The missing heiress. Not yet eight and very unhappy, from the looks of this picture. She seems as lost in the life-size painting as she did in real life, if the photos I've seen of her in the newspapers are anything to go by. There's no hint of a smile at her mouth or flash of personality in those dark eyes. Her olive skin appears out of place among the other pale-skinned Valentine ancestors. Her clothes are old-fashioned and dated too, and I wonder who would dress a child in such an ugly pinafore. The answer comes to me on my next breath: *Jane, of course.*

I'm about to touch Lucy's portrait, to see if I can get a sense of her, when a trickle of childish laughter reaches me. Immediately I withdraw my hand and drop it to my side, in case I should scare away whoever made that sound.

'Lucy? Is that you?' I gasp, hardly daring to believe that the child has reached out to me so soon. Leaving the portrait behind, I go in search of that sound. It leaks enticingly out of a door off the landing, but in a different wing to the blue room Jane put me in.

'Lucy,' I call again, pressing my ear to the door, hoping for more of the same infectious laughter. I'm not disappointed. A child's giggling is heard within. But would the Lucy in that portrait make such a playful sound? Isn't she too sad and serious for such behaviour? The laughter I hear is infused with a love of life that's absent from the eyes of the girl in the painting. I've no idea who is on the other side of the door, but there's only one way to find out. Taking a deep breath, I steady myself before reaching for the doorknob.

14
_____

I'm inside a little girl's bedroom that's unlike any child's bedroom I've seen before. My own daughter's bedroom was, *is*, an oasis of different colours (pinks, mostly) and is filled with dolls and toys, whereas this is sparse and uniform, like a boarding school dormitory. Not that I'd know what one of them looks like. All I know is everywhere is excessively neat and tidy. Not a thing out of place.

The metal-framed single bed has been stripped of bedding as if no one expects a child to return to it. I don't want to be critical of Jane and John, who clearly love their daughter and want her back more than anything – else why involve me – but I can't help thinking what a grey and depressing world this must have been for a child to wake up in.

Wondering where all Lucy's toys are, my eyes alight on an old-fashioned doll's house, which I quickly realise is a replica of Moon Hollow. But even this is creepy. Not at all suited to a child's bedroom. The windows of the doll's house follow me about the room like eyes, reminding me of my arrival here yesterday when I sensed I was being watched. There's a churchyard in the grounds, again like Moon Hollow, with resin black-and-white horses beyond, heads down, munching on felt grass. In the nursery, a miniature couple are looking down on a baby in a cot, while another female figure gazes out of an attic window.

I can't shake off the feeling that she's searching for someone. On closer inspection, I suspect that the doll's house is attempting to tell a story of its own. I don't know who's responsible for arranging the figures in such a way, but my eyes are drawn back to the graveyard, to the figure of a man on a bicycle, who's cycling past the church. That's when I feel my temple begin to throb.

"Dance, then, wherever you may be, I am the Lord of the Dance, said he."

It's the same man's voice from before. Singing that damned hymn. I wish I could place it. If I had my phone, I could google the words and find out, but I surrendered it the minute I arrived here, having agreed with the Valentines beforehand that no contact with the outside world was best. That doesn't stop the outside world intruding on my senses, though. Far from it. At times, my head is so full of voices I sometimes forget which one's my own. That's why I've come to hate this so-called "gift" of mine. It doesn't just come and go when it pleases, it takes over my life. *What life?* I scoff. *I have no life without Grace.*

Deciding this is too painful a reminder, I focus again on the figure on the bike. This time, I hear the spokes of the bicycle wheels turning, and when I close my eyes, I catch a glimpse of a bunched-up trouser leg that's been tucked into a metal clip shaped like an angel's wing. I don't understand the significance of any of this yet, but I sense it's important. That the mystery of this man will, in time, be revealed to me.

I spin around and almost trip myself up when I hear the child's laughter again. Much closer this time, coming from behind a door that I suspect leads to another built-in wardrobe. *What is it with this house and wardrobes?* Edging towards the door, a horrible sense of déjà vu shadows me as if I've lived this moment before.

'Lucy?' Fearful of what I might find, I feel my chest tighten. 'Lucy?' I call again, trying to sound braver than I actually am. In response, there's a shuffling from inside the wardrobe, followed by stifled laughter as if someone's playing a game with me.

When I throw open the door and see my daughter huddled in the corner of the wardrobe with a big grin on her face, I'm surprised I don't pass out on the spot. Grazed knees drawn up to her chest, Grace hugs a doll I'm not familiar with.

'Grace. Oh, Grace.' My heart beats against my chest as if it were a bird trapped against glass. The flood of relief I feel at seeing her makes my head swim until I start to feel sick.

Her face falls as soon as she sees me, and her giggling also ceases abruptly. When I reach out to pull her into my arms, she flinches and shuffles away as if I might hurt her. Horrified by her reaction, I back away and bump straight into Jane, who, unbeknown to me, is standing right behind me, her arms crossed impatiently across her chest.

'You did it, Jane. You kept your word. You did what no one else could do. You brought Grace back to me.' Feeling immensely indebted to her, I'm tempted to hug the woman but think better of it. She's hardly the affectionate type.

'You have found each other, then,' Jane says, rolling her eyes as if what she's done is nothing and doesn't require any thanks.

I itch to touch Grace as I watch her clamber out of the wardrobe, the doll tucked possessively under her arm. But, bypassing me, she goes straight to Jane, drops the doll on the floor as though suddenly bored of it, and tugs at Jane's dress. It seems to me the two of them have already made friends.

'She has been giving me the runaround all morning.' Jane tuts, moving away from my daughter as if she were poison.

Forgetting how grateful I was to Jane a moment ago, the only thing stopping me from grabbing her by the neck – *How dare she reject my child!* – is John's sudden appearance. Acting much jollier than I've seen him before, he seems intent on putting his best foot forward to make up for yesterday.

'There you all are.' John doesn't seem to notice or mind the atmosphere in the room. He's a fool not to feel the chill coming off our female bones.

I observe Jane darting him fierce looks. Perhaps he'd been charged with watching my daughter before she ran loose.

'It seems we've found Grace. You were looking for her too, weren't you, John?' Jane says pointedly.

'Yes, of course.' He grins stupidly, embarrassed, maybe, that he's been caught neglecting his duties.

He receives another scathing look from Jane, yet her

voice is gentle when she asks, 'Why don't you take this little urchin to breakfast?'

John raises a brow at Jane as if she might enjoy that prospect herself.

More fool him, I think, watching Jane's face stretch in disgust. But when her eyes land on the doll lying on the floor, I can tell from her horrified expression that it's important to her.

Wanting the attention to be on her and not the doll, Grace snatches it up in her hands again, and Jane immediately bristles. She clearly doesn't want Grace to have it.

Deciding that I'll be the one to take the doll from my daughter, not Jane, I hold out my hand. 'Give the doll to John first, Grace. Then you can go for breakfast,' I say firmly. But Grace's hand visibly tightens on the doll.

'It's not yours, is it?' I remind her kindly, bending down so that we're both the same height, but not encroaching on her personal space.

I watch Grace's eyes fill with angry tears. 'No. And I don't want it anyway,' she shouts, throwing the doll on the floor before stomping away.

'Grace, come back. You don't know your away around yet, and this is a big house. Not what you're used to.' I want to go after her myself, but Jane shakes her head at me as if that wouldn't be a good idea and runs after my daughter instead.

'Thank you, John. Thank you for keeping your promise and bringing Grace here,' I say tearfully, picking the doll up from the floor. John shuffles on the spot, not knowing what to say. Turning my back on him so he doesn't see my tears, I sit down on Lucy's bed and caress the doll's shorn brown hair, wondering who might've taken a pair of scissors to it.

It hits me then, like a spiteful slap, and I get why Jane acted so possessively just now. A sudden, sure knowledge seeps into my bones like quick-setting cement.

'This was Lucy's favourite.' I gasp. 'She called it Heidi.'

15

'I did what nobody else could. I got your daughter back. Now you have to help me find mine.' With fingers bent into claws that dig into my skin, Jane has hold of my wrist and is trying to force me to touch Lucy's portrait.

'She already has,' John urges, trying to calm Jane down. If only that were possible. She's out of control. Something I'd never have expected of her. My main concern, though, is for Grace, who's gone dangerously quiet and seems incapable of moving.

'Cindy confirmed the doll was Lucy's,' John reminds his wife. 'She knew its name.'

'Do not take me for an idiot, John. Any fool could have found out about the doll.' Jane snarls, lunging for me again.

As John jumps in to separate us, I duck out of the way, managing to grab hold of Grace's hand in the process. As I pull her towards me, I expect her to resist, but she doesn't.

'Touch it and tell me if you see anything,' Jane orders,

pointing again at Lucy's portrait, all the while trying to wriggle out of her husband's arms.

'You have to stop this, Jane. You're frightening Grace,' I say, resting my trembling hands on Grace's thin shoulders. She feels cold, in need of warming up.

'If I have to drag you over here myself, I will,' Jane threatens, not looking in my daughter's direction. 'Why won't you try, Cindy?' she appeals, her mood as changeable as the weather, before glancing furtively at John and stating coldly, 'She owes us that much.'

'But what if she can't tell us anything?' John remonstrates weakly.

Jane is adamant. 'There's only one way to find out.'

'All right, Jane. I'll give it a go,' I blurt out suddenly, surprising everyone, including myself.

John and Jane each hold their breath as I walk towards Lucy's portrait. Grace has stopped sobbing and watches with Bambi-sized eyes. I look from her tearstained face to Jane's hardened blue eyes, which are willing me not to fail, and finally to John's aghast expression. I'm shocked to discover that he's more scared than any of us.

As my hand hovers over the portrait, I feel my heart flutter. If anything has happened to this child, if I'm forced to see it, I won't be able to endure it. Plucking up courage from somewhere, I allow my fingers to graze the different textures and layers of the oil painting, tracing the impressions left behind by the artist's brush. My face is so close to the portrait I can smell the turpentine that would've been used to dilute the paint.

This time, when I gaze into Lucy's muddy brown eyes, I experience a feeling of intense anger. Not at Lucy. Nor at John or Jane. But at someone else. Someone I haven't met yet. I am sure of this. But the sensation is fleeting. Hardly tangible at all and gone on my next breath. I'm left with a sensation of acute loneliness, but I can't place who the feeling belongs to. *Could it be Lucy? Am I feeling her?* It's hard to tell. This house, I won't call it a home, has a sense of isolation about it. As if it breathes loneliness into those who live here.

Where are you, Lucy? Are you still with us?

I dare not speak aloud in case my concerns upset John or Jane. At this stage, I can't be sure if their child is even alive, and because of this, I find myself pitying them. I can't imagine what I would do if anybody took my Grace away, for good, I mean. I'm sure I'd go crazy too. Like Jane. Becoming conscious of the fact that hope may be all that the Valentines have left, I don't want to add to their heartbreak by making the same mistake I did with Adam Lockwood. Before I tell them anything, I must be certain of the facts.

I feel it. Far away and distant at first. Barely there. But it grows stronger. As does the tingling in the middle of my forehead and the throbbing behind my right temple. Closing my eyes, I clear my thoughts and inhale. Three deep breaths. As I do, the room around me disappears, and I fall into a blackness where...

I see *him*. His hands, anyway. Gnarled grey flesh. Dirty fingernails. Sparse black hair sprouting from white knuckles. He holds a pencil in one hand. The tip looks as if it's been sharpened roughly with a knife. Resting on the palm of his other hand is a well-thumbed artist's sketch pad. I don't get to see his face nor any other part of him. Just his hands. But they are enough. They show me what I want to see – Lucy.

Except it's not Lucy at all. But a drawing of her. Lucy is posing uncomfortably in a hard-backed wooden chair. Her hair is uncombed, and her clothes are creased as if she's slept in them. She looks back at the man with dry eyes as though she's done crying. She doesn't break her pose, but I can tell that, mentally, she's not in the same room as him.

Where is he hiding you, Lucy?

As if he knows I'm watching him, the man puts down the sketchpad and gets to his feet. Light floods in behind my eyelids, and I'm immediately transported back to Moon Hollow. My eyes flash open to find John and Jane staring at me as if they'd never expected to see me again.

I'm the first to speak. 'The bastard is drawing her.'

16

JANE

Moon Hollow has been in Jane's family for generations. In its former days, it comprised a 2,200-acre estate of six farms and eighteen cottages, including a family-owned church that was built at the end of the fifteenth century. Nowadays, the house, church, and surrounding parkland are all that is left of her inheritance, the rest having been sold off by necessity over the years. Big houses such as Moon Hollow are expensive and difficult to maintain. A family's reputation more so, Jane has found.

She is on her way to the church now to pray, but she lingers in the graveyard, on the other side of a chain that segregates her Valentine ancestors from the rest of the villagers. Standing under the gloominess of the church tower that can be seen from miles around, Jane likens the weathered gravestones that jut out of the ground at odd angles to wonky teeth, the kind that need pulling. She has nothing to say to these people, *her* people, so she marches towards the church. Taking out a heavy skeletal key from her pocket, she inserts it into the lock, feels it grind like a clenched jaw, and then shoves open the wooden door.

A dull grey light creeps into the building, illuminating a single candle visible from the church entrance. It burns twenty-four hours a day on the main altar and will not be extinguished until Lucy's return.

Once she arrives in the family's private pew, which is segregated from the rest of the nonexistent congregation, Jane pushes aside the kneeling pad and falls dutifully to her knees. She does not mind how much her joints ache from pressing on the concrete floor. This is part of her penance. She is bone tired. All she wants to do is sleep. But instead, she prays. She does so every day. What sort of mother would she be if she did not?

John never comes to see if the candle is still burning, because he has lost his faith. In God and in Jane. He regrets, now, the things they got up to in here, deeming what they did a sacrilege. He believes God is punishing them with the loss of their daughter. He could be right. But when they first made love in the cold confines of the church, behind the chapel screen, it felt as if their union was blessed by God Himself.

Outside, it is late summer. Fledgling birds are trying out their wings. The foals in the park are galloping around on new legs. But in the church, it is winter. The walls are as cold as the tombstones outside, and the lacelike tracing of the glass windows bleed with condensation as if the church itself were weeping. Although John believes the church no longer has a purpose, not since it was made redundant and the parishioners went elsewhere for morning prayers, Jane does not agree. The villagers can shun the church, and *them*, all they like. The only thing that matters is that it remains in the hands of the family who owns it.

Disappointment and anger are aging Jane. Her hair and skin used to be shiny and soft from wealth. But now her hair is course, her skin dry, and her eyes are stained with yellow. Her mother, famed for her beauty, used to say that Jane, her only daughter, was ugly, barren, and incapable of love. Jane wasted years trying to prove her wrong. But she cannot help thinking that Georgina, or Gorgeous Georgie, as she was known, was right all along.

Eyes closed firmly shut, hands pressed tightly together, Jane shuffles on her knees as she tries to fight off cramps. She is meant to be praying for Lucy's safe return, but her mind keeps wandering back to the past. Lucy was supposed to save Jane's relationship, but instead, she is tearing her and John apart. Sometimes, Jane thinks they were better off childless. She knows that as a mother and God-fearing woman, she is not supposed to have such thoughts. Especially at times like this. But they haunt her still.

Jane had originally intended to become a nun. The desire to sacrifice herself to God had been strong in her since she was a child. But then, to everybody's shock and disbelief, John happened, and the rest was history. Although Jane had not been opposed to the idea of having a child, she was less enthusiastic than John. That is not to say she does not want her child back. She would give anything for her safe return.

And if Cindy can be believed, there is every chance that could still happen. Because Lucy is alive. Not dead, as they'd feared. This news should cheer Jane and bring her great relief, but she feels more anxious than ever.

Who is drawing Lucy? What can it mean?

Is Jane right to trust Cindy? Could the girl have got it wrong, as she did before?

Jane remembers the first time she met Cindy and what her initial impressions were. A slut. A tart. A single, unmarried parent living on benefits. In Jane's opinion, girls like that do not deserve to be mothers. When Jane found out what Cindy was guilty of and what that poor child had been through, her point was proven. If Jane had her way, she would lock up all teenage mothers and single parents and throw away the key. They are a disgrace, and Cindy is no better. It's not just the booze and fags that upset Jane, it's the fact Cindy was out partying with friends and having unprotected sex with drug addicts whilst her child was left alone at home.

Cindy Martin must be the worst mother in the world. Yet Jane has entrusted her with finding her own daughter. But without Cindy, they would still be in the dark about Lucy.

There is another reason why she is desperate to get Lucy back. Only then can Jane put her doubts behind her regarding John. She needs to know that he was not responsible for Lucy's disappearance. There, she said it, at last, the words she had hardly dared to think. Jane knows that John would never deliberately hurt Lucy. He was, *is* crazy about her. Perhaps too much at times. But his past cannot be overlooked.

Jane suspects that something might have happened to Lucy, an accident of some kind that John is keeping from her. It would not be the first time. The only thing stopping her from clawing John's lying eyes out is her faith. She will keep the bargain she made with God. If Cindy is wrong about Lucy and she is not returned to them, then John will be punished. As God is her witness, she will see that justice is done. If he dies, then she will follow suit and vice versa. It is a pact they made a long time ago. He might have forgotten it, but she has not. Nothing will part them. They are as one. She knows John better than he knows himself. This is how she knows what he is up to right now. Sniffing around Cindy, like a dog in heat.

17

CINDY

S tanding at the bottom of the secret staircase that lurks at the back of the wardrobe, I take my first step on the wooden stairs. Every fibre of my being warns me that I shouldn't be doing this. Something bad could be waiting up there. Doors don't open by themselves. Everybody knows this. So, when the wardrobe door popped open again just now, I knew it was a sign that somebody wanted my attention. This time I wasn't going to ignore it.

Although I'm meant to be preparing myself for my next potential encounter with the kidnapper, or Lucy Valentine herself, I keep climbing. I must know what's on the other side of the door at the top of the stairs. Whatever it is might bring me closer to Lucy. My bare feet, with their brightly painted orange toenails, follow the same invisible trail of dusty footprints that I saw disappearing up the staircase last night.

Suddenly the temperature drops, and I can see curls of white breath spiralling out of my mouth. I'm reminded of the mist you see in cemeteries, the kind that hovers over graves, like ghostly fingers pointing out the names of the dead. My arms are peppered with goosebumps, and a ghostly prickle runs up my spine, ending at the blood-red dip-dyed ends of my hair. The silence feels unnatural as if I've stepped into another world.

It shouldn't be this cold. Or quiet.

Head swimming, I reach the door. It looks harmless enough, painted white with a tarnished metal doorknob that looks as if it won't put up a fight should I try to turn it. My shoulders deflate somewhat when I see a key protruding from the keyhole, denying me the chance of finding the room locked and inaccessible. A distant hope I'd been clinging to.

I square up to the door in the same way I'd like to do to Jane Valentine, and after taking a deep breath, I push it open. Before I can change my mind, I step inside, and I'm immediately blinded by a surge of sunlight that leaks in through the large overhead glass of an atrium. It's a few seconds before I can see properly, but when my eyes finally adjust, I can see that the windows are too high for me to look out of, even on tiptoe, but I suspect they offer a panoramic view of Moon Hollow and the surrounding Fenland countryside. To watch the stars up here at night must be an incredible sight.

Disappointingly, the room, though large and bright, is empty. Not what I expected at all. The floorboards are covered in a fine, unspoilt layer of dust, but the remains of underlay sticking to the bottom of my feet suggest a carpet has recently been pulled up. The faded off-white walls, which are peppered with square patches of lighter, brighter white paint, hint at having once had pictures hung on them.

A movement. Barely there. The slightest suggestion of

a shadow caressing the wall. The creak of a floorboard. Someone else's breath. Close by. A hint of dirty water. Dampness and something else. The same smell of anaesthetic, heavy in the air, that weakened me before.

'Lucy? Is that you?' I turn like a ballerina in slow motion and search for a watching face or a glimpse of shadow, but there is nothing there. I start to think that I must've imagined it, but then...

I am Lucy.

A voice, tinged with sadness, dances through the room, and a shiver cuts through me like a knife. I open my mouth to scream, but my voice is whipped away, stolen by the shadow in the corner that I can feel watching me. But that was not the voice of a child. Recalling the face in the mirror and the foreign accent, I'm sure the voice belongs to the same woman from before. *Is she called Lucy too? Surely not. That would be too weird. Who is she? And why am I seeing her and not the Lucy I'm meant to be looking for?*

'You can't be Lucy,' I say to the silence gathering around me like a circling mob.

This room is flooded with light, but I sense that something dark happened in here. *To who, though? The child Lucy or this other Lucy, the mysterious young woman whose eyes, I remember, were haunted by fear. Why is she so desperate to connect with me? What does she want me to know?* Making a silent promise to myself that I won't force the image of the woman with the birthmark back into the shadows as I did before, I close my eyes and concentrate on reaching out to her.

A throbbing behind my eye. A tingling sensation in the

middle of my forehead. Something. Someone. I can almost feel it. *Her.* It won't be long now...

'It was going to be a playroom for Lucy.'

Catapulted back to the present, my eyes snap open as I spin around to face John, who hovers outside the doorway, not entering. *Why doesn't he come in? Why?*

'John. You scared me half to death.' I clasp both hands to my chest as if that will calm the palpitations.

'Sorry.' He laughs, sounding as if he means it, but he doesn't smile.

'Do you mean your Lucy?' I ask, only now absorbing what John has told me.

'Yes, of course. Who else?' His eyes narrow with confusion. 'She was too frightened to come up here on her own.' He shrugs as if it doesn't matter. As if there are no tears shining in his eyes, waiting to fall on his immaculately pressed shirt.

My eyes drop automatically to his hands. I'm relieved to find that his are too well-manicured to be the kidnapper's. The hairs on the back of his hands are as blond as the rest of him. When I glance up at John's face, I can tell by his horrified expression that he's guessed what I've been thinking, so I look away again, unable to meet his eyes.

'I can see why she wouldn't want to come up here alone.' I twist around to take another look at the room. As I do, I feel my face stretching into a frown because whatever I felt before has gone. She vanished the second John showed up.

'Thank you for earlier...for...' John shuffles on the spot, looking uncomfortable. As if he doesn't quite know what to make of it all, especially my part in this.

'Where's Grace?' I ask, desperate to have her in my sights. To know that she's safe, unlike his daughter.

I watch John hesitate, and for a sickening moment, I fear that Jane has sent my daughter away again. Then he smiles, and this time the smile reaches his eyes. Relief overwhelms me.

'Playing outside in the garden.' His voice implies surprise as if I should know this.

'With Jane, I take it?' A fit of unnatural jealousy stirs within my bones. I hope it doesn't show, but John shrugs noncommittally like he has no idea what I'm feeling.

'I ought to go and find her. She seemed upset earlier,' I say lamely, feeling as uncomfortable as John looks. When Jane's there, we get on fine, but when we're alone, like now, we go back to being awkward around each other. I have no idea why.

18

I head in the opposite direction to the garden where I've been told Grace is playing, *with Jane*, not only because I'm dying for a fag (Grace hates my addiction and refuses to kiss me goodnight if she smells any trace of cigarette smoke on my breath) but because I need time to think about what I'm going to say to her to win her around. Too many apologies and promises to do better have already fallen on deaf ears.

Pulling a crumpled packet of Lambert & Butler out of my jeans pocket, I light up. Jesus, it feels good. God knows I've tried to quit, but it's so fucking hard. Christ, am I expected to give up everything I enjoy – sex, booze, and fags? Nobody told me being a mother was going to involve so many sacrifices. Realising I've blasphemed three times in a row, I'm relieved Jane isn't around to hear me. My mother is the same. Hates hearing anyone taking God's name in vain. They're similar, Jane and my mother. Both are religious freaks.

Not wanting to come face-to-face with the horses

grazing in the adjacent parkland, I take another much-needed drag on my cigarette and head towards a small wooded area, which looks invitingly private, but over-hanging thorns pull at my clothes and brambles whip at my bare legs as I try to reach it. I guess a vest top with a bright pink push-up bra and fashionably ripped denim shorts aren't standard country gear.

When I come across a clearing in the middle of the trees, circular with grass that looks as if it's recently been cut, I worry in case I've trespassed onto someone else's land. I've heard that farmers can be arsey about stuff like that. I could end up getting shot if I'm not careful. But then I spot something that makes me forget my concerns. On the ground, partially hidden under the branches of a tree, there's a cage, constructed of wood and wire mesh, with a black-and-white bird inside. A magpie, I think. Not that I'm an expert on birds. *Aren't they meant to be lucky, or is it unlucky?* As I draw closer to the cage, the bird squawks angrily, as if it holds me personally responsible for its capture.

'How did you get in there?' I say to it as it hops closer.

We weigh each other up. Its eyes are a reddish brown, with small black pupils that appear like full stops. The black dots blink at me, demonstrating a level of intelli-gence that takes me by surprise. Poor thing. You'd think it would be terrified, but it isn't a bit scared, not of me, anyway. It assesses me in much the same manner Jane Valentine did when we first met.

I'm the first to admit I was not looking my best back then. Grace had been taken away from me by this point, and I'd been fired from my job at the supermarket cigarette kiosk – something else Social Services intended to hold against me in the fight to get my daughter back. I wasn't suitable, they claimed. There were a lot of not-suitable glances being thrown around by officials at that time. I saw the same judgement reflected in Jane's eyes.

Ordinarily, people feel sorry for those who, through no fault of their own, lose their jobs. But not me. I should've been more responsible, they said. How could I have known that queues of people would turn up at the kiosk, not to buy packets of cigarettes and vaping pods but to seek advice on whether their husbands were having affairs or to find out where so-and-so's wedding ring had disappeared to.

Oh, and a few simply demanded to be told what numbers would get called on the lotto that week. As if I would be standing there in my ugly uniform, earning minimum wage, if I knew that. Word gets around in a town the size of Stamford, though, and the press coverage of my involvement in the Adam Lockwood case didn't put everybody off. An unreliable psychic was better than none.

Anyway, back to the bird with the analytical eyes and the confidence of Jane Valentine. Figuring I ought to release it, make it my good deed of the day, I look for an opening in the cage. If it got in there by itself, and I assume it did, then there must be a way out.

'You wouldn't be thinking of letting that bird go, would you?'

I spin around to catch the man from this morning, the one who argued with John, watching me. *How could I have allowed him to creep up on me like that? The papers are right. I'm losing my touch. So much for sixth sense!* He's younger than I first thought. Mid-thirties, I'd say. Wearing the same country attire as before, he looks how I imagine Lady Chatterley's lover would. Not that I'm much of a one for classic English literature, being more of a gossip-mag person.

'You scared me,' I say, guiltily stepping back from the cage in case I'm in trouble.

'It's a decoy bird.' His chin juts in the direction of the cage. 'Used to attract others.'

'What are you trapping them for? What harm can they do?' I'm on the bird's side although, as a rule, I'm nervous around anything that flaps, stings, bites, pecks, or kicks.

'Nest predation,' he states as if I ought to know this. Then he saunters over to tower over me. I step further away from the trap and him, avoiding eye contact. Is he safe?

'Magpies are notorious for preying on other birds' nests,' he explains. 'Stealing eggs and taking young that don't belong to them.' His eyes blaze suddenly like someone's lit a fire behind them. I wonder if he's thinking of Lucy Valentine at this moment.

'I didn't know. I'm sorry.'

'Some say the magpie is jealous of any bird with more colourful plumage than itself and that's why they ransack songbirds' nests.'

That's all very well, I think, *but I don't need a lesson in ornithology, a big word for me, I know. That's not what I'm here for.*

'I saw you earlier with John Valentine,' I point out.

'So?'

'What were you arguing about?'

He's amused by my bluntness, I can tell. His cheeks grow pink, and he takes off his tweed cap and runs a gloved hand through his curly brown hair, as I saw him do before.

'Foxes.' He laughs, but, really, he might as well have told me to mind my own business. I would have admired him for that. Still, there's something likeable about him. His eyes are a countryside olive and lively with laughter, which I like. Before I can make up my mind about him, I need to see his hands. Until I do, he's as much a suspect as everyone else.

'I'm Cindy Martin.' I hold out my hand, but he cleverly avoids it by thrusting his hands in his pockets.

'I know who you are. You're here to look for the missing lass.'

I nod, trying to sum him up. He's quite a mystery. *Why is he wearing gloves on a hot day like this? What's he trying to hide?*

Moving slowly yet purposefully, he ambles over to the cage and peels back the wire door I had trouble finding. Dipping his hand inside, he drags the magpie out before it knows what's happening. A flurry of beating wings and an ungrateful, indignant screech and it's gone, soaring unsteadily towards the treetops. After what he said, I wasn't expecting him to free the bird, but I'm pleased he did. He throws me a half-friendly, half-hostile smile, as if I owe him one, before turning his back on me and stomping away.

He looks over his shoulder and barks, 'I'd start with the treehouse if I were you.'

19

Whoever built this treehouse doesn't know anything about children. They certainly didn't consider how treacherous the climb up to it might be for a child. It's too high, and the wooden ladder nailed to the trunk of the tree is likewise too steep. Hanging precariously on the edge of a massive branch with exposed bark, the treehouse looks as if it's been dropped carelessly into the decrepit tree that houses it. Craning my neck to look up, I feel my heart lurch as I imagine Grace or any other small child tumbling out of it.

I'm surrounded by trees so tall there's barely any room for the sky. For a town girl like me, this makes me uneasy. As I begin to climb, I don't look down. I'm not afraid of heights, but up here I'm made to feel small and so light I might get blown away on the slightest of breezes. I think I hear a rustle close by as if someone is parting a branch to pass through the trees, followed by a twig breaking, but I still don't look down.

"Dance, then, wherever you may be, I am the Lord of the Dance, said he."

No. I will not listen to you now, I think, berating the voice that comes and goes as it pleases. *I'm here for Lucy,* I tell it, forcing the song from my head.

Having made it up to the top in one piece – I'm not looking forward to the climb back down – I step into the interior of the treehouse, surprised by how sturdy it feels underfoot. *That's something, I suppose.* I forget all about the climb, everything, in fact, when I see the gathering of teddy bears and dolls. So, this is where Lucy kept her toys. They're positioned carefully on a rug in the middle of the floor, no doubt organised by Lucy in ascending order of preference, as Grace would do.

If I didn't know better, I'd suspect somebody had deliberately arranged them as if they were willing participants in a Ouija board game. The thought makes me smile. Only a clairvoyant would think like this. But when I see the remnants of a smashed china tea set scattered over the rug, the smile drops from my mouth; everything around me blurs, and I sink to my knees.

I see her. For the first time, I see her. Lucy Valentine...

She's helping her toys to sips of imaginary tea, balancing the delicate china cup in her hand and sticking out her little finger in a ladylike way, no doubt imitating her mother. Her dark hair is cut in an aggressive bob, and she wears a stern pinafore dress too old for her. With black patent shoes and white ankle socks, she's dressed as if she were a make-believe child that stepped out of the pages of an old-fashioned nursery rhyme. Perched next to her, taking pride of place among the other toys is her favourite doll, Heidi, the one with the shorn hair. The one that Grace refused to let go of.

A crow caws nearby, making me jump. At first, I think it's only me that can hear it, but Lucy hears it too. Raising a finger to her lips, which look as if they've been drawn on with a red crayon, she shushes her toys, then cricks her head to look out of the open window.

The pale blue sky fades to black as a murmuration of starlings takes flight, twisting and turning as one massive shape. I don't know what made the starlings take to the sky, but I sense that something bad is about to happen, and they know it. Closing my eyes, I will myself to feel it.

He's out there. Hiding among the trees. Waiting. Watching. I sense his excitement and fear. Feel him holding on to his breath. See the hunch of his shoulder as he bends down, keeping himself hidden in the under-growth. A hand comes out to part the branches, the same sound I imagined earlier. Gnarled grey flesh. Dirty finger-nails. Sparse black hair on his knuckles. A twig breaks underfoot as he approaches.

He's coming. I spin around, wanting to warn Lucy, but I can't reach her. I can still see her, but she's distant. Too far away. I've no idea why I'm finding it so difficult to keep her within my vision. Something's getting in the way. I get the feeling that someone is deliberately trying to prevent me from reaching out to her. But who?

I try to clear them out of my mind. I won't let them run riot in my head nor prevent me from finding Lucy, who desperately needs my help. But when I try to see through the fogginess of my mind to look for her again, she's gone. Only the kidnapper remains. Everything grinds to slow motion.

Go away. Leave her alone, I want to shout, fearing that I'm about to relive the moment, *the actual moment* when Lucy disappeared. Oh God, how can I witness this, knowing there's nothing I can do? This event might already have taken place in the past, but it's going to feel very real to me. I'm not meant to be here. It isn't right. Isn't fair.

I hold my breath as I wait, willing my racing heartbeat to slow. For a long time, nothing happens. The tension becomes unbearable. I wonder if Lucy feels it too. I almost become desperate for the kidnapper to be on the move again. *Just get it over with, you bastard.*

At last, the door squeaks open, and there's a shuffling of heavy boots that don't quite make it inside. He's cleverer than I thought. He doesn't want to frighten her. Not yet, anyway. Moon Hollow is close by. A child's scream is within hearing distance. On that thought, I wonder why Lucy isn't already screaming. *I know I would be.*

I see her then. Just as she was before. Sitting on the rug in the middle of the floor, surrounded by her toys. I'm so relieved to have her back again, I could cry. Like me, she's focused on the kidnapper, whose face I can't see, but rather than show alarm at having an intruder enter her lonely world, she appears intrigued. I expected her to be frightened, terrified, but she seems pleased at the prospect of having a real-life playmate. I watch in horror as she smiles invitingly and holds out the cup and saucer as if offering it to a friend.

The vision fades. Lucy and the kidnapper vanish. I find myself alone again. That's when it hits me. He's not the stranger we thought he was. She knows him. A monster he may be, but I'd stake my life on it that he's a local man. He might even be known to Lucy's parents. This sickening thought fills me with dread. How am I to break this news to John and Jane?

John and Jane. There's something not quite right about them. I've known this from the start. Closing my eyes, I try to see what it is they're hiding. First nothing, then comes the tingling in my forehead and a throbbing behind my temple. I see glimpses of naked flesh, the limbs of a man and a woman twisted together, the murmur of voices full of desire. The air around me is cold and damp. There are echoing stone walls and stained-glass windows. I think we're inside a church.

I'm reminded of the times spent with my mother attending family weddings and funerals. Distracted by my memories, I lose sight of John and Jane, and whatever it is they're trying to hide evades me too. I'm about to give up concentrating on them when out of nowhere, I hear Jane's voice calling out to Lucy. She sounds angry.

"Lucy. Lucy. Wherever you are, come out this minute."

I get the sense that, wherever this scene played out in the past, Lucy was deliberately hiding from Jane. I can't say I blame her. I wouldn't come out of my hiding place either if Jane was in a bad mood. *Was Lucy frightened of her mother?* I wonder. What a terrible thought. It would kill me to know that my child feared me.

Grace. Watching me from one of the upstairs windows at Moon Hollow.

I didn't realise how close the house was until now. She's a lonely face in a grey window. At first, I think she's a vision, that I've conjured her up in my mind, but then I remember I'm not able to see Grace or reach out to her as I can others. This is real. She is real. I do a quick count of the windows and conclude that she's in Lucy's bedroom. What's she doing in there? And why is she on her own? John and Jane are meant to be looking after her. Besides, didn't John say she was playing in the garden?

Did he purposefully send me on a wild goose chase to get me out of the way? Feeling a rush of irritation towards them both, I'm about to leave the treehouse and go in search of my daughter when I see Grace breathing on the glass, then writing something on the misted-up window.

Lucy.

Grace's eyes are angry. She's mad at me for something. But apart from the obvious, I don't know what I'm in trouble for this time. Her eyes lock with mine, and I watch, spellbound, as she opens her mouth to form the word.

Lucy.

I can't be certain that what I'm seeing is real. The house is close but not close enough for me to see inside Lucy Valentine's bedroom. Grace is the one who's blocking me from finding Lucy. I think I've known this all along.

20

Grace won't look at me. All her attention is on the book in her hands. She's sitting on the floor in Lucy's bedroom, her bruised knees poking out to one side, while I remain hovering uncertainly in the doorway. Not getting any response, I come in and sit down anyway on the edge of the bed, unsure how close she'll allow me to get to her.

I can't remember the last time she let me touch her. I want to badly. But I can remember a time, not so long ago, when I took her outstretched arms for granted.

'Do John and Jane know you're in here, in Lucy's bedroom?' I ask gently.

'It isn't Lucy's bedroom. Not anymore.'

'Perhaps not,' I agree, hoping she isn't right, although it's true I never get a sense of the little girl in this room either. Does that mean she's never going to return to it? She must make it home. Not just for my and Grace's sake. But for John's and Jane's too.

'What were you doing in the window, Grace?'

She doesn't answer, but I can tell she's no longer reading the book, only pretending to.

'Were you trying to stop me from finding Lucy?' I persist, knowing this could end badly.

'I don't care for her,' Grace mutters through gritted teeth.

Grace is jealous. This should have been obvious to me from the start. As an only child, she has been spoilt rotten, although not by me. Obviously. Or my mother. Mainly by her grandfather. Now that I know this, it makes perfect sense. Having spent all that time apart from me, Grace now finds herself among strangers, and it must seem to her that I care only for Lucy, someone else's child. She might not have forgiven me for the things I did, but that doesn't mean she wants to share me with anyone else.

Oh, Grace. How can I make you understand?

'Do you see things? Things you don't understand?' I ask.

My daughter nods. The tear sliding down her cheek is hard for me to take. I want to comfort her, but I'm afraid if I do, she'll push me away.

'What do you see, Grace?' I slide onto the floor next to her and curl my knees under me. Our skin touches, but she doesn't jump away, as if electrocuted, as I expected her to. This is a good sign. 'Tell me. I might be able to help you understand what's happening to you.'

There's no excuse for me not guessing that my daughter has second sight too. I'm her mother as well as a psychic, albeit a reluctant one, so I should have known. Fuck knows it isn't something I would wish on my worst enemy, let alone my daughter.

From now on, I mustn't let her see how much I hate the

so-called gift I was handed at birth. It'll only make her feel worse. A feeling of helplessness overwhelms me until I feel a single tear slide down my cheek, matching Grace's. What am I doing here? How the fuck did I get us into this mess? I can't help anyone. Not Lucy. Not Grace. I can't even help myself.

'I see *you*, Mummy. All the time,' Grace accuses, finally glancing up at me.

21

JANE

The next day, Jane is going about her chores, preparing breakfast as she does every morning in the vast kitchen, which boasts a central island with a sitting area and a more formal breakfast room going off it. The room is as unfussy as Jane. That is the way she likes things.

A long table that seats twenty-four at full capacity looks out through French doors onto the pretty rose garden that for years was cultivated by Jane's mother. These days, it is left to itself. As Jane wishes to be. Except today, *they* are not allowing that to happen. Instead, everybody is ganging up on her. Or, at least, that is how it feels to her.

John grips hold of the edge of the table and wears a hunted expression. There is a sprinkling of crow's feet at his eyes and a sagging of the jowls that Jane has not noticed before, no doubt brought on by stress and exhaustion. She tries not to feel smug about this but wonders how a man as vain as her husband will cope with the aging process.

Cindy has black mascara running down her face, giving the impression that she has been crying black tears. Her slim arms look as if they long to have a man's arms wrapped around them. She is much smaller than Jane, being barely five feet tall. Jane supposes men find petite women like her appealing, bringing out the protector in them. Cindy's face is white and pinched, though, as Jane imagines her own to be.

Jane does not know whom she is angrier with. Herself, for bringing Cindy here, or John for immediately befriending her. After all they have been through together as Lucy's parents, Jane does not deserve this. Later she will recall that John's disloyalty is not so surprising. His latest betrayal is one in a long line of treachery. A sneaky rat. That is what he is.

'You are agreeing with her! Siding with her,' Jane shrieks.

'In this, I am right, Jane. You know I am,' he tells her with a new authority that Jane suspects is for Cindy's benefit. He always did like to impress.

'They won't believe us. I mean me. Not after what happened with Adam Lockwood. Don't you think it'll complicate things?' Cindy avoids looking at Jane when she says this.

Jane catches the private glance that passes between John and the girl who is quickly becoming a thorn in her side, and feels herself bristle. The pair of them are already in cahoots. John is moving faster than she gave him credit for. And alone, without Jane. She could almost admire him for that. Almost. One way or another, she will put a stop to this; see if she doesn't. John must not be allowed to do things his own way. It is not safe.

'It is clear to me, John,' Jane says scathingly as the doubts she has about him return, 'that you don't want the police to find our daughter's kidnapper.'

'That's not what I meant, Jane, and you know it. But if we tell them what Cindy told us, that we think the man might be a local, they will think we're making it up. They have scoured every inch of this village and interviewed everyone from the vicar to the dustbin man. Don't you see? They'll stop looking for Lucy and concentrate on us.'

This is a long speech for John, making him seem desperate. Jane wonders again what it is he is trying to hide. What doesn't he want the police, or her, to find out?

'Let them,' she says coldly, making up her mind to kill him herself, with her bare hands, if she finds out he is involved in Lucy's disappearance.

John cannot hold her gaze. He gives up and turns away.

'If you tell the police and they decide to resume their search, there's a chance the kidnapper could panic and run,' Cindy warns Jane.

'And take Lucy with him?' *Or worse*, Jane thinks, wringing her hands. She had not considered this option. The girl could be right.

'We can't run that risk,' John pipes up lamely.

Jane wants to tell him that nobody cares what he thinks. She cannot remember the last time she listened to anything he had to say. It will be her and Cindy who decide what to do. Isn't that what women all over the world do?

'What do you suggest?' Jane confronts Cindy, trying and failing not to judge the younger woman's appearance. *Whatever made her dye the ends of her hair red like that? She looks like a woman of the night. And as for those shorts. You can almost see what she ate for breakfast!*

'Can you think of anyone who might want to hurt you?' Cindy appeals. 'Someone you know or once knew? Lucy wasn't afraid of her kidnapper. He must be known to her.'

Jane looks at John and vice versa. She knows what he is thinking. *George, the black sheep.* She is thinking the same. But she is not sure how much she wants Cindy to know about their past. She is reluctant to let the girl in, but if it means finding Lucy...

She is about to say something. Really she is, although John would hate it, when Cindy interrupts.

'What about the man from yesterday morning?'

'What man?' Jane snaps.

'The one John was arguing with.' Cindy apologetically slides her eyes in John's direction, as if worried she might have got him in trouble.

'She is talking about Hugh.' John sighs. 'His name is Hugh Hunter,' he says, looking directly at Cindy, 'and he is, or used to be, our gamekeeper. More of a friend now.'

'Friend!' Jane scoffs. The idea makes her want to laugh out loud. She wonders where John gets his ridiculous notions. He is like a child. She blames herself. She has always been more mother than partner where he is concerned. Until Lucy came along, Jane had smothered him. She supposes the eight-year age gap did not help.

'Hugh wouldn't hurt a fly.' John pauses, thumb on chin, pondering. 'And we wouldn't want you bothering him, asking him questions, not after everything he has been through.'

Jane overrides her husband. 'You can ask him all you want. Lucy is all that matters.'

'But he isn't a suspect, Jane. He never was. Even the police said so.'

Cindy shakes her head. 'Until I get to see the kidnapper's face, everyone is a suspect.'

22

CINDY

The felt-tip picture Grace gave me earlier, showing her sitting on the handlebars of a bike, laughing and smiling up at her dad as he pedals her around the garden of our home, saddens me because I'm not in it. Skid, her dad, ducked out of her life years ago, but Grace adores him anyway. I don't know why the picture bothers me as much as it does. It's not as if I have a soft spot for him or anything. Couldn't wait to be shot of him, if I'm honest. Him *and* his shit-stained underpants, hence the dumb nickname.

Fighting back tears, and losing that battle, I screw the paper into a ball before firing it into a wastepaper bin next to the bed. Despite being a useless twat, Skid will always be Grace's dad. And my ex. On that note, I find myself smiling. It's good to swear, if only in my head. I'm not used to having to mind my language, except around my mother. Dad, on the other hand, is like me. Swears like a trooper. He's the only one back home who'll be missing me. I feel bad that I couldn't tell him where I was going. He'll be worried sick.

Rather than think about my dad, or the drawing without a mum in it, I go back to pouring over the list of names the Valentines gave to the police, in the hope of stumbling across something they missed. But I'm not having much luck. The Valentines don't have any friends. Just people they know in passing. The kind they nod to. All their relatives are dead too, according to this statement, and they haven't employed any staff in years.

That only leaves Hugh Hunter and the man on the bicycle, the one who keeps popping into my head, singing that stupid hymn. I wonder if his name is somewhere on this list. John and Jane insist that they haven't seen or heard of anyone like him in the village, and they come across as telling the truth. So, I'm at a loss as to who he is and where I can find him. Unable to connect with the child, and God knows I've tried, and with nothing else to go on, I realise that looking for Lucy is going to be much harder than I thought.

When the bedroom door opens unexpectedly, I grab at my dressing gown, not wanting anyone to catch me sitting on the bed in my underwear, which clings to my body as if it were painted on. *What if it's John? Do I want it to be John? Am I expecting it to be John?*

'Jane,' I exclaim in irritation, quickly covering myself with the silky folds of the dressing gown. 'I didn't hear you knock.'

'That's because I didn't,' Jane says dismissively, coming into the room and placing a bundle of folded clothes on the bed.

The swish of her long skirt on the carpet makes me

shudder, reminding me of the creepy housekeeper from that old black-and-white movie *Rebecca*. I watched it on the TV once when I had a terrible attack of period pain and couldn't get up from the sofa. When I remember that Grace brought me a glass of milk and some biscuits on a plate to cheer me up, I feel a lump catch in my throat. *Oh, Grace. How can I ever make it up to you?*

Turning my attention back to Jane, I watch her standing there, not saying anything but boldly appraising me. Arching my eyebrows at her, I slip on the dressing gown, noticing how her eyes crawl enviously over my young body.

'I have bought you some appropriate clothing to wear. I hope you don't mind.' Jane stands back, looking awkward. Not quite embarrassed, but uncomfortable.

'Thank you,' I say, not meaning it. I can easily imagine the sort of clothing she would consider appropriate. Shapeless and matronly, I'll bet. The kind that Jane wears. Add to that the fact that they're bound to drown me, Jane being at least two sizes bigger, it's clear that she intends to make me look hideous.

Well, I won't wear them, I tell myself. *Yes, you will, Cindy. You'll do everything this woman says, even if she orders you to go down on your knees and give her husband the blow job he so desperately needs.*

Where the fuck that thought came from, I've no idea. But I'm bloody angry with Jane for trying to control me in this way. Overstepping the mark, that's what she's doing. To teach her a lesson, I let the dressing gown slide open and thrust out my chest.

'I'll still have the same firm young body underneath,

Jane, whatever I wear,' I say cruelly, regretting my words as soon as they're out of my mouth. *What a bitch I am.*

'A friendly word of advice about my husband.' Jane folds her arms, unmoved by my childish gesture. 'His taste for young women—' she pauses to look me up and down, her lip curling with distaste '—is legendary and should not be taken as a compliment.'

Jane has out-bitched me. I can hardly believe it. But I'm determined she won't have the last word. If the gloves are off, then I'm up for it as much as she is.

'You talk as if you stepped out of an old black-and-white movie,' I taunt, knowing the reference to being old will hurt.

Did Jane almost blush then? I would never have thought it possible. Perhaps she's not so tough after all. What she says next, though, convinces me otherwise.

'Anyone would think you did not want Lucy found, Cindy, and yet that is the only reason your child is here.' Jane's eyes dart away as if it pains her to think of my daughter when her own is missing. 'Surely, that is worth remembering.'

As soon as the door closes on Jane, I do recall something that's worth remembering. If I'm right about my daughter and she really is trying to stop me from finding Lucy, then I can't believe anything she says or does. Acting impulsively, I retrieve the crumpled piece of paper from the bin. Grace wouldn't have drawn her father giving her a ride on a bike outside our house. I never once saw Skid on a bike. I don't think he even owned one. He wasn't that cool a dad. Besides, he always took her to the park. Grace would've drawn him pushing her on a swing.

Shit. I was right all along. Talk about being bloody

Miss Marple. Who'd have thought Cindy Martin, the reluctant, pissed-up psychic, could turn all Agatha Christy? The little girl in the drawing isn't Grace at all. I was wrong before. That was a red herring, put there by my daughter to distract me from what I should be doing so I would focus on her, not Lucy.

The child in the drawing has short dark hair, and she isn't smiling as Grace would have done. Rather, she's sad-faced and perched on the handlebars of an old-fashioned bike, and her small, sad body is partially hidden in the long coat worn by the man riding it, who isn't Skid. This man's hands rest on the handles of the bike, where the girl – *Lucy* – sits, and his trousers balloon clownishly at the bottom as if tucked inside his socks. I bet if I looked hard enough at the picture, I could imagine his knuckles are peppered with sparse black hairs.

Like a lone firework straddling the sky, his song goes off in my head.

"Dance, then, wherever you may be, I am the Lord of the Dance, said he."

It's him. The man I think of as Lord of the Dance. If Grace can see him too, then this is evidence that he exists, not only in my visions but in hers too. Does that make him real? If so, then that makes him the prime suspect.

23

It feels as if I'm falling, but I sense I'm not in any immediate danger because my descent is unhurried yet deliberate. The ground beneath me slowly rises to greet me, and I see glimpses of the moon blinking sleepily through the trees as if I were in a fast car. When I land, it's like somebody has spun me around on the spot, too fast and too many times.

Bright lights race towards me, blinding me, and it's impossible to focus on anything else, like *where am I?* My head feels fuzzy, and my legs are weak. I worry they'll crumple beneath me. When I realise that the lights belong to a car and I'm standing in the middle of a dark, unlit road, I will myself to move out of the way, but I can't. So, I stare transfixed as it hurtles towards me, gathering speed like a bolting horse. Faster and faster.

Just as I think it's about to hit me, I'm transported into the back of the car – a taxi, I think, judging by the signs on the doors and the flashing digital display on the dash. The driver's eyes, mean and dark in the rearview mirror, are all over me. Everywhere except on the road where they're meant to be, taking in my laddered tights, short skirt, stiletto heels, and glimpses of red underwear.

I tear my eyes away from his and pull at my skirt, conscious of what a mess I must look. "Once a tramp, always a tramp," my mother would have sniped. She liked to save her harshest words for me. But on this occasion, she would've been right. I look like a hooker. No wonder he stares. My hair is knotty and wild as if unkind hands have raked through it, and one of my fake fingernails is missing.

Flashes of a dark-skinned man leading me by the hand come back to me. His lips are as red as my nails, his breath hot and spicy. A yellow Molly tablet is on his tongue one minute and on mine the next. Other bodies graze ours on the dance floor, but we barely notice. Daft Punk plays in the background, but we don't need music to know how to move against each other in the dark.

The next thing I know, the man – Zak, I think his name was – is gone and I'm back in the cab. All I can see is the driver's eyes. He's without a face. Staring at me. I want to scream, and I open my mouth to do so, but someone beats me to it.

Grace. Standing in the middle of the road, her face lit up by the glare of the car's headlights as it accelerates towards her. Her face is turned in my direction as if she knows I'm inside the car. I watch her mouth form a black hole as she screams out one word.

"Mummy!"

. . .

I WAKE UP COVERED IN SWEAT. HOT AND THIRSTY WITH A bastard of a headache. *Oh God*, I think, terrified in case I haven't yet left the nightmare behind me. Pushing the damp sheet aside, I sit up, not wanting to remember. Then, desperate for a glass of water, I get out of bed, but as soon as my feet land on the carpet, flashes of the dream come back to me.

When I see a gleam of white light shining through the curtains like a slice of fresh air, I fear that my ordeal isn't yet over. The night is not done with me.

Peering out of the window, down at the rose garden where I saw John arguing with the man the Valentines call Hugh Hunter, there's a car. I can't tell what make it is, but its engine purrs softly, and the driver's door has been left open as if somebody got out in a hurry. The car headlights, left on full beam, illuminate the lawns of Moon Hollow that dip down towards a lake that glimmers in the distance. The water on the lake takes on an unnatural shine in the dark, making it appear like ice.

By the edge of the lake, I see the shadowy silhouettes of two people running. One of them – a woman, I think – stumbles often, always picking herself up again. The other – a man, I assume by his body shape – chases silently after her, never making a sound.

Help me. Oh God. Somebody, please help me.

I recognise the voice and its Eastern European twang, and my heart somersaults. It belongs to the young woman I saw in the mirror. The other Lucy, from the secret room. I hold my breath, feeling her fear as if it were my own. *Who is chasing her? What do they want? Why is she so terrified? And what can I do to help?*

'What is it, Lucy? What's happening? Tell me,' I urge as if I ever had a hope of distracting her from her terrifying past. And with that, she vanishes, like a magic trick gone wrong. The car also disappears, robbing the scene in front of me of any light. The lake is now as invisible as I felt watching the shadows run towards it.

Not knowing what to do, I turn away from the window, wondering if the ghosts have finished with me for tonight. That's when I hear it. The distinct sound of somebody turning a key in a lock. Locking me in.

I want to fly across the room and try the door handle to be sure. Raise the bloody roof – how dare they! – but I know if I do, I'll disturb and frighten Grace, who's asleep in the bed, looking so small in the vast expanse she barely makes a dent in the covers. This is the first time in a long while she's felt safe being alone with me, and I can't risk upsetting her.

Earlier, I asked her if she wanted to sleep in my bed, and she nodded solemnly, not giving much away. It was the start I'd been hoping for. A beginning I knew I didn't deserve.

'Are we friends again, Grace?' I asked once she'd slipped in beside me. Her toes, scrunched up with cold, scratched against my skin as she curled herself into the nook of my arm. Knowing she wouldn't want me to notice or comment on this, I sighed into my pillow, fighting back the tears and heartache that are always threatening to tear me apart.

The thaw with my daughter had begun an hour before we went to bed, after I'd promised her a bedtime story, but not before prying her hand away from Jane's on the landing outside our bedroom. Jane had tutted as if it didn't matter. But her dagger eyes and twitchy mouth told me differently.

As soon as I had my daughter to myself, I closed the door, hoping it would provide a barrier to the Valentines' interference. There was no sign of any key in the lock then, I recall; otherwise, I would've locked it myself. From the inside. I decided against tackling Grace about the drawing of Lucy and the man on the bike, though, sensing it would put her in a bad mood. I dared not risk spoiling tonight, not when everything was going so well.

'You don't smell of fags anymore,' Grace observed once we were alone.

'I gave them up,' I told her, opening the pages to her favourite book, *The Tiger Who Came to Tea*. I wasn't going to admit to the odd one or two I smoked on the quiet.

'You did?' she asked, wide-eyed.

'I gave up a lot of things when you went away.'

I placed my hand on top of hers then, but it was too soon, and she pulled away, wrinkling her nose as if at an unpleasant smell.

'What about the booze?' she protested, still refusing to look at me.

'Just wine sometimes when I have trouble sleeping. Not much,' I reassured her. This, at least, was true. Mostly. Even so, I crossed my fingers under the book so she couldn't see.

'Shall I read to you now?' I asked, wanting to change the subject.

'You may,' Grace deigned in that princess-like way of hers. And with each word I read, she drew closer until she was leaning sleepily against me, her hot breath tickling my skin. She smelt as I remembered. Coconut shampoo, fizzy cola, and toothpaste.

Not long after that, I'd drifted off to sleep. After what just happened tonight, I doubt I'll be doing that again soon.

24

JANE

J ane is aware that she and John behave in ways that would appear strange to others. Embarrassment does not exist between them as it does with some couples, which is why she can sit on the toilet with her knickers around her ankles and pee while John is in the room with her, flossing his already incredibly white teeth in the mirror.

'You never mentioned George to Cindy. Why not?' Jane asks, folding a diamond shape in the toilet roll. A habit she knows annoys John. Reminds him of cheap hotels, he says. Jane has not been to any cheap hotels with John and does not like to think about when he might have visited them and with whom.

'I could ask you the same thing,' John replies with an edge to his voice, not once taking his eyes off his good-looking reflection in the mirror.

'I nearly did but stopped myself just in time.'

'It wouldn't have made any difference anyway. Leave the dead in peace, that's what I say.'

Jane persists. 'But we don't know for sure he *is* dead.'

'He has been gone a long time, Jane.' John's eyes meet hers in the mirror, and she imagines a softening in them. It lasts only a few seconds.

'Do you ever think about him?' Jane stands up and flushes the chain, not wanting John to see how watery her eyes have become. He notices anyway. Lately, he has a habit of doing the opposite of what she wants.

'It is what it is, Jane.' John is gruff. His words final. He does not want to talk about it, so Jane changes the subject.

'She is menstruating.'

'Who is? What on earth are you talking about?' Taken aback by his wife's remark, John drops his toothbrush in the sink.

'Cindy is on her period,' Jane says smugly, finding John's toothbrush before he does. Before he can stop her, she slips it into her own mouth and begins brushing. She will force him to be intimate with her if it kills her.

'How would you know that? More importantly, why are you telling me?'

Jane understands that her husband is mortified by such talk. He has never been one for discussing women's problems. In his own way, he is as prudish as she is.

'She can easily have another baby, whereas I...' Jane unconsciously places a hand on her flat, ever so slightly wrinkled stomach as she says this. Again, John is quick to notice.

'Try not to let it get you down.' His words are meant kindly, but they do not begin to smooth away Jane's jealousy and sense of injustice. Why should a slut like Cindy be so fertile? After what she did, she does not deserve to be a mother at all.

'She's lucky, that's all I'm saying.' Jane does not want this conversation to end. She must find out John's stance on what they both know she is secretly suggesting, but is he man enough to openly acknowledge it? Finished with the toothbrush, Jane gargles a mouthful of water and spits it into the sink in a surprisingly unfeminine way. John narrows his eyes at her. He can be such a bore about how he expects women to behave.

'So long as that *is* all you're saying,' he warns, wiping toothpaste from his mouth.

25

CINDY

My skin prickles as I make my way downstairs. No matter where I go, I can't shake off the sensation that someone's eyes are on me. An old man, hidden in the walls. Driven there through fear, by relatives wanting him dead, I suspect. Since stepping off the bus that brought me here, the fear of this house and its inhabitants has gripped me. Whenever I roam the darkened hallways, trying to find traces of little Lucy, I stumble into people who are not there. Like the elderly man. Old inhabitants, long dead.

Coming into the grand hallway, where the past lingers even more determinedly – evident in the scrape of a boot, the thudding of children's feet on the stone floor, a tinkle of piano keys, the distant echo of horses' hooves and a carriage's wheels on gravel accompanied by a flick of a whip – I catch a glimpse of the outdoors through the partially open double oak doors. Hollow Fen is a fitting name for the dreary village Moon Hollow presides over, except it's not what I would call a proper village, just a few farms and cottages, not even a pub or post office. The surrounding countryside's no better. Everywhere is flat and barren. Depressing, really, unlike the picturesque, cobbled lanes of Stamford, my hometown.

When I make it down to the breakfast room at five minutes past the hour – timekeeping has never been one of my strengths – Jane's already seated, wearing a face as long as the table. She's spooning small amounts of muesli into her mouth, chewing the recommended number of times between each mouthful, but I get the impression she's as uninterested in food as I am. John's chair, scraped back from the head of the table as he must have left it, is vacant. Judging by the crumbs and blob of bright orange marmalade left behind on his plate, I guess I'm not going to see him this morning. *Just Jane*. I sigh inwardly, returning Jane's unwelcoming stare.

Grace sits next to her, closer than she needs to, and they each roll their eyes at me as I fall into my seat, careful not to disrupt the carefully laid table setting in front of me, complete with silver and white linen napkins. I was hoping to get my daughter on her own so I can ask her about the drawing of the man on the bike with Lucy, but Grace is glued to Jane's side. If I tried to pry her away, she would fight like a little wildcat.

Pouring filtered coffee that's as rich and dark as chocolate, the likes of which I've never smelt before, I wince, almost overfilling my cup as another spasm of pain spreads over my stomach, causing my muscles to contract. I've suffered from acute period pain since I was twelve. It got worse, not better as I was advised it would after having Grace.

Since then, I've considered getting myself sterilised, as I've heard that puts an end to the monthly torture, but it always seems too final a decision, so I've held off, in case I'd miss out on the chance to have another baby further down the line. At this stage in my life, I haven't ruled out the possibility of meeting someone. Of course, everything changed after the accident. Nobody in their right mind would want to have a baby with me now.

'I'm going to see Mr Hunter today,' I blurt out, avoiding Jane's gaze. 'I take it you don't have any objection?'

Jane stops chewing and wipes her mouth on a napkin. 'As I said last night, if you think it will do any good, you are welcome, but he is a dark horse, so I doubt it will get you anywhere.'

'I'm good at figuring people out,' I say, a tad too smugly for Jane's liking.

'You can't believe anything he says. He is a liar.'

'I thought John said—'

'John's not here. And he does not read people the way we do, Cindy.'

I'm not sure what she means by this, but I decide that I don't need to know. I'll make my own mind up about Hugh Hunter and won't be swayed by either of the Valentines. I've not yet been able to find out where Lord of the Dance lives or even if he's a living, breathing person for sure, but Hugh Hunter isn't so lucky.

As I think this, another debilitating shot of pain creases through me. I want more than anything to go for a lie-down with a hot water bottle, but I fight the temptation. Luckily for me, my periods never last long, and this misery will be over by tomorrow.

'Is he really your gamekeeper?' I ask, to take my mind off the pain.

'Nobody works for us anymore,' Jane says mysteriously, shaking her head.

'You'll keep an eye on Grace while I'm gone?' I stare pointedly at my daughter.

Jane's eyes track mine, coming to rest in alarm on Grace's jam-streaked face as if she hadn't noticed her sitting there before.

'Of course. I do not break my promises, Cindy. You will find me firm but fair.'

Firm but fair, the same words my mother used to describe her own nonexistent parenting skills. Except there's nothing fair about Jane, and Esther Martin wouldn't know the meaning of the word if it smacked her in her self-righteous, Bible-spewing face.

26

On the way to Hugh's house, I catch a glimpse of the lake, the one I saw in my vision last night. Mist still clings to its surface, like smoke from a bonfire, but luckily no shadows are running around it today. Even so, I keep my distance. Earlier, when I'd asked Jane about the lake, she told me it was a man-made affair, originally dug out by prisoners of war.

Then, rather curtly, as if she didn't want to discuss it anymore, she handed me a slip of paper with Hugh's address on it. Rather than go through the village, I've taken a shortcut across country. My sense of direction is appalling, but as most of the surrounding land belongs to Moon Hollow, I shouldn't get lost. The white geese that patrol the striped lawns honked fiercely when they first saw me, but they're far behind me now, and away from the shadow of Moon Hollow, I can finally stop searching its windows for watching faces.

Thanks to Jane, although I don't like to admit it, I'm appropriately kitted out for a trek in the countryside.

There's nothing sexy about what I'm wearing, but at least I won't get scratched or stung like before. My new look – hiking boots, a checked shirt with the sleeves rolled up, and baggier-than-usual jeans – suits me.

The front entrance to Moon Hollow, with its rolling lawns, teardrop driveway, and wisteria-clad walls, is nothing like the rear, which has been allowed to grow wild. Deciding I prefer it this way, I pluck an apple from a loaded tree, just to stare at it before tossing it. I'm no Snow White, that's for sure, and I don't eat apples. But the disused tennis court that I can see through the sagging netting that surrounds it does interest me. Crusty leaves from several seasons ago gather at its edges, and weeds grow through its cracked concrete floor.

A sudden prickling sensation in the middle of my forehead and a throbbing at my temple alerts me to the fact that I'm about to see a glimpse of the past. The whack of a tennis racket slices through the air, accompanied by a thud as an invisible ball bounces on concrete. This is followed by a rumble of laughter and a flash of white skirt. Mixed doubles with attractive people who all talk like John and Jane. The chink of glass, the aroma of Pimm's and strawberries. *How the other half lives or lived*, I think jealously.

I force myself to move on and put the scene behind me, but traces of it linger, highlighting how different my life is compared to the Valentines'. Moon Hollow is affecting me in ways I can't shake off. After a short time living with the Valentines, I feel myself changing. Regardless of whether Lucy Valentine is found – and I hope to God she is, or else how will I live with myself – I may have to accept that my old life is no longer good enough.

Nobody can blame me for wanting to improve my lot

in life. Pregnant at twenty, lumbered with a partner who was a minor drug dealer and who now dips in and out of Grace's life when he feels like it, was all my own doing, but I'm not to blame for my childhood.

Raised by a religious freak who thought I was a devil for knowing things I shouldn't, I count myself lucky my mother never drowned me or got the local priest to perform an exorcism. There are no pictures of me or Grace in my mother's house. But there are plenty of photos of my brother, whom she adores, and his twin boys. I've got used to this over the years and try not to let it bother me, but of course it still does. My cold, indifferent childhood isn't something I can easily erase. It shapes who I am today.

Before the accident, I admit to being hungover most weekends. Anything was better than being me. I even grew to resent my daughter for the way she looked at me. For catching me vomiting on the stairs, or for the way she crinkled up her nose when she smelt fags and booze on my breath. Seeing her turn away from me like that hurt like hell. But not enough, obviously, otherwise I wouldn't be in the predicament I'm in now.

27

JANE

J ane was wrong to dress Cindy in those clothes. She sees that now. When it is too late. Rather than make Cindy appear drab and uninteresting, like Jane, the girl is more appealing than ever. Even worse, there is a mystery to Cindy's small, impossibly bouncy body that was not there before. Cindy is a pretty plaything, a doll, in fact, and just as easily breakable.

The thought brings Jane pleasure. This makes her sound bitter and twisted, an irreparably damaged person, but she is no fool. She would not dare harm a hair on the girl's head.

'I take it back. I *am* a fool,' Jane says out loud, raking her hands through her perfectly coiffed hair, only to immediately smooth it down again. 'Worse than that. I am a jealous fool. Exactly the kind of woman John despises.'

Reminding herself that there is only one type of woman John does not despise – the young and beautiful kind – Jane's eyes narrow to angry slits. Picking up her coffee cup, her sixth of the day already, she gazes at the cold grey disc that has formed on its surface and tips the contents down the sink. She must do something about her wayward husband.

While it is important he keeps Cindy on side, even if it means manipulating her with some of that public-schoolboy charm of his, Jane wants it to be at her insistence, not his. She cannot bear the thought of him becoming enamoured. She will not let that happen again.

But is it already too late? She has spotted how he looks at Cindy. The same way he's looked at the others, but with more intensity. The last girl never messed with his head the way Cindy is doing. *What is so special about her?* Is the clairvoyance element responsible for his growing fascination? That could explain why he is desperate to impress her.

Does John fear Cindy will use her psychic powers to expose who he really is? If that should happen, he will turn to Jane for protection as he always does, but how can she stop Cindy from uncovering his dirty little secret? The girl is a psychic when all is said and done, and if she sticks around long enough, she is bound to work it out. It is only a matter of time.

Despite feeling humiliated by her husband's weakness for younger women, John is, and always will be, Jane's life. No girl, however beautiful, will get in the way of that. It occurs to Jane that she might be worrying over nothing, as Hugh might yet beat John to it. Hugh can be a fast mover when he wants to be where women are concerned. She has seen that firsthand. He might be a rough diamond, but he has a certain rugged magnetism, and he has got to be a step up for someone like Cindy.

Smiling to herself, Jane crosses the room, de-heading

flowers in vases as she goes before picking up the receiver of an old-fashioned telephone with a curly cord. It is probably older than the woman playing on Jane's mind. Knowing Hugh's number off by heart, she quickly makes the call.

'Pick up. Pick up,' she commands, smoothing down her linen skirt and rubbing at an imaginary smudge on her espadrilles.

Deciding that she could potentially solve two problems with one phone call, she intends to warn Hugh off the girl as well as remind him of his promise of silence. That should be enough to get him to do the opposite where Cindy Martin is concerned. Like her husband, Hugh is a lady's man. She supposes that is why John and he remain friends. But *unlike* John, Hugh is his own man. A proper man, her mother would have said.

Wishing she had thought of this tactic sooner, Jane feels she has nothing to lose. Hugh is not daft. He knows if he tells Cindy anything he shouldn't, then Jane will personally see to it that he loses his cottage. It has always irked her that John allows him to live rent-free on her, *their*, estate for old time's sake. Legally, John does not have a say in such matters. Moon Hollow belongs to her. As the eldest of her family, she inherited it fair and square. But it does not hurt to let John have his own way now and again to make him feel like an equal. A laugh, sounding dangerous to her ears, escapes from Jane's mouth.

'As if we could ever be equal,' she sneers, slamming down the phone on its thirteenth unanswered ring. Forgetting for the moment what she is supposed to be doing, Jane suddenly remembers that she is meant to be looking after

Cindy's daughter. What a joke that is. She is hardly the babysitting type anyway. Before Lucy came along, she was not remotely interested in children. In her absence, she finds nothing has changed.

28

CINDY

Hugh Hunter's cottage is not what I was expecting. It's ordinary-looking. Ugly, in fact. And back to front. The front has no access. Not even a path. You're forced to go around to the rear of the property, where there's an old barn housing a jeep with a wet dog inside, to access the back door, which incidentally has been left open. Pairs of dirty wellies, all a similar size, have been kicked off in a muddled pile outside the door.

The windows are small, and I suspect they make the rooms feel dark inside. I wonder how someone as tall as Hugh copes with the low ceilings. I bet he hits his head a lot. The garden is overgrown with grass and creeping weed, and there are random bits of wood everywhere.

When I raise the knocker and let it fall gently against the top half of the stable door, the dog in the jeep opens its eyes and barks a panicked alarm before springing to its feet. Claws frantically scratching at the glass, its saliva flies everywhere. Thank God it's unable to get out. I would've shit myself if it had. I can't stand dogs. When no one comes to the door, I'm not all that surprised. My knocking was barely loud enough to register. The plan was always to have a nose around first. Careful not to make a sound, I ease my way in.

The kitchen is sparse and masculine. No ornaments or clutter. A yellowing, old-fashioned range cooker, a checked blind, and a pile of neatly folded tea towels is all that catches my eye, so I go through to the living room. This is more like it. It's cosy and inviting. My kind of tidy too. Not over-the-top. I would be more than happy to sit in the comfy armchair next to the fire and drink a glass of wine.

My mouth salivates at the thought of chilled chardonnay slipping down my throat. It's been too long. Although the fire is unlit, I imagine the cottage comes to life at night when flames dance around the room, landing on the covers of Hugh's books, which are displayed on shelves either side of the brick fireplace. I'm about to investigate their titles when I hear him tripping down the stairs.

'Sorry. I did shout and knock,' I say loudly, compensating for the fact that I pretty much broke into his house. I still catch him off guard, though. Judging by the mixture of confusion and alarm on his face, I would say he's one of those types that are easily spooked. I want to laugh at his expression but decide against it.

'The door was open,' I add hastily.

'What are you doing here?' he asks bemusedly, checking out the room as if he thinks I've robbed him of something.

'You gave me some good advice the other day. I wanted to thank you for it.' I sit down before he can throw me out. I'm sure he's already figuring out how to ask me to leave.

'You mean the treehouse?' He rubs his stubbly chin.

I'm quick to check out his bare hands and feel my heart settle when I see they're nothing like the kidnapper's. Though relieved, I realise I haven't come prepared. *What if he'd turned out to be the kidnapper? What then? Would I have been able to get away from him?* As always, I've barged in without thinking of the consequences. *What an idiot.*

'The tip proved useful,' I say, not wanting to admit to any more than that.

He waits for me to continue the conversation. I feel him willing me to speak. Say something. But I don't help him out. I can keep up silence for as long as you like. My mother and I could go weeks without saying a word to each other.

He's forced to say something at last. 'Drink?' I win.

'What've you got?'

'Builder's tea. Instant coffee?'

'No booze, then?' I feel desperate asking.

'I don't drink,' he apologises as if he intends to take up the habit very soon.

I sigh in disgust. Away from Moon Hollow, I thought I might be able to rustle up a sneaky glass of wine from somewhere, but, sadly, it's not to be.

'Coffee, then. Black.' I don't thank him. I'm too disappointed to do that.

As soon as he goes into the kitchen, I'm out of my seat, stalking him like a mad collie. I watch him spoon sugar into chipped mugs, three spoonfuls for me when I gesture for him to keep going and a half for him. He has crinkly eyes that have a habit of really looking at you.

I've never been one to blush and I'm not about to start now, so I take my coffee back into the room and reclaim my seat. He sits opposite me in a matching armchair but moves all the cushions off first, piling them neatly on the floor. They remind me, somehow, of a shaggy dog at his feet.

'How is it going with the search?' he asks noncommittally.

'No comment.' I wink at him. Flirting comes naturally to me. I'm a pro at it.

'The Valentines, then?' He laughs.

'Fuck them.' I don't want to talk about John and Jane when I could be having fun. But I don't want Hugh to think me a bitch either, so I feel obliged to add to that statement. 'The jury's still out on the Valentines. I don't know what to make of them.' I worry I'm saying too much, but Hugh nods along as if he shares my opinion.

'Losing a child can screw you up pretty badly,' Hugh says, sounding like he knows what he's talking about. *What was it John had said about him?* Something along the lines of "We wouldn't want you bothering him, not after everything he has been through."

'Jane thinks I'm after her husband.' I grin.

'Are you?' Hugh is smiling again.

I suspect he's flirting with me now, but Hugh Hunter is no match for me. I like him, though. I've always enjoyed being around men. I'm better with them than I am with ghosts.

He changes the subject. Clever man. 'So, where *do* these visions of yours come from?'

'You avoided shaking my hand the other day. Why was that?'

'I didn't realise I had.' Guiltily he looks away, anywhere but at me.

'You're lying.' I smile to let him know it's okay, that I'm not accusing him of anything. 'I won't automatically know things about you if I touch you. It doesn't necessarily work like that.'

'But sometimes it does.' He's wary. Unsure of me.

Knocking back the last of his coffee, Hugh leans forward in his chair and somehow invites me in. I can feel it happening although he's not yet aware of it himself.

'How *does* it work? I'm curious.'

I bet you are, I think, noticing the subtle way his eyes stray involuntarily to parts of my body. Not in a creepy tits-and-arse way, which is what I'm used to. He starts with my hair first, then lingers on my eyes before moving to the skin on my arms.

'As you can tell by the predicament I'm in, I don't get to see things about my own life or those close to me. I guess that's why, deep down, I've always been reluctant to help others. That makes me selfish, doesn't it?'

'You have to be selfish to survive. It's what animals do.'

Hugh gazes into his empty cup, and for a minute I think he's going to offer me another drink. I hope so, as I'd like to stay a while longer. I want to ask him about Lord of the Dance. Find out if John and Jane are telling the truth about having no close friends or living relatives.

'From what you're saying, it sounds like my secrets will be safer the more I get to know you,' he jokes.

'Ah, but until then, I could still read you, given the chance,' I tease.

'But you haven't answered my question yet.'

'What question?'

'The one I've subconsciously been trying to communicate the last five minutes.'

'Does it have anything to do with my number?' I catch on quickly.

He passes me his phone so I can enter my number in it – not that he'll be able to contact me until after I leave Moon Hollow, due to the fact Jane has locked my phone away – but it startles us both when it rings. His face darkens as he answers it. 'Yes.' He's abrupt with whoever is on the other end of the line.

Gesturing to me that he'll take the call in the kitchen, I get to my feet and go back to what I wanted to do earlier, browse Hugh's bookshelves. His tastes run to cars and sport. There are no accompanying photographs on the shelves. This makes me wonder who's missing from Hugh's life.

I'm reminded once again of the absence of any photographs of me and Grace in my mother's house and feel a familiar twist of pain. My old school photographs have been put in a drawer to make way for Anthony's boys' pictures. My brother, four years older than me, has always been her favourite.

I push these painful memories aside and glance around the room. There are no pictures on these walls either. They've been removed, leaving behind lighter patches on the walls.

Just like in the secret room.

Hugh's voice, angry-sounding and slightly raised,

drifts in from the kitchen, and I wander into the hallway to get away from it. I don't want him to accuse me of listening in. A brightly patterned carpet, like the one I have in my own hallway, leads up to a steep staircase.

Much as I'd like to, I dare not venture up there. I would have a hard job explaining how I ended up in his bedroom. So, I push open a door that looks like it might lead to a garage rather than another room. I'm right. Cold air hits me as soon as I step inside. I fumble for a light switch but don't find one. In the darkness, I can pick out shapes of machinery and tools.

At first, I think it's the cold making my nose run, but when I go to wipe it, I realise it's blood. A throbbing pain in my eye, far worse than normal, followed by a tingling sensation in the middle of my forehead thrusts me into a different timeline.

THE TWIST OF A KEY IN A LOCK THAT'S DIFFICULT TO TURN. A car door slamming shut in the dark. The growl of a diesel engine firing up. Exhaust fumes and white smoke. A flash of yellow as an interior light comes on before being extinguished again. Shadows in the back seat of the car. Bodies clinging on to one another. Somebody crying. Somebody screaming.

'CINDY, WHAT ARE YOU DOING OUT HERE?'

Hugh brings me back to the present, but it's not a pleasant reunion. He's furious.

'Sorry, I...' Words fail me. The scene in the garage has upset me so much I don't know what to think. *What happened in here? Who were those people? Has this got something to do with Hugh?*

He sees through me. Of course he does. Just when we were getting on so well, I've come across something I hadn't bargained on. There's a secret here that he doesn't want me to know. *What are you hiding, Hugh?* Making up my mind that I will find out, I barge past him.

He gets to the back door before me. Blocks my way. *Am I in any danger? Is he safe?*

'What are you really doing here, Cindy?'

'I want to know who Lucy is. Not the child. The woman,' I bark, as angry as he is.

That floors him. He staggers backward. It dawns on me then that he knows something. The look of horror on his face gives him away. Too late, he tries to hide his distress.

'I can't help you,' he says, getting out of my way at last.

'Can't or won't?'

'Both,' he tells me, pointedly holding open the door.

29

JANE

They are downstairs drinking. At John's request, Jane has given in and allowed it, even though she knows that drunkenness displeases God. She would not dream of having anything brought up from the cellar for someone like Cindy, whose tastes no doubt run to cheap white plonk, so Jane went out and bought the wine herself. From a supermarket.

Jane enjoyed the trip out in her MINI Clubman. She does not miss the police and press presence outside the gates of Moon Hollow, but their absence means they have given up on finding Lucy. Everyone will in the end, she fears.

Cindy is under the mistaken impression that Jane is minding Grace, but nothing could be further from the truth. Jane has come into Lucy's room to be alone. She would give anything to stretch out her weary body on the single mattress and close her eyes. Block out everything that is bothering her – Lucy, John, Cindy, Hugh, the police investigation, or lack of it. But before she can do that, she needs to check on something...

The doll's house is how Jane left it. The figures remain in the same place, doing their own thing. They represent Jane's hopes. She wants nothing more than to go back to how things were. Just the three of them. The pink replica baby, which symbolises Lucy, is tucked up in her cot as usual with blond John and Jane dolls looking down on her, but when Jane sees the figure of a woman peering out of one of the attic windows, she takes a step back in fear.

Who put it there? Was it Cindy, or could it have been John? If this is meant to be a joke, it is not in the least bit funny. Snatching up the dark-haired figure that appears to have black shadows under its eyes, Jane slams it to the floor. Landing with an eerie thud, Jane stamps on it before it can roll out of the way. The heel of her shoe snaps off the figure's head, so it can no longer point the finger of blame at Jane.

Laughter drifts up the stairs and creeps into the room, a reminder of what is going on downstairs. It feels wrong to fill this house with laughter when her daughter is missing. Lucy could be dead for all they know. But Jane must not think like this. The doctor warned her it was not good for her.

Hope is all she has left, and it sickens her that she is forced to depend on that girl for answers. Jane wonders if the wine will work. If Cindy is to be believed, then it helps her see the missing pieces she cannot find any other way. Jane hopes so. The sooner Lucy is found, the better.

Once that happens, Cindy will disappear, and they can go back to their old life. The girl was rather vague about Hugh, claiming she did not find out anything new. This means that their secret is safe for now, but for how long, Jane cannot tell. One of these days, Hugh Hunter will talk.

On the phone earlier, he had accused Jane of stirring up trouble. "You should not have involved Cindy in any of this," he told her. How dare he? After all they've done for him, this is how he repays them. If it weren't for Hugh, then perhaps none of this would have happened. He is as much to blame as anybody else.

Sitting on Lucy's bed, Jane picks up the doll, Heidi, and straightens her dress so that her frilly knickers do not show. This immediately makes her think of Cindy, the cheap slut, so Jane puts it facedown on the bed, not wanting to look at it anymore. Must everything that girl touches become contaminated? Soon, it will be John's turn.

The Bible preaches that it is not a sin to drink alcohol in moderation but warns that overdrinking can lead to debauchery. Tonight, the fornicators downstairs may end up sleeping together – if John gets his way. And he usually does.

Jane is not sure how she feels about this. In one way it could be a good outcome. Extracting some sort of allegiance from Cindy, enough for her to keep on looking for Lucy, would do no harm – but the downside of that is the danger of John falling for her. Jane is not too concerned about the sex act itself. Her jealousy runs far deeper than that. But if the girl were to get pregnant, that would be a different matter.

30

CINDY

W e've continued our drinking in the games room. I admit I was surprised to find out the Valentines had one. It's a new addition, apparently, but seems at odds with the older, more traditional parts of the house. From the dark green walls with their low, intimate lighting to the oak wooden floor and beams, everything smacks of John's middle-aged tastes.

Bi-folding glass doors open onto a terraced area with comfy seating and views of the parkland, and there are contemporary abstract prints of fashionably thin nudes on the walls. They're meant to be artistic and tasteful, but they look like posh porn to me. I know I'm supposed to be impressed by this room, but the only two things I like about it so far are the pool table and the bar. I'm always up for a game of pool. But a bar, for Christ's sake! They don't know how lucky they are. Then I remember Lucy and take back my words.

John's behind the bar making cocktails. He's promised to make me any concoction I want. But so far, I haven't succumbed to his offers of "Sex on the Beach" or an "Orgasm", however tempting. I'm not drinking anywhere near as much as he thinks I am. John, on the other hand, is already slurring his words. He's ditched his customary shirt and blazer and is wearing a designer polo shirt, chinos with rolled-up trouser bottoms, and white trainers. He seems dead chuffed with himself, but I prefer the old John.

'Jane never comes in here,' he boasts, throwing ice into the cocktail shaker. 'It's called a games room for a reason, and Jane isn't exactly a fan of…'

'Games,' I finish for him.

'You're a fast learner, Cindy. I've said so from the start.'

I suspect them both of being game players, but for different reasons, and I guess what he really means by that comment is that he thinks I'm fast, but I don't say so. Instead, I raise my eyebrows and do my best to look suitably impressed as he juggles the cocktail shaker over one shoulder before removing the cap and tipping the liquid into two frosted glasses.

We touch glasses. 'Cheers,' I say, taking a sip of my piña colada before swinging my barstool around to inspect more of the room. In one corner, a vintage jukebox spews out a-ha on repeat. "Cry Wolf" followed by "Take On Me" and then "Hunting High and Low". I suppress a smile, wondering which one of us is the wolf and who's doing the hunting. Me or John?

At the far end of the room, a giant TV screen dominates a multicoloured LED-lit wall. Parked in front of it is a plush velvet sofa that's the same inflamed red as John's eyes. It occurs to me that I must never find myself alone with him on it.

Try as I might, I cannot imagine Jane hanging out in this room, downing cocktails at the bar or challenging John to a game of pool as I intend to do.

'I agree. It's hardly Jane's style,' I say at last, thinking how sad it is that John is apart from his wife, hiding in his man cave when she's grieving for their missing daughter. Not for the first time, I wonder if John isn't as nice as I once thought him. I can't seem to make him or Jane out. Every time I think I'm getting to know them, they throw me a curveball.

'I hope you think it's mine,' he says, sounding smug.

If John thinks I'm about to compliment him on how young he looks for his age, he's mistaken. There's no denying he's a handsome man, better-looking than the less polished Hugh Hunter, but by now his cheeks are flushed red with alcohol and sweat runs off his shiny nose. John may not know his limits as far as booze is concerned, but I do.

'I hear you paid old Hugh a visit this afternoon,' John teases. At the same time, he tops up my glass so it overflows.

I take a sip of my drink and lick my lips. This alone causes John's eyes to burn with desire. When he's not looking, I pour some of my drink back into his glass. I'm nobody's fool. I've already cottoned on to the fact that John's trying to get me drunk, but I'm not entirely sure what his plans are. *Does he really mean to bed me?*

'How did you find him?' John persists, way too obviously.

Jane has put him up to this. She's desperate to know

what Hugh and I talked about this afternoon. I told her there was nothing to tell, but the truth wasn't good enough for Jane. What I didn't mention was that, although Hugh had divulged absolutely nothing, he'd given himself away anyway. He knew exactly who I was referring to when I'd asked him who Lucy was.

'A bit changeable, if I'm honest,' I quip, casually swinging my bare legs back and forth in time with the music.

I've changed for this evening, reverting to my customary denim shorts. Short shorts, I like to call them. I've gone without a bra too. Jane clocked that the moment she saw me, even before John did. 'Friendly one minute, then…'

I let my words hang in the air, curious to see if John will finish my sentence for me, like Jane does his sometimes.

'Not.' He laughs. I don't think I've heard John laugh before. It sounds strange to my ears. Over-boisterous, like a bull terrier that's been locked up for too long. 'That's Hugh for you. He's a good egg, really, Cindy. Once you get beyond the prickliness.'

'What about Jane?'

'What about Jane?' John's sudden terseness takes me by surprise.

'Does she get on with him?'

'Oh, I see.' He relaxes, dumbfounding me yet again by lighting up a cigarette. 'Does Jane get on with anyone?' he jokes, offering the packet to me.

This night keeps on getting better and better, I think, taking one.

'I bet Jane doesn't know you smoke,' I taunt, noticing how his hands quiver as he lights my cigarette.

'Jane doesn't need to know what I get up to. Best that way,' he boasts, touching the side of his nose.

There's a hidden meaning to his words, of course. I get that. But John is fooling himself. I'm under the impression that Jane knows everything there is to know about her husband.

He comes to stand next to me. Close up, he's not so attractive after all, and I start to go off him. An odour of sweat clings to his clothes, and his middle-aged paunch rests against my leg. What John doesn't know is that I wouldn't trust any man who's prepared to cheat on his wife, especially under her own roof. Not that I owe Jane anything, mind.

I've done some bad things in my time, using men for sex, but I've never slept with a married man. Not to my knowledge, anyway. Flirted, yes. I can't help myself, but no more than that. It's one of my few no-go areas. Decency instilled in me by my parents, no doubt, that I can't shake off. I'm not the kind of girl John takes me for, and I bet it would surprise him and Jane to know this. I shouldn't think he takes kindly to being turned down either.

Realising it's not in my interest to do so yet, I move away. Picking up one of the pool cues, I give the end a provocative rub of chalk, then remove the triangle rack from the stack of balls. With my eye on the number eight in the middle of the pyramid, I lean over the table and take a shot, making sure John gets an eyeful of leg and thigh.

When I sneak a look in his direction, I see that his eyes, though slightly glazed, are devouring every inch of me. Now that I have him where I want him, I fire at him the one question I've been waiting all night to ask him. 'Who is the other Lucy I keep seeing, John?'

'Other Lucy?' he blubbers unconvincingly. 'I don't know what you mean.'

The lie drops from his mouth like coal spilling out of a fire.

31

Night has fallen, and the scene stretching out in front of us could be straight out of Africa. I've always wanted to go, but, so far, I've only ventured as far as Lanzarote. Even then I had to take sedatives before stepping foot on the plane. Life's not much fun when you can see the future, and I've seen enough visions of planes nose-diving to put me off long-haul flights. It seems I'm always to be haunted by one accident or another.

On that thought, I dig my fingernails into my palm and try to force the image of the car hitting Grace back into the shadows. That night remains blurred in part. The facts are hazy, but the blackness of it had swallowed me up as if I were nothing. Days and nights, weeks, and months lost in a fog.

Eventually, the mist in my head clears, and I notice that the surrounding parkland has been dipped in blue by the moon. The buzzing of insects helps feed the fantasy that we're far away from Moon Hollow and Hollow Fen. *I wish.*

But we're only a few feet away – sitting outside on the terrace, our rattan chairs pulled under a patio light that draws moths from far and wide. Their papery wings fluttering around us create no sound, but the silence is filled by Adele playing in the background. I prefer this to John's '80s Norwegian boy band.

For someone who claims to only smoke socially, John lights one cigarette after another. Black coffee has helped to sober him up, but his mood is still dark. He's absent, morose in a way I've not witnessed before. Like a condemned man. Like Adam Lockwood.

'So, her name was Lucy Benedict? And she was your au pair?' I prompt him to continue with his story.

'Lucia. She was called Lucia, but we, I, called her Lucy for short.' John mopes.

'And she was from Romania?'

'Yes. Somewhere near Bârsana. Wherever that is.'

'And when she lived with you, what room did she sleep in?'

'What difference does that make?' John wants to know. 'She was only with us five minutes.'

'Eleven months isn't five minutes,' I gently remind him.

'In your room, if you must know. Not that it matters,' he snaps.

'It matters, John, because I see her.'

John's face pales at that, and his lips part as if he's about to say something, only for him to fall silent again. He picks up his glass, remembers that it's empty, and reaches instead for another cigarette.

'Good God,' he utters at last. 'You really see her?'

I nod. 'Everywhere I go. I see her when I should be

looking for Lucy. If I'm to find your daughter, John, then I have to know what happened to this other Lucy.'

'Nothing happened. She left, that's all. Why? You don't think—?' His jaw drops open as it registers that she might actually be dead.

'I'm not in the habit of coming across living ghosts,' I point out.

'But you've seen Lucy and the kidnapper. And they're...'

'That is vastly different from how it feels when I see Lucy Benedict. She speaks to me, John. She can only do that from the other side of the grave.'

John looks horrified, and I almost feel sorry for him, but I resist reaching out and patting his arm. I don't want to lead him on or give him false hope that everything is all right when it clearly isn't and may never be again.

'What does she say?' he asks.

'I'm still trying to figure out what she wants me to know,' I confess. 'Until then, I need you to tell me everything you can about her.'

'There's not much to tell.'

'Then tell me what you *do* know.'

'She came to us the year before we had Lucy. She wanted to improve her English, and Jane needed some help in the house, said she was fed up employing local people. She didn't like them knowing our business. You know what Jane can be like.'

John's eyes, clearer and livelier than they were an hour ago, rest on me as if he needs my approval to go on. I nod eagerly to show I understand.

'Jane went through an agency in Peterborough. That's all I know about how Lucy came to live with us.'

'She never knew your Lucy, then?'

'No. She left long before Jane fell pregnant.'

'And how did Jane get on with her?'

'Fine. They got on fine.'

John is being flippant. That's how I know he's lying.

'It must have been hard for her having another woman living under her roof. And we both know Jane doesn't get along well with people. You said so yourself, remember?'

That's got to get him in the gonads. And it's true. The look he bestows on me is one of contempt. He thinks I'm hitting below the belt. As if he were a witness in a court case, John lowers his head and refuses to say another word. My irritation flares.

'What happened the night she left? Was there an argument, or did she leave amicably?'

John has his head in his hands, and his body is shaking. I don't know whether I should press him anymore. He's obviously distressed. But I don't feel any sympathy for him. Not a whisper.

'It's clear there's something you're not telling me, John. The way I see it, we have two choices. You can either tell me the truth about what happened to Lucy Benedict or we can wait until she decides to tell me herself. And in the meantime, she will continue to get in the way of my search for your daughter. Is that what you want?'

His head bounces up at that. There are real tears in his eyes, which surprises me no end. I didn't think men of John's type and status displayed emotion. I thought they had any softness beaten out of them while they were still at boarding school.

'Jane threw her out,' he blurts.

Before I can ask why, he's speaking again. The desire to talk, to get it all out in the open, becomes apparent.

'She had this birthmark on her face. I think secretly that's why Jane hired her, thinking it would put me off, but even with it, she was lovely. Quite beautiful.' He sighs.

'You cared for her.'

Knowing what I do about John and his way with the ladies, I'm still shocked. His words have me sitting upright in my chair, longing to know more.

'It didn't last long,' John admits with regret. 'Somehow or other, I don't know how, Jane found out. Poor Lucy was sent packing the same night. I didn't get a chance to say goodbye.'

John is looking at me with lovelorn eyes. It's clear he wants me to take pity on him, and part of me does now that I know he cared for this woman. The harsher side of me judges him, though. Poor Jane. She's no angel, but an affair with the au pair, for Christ's sake. *What was John thinking?* No wonder Jane won't employ anyone to help in the house.

Deciding that I'll delay offering John a shoulder to cry on until I find out what really happened to Lucy Benedict, and it's clear that something did or else I wouldn't keep seeing her in my visions, I'm struck with a terrible thought. *Surely not Jane. She wouldn't. Couldn't. Could she? Understandably, Jane would've been angry with Lucy that night, but did she do something to her? And is John covering for her?*

I'm about to ask John what he thinks happened that night when a scream, the likes of which I've never heard before, rips through the house.

32

JANE

'She has gone. Lucy has gone.' Jane screams, clawing wildly at her hair as she paces agitatedly up and down the room, stopping only when she sees John and Cindy gaping at her from the doorway. At once, Jane throws herself into John's unwelcoming arms. She will make him care for her. Put her first. Even if it kills her.

'Someone took her.' Jane almost retches when she smells Cindy's cheap perfume on John. He lets her rest on his shoulder only for a few seconds before pushing her away again. He still has hold of her arms, though, Jane notices – not to support her, rather, to restrain her. He does not like to see her distressed like this. Like most men of John's kind, he does not think it seemly for a woman of her age and position to lose control. But he will not say so in front of Cindy.

'What's this all about, Jane?' he demands, peering into her anguished face, looking for clues that he is too stupid to find. But Jane does not care if he disapproves. She was foolish to think John would be any support to her in her hour of need. Deciding she does not need his sympathy or understanding, she thrusts him off as if to prove it. But she is not strong enough to prevent the tears from coming. They roll down her face freely.

Cindy pipes up from somewhere behind John. 'Are you all right, Jane? Did something happen?'

At least she sounds genuinely concerned, Jane observes. Unlike John, who simply does not want her to make a scene. Again.

'What has brought this on?' John attempts to be kind. More for Cindy's benefit, Jane suspects.

'I went to look for her, and she wasn't there.' Jane can hear the tremor in her own voice. God, she sounds weak. Like the pathetic, needy type of woman, she secretly scorns. Worried her knees are about to crumple beneath her, and she certainly would not want Cindy to witness that, she flops down on Lucy's bed. Try as she might, she cannot stop shaking.

'I know, love. I know.' John pats her trembling hand. The gesture is meant to be tender, but it comes across as formal and awkward.

'I'll get her a glass of water,' Cindy says, rushing into the adjoining bathroom.

Since when did I become her? Jane seethes. Her mind clouded with confusion, she allows the paranoia to set in. It can happen at any time. The steaming red mist is never far away. But John is talking, and she must concentrate on what he is saying, otherwise he may insist on sending for the doctor again. Like he did the last time she became hysterical.

'But there is every chance she will still be found. We

can't give up hope yet.' John attempts to reassure her. Jane wants to laugh in his face but resists.

'That's not what I mean. I'm not talking about our little girl but the doll.' She is scathing.

'Doll? What doll?' John is bemused.

A glass of water is handed to Jane, and she takes a large gulp of it before replying.

'The one from the doll's house.' Jane points to the replica of Moon Hollow but cannot bring herself to look at it.

'You mean the baby in the cot?' Cindy asks.

Jane nods, grateful to Cindy for once. She seems to understand where Jane is coming from.

'I don't see the significance.' John is losing interest. Jane can read him like a book. He is thinking that if this conversation starts getting fanciful or, worse still, hormonal, then he should escape while he has the chance.

'The baby in the cot represents Lucy,' Cindy explains, helping Jane out. But when John shrugs, clearly still baffled, Cindy walks over to the doll's house and peers inside.

Eyes brimming with tears, Jane watches Cindy search for the missing piece until the tension becomes unbearable. Judging by the girl's expression, she is almost as upset by the disappearance of the figure as Jane is.

'It was there earlier,' Jane insists before anyone can contradict her. 'Before I fell asleep on the bed. When I woke up, it was gone.'

'But who could have taken it?' Cindy enquires, raising her eyebrows.

'I thought one of you might have come in while I was resting,' Jane says nonchalantly, to disguise how desperate she is for the doll to have been taken by one of them – because if not, who? A shiver runs down Jane's spine. Likening it to somebody walking over her grave, a creeping horror seeps into her, as if somebody else's blood were invading her veins.

John and Cindy look at each other before shaking their heads.

'We were downstairs the whole time,' John confirms guiltily.

'What does it mean?' Jane addresses Cindy, as John is no use to her now.

The girl whispers, paling with fear, 'I don't know.'

33

CINDY

A t Moon Hollow, characters such as the Lord of the Dance dip in and out of my head without any introduction or goodbye. Earlier tonight, on my way up to my room, an old man, the same one I suspect of spying on me through the walls, passed me on the galleried landing and nodded at me politely. He might've taken this in his stride, like it's an everyday occurrence, but I bloody well didn't. When I first clapped eyes on the old git, my stomach was in knots. I was so scared I couldn't move an inch.

Grace was already asleep when I finally did make it up to bed, so I crept in next to her, careful not to disturb her. Once there, I pulled the duvet over my head like a child scared of the dark, not wanting to see any more ghosts. I can't remember when I last felt this tired. How long has it been since I slept? Two days? It feels like two years. An entire lifetime.

This house with its terrible secrets, intrusive stillness, and oppressive atmosphere is taking its toll on me. *On all of us*, I correct myself. It's gone midnight, but I'm unable to sleep despite the late hour. The house has finally settled. By that, I mean it's quiet. I wouldn't say peaceful. That's not a word I'd ever use to describe Moon Hollow or its inhabitants, living or dead. Noticing that the sheets are like ice around us and that we're both shivering with cold, I move closer to my daughter in the hope of warming us both up, only to find she's now awake and staring back at me from under the folds of the cover. 'What's wrong, Grace?' I ask wearily, sensing she's in another of her moods.

She goes on ignoring me. Normally, I would give her a friendly poke and tell her to stop being a "sulky little shit", and she would respond by pursing her lip and telling me off for swearing. She's always been the adult in our relationship. At times it's felt as if our roles were reversed. In our previous life in Wharf Road, that's how Grace and I were.

I miss how we were together. But tonight, I'm too exhausted to deal with one of her sulks, and I'm about to roll over and try to get some sleep when I spot Grace's clenched-up hand under the sheet. For some reason I can't explain, a tiny shiver of fear runs down my spine. From experience, I know this isn't a good sign.

'What have you got there?'

Grace narrows her eyes at me, still clutching at whatever is in her hand. I owe my daughter many things, including the truth, but I figure we're in this relationship together whether she likes it or not, so I refuse to go on being ignored.

'Grace,' I say firmly, pulling the bed cover away from her. 'Please show me what it is.'

My daughter smiles at me then. An odd sort of smile

that makes me feel afraid without knowing why. But I don't stare at her face for long, not because I can't bear to, but because she's opening her hand, suddenly eager for me to see—

'You took the baby from the doll's house.' I'm more shocked than I should be. She's a child, after all. A little girl who likes dolls and doll's houses and who, through no fault of her own, has been left to her own devices in this rambling old house. For all her talk of providing a home that Social Services would approve of, Jane's not much of a childminder.

'Lucy doesn't need it anymore.' Grace's crazed eyeballs turn nasty with jealousy. 'She's never coming back to this house. I live here now.'

'Don't say that, Grace.' I gasp, hardly believing that my lovely, kind daughter would say such a thing. But then I remember that she, too, has been given the so-called gift of second sight. Perhaps she knows something I don't.

'We have to believe that Lucy is still alive,' I remind her.

Grace claws herself into a sitting position and places the figure in the middle of the bed, creating even more of a barrier between us.

'Why is she so important to you?' She crosses her arms.

'Because she's lost, and her mummy and daddy need my help to find her.'

'I don't care if she's dead, and neither does Jane.'

'What a thing to say, Grace. You don't mean that.'

'I do,' Grace exclaims in a voice edged with hatred. 'You don't care about me. Why should I care about her?'

'Grace, I care about you more than anything…'

Grace clambers out of bed. Her eyes are little dark slits. She hurls the plastic baby, aiming it right at me, and I'm forced to duck to avoid it striking my face. *Enough is enough*, I think. So, I get out of bed too, determined to take charge of this situation, but I'm not quick enough. As soon as I get to my feet, Grace is on the retreat, running towards the door.

'They're not her parents!' Grace yells over her shoulder as if she's done with me. But when she reaches the door and finds it locked, she turns accusing eyes on me. I want to tell her that I didn't lock it, that someone else did. It happens every night. But I can tell by the reproachful way she's staring at me that she wouldn't believe me.

'What do you mean by that?' I ask gently, resisting the urge to move any closer, because I don't want her to feel cornered, but wondering at the same time who's fed my daughter this terrible lie. But Grace refuses to say any more.

'Are you trying to tell me that the Valentines aren't Lucy's parents?' There's an edge to my voice that wasn't there before, and Grace immediately picks up on it. Deciding that I must stamp on this nonsense quickly before the Valentines get to hear about it, I dare to contradict her. 'You know that isn't true.'

'It is true,' Grace insists defiantly, but there's fear in her eyes too as if she knows she's been caught out in a lie. 'I heard them talking. They don't want you to find Lucy.'

At first, I think Grace is throwing me a clue to something I might've previously overlooked regarding John and Jane, but I'm wrong. I finally understand that Grace is telling the truth when she says she heard John and Jane talking about Lucy, but they were referring to Lucy Benedict, not their daughter.

Knowing this convinces me they're covering something up about the night the au pair went missing. Grace is right about one thing – the Valentines don't want me to find Lucy Benedict. But find her I will.

34

I see her. Again. Grace. Alone in the dark. Standing in the middle of the road. Her face is lit up by the glare of headlights as a car accelerates towards her. As before, her face is turned in my direction as if she can see me. I mean *really* see me. But that's impossible. How could she? I watch her mouth form a black hole as she screams out one word.

"Mummy!"

I'm in the backseat of a taxi, too smashed to care. I want to laugh because this isn't really happening. It can't be. If it were real, then Grace would run out of the way of the oncoming car. In the rearview mirror, the driver checks me out. I part my legs and give the perv something to get off on – a flash of red underwear.

There's a bang, followed by a sickening thud – as we hit something.

The screaming stops. I wake up.

Snot and tears, the saddest of couples, stream down my face. Everything about that night is a snatched memory.

No matter how many times I have the nightmare, I always wake from it feeling exhausted and numb. Knowing from experience that I won't fall back to sleep again, I push the bedcovers away and sit up. Grace's body beside me makes the smallest of mounds. She doesn't stir. I'm glad that at least one of us is getting some sleep.

That's when I see it—

The wardrobe door is open. Yet I know I shut it before coming to bed.

That's when I hear it.

The voice.

Lucy Benedict's voice.

She doesn't call out my name as she did before. This time, she's moaning as if in a great deal of pain. The sound echoes around the room. I look at Grace, but she remains asleep. I understand then that Lucy Benedict wants only me to hear her.

I feel I've no choice but to go in search of her. Perhaps if I do, I'll learn something new. The worst part is finding the courage to enter the wardrobe again. Knowing how much pain she's in drives me on. My hand trembles, though, as I slide open the hidden partition at the back of the wardrobe. Using my arms and elbows to guide me, I edge myself into the confined space that leads up to the secret staircase. It's like being in a small coffin. A child-sized one at best. The thought causes me to shudder.

The steps are dusty, but this time there aren't any ghostly footprints to guide me up them. Never mind. I can feel my way in the dark. But as I begin my ascent, a cold-ness seeps into my bones, and I get the feeling once more that I'm being watched. A pair of watery eyes, belonging to the same old man as before, peering down from the walls. I sense that he's on the lookout for his relatives again, the ones who're after his money and want him dead. But instead, he's found me. The thought of him being there makes me want to creep back into the shadows and hide, but knowing he can't hurt me, I keep on going.

When I reach the top of the stairs, the dampness I experienced before, which reminds me of dirty water, is present in the air, accompanied by the familiar smell of anaesthetic. By now, the throbbing behind my right temple has me wanting to call out in pain, as Lucy Benedict is doing. The symptoms I experience whenever I have a vision are getting worse. I blame Moon Hollow for this.

Before I can reach for the key protruding out of the lock, I see two rusted bolts, one at the top of the door and one at the bottom, sliding slowly open. They make an eerie screeching sound that has me clenching my jaw, but I stand my ground, wondering why I didn't notice the bolts before on my last visit to this room. *Were they even there then? Why would anyone put bolts on the outside of a door if not to keep someone locked inside?*

Feeling weak with fear and anticipation but equally determined that nothing will bar my entry into the room, I force myself to push open the door and step inside.

I'm immediately blinded by powerful overhead lighting that wasn't there before. And when my eyesight adjusts to the artificial lighting, I see that the room is also different.

Peering through my fingers, I'm stunned to discover that the room is no longer empty. I don't waste time asking myself how this is possible, because I know from experience that what I'm seeing is a vision and no more than that. Keeping my rational head on, I observe that the pictures are back on the walls – calming prints of sunflowers and green forests.

The floor is now carpeted, and the looping cobwebs are nowhere to be seen. Unlike before, everywhere is spotlessly clean. But I barely acknowledge any of these changes because all I can focus on is the pregnant woman lying naked on a bed in front of me.

The metal hospital-style bed is parked under the glass atrium roof, and a circle of blood surrounds the girl in it. At first, I don't know her. Her long black hair is tied back, away from her gaunt face, and her skin is oily with sweat. Thick purple veins, which throb and pulse like they have a life of their own, protrude from her swollen abdomen.

It's hard to pull my eyes away from it, but when I do, I see that her unseeing eyes are half open with the whites revealed. It's only when she pushes herself up onto her elbows, bares her teeth, and emits a groan as loud as any beast's that I recognise Lucy Benedict's birthmarked face.

'Lucia. Oh my God, Lucia.' I rush over to help her. But when I try to take hold of her hand, my own slices through the air, landing on nothing. As usual, I'm not allowed to interfere, which means there's nothing I can do to ease her pain. I back away, terrified, not knowing what to do except exist as a macabre witness.

That's when I see the drip stand next to the bed, with a saline bag hanging from it. My eyes scan the tubing that has a yellow liquid pumping through it, following it to where it ends, inserted into the back of her hand. It must have been there some time, because the skin is puckered and bruised around the needle entry point.

Footsteps. Coming up the stairs. Two sets of them. Lucy Benedict and I both look towards the door. It appears we can hear and see the same things even if we exist in different timelines. We're fenced in by whispers. A low murmuring of muffled voices. First a man, then a woman.

When the door finally creaks open and they come in, I don't know who is more terrified – me or her. The blurred figures of John and Jane Valentine surround the bed. I catch glimpses of their plastic doll-like faces, a stark reminder of the figures in the doll's house who, thanks to Grace, now look down on an empty cot. I can't see them properly, no matter how hard I try, nor hear what they're saying, but I suspect Lucy Benedict can.

I watch her shrink back in fear and try to pull a sheet over her nakedness as if determined to hide her belly from them, but it's too late. She looks like she's about to have the baby any minute. It hits me then that she might die. This amount of blood can't be normal. *Is that what happened to her? Is this what the Valentines have been trying to cover up?*

I put a hand over my mouth to stifle the scream that's about to erupt from it and back myself into a corner. I can't bear to see what happens next. I don't want to go anywhere near the bed, the Valentines, or Lucy Benedict. God forgive me, all I want is to wake up in my own house, with Grace by my side. I wish I'd never come to Moon Hollow. Never set eyes on the Valentines or Lucy Benedict.

I close my eyes, wanting to block out the scene in front of me. Blood, so much blood, the stench of anaesthetic, and Lucy Benedict's eyes rolling backward, a sense of betrayal in them as they close, *possibly for good.*

I take several deep breaths and wait for it to end. Nothing will make me open my eyes again until I'm sure they're gone. At last, I feel a silence settling around me like snow on someone's eyelashes. When my eyes do eventually open, I'm relieved to find myself alone, not in the corner of the room where I'd positioned myself but sitting in the middle of the floor, raised on my elbows with my legs apart.

Shocked to find myself in the same birthing position that Lucy Benedict adopted, I search the empty room, looking for traces left over from my vision. But the bed has disappeared along with the young woman in it. The pictures have vanished too, so has the drip and the carpet. The room is as it was when I first came across it. Not a drop of blood is left behind. There's no lingering waft of anaesthetic, and the dampness that I now associate with Lucy Benedict has also gone.

I'm about to get to my feet, dust myself down, and take a moment to recover when a glint of silver catches my eye. Peering closer, I see a chain of some kind is wedged between the floorboards. Although it wouldn't be immediately obvious to anybody entering the room, it's close enough to the surface for me to be able to forage it out with my fingernails. Once it's resting in my hand, I see that it's a silver bracelet with one word engraved on it—

Lucia.

I slip it over my hand and, once the catch is closed, allow it to slide onto my child-sized wrist. Although too big for me, I promise myself that I won't take it off until I find out what happened to Lucy Benedict. Knowing how much my own engraved ankle bracelet means to me, the one my dad gave me for my twenty-first, I'm certain she wouldn't have left Moon Hollow without it.

'What did they do to you, Lucia?'

35

As soon as I hear the door being unlocked at the ungodly hour of six a.m., I leap out of bed, ready to do battle. After what happened last night, I didn't go to sleep at all and instead spent the whole time awake, lying fully clothed on the bed, next to Grace, who, despite being in a foul mood all night, had gone back to sleep as soon as her face hit the pillow.

If it weren't for my daughter, I would have banged on the door and screamed blue murder until Jane came down and let me out. Although I've had all night to mull over things, I'm just as fucking furious as ever.

Creeping out of the room, careful not to disturb Grace, I now make my way up the second staircase of the house, as this is the only way, *apparently*, to access John and Jane's suite of rooms in the west wing. For a council-house girl like me, the idea of having wings in houses is mental. Each to their own, I suppose.

Except this staircase is not as grand as the one leading up to my room. When I say *my* room, I am, of course, referring to the Valentines' guest room, which couldn't be any less mine.

The stone steps are covered in dust, and if I didn't know better, I'd swear that nobody ever came up here. In my rush to get to the top, I stumble and put out a hand to stop myself from falling. My palm comes away from the wall covered in a thick layer of dust that's as fine as face powder. That's when I notice something painted on the wall – a mural of some kind, hidden beneath the grime. Despite being keen to tackle John and Jane about all I learned last night, I'm intrigued.

So, I pause on the stairs to wipe away the dirt that must've taken months if not years to accumulate, until more of the mural is revealed. It appears to tell a story of some kind. But, like the past, it's faded in places, as if it doesn't remember things properly.

On closer inspection, I realise it's one of those trompe l'oeil paintings I learned about at school as part of my art GCSE. It's a technique that uses imagery to create an optical illusion, making the people and objects in the painting appear in 3D. If I remember rightly, the translation for trompe l'oeil is "deceive the eye".

How appropriate for this house, I think, leaning in for a closer look, careful not to breathe in the swirling particles of dust that I've disturbed. My eyes are drawn first to the unmistakable conical spires of the church, which I instantly recognise, and then to a family of blue-eyed, blond-haired Valentine ancestors posing on the lawns of Moon Hollow. But instead of the house, a yellow-stoned castle hovers imperiously in the background.

This must be the castle that was demolished to make way for the existing house. Even more intrigued, I study the family in greater detail. They're surrounded by tall hunting dogs, who each hold the gaze of the woman dominating the scene, as if desperate to be commanded by her.

Something about the tallest dog's cropped, mutilated ears and human blue eyes has my stomach doing somersaults. The feeling that I've met this dog before or that I'm quite likely to in the future makes my skin prickle. Confronting such a dog would be one of my worst fears. Cowardly lowering my eyes, as if it were really stood in front of me, I turn my attention back to the family members, seeing something of Jane in the little girl. If it is her, then she's taller than her two male siblings, which I assume makes her the eldest.

I wonder what happened to the boys. They're similar in looks, but they're not twins. One of them is stunted and deformed-looking. The runt of the litter, my mother would have said. There's something about the over-smiley eyes that make me suspect he has behavioural difficulties. I find it odd that Jane has never mentioned having brothers. This makes me distrust her even more. They promised to be honest with me and to tell me everything. But their version of the truth is different to anyone else's.

Despite feeling angry, I almost smile when I see that the artist has captured Jane in a temper. Her eyes are shining with anger, and her mouth is tugged into a snarl as if she's longing to escape from the hand that's holding hers captive. The woman responsible for Jane's anger looks full of self-importance. Her fingers, adorned with jewelled rings, seem to nip cruelly at her daughter's skin. This makes me wonder if Jane's mother was unkind to her, as my own was. Does this mean we have something in common?

I dismiss that thought when I see how breathtakingly beautiful Jane's mother was. Yet the woman's painted-on smile appears fake, as though only there to impress. Judging by the manipulative glint in her eye, I imagine her capable of twisting anyone, men especially, around her little finger. Her waist-long blond hair has been teased into playful curls, and her pink lips and English-rose complexion complete the high-society look.

My mother was rather plain in contrast, so I've no idea what it must have been like for Jane having to compare herself to her mother every day, as I'm sure she did.

With a mother like that, I almost feel sorry for Jane, but then I remember that, along with her husband, she's been lying to me the whole time. When I think about the way Lucy Benedict was kept locked up in that room for God knows how long, my blood boils. I also can't forget the words that Grace threw at me in anger.

"They're not her parents."

How she guessed before I did, I'll never know, but everything I learned last night tends to support the conclusion that the Valentines are not Lucy's real parents, yet I still have my doubts. They could've gone on to have their own baby after Lucy gave birth to hers, but if that were the case, then where is Lucy Benedict's child? All I know for sure is both Lucys are missing and one of them didn't make it. But are John and Jane capable of hurting another human being or doing something to Lucy Benedict's child to cover up the fact that things went wrong that night?

John and Jane were both there in my vision, at Lucy Benedict's bedside, helping to deliver her baby. *Oh my God, I hope they were helping her, because I can't bear to think of the alternative.* As I keep telling myself, that amount of blood was not normal. Something must have happened to Lucy.

Reminding myself that there's only one way to find out, I hurriedly climb the remaining stairs, the painting quite forgotten about. Whispers from the past nudge me up each step, encouraging me to move faster.

I don't know how, but Jane found out.

Poor Lucy was sent packing the same night.

I didn't get the chance to say goodbye.

Lies. All lies.

36

As if my banging on their bedroom door before sunrise is a normal occurrence for the Valentines, I hear them moving around unhurriedly inside the room. I imagine them slipping on dressing gowns and slippers like there's no need to rush, and sense the pair of them are exchanging inquisitive looks and raising their eyebrows as if to say, "What now?"

Hating that the world on the other side of their door hasn't yet been impacted by what I've had to endure tonight, I pound on it again until my knuckles throb.

'Who's there?' John's sleep-deprived voice calls out from the other side of the door.

'Well, it's not bloody Lucy Benedict. That much I do know,' I yell belligerently.

My words are met with silence. *Hallelujah*, I think, though that's my mother's voice creeping unwittingly into my head. I rectify that immediately with my next thought. *How fucking good does that feel? Knowing I've shocked them into silence.*

The door opens abruptly, almost unexpectedly, and I stumble through it. The look of dread on John's face as he shakily attempts to tie the belt on his dressing gown is priceless. His eyes plead with mine as I march past him into the room, but I look right through him. I was an idiot before, worse than that, a fool, for being taken in by John's crocodile tears and sob story, but there's no chance of that happening again.

Before I can say anything, I'm brought up short by the sight of Jane innocently sitting up in bed, naked beneath the covers, as if she hadn't already got up once to unlock my bedroom door. Seeing her like this throws me, because if Jane isn't the one locking me in at night and letting me out each morning, who is? Somebody doesn't want me roaming the corridors of Moon Hollow at night. That's for sure.

Shuddering at the thought, I accidentally let back in flashes of the vision I had before of the couple making love in the church. *Could that have been John and Jane?* I shouldn't be surprised. These religious types are always the worst. I should know. I grew up with one. My mother was the biggest hypocrite of all, declining to do her godly duty by refusing to take me and Grace in when we needed her help, even though she knew I could end up losing my daughter for good.

"As far as I'm concerned, after what you did, both my daughter and granddaughter are dead to me," she'd spat cruelly. Who was she to lecture me about parenting? And why punish Grace as well? If it hadn't been for my father, I would have clawed out her eyes for that.

Returning to the present, I get the feeling that Jane would like to do the same to me, judging by the hate-filled stare she's levelling at me. But I ignore her for now. John is the one who lied to my face. He'll be the first to break. Not Jane.

'You lied to me, John.' I jab a finger in his chest. I've never wanted to punch someone's lights out as much as I do him right now.

'What…about?' he stutters. 'I don't know what you mean.'

'You know what I mean, all right. Lucy Benedict.'

'What about her?' His guilty eyes dart to Jane's and then back to mine.

'You kept her here against her will,' I point out.

John shakes his head. 'We most certainly did not.'

'I saw what you did. The pair of you. In the secret room.'

This time, when John's eyes slide across to his wife's, and remain there, I feel a small shiver of fear run through me. *Should I be saying so much?* For the first time, it occurs to me that by accusing them of what potentially could be murder, I could be placing myself and Grace in danger. If they could harm a pregnant woman, there's no telling what they would do to me. But it's too late to back down now.

'What exactly did you see, Cindy?' John wants to know.

'You tell me,' I say, dodging around the fact that, other than what I saw tonight, I don't know everything yet, and I can't risk them knowing this. I still don't know how Lucy Benedict died, only that she had a baby and was held captive against her will.

'It sounds like you've made your mind up about us

already.' Jane sounds bored. For a minute, I think she's about to order me out of the room, but then I see her fingers are clutching tightly at the duvet, and I know then that she's not as calm and collected as she's making out to be. This gives me the confidence to go on.

I renew my interrogation of John. 'You said that Lucy Benedict left here the night Jane found out about your sordid affair.'

'That's right.' He gulps.

'But we both know that isn't true. She didn't leave when you said she did because she went on to have a baby. A baby she gave birth to, here, at Moon Hollow.'

'We wanted to help the girl out of a spot of bother, didn't we Jane?' John looks to his wife for signs of encouragement but receives none. He doesn't notice that her grip on the duvet has intensified, but I do. This tells me more than all their lies put together.

'We didn't tell you because we thought it would complicate things. Besides...' John wheedles, 'it had nothing to do with our Lucy going missing.'

'But she wasn't your Lucy, was she, John?' I say, thinking back to what Grace told me. *They're not her parents.* Finally, it twigs. John lied about the dates. About how long Lucy Benedict had stayed with them. He lied about everything. As did Jane. Neither of them is to be trusted. I wonder why I didn't get to the truth sooner. I must be the world's worst clairvoyant.

'She was Lucy Benedict's baby. Not yours,' I screech, wanting to lash out at the pair of them. The lying bastards. 'And you'll pay for what you did to that poor woman. I'll make sure of that.'

'Before you do,' Jane says huffily, 'you ought to know that you are wrong about one thing. You see, I might not be Lucy's real mother, but John was, is, her father.'

37

JANE

J ane stares at her reflection in the dressing table mirror that once belonged to her mother and frowns at the crack spreading from one corner of the glass to the other, a reminder of the last time she and John fought when things turned nasty. She feels a similar fracture spreading inside herself, tearing her apart. She does not know why she has kept hold of the damaged family heirloom. It is not as if it has any sentimental value or, indeed, any financial worth, which is how she feels about herself most days.

But then she reminds herself that nothing in Moon Hollow has ever been purchased from new. Everything is inherited. Even the house, built to replace the crumbling-down castle that was once her ancestral home, retains parts of the castle walls. Its old bones are kept alive, enclosing them within its grasp still. Jane fears it will outlive them all. She had hoped Lucy would one day inherit this house, becoming its next custodian. Now, she is not so sure.

Knowing the house's history as she does, would she really wish that on her only child?

After Cindy's unsettling visit, when the girl accused them of just about everything under the sun, Jane had got out of bed, slipped on her dressing gown, and went to sit at the dressing table, intent on brushing her hair one hundred times as she does every morning and night like her mother taught her to do. Jane used to do the same for Lucy, hoping she would find the experience calming and therapeutic. But the child refused to sit still and would cry out when Jane tackled her knots with the silver-plated comb.

Jane regrets her decision to have Lucy's hair cut short. Her daughter loved her long hair. She loved it more than her own mother. Correction. She loved everything more than her mother – her doll Heidi, the treehouse, but most of all her daddy who could do no wrong. Wondering if anybody is brushing Lucy's hair right now has the power to bring tears to Jane's eyes.

These days when Jane sees herself in the mirror, she is reminded of her mother's beloved dog Monty, a majestic Great Dane whose bloodlines were almost as worthy as the Valentines'. Jane remembers being horrified by its glazed-over eyes on the day they found it dead. Her mother wept over the loss of that dog as if it were a child, making Jane feel intense jealousy towards it. It was the only time she had ever seen her mother shed tears.

Like Monty, the life has gone out of Jane's eyes. She would never stoop so low as to cry over an animal, but going back to being publicly barren, a woman unable to have children, has left her feeling dead inside.

Beneath the dressing gown, which comes up to her chin, Jane's skin is white and flawless. She inherited her mother's complexion, if not her beauty and wit, and she longs to claw at it – mark it and make it bleed.

But if she did, John would look at her in disgust before calling for the doctor. He has never been able to cope with women's moods, let alone hormones, menopause, or childbirth. He almost passed out when he saw Lucy being born. One look at the state poor Lucy Benedict was in would have put him off her forever if he hadn't already lost interest by then.

Jane hears the flush of a toilet and watches John come into the room, as agitated as he was earlier when Cindy flung her wild accusations at them. The girl must have been unhinged to suspect them of plotting to murder the mother of their child when they had done all they could to bring the baby into the world alive and kicking. Why would they even consider it when everything had been settled between them?

Everyone had agreed that Lucy was in no state, emotionally or financially, to raise the child herself, so it made perfect sense for John, the natural father, and Jane, his barren wife, to take it on. Lucy Benedict had been paid handsomely for surrendering her baby, so nobody could accuse them of taking advantage of the girl.

Breaking from her thoughts, Jane slyly observes John doing up the belt on his trousers and takes pleasure in the fact that his waistline is expanding. He is having to add an extra notch to his belt these days.

When he sees her watching him, he frowns as if trying to figure out what she is thinking – *good luck with that* – and then paces up and down the room, wringing his hands. She is reminded of his father, who had been a general in the army. An officer of rank who believed in courage, discipline, and selfless commitment, values that John lacks. Sadly, putting his country first, before his own family, meant he was not around much when John grew up.

'I think she believed us,' John says shakily, trying and failing to secure his cuff links. Normally, Jane would help him with this task, but she does not feel like it today. Holding his gaze, she waits for him to elaborate. But he does not. Instead, he turns away, a sheepish look on his face that Jane is well acquainted with.

She sometimes glimpses it after he has stayed overnight at the gentleman's club in London that he still insists on frequenting. A habit that has fallen out of favour with most of the upper classes these days. But John is a dinosaur and refuses to give up his way of life. Anyone would think he had earned it.

'Why shouldn't she? It is the truth, after all,' Jane tells him snootily.

'If you say so, Jane.'

It surprises Jane to know that John is as rattled as he was earlier. He seems surprised, irritated, that she does not share his concern.

Jane goes to some lengths to reassure him. 'She knows I would never adopt a child who wasn't a blood relation. I could see it in her eyes that she believed me.'

'We didn't technically adopt Lucy.'

'No.' Jane grits her teeth, annoyed by his nit-picking. 'She was given to us.'

'It isn't the same thing.'

'It absolutely is.' Jane wants to throw something at her husband. 'You must never let on to Cindy that this was a business transaction and nothing more. It is far better that she continues to believe Lucy was born as a result of your being infatuated with the girl.'

'As indeed I was,' John taunts cruelly.

Jane wants to tell him he is wrong about that too but decides against it. Her days of begging, crying, and placating are over. These days, she saves such emotion for God and Lucy. Indeed, her husband might once have been beguiled by Lucy Benedict. At first, he thought her exotic, and Jane had put this down to the girl's accent and disfigured face, believing it brought the protector out in John.

But as soon as he had her, he moved on to the next one while Jane waited desperately to find out if there would be a result of their dalliance. And there was, and Jane went down on her knees and thanked God for John's bastard, especially when Lucy agreed to give up her baby.

'You are a cold fish, Jane. I've always said so.' John has resorted to scorning her when he did not get the response he was hoping for.

'Well, you must remember, John' – Jane continues to brush her hair, counting each stroke in her head, *eighty-seven, eighty-eight, eighty-nine* – 'that fish have a habit of escaping the net when it suits them.'

'You wouldn't betray me?' He sounds like the same scared boy she took on all those years ago when they first fell in love and he looked up to her. Adored her, even. Whenever he wants something from her these days, he deliberately uses the same tone of voice he knows gives her butterflies. She has always wanted to wrap herself up in John's voice. She used to be fond of saying that it was better than any fur coat. But that was then, and this is now, and the truth is like a rock being thrown at her head.

'Isn't that what you do every time you go off with someone else?' she asks softly.

'I didn't think you minded.' He sulks, again like a little boy.

'While we are being honest, which is something we both seem incapable of these days' – Jane swings around in her chair to show him that he has her full attention – 'you ought to know that I do care, and I do mind, but that has never been enough to make you stop.'

'You should have said.' John shoves his hands in his pockets and looks at the floor, his face ugly and twisted with guilt.

'I absolutely should not,' Jane argues, angry that John has caused her to lose count of the number of brush strokes. She has no idea where she was up to, ninety or ninety-one? Deciding that she will have to start again, Jane savagely tugs the brush through her bouncy blond waves. One, two, three…

'Did you see what she was wearing?' she asks, changing the subject.

John shrugs, insinuating he has no idea what she is talking about. For some reason this annoys Jane, more so than usual, and now it is her turn to want to lash out.

'For a man who claims to love women's bodies, you do not notice much, do you?'

'Now, Jane,' John warns.

'The bracelet. Lucy Benedict's bracelet. Cindy had it on her wrist. She was wearing it,' Jane screeches. Honestly, he can be so dumb at times. 'I asked her about it when you went down to make us all coffee. She said she found it in a drawer somewhere.'

'But why would she lie?' John scratches his chin and pulls a bemused expression.

Poor John. Always confused about something or other, Jane cannot help thinking.

'I don't know, John. But we searched every inch of this house looking for it, and it was not in any drawer.'

'Then, that must mean she is…' John pauses as it sinks in.

Jane finishes his sentence. 'Lying too.'

38

CINDY

Having been woken at first light by another presence lingering on the bed, not a child this time but a weeping woman with paper-thin skin and sunken cheeks, who'd lived through the Boer War, I've come outside wanting fresh air. But it feels as if the scream that was trapped in my throat when I first saw her is still there, crushing my chest. My stomach is in terrible knots even now. Gives me the jitters just thinking about it.

Its name was Mary, and her thoughts, hopes, and dreams ran riot in my mind for a while, driving all thoughts of Lucy away. There was a cancer spreading through the woman's skeletal body, making her wheeze and cough up phlegm into a blood-soaked handkerchief. Another distant relative of Jane Valentine's, Mary had cruelly been branded an old maid by her many nephews and nieces who ridiculed her for constantly weeping over the man she'd loved and lost in the war. One of the thousands who didn't make it home.

Mary's eyes hungrily devoured me as I leapt out of

bed and tugged on some clothes, relieved to discover she was too weak to follow. She didn't reach out to me as fiercely as some do, but I could tell she was jealous of my ability to breathe. Her hands itched to claw at me. Fear of her stealing the breath from my body is what drove me out of the room. And into the sunshine. Wanting to fucking run because I was alive, and she wasn't.

I haven't jogged in over three years, so I find I'm easily out of breath and having to stop and rest a lot. This makes me glad, for once, that I'm in a quiet country lane where nobody can see me. I would be a laughingstock back home if my friends caught me out jogging in baggy pants and ancient trainers, wheezing like the old woman on the bed.

It's still really early, and the grass is wet with dew, but I can already feel the warmth from the rising sun on my skin. I avoid the grass verges because they grow wild and there's evidence of rabbit burrows. The last thing I need is to sprain or break an ankle. So, I keep to the tarmac, which is cracked in places, broken down over time by the tractors and combines that use these lanes.

I'd quite forgotten the high I used to get from exercise before booze, fags, and recreational drugs took its place. Despite Jane and I calling a truce, I'm still not allowed my phone. I don't understand why, not now that their secret is out in the open, but I'll go along with it for now. I only wanted it so I could listen to music on my run, but yesterday when John lent me an old MP3 player and earphones on the quiet, on the understanding that I wouldn't mention it to Jane, I could hardly believe my luck. The music might not be to my taste – a compilation of Guns N' Roses, Def Leppard, and Bryan Adams – but it'll do.

The back lanes are winding with unruly trees and over-grown hedgerows, so I can't see what's coming around the next bend. It never occurs to me that I should be worried about traffic coming from the other direction, so I've only got myself to blame for what happens next. With all that rock music turned up full volume, blasting in my ear, it's no wonder I don't hear the car approaching from behind. When it does race by, angrily pipping its horn, I'm forced to jump out of its way onto the grass verge and almost tumble face-first into a prickly hedge, causing a flock of sparrows to spill angrily out of it.

I want to yell after the driver and call them a crazy bastard – they could have killed me – but I recognise the midnight-blue Jaguar and private number plate as John's. It's usually parked in the driveway of Moon Hollow, unused and gleaming with wax, and this is the first time I've seen its owner behind the wheel.

John doesn't slow down or check to see if I'm okay. Did he mean to try to run me over, knowing I wouldn't be able to hear? He must have known what direction I'd be heading in. He might have even watched me leaving the house. But why would he want me dead or injured when I'm here to find his daughter? It doesn't make sense. It's more likely he's angry with me. Or himself. That must be why he didn't raise a hand to acknowledge me.

John is quickly forgotten about when the music ceases abruptly in my ear and is spookily replaced with a strange hissing, quickly followed by a man's voice—

"Dance, then, wherever you may be, I am the Lord of the Dance, said he."

I recognise the hymn and the man's voice straightaway. I've heard it enough times by now to have become frustrated by it. Taking out the earpiece, I give it a shake, then cautiously pop it back in my ear. This time, I welcome the classic rock sound of "Pour Some Sugar On Me". *Much better than that ghastly old hymn.*

Unable to put the elusive Lord of the Dance out of my mind, though, I slyly check out my surroundings in case I'm being watched, fearing that the ghosts have left Moon Hollow and followed me outside. *Who are you? What do you want from me?* Out here, alone in the middle of nowhere, anyone could be playing tricks on me. As usual, there's nothing to see. Hollow Fen is eerily silent.

My mind goes back to mulling over last night. *Why is John angry with me?* If Lucy Benedict left of her own free will, agreeing to hand over her baby to them after giving birth, as John and Jane claim she did, then I don't get why he should be holding a grudge. I was wrong to suspect the Valentines of something more sinister, of keeping a pregnant woman captive and killing her so they could get their hands on her baby – but I'm the first to admit this. As I did last night.

I still feel sorry for Lucy Benedict, but I'm glad everything is out in the open. Knowing that John and Jane are not murderers, that they did everything they could to ensure the baby was delivered safely and that Lucy Benedict was properly cared for right up until the day she decided to leave, is a huge relief. I may never find out what happened to her after she left Moon Hollow, but her decision to hand over her baby to the Valentines is none of my business.

I can't help wondering, though, if Lucy Benedict had

any regrets. I understand that she felt she didn't have any choice other than to give up her child, but, at the same time, I don't think I could have done what she did, no matter the circumstances. I've fought tooth and nail to keep Grace with me, and I would do the same all over again if I had to.

But if everything John and Jane told me is true, and I no longer have any reason to doubt them, then Lucy Benedict came from a poor and deeply religious family who would have disowned her for having a baby out of wedlock.

Returning to the rural Romanian village she'd grown up in was not an option for her. Knowing what it's like to be rejected by family, I try not to judge her. On the other hand, I completely get why she left the way she did, suddenly and without warning, because that's exactly what I would have done in her shoes. Last-minute cuddles with the baby would have been too much to bear.

The Valentines might have been shocked by Lucy Benedict's sudden departure after everything they did for her, but I'm not. It seems a shame, though, that the money the Valentines gave her – an "adoption fee" they called it, which would have set her up in a new life somewhere else – went unspent.

One thing I do know is that Lucy Benedict is no longer of this world. How she died isn't important, but I hope that somewhere there's a gravestone with her name on it. I should like one day to go there and pay my respects. A part of me clings to the possibility that her spirit lingers at Moon Hollow so she can be close to the baby she gave up.

I probably won't ever grow to like John or Jane, but they're not the cold-blooded killers I took them for. What they *are* guilty of is withholding information, and who isn't guilty of keeping secrets? Not me, that's for sure. Knowing this frees me up to concentrate on what I came here to do. Look for Lucy. I'm convinced this is what Lucy's real mother would want me to do. Only then will all the ghosts in this house finally be put to rest.

First, I need to find out what happened in Hugh Hunter's garage. Something bad happened there. I sensed it then, and I feel it now. His white, bare-knuckled farming hands might have cleared him of being the man drawing Lucy, but for all I know, the kidnapper has an accomplice.

Until I know for sure Hugh has nothing to do with Lucy's kidnapping, I can't rule him out of my investigation. To do this, I need access to a computer. And now that John's out of the way, nothing is stopping me.

39

I come in the back way to avoid being seen, removing my trainers so I don't leave a trail of footprints behind me. I'm on the way to John's study, which I've only glimpsed in passing before, but I must first access the garden room and then the library to do so.

The smell of flowers in the garden room is overpowering. Anyone would think I'd stumbled across a freshly laid grave. Jane must have been outside picking flowers, as armfuls of white lilies, chrysanthemums, and red roses have been gathered.

Noticing a few droplets of scarlet on the drainer, I walk over to the sink and pick up the razor-sharp secateurs that have been abandoned next to a splattering of blood. I can do nothing about the sudden tingling in the middle of my forehead or the throbbing behind my right temple.

Without warning, I am Jane, manically hacking away at the flowers and sending sprays of stems and petals everywhere. Darkness envelops Jane, but she feels at home there. Unsurprisingly, her head is full of Lucy and me.

Equal amounts of hatred and outpourings of love catch me off guard, like one of my mother's backhanded cuffs around the head.

If I ever find out who took my daughter, I will rip them limb from limb. John will not help. He is too feeble. He won't even try to find out what happened, whereas I will make it my life's work. In the meantime, I must pray for our poor, darling girl and ask that God punish only us and spare her. Even though she is not mine. Not mine! All her fault. That bloody girl. Oh, how I wish I had never asked her to come here.

The same involuntary shudder that Jane experienced passes through me as the blade of the secateurs pierces her thumb. *Blast and Goddamn it,* I hear her cuss in a surprisingly unladylike way as she sucks at the blood on her hand to stop its flow. I taste Jane's blood in my own mouth. Then I feel the swishing of her skirt against my thigh as she leaves the room. Forcing these unwelcome images from my mind, I return to being me.

Parts of Jane linger, though. A coldness has invaded my veins, and my clenched fingers, numb with cold, feel as if they'll never unwind. The iciness I experienced being her was terrifying. I shall never hope to know what goes on in her mind again. Even if it were to help me find Lucy.

Relieved to be leaving the garden room behind, I pass through the library, which, as you'd expect, is fitted out floor to ceiling with books, the kind I imagine nobody reads. I don't stay long, just enough to glimpse Jane's writing desk. Light leaks through tall windows to shine on it, illuminating silver picture frames, a pearl letter opener, and monogrammed writing paper stacked in neat piles.

I wonder who Jane writes to? I can't imagine any

correspondence from her would be filled with warmth or light gossip. *Hasn't she heard of email or texting?* I don't want to get any closer to the picture frames, nor see whose eyes might be shining out from them, in case they seek me out, so I move quickly on, diverting my eyes.

John's study is as I imagined. It has a masculine air and smacks of an authority I suspect he hungers for but lacks. It's dark and gloomy inside and smells of old books and stale cigar smoke. The desk is large and made of mahogany. It has a glossy green top, like fresh grass, and a heavy button-backed leather chair is pushed up to it.

The walls are covered in black-and-white photographs of saluting servicemen lined up outside a military head-quarters. I don't know what significance they have, as John doesn't appear in any of them, but I certainly wouldn't have had him down as a military man.

The curtains are closed, but a tiny gap of light oozes through them into the room. I guess John doesn't like to be spied on. Although it's left open today, I imagine he usually keeps the door locked when he's working. *Work. Now there's a word I don't normally associate with John.* I'm not convinced he's ever held down a regular job.

I remember Jane once boasting that after gaining a degree in architectural history, John had gone on to train as a barrister, but there was no further talk of him donning a wig and gown or ever going into practice. He would make a terrible prosecutor and an even worse defence lawyer. You don't need to be clairvoyant to see through his lies.

There's something creepy about John that escaped my notice when I first met him. It took me a while to figure out exactly what it was about him that bothered me, but now I know the word I'm looking for to describe him is –

predatory. "Rapey" is how my so-called girlfriends back home would have described him.

Now that I know him better, I don't disagree. Distractedly, I try to pull open the desk drawers, but they're locked, with no sign of a key anywhere, so I sit down in the leather chair and open John's dated laptop.

When I manage to access it straightaway, I can hardly believe my luck. I don't know anyone who doesn't use a password these days, but apparently John is in the minority. I guess there isn't much of a need when his wife is a technophobe. On the downside, there's only one bar of battery life left, so I'll have to be quick.

Checking out John's recent online search history, I'm not surprised to find bookmarked pages of Russian and Ukrainian girls – blondes and brunettes, tasteful not trashy, with names like Olga and Tatyana. They remind me of Lucy Benedict, and I feel my heart go out to her and every single one of these young women who get used by rich dirty old men like John.

Having clicked through pages of similarly young and beautiful girls, I eventually come across a stash of porn websites. Because I'm not averse to a bit of soft porn myself, I don't judge John too harshly, although I'm not sure Jane would be as forgiving. Thinking about sex under John and Jane's roof makes me uncomfortable, so, looking for a distraction, I type in my own search—

Hugh Hunter.

This reveals a couple of tired Facebook profiles, but when I click on them, I quickly establish that they're not the Hugh Hunter I'm looking for. So, I try again.

Hugh Hunter Hollow Fen.

Immediately, the screen fills with newspaper reports

and blurred images of a younger Hugh Hunter with startled eyes. I don't instantly focus on the pictures because the words on the screen are yelling at me in bold capitals and lots of shouty exclamation marks.

DID HUGH HUNTER KILL HIS WIFE AND DAUGHTER AS PREVIOUSLY SUSPECTED? OR IS HE AS INNOCENT AS HE CLAIMS TO BE? CLEARED DOESN'T NECESSARILY MEAN NOT GUILTY!

The words dance in front of my eyes, some not making any sense at all, others filling in the missing pieces that I always suspected were there. From what I can make out, Hugh Hunter was arrested and charged with the murder of his wife, Tess, and their five-year-old daughter, Katie, who were found dead in the family car in the garage of their home, but he was later released due to lack of evidence, with the judge eventually delivering one verdict of death by suicide by carbon monoxide poisoning and one count of murder against the mother, Tess Hunter.

According to the papers, Hugh Hunter claimed he had nothing to do with the deaths, insisting that his wife took her and their daughter's lives in a cruel, revengeful suicide pact that deliberately pointed the finger at him.

During the court case, the prosecution argued that a woman like Tess Hunter, who was a quiet and some would say shy stay-at-home mum, with no knowledge of vehicles except to drive them, could not have known that the catalytic converter on her car would need to be removed to enable death by carbon monoxide poisoning.

Instead, they pointed the finger at the husband, who, well acquainted with all types of farm machinery and vehicles, would have known this. They went on to add that it would have taken someone with his considerable knowledge less than a minute to saw it off his wife's family saloon. The fact that the missing converter was found in a bin one mile from home without his fingerprints on it helped him get acquitted. But further investigation into Tess Hunter's mental state also supported his case.

I feel sick thinking about what happened to Hugh's daughter, how frightened she must have been. *Could a mother really have done that to her child, even if she was as sick as the courts made out?* As a mother, I find it hard to believe, which means I'm left feeling unsure what to think of Hugh Hunter, who seems to have narrowly escaped a murder conviction.

Reading between the lines, I suspect the police and the local news teams all considered him guilty, rather than accepting the verdict that was given. They wanted a monster to grace their pages, not a stay-at-home mum. One police officer took great pleasure in stating that they weren't looking for anyone else in their investigation, although they believed Mrs Hunter could not have acted alone.

Making up my mind that I must go back to Hugh's cottage as soon as possible to find out what really happened that day, and knowing I won't rest until I do, I'm about to exit the study when I hear the sound of a child's laughter floating in through the window.

40

This morning when I went for my run, I'd left Grace asleep in bed, a small dimple in a vast expanse of mattress and duvet, with feet as cold as a dead person's. I had no qualms about leaving her, even though I know about the ghosts that prowl our room. I've intuitively guessed that they're intent only on seeking me out. Besides, Grace never was an early riser and wouldn't have thanked me for waking her, so I'm surprised to see her now, running around on the lawns of Moon Hollow, shrieking with laughter.

Peering through the gap in the curtains, my gaze comes to rest on Grace's companion – Jane – and I hold my breath when I see the way she's watching my daughter. There's a faraway look on her face that I haven't seen before, and she's smiling. *Actually* smiling. *Content* is the word I'd use to describe Jane's expression.

This puts the fear of God in me. Makes me want to rush outside, grab hold of Grace, and remove her from Jane's clutches.

Until today, I've never known Jane to show any interest in my daughter. At best, she's been a reluctant babysitter, tolerating Grace only so I can get on with the task of looking for Lucy. Yet Grace has been enthralled with the woman since first meeting her. I've not been the most reliable of parents, but I consider myself more maternal than Jane. Knowing that Grace has second sight too, I wonder why she doesn't see through Jane as I do.

The last time I saw Jane, she was a broken woman. I almost felt sorry for her. But I begin to think I was wrong to pity her. The woman before me is a quite different Jane to any I've come across before, and I'm not sure I'm going to like this version either. I've never seen Jane fight for her child, not really, but judging by the protective look she's bestowing on Grace, she looks as if she might do so for the first time now, only over my child, not hers.

I want to tell Jane that she can't have her. Not even the tiniest part of her, because I've fought so bloody hard to keep her, risked everything, in fact. I won't lose my daughter now, especially to the likes of Jane Valentine. We're neither of us perfect women nor natural mothers, that much is obvious, but I love my daughter with a passion that I only came to realise when it was almost too late.

I wonder what's changed to make Jane suddenly show an interest in Grace. Has she given up on Lucy? Is she looking for a replacement? As I now know, Lucy isn't Jane's real daughter but a by-product of John's adultery, which must sting like hell for a woman as proud as Jane Valentine.

My attention flickers between my daughter and Jane, and I find myself torn between them, not knowing who I should be paying more attention to. Grace wins, of course. I could watch her all day, given the chance, but not like this – chasing the geese that have more of a right to be at Moon Hollow than she does. They run away from her, noisily honking, hissing with indignation, and dropping their feathers over the striped lawns. It seems a cruel thing to do. I'm not one for animals as a rule, mostly due to fear of them, but I wouldn't allow anyone to harm them. Yet Grace seems unaware of the distress she's causing them.

I can't remember the last time I heard her laughing this freely. She appears carefree and innocent, exactly how she used to look before the accident. God, I wish I didn't have to keep bringing up that terrible night. I must somehow get beyond it if I'm to move on.

As if sensing my presence, Grace's eyes come to the rest on the study window. She appears angry as if I've somehow betrayed her. Knowing that look well, I take a step back, out of sight. Suddenly, the room is without air, like an over-warm funeral parlour. I imagine I can hear the wheels of a car plunging through gravel, a door slamming somewhere inside the house, the sound of footsteps, of shuffling – and I freeze, not knowing what else to do.

Am I about to be found out? Has John returned home? Do these sounds belong in the past or the future? Even as these thoughts are rushing around in my head, I can't take my eyes off my daughter, who I suspect, once again, is trying to stop me from finding something out. *Why doesn't she want me to find Lucy? Is it because she fears going home with me when my job here is done? Or am I the one who's secretly afraid of returning home with my daughter, in case I find out I'm still a bad mum who can't take care of her properly?*

Now that I come to think of it, Grace even looks different. She's wearing clothes I would've never put her in, and her long blond hair has been styled into a French plait that goes all the way down her back. Her skin appears fresher and cleaner. And as much as it kills me to acknowledge it, she looks like a much happier version of herself.

I'll be having words with Jane when I next see her. How dare she? But what can I say to her that would make any sense? *Stop liking my daughter. Don't be so nice to her. Stop forcing Grace to like you.* Whatever way I look at it, it makes me sound childish and petty. I should be relieved, pleased, even, that Grace is being looked after when I can't be with her, and I guess that this is the telling part. I can't be with my daughter, putting things right as I've promised to do, when I'm out looking for someone else's.

When the geese take to the water on the pond, finally putting themselves out of reach of my daughter, Grace shrieks with glee and dances excitedly on the spot.

'Look, Jane. Look,' she calls animatedly, looking up to Jane in every sense of the word, as if she wants nothing more than to be like her when she grows up. Grace has never looked at me in the same way. Nor is she likely to. Not after what I did to her.

Returning to the night of the accident yet again, I fight off the horrible reminder as best as I can. There's plenty of time to dwell on my mistakes when I leave Moon Hollow. Making up my mind that as soon as I find Lucy, Grace and I are out of here, I close the gap in the curtains and shut out my daughter's laughter.

Echoes surround me almost immediately. This house is so full of ghosts, the living and the dead seem almost to collide. Most of the time, I close my eyes and ears to what is going on; otherwise, the spirits that exist here would overwhelm me.

To find Lucy, I must push them aside, as I must ignore my own daughter and the increasingly disturbing hold Jane Valentine has over her.

41

JANE

Jane has looked everywhere for Cindy, but the bloody girl is nowhere to be seen. Although Jane has since forgotten why she went looking for her, she is irritated at not being able to find her. Everybody seems to be escaping her these days. The house is big but not that big.

Having searched upstairs and downstairs to no avail, she is drawn to her husband's study, the last place she wants to be, if she is honest. It pains her to be in here when every day John sits at this desk, staring out of the gap in the curtains, mulling over thoughts that exclude her.

Once upon a time, like the best of fairy tales, she could read his mind and finish his sentences for him, but he is a stranger now. Someone who isolates himself away from her. Instead of growing closer over their tragic circumstances, they are more distant than ever. Jane begins to think they will never get back their close bond.

Noticing straightaway that something is out of kilter in here, she gazes around the room, pondering on what this could be. Nothing has been disturbed. John's laptop is in its usual place on top of the desk, the lid closed like a clenched jaw.

Despite being intrigued, Jane has never tried to gain access to it. She is hopeless at that sort of thing. Would not have a clue where to start. The drawers will of course be locked as they always are. Lord knows Jane has tried opening them enough times.

Just as she is about to give up trying to solve the puzzle, it hits her. Cindy's cheap perfume. Its awful smell lingers on the shiny surface of the laptop and amongst the heavy folds of the curtain lining. Jane cannot think why she didn't recognise it sooner. She hopes she is not growing accustomed to it.

What was Cindy doing in here? Did she find out something? Is that why she is nowhere to be seen? Dread gathers in the pit of Jane's stomach. If John has done anything to sabotage the search for Lucy, she will punish him for the rest of his days. Surely, he would not be stupid enough to leave behind any clues.

Then Jane remembers Lucy Benedict's silver bracelet, and suddenly she is not so sure. He did not do a good job of getting rid of that. The uneasiness in the pit of Jane's stomach intensifies, making her want to retch. Her hands flutter down to grasp her stomach, where no child has ever resided.

Her hands drop guiltily away again when John's car pulls into the driveway and comes to a jerky boy-racer stop, gravel spiralling off the wheel arches and forming a spray. She is dying to know where he has been, but she will not ask. Sometimes it is best not knowing.

Suspecting that John is still sulking over Cindy's allegations, she watches him slam the car door shut, then trudge miserably through the gravel before climbing the steps to the front entrance. Before letting himself in, he squints up at the window as if he knows he is being watched. Jane is satisfied she cannot be seen so does not step back from the window.

Seeing him like this, depressed and worried, makes her want to reach out and help him, mother him as she has always done. She still gets butterflies in her stomach from looking at him. Reminding herself that this is an inappropriate reaction for a woman of her age and situation, she becomes conscious of the promise she made to God. Until Lucy is found, Jane will not break her side of the bargain she made with Him. Not that John has noticed her self-imposed vow of celibacy. He is too infatuated with Cindy.

Jane finds it both annoying and surprising that Cindy has so far refused all of John's advances. *Does she think she can do better?*

Unlike the others, who mistakenly believed the wealth was all John's, *and they could not have been more wrong*, this girl shows no desire to steal John away from her. This should offer Jane contentment, but it does not. Nor does it soften her animosity towards Cindy. The truth is, she cannot wait to see the back of her.

The shame and humiliation John has put Jane through over the years with his various dalliances never diminishes, but if it means one day securing another child, then she considers it a necessary evil. The only thing she would ask is that he not enjoy the experience quite so much. While Cindy has not yet succumbed to her husband's charms, Jane is convinced that she will. Nobody has ever been able to resist John. She only has to look at her own situation to know this. Jane went against everyone's wishes, including God's, to be with John, the charmer. John, the womaniser. Now she is paying the price.

But if Cindy agreed to give them a child, everything in the world would be right again. A sister for Lucy, *if she comes back*, would complete their family. And if Lucy is not found, a new baby would guarantee them a fresh start. Having a child, any child, is what occupies Jane's mind most of the time, except, that is, when she is worrying over John's infidelities.

She tells herself that such yearnings are understandable. Cindy has already given birth to one child so having another should not be a problem. She is young, healthy, and fertile. So why not? Girls like her fall pregnant at the drop of a hat! Besides, Cindy needs money, and the Valentines have lots of it. Moon Hollow might be falling around their ears, and enormously expensive to maintain, but Jane's trust fund remains intact. That is the one thing she has never allowed John to get his greedy hands on.

If Cindy ends up finding Lucy, then so be it; this will be a terrific bonus, as Jane wants desperately to be reunited with her daughter, but this hope pales into significance against her desire for another baby. Whatever way she looks at things, if all goes to plan, then she will get a daughter out of this tragedy. A replacement daughter for Lucy if need be. For that reason, Jane intends not to let Cindy out of her sight. Jane will keep her under lock and key for as long as is necessary.

Jane's fists clench involuntarily, and her heart races with fear when she spots a distant shadow, as small as one of Lowry's stick people, out by the lake. Gasping and holding her breath, Jane immediately recognises the womanly profile. Only Cindy Martin could strut like a stripper while wearing camouflage trousers and hiking boots.

What is she doing out there? On the lake of all places. What does she know? Jane's brain pounds as she comes up with numerous excuses for Cindy being out on the lake, but she keeps returning to the same conclusion – the girl clearly knows more than she lets on. If true, this could ruin all of Jane's plans and desires. For now, she cannot decide if this places her or John in any immediate danger, but she intends to make it her business to find out.

They might be under the girl's power, but there is only so much Jane will tolerate. As for John's reaction, Jane decides she should not think about that right now. Not after what happened last time. Everything will depend on how much the girl knows. Until then, Cindy must not be allowed to leave.

42

CINDY

As I trudge along in my borrowed boots that are several sizes too big, I ask myself what I've learned about John and Jane, both Lucys, and Hugh Hunter since coming to Moon Hollow and decide I don't know shit. The mystery of it all is like a claustrophobic hug that won't let go no matter how much I resist.

The fact that I no longer see Lucy Benedict bothers me a great deal. More so than the missing child's continued absence. I begin to think that I'll never find one without the other. That's why I can't stop thinking about Lucy Benedict, who I'm sure is the key to finding little Lucy. *Where has she gone? Why doesn't she reach out to me anymore?* Since the truce with John and Jane, there's been no sign of her. Every time I go up to the secret room, clinging to the hope I'll find her, she's not there.

I try telling myself that perhaps now her story has been told, she's finally at peace, but this doesn't ring true either. I definitely got the impression that Lucy Benedict hadn't finished her story, that there was more she wanted to say.

As for her daughter – no matter how hard I try to connect with little Lucy, I can't catch a glimpse of her. If things carry on like this, Jane will throw me out on my ear, as she did Lucy Benedict, and Grace will go straight back to the children's home or be allowed to remain with the Valentines, with or without my consent.

It's not as if I'm not trying. I think about Lucy Valentine all the time. But I always end up focusing on the other Lucy, which is the last thing John and Jane want me to do, but this house has other ideas. I only hope little Lucy's disappearance from my visions doesn't mean anything bad has happened to her.

This brings me back to Hugh. Next to Lord of the Dance, he's the only other suspect. He knows the Valentines well and was a friend to little Lucy too by all accounts. It's highly likely that she would've gone off with him without thinking anything of it. Knowing I've a much better chance of reconnecting with both Lucys once I've pushed all thoughts of Hugh Hunter from my mind, which is turning out to be a dangerously overcrowded place, I speed up. I'm on my way to his house now, determined to find out if he's involved in the little girl's disappearance. For all I know, he intends to blackmail the Valentines for money.

But I also want to get to the bottom of what happened to his wife and child. I have the feeling that it's somehow connected to both Lucys going missing. But I need to prove it. Somehow or other, I've got to get inside that garage without him knowing. I must know if the man that I instantly warmed to, which is so unlike me, is who he makes out to be.

The thought of him being a kidnapper or killer hangs

over me like a dark cloud. I know that Adam Lockwood turned out to be innocent in the end, but that doesn't mean Hugh Hunter is. *I can't be wrong again, can I?*

Grace's laughter, ringing loudly in my ears, haunts me. I hear it everywhere, in the rustling leaves, the swaying of the trees, the cooing of pigeons, each breath of air – until I feel my body tense with anger and resentment. No matter how hard I try, I can't get the image of her grinning happily at Jane out of my head.

I know that now is not the time to worry about how I'm going to get Jane to relinquish her hold over my daughter, so rather than give in to my jealousy, I concentrate on calming my rising anger. I can't let it take hold. I have a job to do. Lucy Benedict's silver bracelet jangling against my wrist urges me on, faster and faster, lending me courage until, at last, confidence washes over me like a seductive hand getting to know my body for the first time. As a result, I'm hit by a wave of energy I haven't felt in ages.

But when I see a large dog slipping into the surrounding woodland, nose down as if on the hunt for something, I feel ghostly fingers pressing into my spine, paralysing me. It's the dog from the painting. I know it is. The ghostlike creature has the same steel-blue coat and cropped ears that point upwards like a shark's fin. I'm certain it hasn't seen me, thank fuck, but even when it slinks out of sight behind a tree, I find myself wanting to run.

Then I go down. A long, steep descent. It takes a few seconds for me to realise that I am, in fact, falling down a grass bank. When I see the shimmer of the lake looming at the bottom, I claw frantically at clods of earth to prevent me from tumbling into the water. Clumps of sharp grass come away in my hands, cutting into flesh, but my slide continues.

Luckily, I don't land up in the water, as I feared I would, but come to a slow, painful halt at the edge of the lake, feeling as if the skin on my arms, elbows, and knees has been scraped off with a knife.

Heart racing madly, I pull myself up, but getting to my feet is more of a struggle than I expected. A stab of pain in my right side lets me know that I'm badly winded, and a film of tears instantly glazes my eyes. When I feel the first drop of rain on my skin, I turn my face up to the sky that was blue a minute ago but is now as black as the soil under my fingernails.

'Thanks for that. Nice one,' I grumble out loud to a god I've never got along with.

Then, eyeing up the sloping grass bank, which is a good ten metres high, I try to work out if I'll be able to climb it, feeling as I do. It's going to be a lot harder going up than it was coming down. Deciding that I don't have a choice, it's that or swimming across the lake to the other side where the grass is level with the water – *fuck that* – I'm about to begin my scramble up the slope when I notice something bobbing in the water.

I lean in for a closer look, not wanting to go too near the murky-looking water. Although I'm a good swimmer, I have a deep-rooted fear of drowning in open water. Even the strongest of swimmers get caught out and drown in lakes and rivers. I don't even paddle in the sea, let alone swim in it. I'm much more of a "beside the pool" girl, given the chance.

The thought of falling into the cold water, which is full

of grasping plants that can tangle around your legs, gives me the creeps. I try reaching for the floating item, which from here looks like a glass bottle, but it slides away from my grasp, mocking me. My stomach pitches when the smell of the water reaches my nostrils. It reminds me of death and decay and is accompanied by a taste of aniseed on my tongue that wasn't there before.

It's a familiar smell, but I can't place it. Something in my memory flares, but it melts away quickly, leaving me none the wiser.

The bottle is too far away for me to chance trying again. Risking a glance around, careful where I place my feet, as it's wet and slippery by the edge of the lake, I try to see if there's anything I can use to reach it with, but these are private grounds, so there's no rubbish lying around. I've no choice but to give up, but if I had to guess at what sort of bottle it was, I'd say it was used to keep perfume in. It has an hourglass figure much like my own.

As I straighten up, I glimpse my blurred reflection in the black water. It catches me off guard because I hardly recognise myself. A shock of horror passes through me as I realise I'm looking at Grace's face and not my own. Her thumb wedged in mouth and eyes closed, I watch her drifting away from me. A rising panic fills me, and I begin to struggle for breath. My chest is tight as if someone has hold of my heart in a tight, unrelenting grasp.

The squeaky whistle of a red kite hovering high in the sky brings me to my senses, and I find I'm staring at nothing but mud-stirred water. So, I blink away my tears and wipe the snot away from my nose on the sleeve of my shirt like a child.

Throwing myself at the grass bank, clutching at rain-dampened grass and soil, anything I can get hold of for leverage, I hurl myself up it as fast as I can. Helplessly, I slide down again several times before I realise what the problem is – the bottoms of my boots are covered in slimy, foul-smelling black shit. That must've been what caused me to slip and fall in the first place.

'Fucking countryside!' I scream, hating to be beaten by something as trivial as animal shit. I don't want to admit to myself how much I want to collapse in a heap and sob my eyes out, but after wiping the soles of my boots on the grass, I have another go, and this time I make it to the top of the bank, having to stop and rest until I get my breath back.

From here, I can just about make out the pitched rooftop of Hugh Hunter's back-to-front house. A curl of grey smoke escapes from its chimney, reminding me sombrely of a crematorium.

43

'Well, here we are, Cindy girl,' I tell myself, staring with trepidation at the peeling paint on Hugh Hunter's weathered door. Today, both halves of the stable door are shut, and only one pair of Wellington boots, soaked with rain, is sprawled across the faded welcome mat. Peering through my rain-plastered hair, I notice that the sun is starting to come out again.

By now, the rain has stopped, and the sky is as blue as the Valentines' eyes. *Typical,* I think, shaking myself off like a wet dog before trying the door handle. Although smoke trickles from the chimney, I don't think there's anyone home. Hugh Hunter's jeep is missing from the open barn, so I'm guessing he's out. For how long is another matter.

The door is locked. This surprises me. I never had Hugh down as the security-conscious type. Unlike us townies, I thought country people always left their doors open, so perhaps he does have something to hide after all. Thinking on my feet, I bend down and flip over the soaking wet mat. When I see the key hidden beneath it, I thank my lucky stars.

Picking it up, I put the cold metal against my lip, thanking it with a brief kiss, and instantly feel the brush of Hugh's hand against mine. This happened only once before, when he passed me a mug of coffee. He didn't notice, but I did. It told me nothing, though. More's the pity. Counting to three, I check to make sure nobody is around. On four, I listen out for the dreaded sound of a diesel engine returning, and on five, six, seven, eight, when I'm sure it's safe to do so, I open the door.

I'm in.

But I'm not alone.

Someone else is in the house with me. I sense their presence immediately. Not Hugh. No. Nobody living could make my temple throb quite so violently.

'Hello.' My voice comes out as a squeak.

As I reach for the living room door handle, my throat dries up with fear. Bracing myself, I count to three and take the same amount of breaths before throwing it open. When nobody fills the doorway to confront me, I tiptoe inside, relieved to find myself alone.

A barely there fire, struggling for breath, is dying in the grate, but I'm thankful for its tiny offering of warmth. Although it's summer, it's surprisingly cold in Hugh's house. When you're clairvoyant as I am, this is never a good sign. Under any other circumstances, I would stir the fire and sit by it for a while to dry myself off, but I dare not linger. Hugh could return any minute. Silence gathers around me, and out of the window I notice the light is beginning to fade. A summer storm is on its way, and more rain will follow, I'm sure of it.

I start to think that I was wrong before and that no spirit lingers here. Sometimes that can happen when sudden changes in the temperature and weather occur. I'm not sure why. I don't question these imbalances in my psychic abilities. They just exist. Like the mother-and-daughter blind spot and not being able to predict my own future. To be on the safe side, I close my eyes and reach out anyway, in case I've missed something.

When one of the books on the shelf shakes violently, my eyes flash open, and I stand there like a statue, hating myself for not being able to move. *Who are you? What do you want?* There's a change in the air as someone brushes past me. They go to the bookshelf, take out the book, and flick through the pages that are thumbed with large oily fingerprints. Hugh's hands.

I feel her then, glimpse her despair.

A haunting sadness settles on this house, much as it does Moon Hollow, only here there is a danger, a threat that I've not come across before. It's as tangible as the cold damp clothes I'm wearing.

The ring on her wedding finger is looser than it was. Her fingernails have been nibbled down to angry red stumps. Her movements are quick and furious. The pages do not turn quickly enough, so she rips them out, one by one, until she comes to page ninety-two. I see the number in my head as clearly as I do the fireplace, the clock on the mantel, the empty patches on the walls where pictures once hung, and the neatly plumped cushions on the sofa. We read this page together, she and I, but she is much quicker than me.

Although it is illegal to remove the catalytic converter from any car, thieves can cut them out with a saw in less than one minute and then sell on the precious metal. Catalytic converters cut emissions by 90% and are thought to save lives, as it is difficult to end your life with one fitted to your car. In 1993, they became mandatory for all vehicles in the UK, putting a stop to suicides caused by piping exhaust fumes into cars. Without one, death by carbon monoxide poisoning would occur within half an hour.

Is this a warning? Is Tess Hunter trying to tell me that she knew something bad was going to happen to her? If so, this could mean Hugh was guilty of planning to murder his wife and child and covering up their deaths. And here I am, alone, in his house. Anything could happen if he were to come home unannounced. Nobody knows I'm here. When I hear the scrape of a boot outside, I go cold all over, and my legs threaten to buckle.

'Is that you, Hugh?'

Her voice, not mine, rings out. It has a nervous, flirtatious sound as if she's desperate to convince him nothing is wrong. I sense that she wasn't expecting him back this early and wonder if it had become a habit of his to check up on her. Her fingers are shaking as she slides the book back on the shelf, and I begin to suspect that she's frightened of him. A fresh spike of pain stabs at my temple as I feel a current of her breath on my neck, making my skin prickle. I feel her lean in close like one would to confide a secret in a friend.

'We mustn't tell him where we are,' she whispers in my ear.

I want to shrug her off, to bolt from this house and its terrible secrets, but instead I follow her. There's something she wants to show me. She needs me to understand.

44

The little girl, Katie, doesn't want to get into the car with her mother. She wants to be somewhere else. With Bonnie. Not another child, no. A chestnut pony with a white blaze who loves sugar and stands eleven hands high, the perfect size for a five-year-old. Katie stomps her foot when Tess Hunter orders her to get in the back seat, telling her that there will be no riding lesson today, but she does as she's told anyway.

The tension I feel between the two of them isn't new. She's a daddy's girl, like Lucy Valentine, and there's a distance between mother and daughter that cuts at my heart because I know exactly what that feels like.

Tess Hunter is small and thin with shoulder-length brown hair that lacks shine. She wears skinny jeans and a baggy sweater with sleeves that hang below her wrists. Her face is free of makeup, and she has a smattering of ginger freckles across her nose. She could be pretty if she wanted to be, but I get the impression she no longer cares. An air of hopelessness clings to her stooped shoulders as she gets into the driver's side of the car and closes the door.

The click of the doors locking and the throaty growl of the car's engine starting up causes my heart to thump. I'm in the car with them. Tess is fiddling with the controls and screaming at her daughter to stay in the back. But Katie never sits in the back. Always up front. She doesn't see why she should have to change now.

When Tess Hunter punches her daughter in the face, sending her flying backward onto the back seat, I whimper. *No. Not this. Anything but this.*

On the back seat, in a crumpled pile, Katie is crying and holding her bloodied nose. Tess is staring into the rearview mirror as if trying to identify who the person is looking back at her, like she no longer recognises herself. When our eyes meet in the mirror, her gaze fixes knowingly on me, as though she suspects I'm going to be the next woman in Hugh's life. She sneers, and the word *bitch* repeats over in her head.

As if to prove that I'll never replace her, she takes me on a journey, pointing out fragments of her happy life. Confetti flutters down onto my eyelids, sticking to my face, as she shows me with her eyes how perfect everything was. There's a wedding day speech, short and to the point, with little laughter. Then their first anniversary, soon followed by the birth of a child – Katie Marie, named after Hugh's mother. A family holiday somewhere abroad and by the beach, sun cream, cocktails, and burnt skin followed by the rough sex that Tess relished. Oral sex was something else she couldn't get enough of, although Hugh wasn't that keen on going down on her.

Such knowledge makes my cheeks burn, but I fall

deeper into her life until I become invisible. Only her heart beats now. Suddenly, she's pulling away, into the darkness, trying to hide from what happens next. I stretch out my fingers to bring her back. There's no escaping the past. We both know this.

Snapshots of Hugh and Lucy Benedict flirting and laughing together race by as if somebody is fast-forwarding through a honeymoon album. I watch them kiss greedily, swapping tongues, and I know a moment's jealousy. The bitterness exuding from Tess Hunter is something else. It's toxic, revengeful, and out of control. I see Hugh stroking the birthmark on Lucy's face and hear him telling her that she's beautiful.

Then, flashes of the girl's belly getting bigger and Hugh turning distant and cold. His expression growing haunted with guilt, more so every day until he snaps at the family he loves, even his daughter. A feeling of shame and disappointment washes over me as Hugh reveals his cruel treatment of Lucy Benedict. It's hard to believe that he'd behave in this way. How could he deny he was the father of their child and dare her to prove it? This seems so unlike him.

But then I realise these were desperate times and his wife was mentally ill, more so than anyone knew. Perhaps Hugh guessed that news of the affair coming out would push her over the edge. He might not have felt anything for Tess anymore, but he was besotted with his daughter.

I feel myself swaying as sudden dizziness comes over me. My head pounds with pain as if I've swallowed too many paracetamols. I'm no longer sure where I am. I can't remember why I'm here in this pokey old garage that smells of oil and exhaust fumes.

Slumping against a wall, I'm about to give in to the tiredness when I see a hand appear in the back window of the car. It seems to reach out in desperation, so I place my palm against it, wanting to reassure whoever it belongs to. The hand is smaller than my own, smaller, even, than Grace's. When it fades away, leaving a misted print behind, I'm jolted back into the past with a speed I haven't experienced before.

The next thing I know is that I'm in the car, peering out of the window from the back seat, my hand resting on the steamed-up glass. The car is fogged up, and it's difficult to see through the smoke. It burns my eyes, blinding me, but I search for mother and daughter anyway. *Where are you, Katie?* I want to shout, but my mouth refuses to open.

Batting away the fumes that are threatening to choke me, I drag air into my lungs and clutch desperately along the backseat, finding nothing. Weak from inhaling the toxic fumes, I'm about to give up and go to sleep when my hands land on rumpled clothing.

Towards the end, Tess must have relented and climbed into the back to be with her daughter, because there they are, the two of them, clinging on to each other, eyes closed in what looks like regular sleep. Even in death, the sneer I saw on Tess's face in the rearview mirror remains. It doesn't fade. Nor does the anger or pain etched into the creases of her forehead.

Everything fades to a black cloak of mourning, and I'm sucked into a void of nothingness that transports me somewhere else. When I open my eyes, I'm standing in front of the garage door that I can remember opening now that my memory is returning.

The urge to escape takes over, and I snatch at the

handle and burst through the doorway, only stopping to fill my lungs with clean air. But when I look up and see Hugh's dog standing in the hallway, hackles raised, blocking my exit, I piss myself a little. *Seriously! Who has this much fucking bad luck in one day?*

'Nice dog. Good dog,' I say, for time more than anything, as I don't know anything about dogs. Slyly, I search for a way out that won't involve contact with its bared teeth. I've never seen a dog like this one before. It has one pale blue eye; the other is brown. *I didn't know you could get dogs with mismatched eyes like that.*

But worse, it has matted fur and a stiff tail that looks incapable of wagging. The strangled growling it's making in the back of its throat sends every red blood cell in my body to a faraway place until I feel the blood draining away from me.

We weigh each other up, this bastard dog and I, but I'm the first to make a move. *Sucker.* Surprised into action, the dog is instantly on my tail, fur and saliva flying off its tensed-up body. I run into the living room, convinced I'm going to have my throat ripped open, and bounce straight off Hugh Hunter's chest, which smells of hay and old jumpers.

Before I lose consciousness, I remind myself that he's not the man I thought he was. He may not be a murderer, but he's a cheat and a liar. Not somebody to be trusted. Yet, as my eyelids close, I can't shake off the sensation of his chest being broad and reliable, the kind of place a woman can safely lay her head.

45

I couldn't bear to be in that cottage a second longer, so as though I were under arrest, Hugh had marched me to the treehouse, stopping only to wipe away the crusted streaks of blood from around my nose. I must have suffered one of the worst nosebleeds ever, not surprising after what I'd witnessed, but I was sobbing so much I hadn't noticed.

As if I were a child, Hugh must've helped me up the ladder, as I've no recollection of getting to the top. Yet here we stand – facing the church spire and the watchful windows of Moon Hollow, ignoring the unbroken circle of forgotten dolls and teddy bears, whose empty eyes appear shocked to see us. Eerily, their plastic fingers are closed in midair as if around invisible china cups, mimicking Lucy Valentine's posture that first time I saw her.

My gaze lingers on the bits of broken china tea set scattered on the rug in front of these ghoulish-looking figures, and I decide that they represent the most macabre and twisted children's tea party I've ever seen.

Hugh is still angry with me. But I don't care. Anger is nothing in the great scheme of things. Not after what I saw.

'What were you doing in there, Cindy? What were you thinking?' He lights a rolled-up cigarette and offers me a drag. I take it without thanking him.

'Another secret smoker,' I quip inappropriately.

'That's all we do in the country, smoke and drink. Didn't you know?' His sarcasm doesn't suit him.

'And have affairs,' I point out, then remember he once told me he didn't drink. *Was that another lie?* He doesn't come across as a dishonest person and seems innocently unaware of what I'm hinting at, so I remind myself that he knows nothing yet of my discovery.

'I thought you were here to find Lucy, not poke around in other people's business and break into their houses.'

Home. He doesn't use that word, I notice. And who could blame him?

'Technically, I didn't break in. I used your key,' I say flatly, inhaling greedily on the roll-up, which is hot against my mouth and burns bright red at the end, like blood, reminding me of Katie's poor little broken face and nose.

When I glance up at Hugh with tear-filled eyes, I see that he's trying to hold himself together. Jane Valentine could do with some of his restraint. She'll be fuming by now, wondering where I am. I can't bring myself to think about Grace. Being absent for most of the day won't have gone down well with her either.

'I know,' I say, struggling to get my words out. The sound of the engine rings in my ears, and I can still smell oil and exhaust fumes on my clothes. 'I know about you and Lucy Benedict.'

His mouth drops open as if he's about to deny everything, but when his shoulders sink and a loud sigh escapes
him, I know I was right about him. He's not a liar.

'How?' he asks simply, gazing at the setting sun as if
he'd like to keep it at bay along with the rest of the world.
I get this. I wouldn't want to be Hugh Hunter either, alone
in that cottage, in the dark, with his memories. There's
such an air of desperation about him that I want to push
away the stray lock of curly hair that's escaped from his
cap. A blanket of fading sunlight hugs the flat Fenland
landscape, reflecting fire in his eyes. But I'm so cold
standing by the open window in my damp clothes that my
teeth are chattering.

He wraps me in his jumper and pulls me against his
chest, where it's warm and strangely comforting. He does
so roughly, wanting me to know that he hasn't yet forgiven
me.

'Lucia. I called her Lucia. I was the only one to do so.'
He offers me a half smile that doesn't even begin to
disguise the pain I can see in his eyes.

'I'm sorry, Hugh, about your wife and child...'

'Don't.' He cuts me off and stamps his shoe on the
cigarette butt.

'You built this treehouse, didn't you?' This is a guess.
Nothing more. Brought to me unexpectedly by the smell of
sawn wood on his jumper.

'For little Lucy.' He nods. 'It was the least I could do.'

I gesture towards Moon Hollow. 'They think Lucy is
John's.'

'Lucia didn't even like John,' Hugh admits miserably,
as if he wishes he could turn back the clock and make her
fall in love with his friend, anyone other than him. 'She

got drunk one night and slept with him, I suspect to get back at me for refusing to leave my wife. She was already pregnant by then, although I didn't know it at that point. She saved that bombshell for a few weeks later and tried to force my hand.' Hugh sighs heavily, and his eyes seem to change from green to grey. 'Lucia was like Tess, thinking she could blackmail me and bring me to heel. Some women are like that,' he adds bitterly, like he's had his fill of such types.

'Not all women, Hugh,' I say, stupidly wanting him to know I'm not like that. *I, Cindy Martin, am different,* I want to proclaim. But am I? Deep down, probably not.

'Anyway, John was happy enough to shoulder the blame, so I thought it was probably better for everyone that way.' Hugh comes clean with an embarrassed cough.

'For who?' I demand, feeling irritated by his weak response. 'If you knew Lucy was yours and not John's, why didn't you say something?'

'After what happened to my wife and Katie, they, the Valentines, especially John, were good to me.' Here, Hugh pauses and licks his lips. 'They gave me odd jobs to keep me busy and kept me going emotionally as well as financially. I honestly don't think I could have got through it all without them. That's why, well, I decided to keep quiet, although I suspected John secretly knew I was Lucy's real father. I knew he wouldn't let on, as it would kill Jane to know this. Neither of us could do that to her. I'd never seen her so happy.'

This is the most I've heard Hugh speak in one go, and I absorb every word. What he says rings of such honest, raw truth that I make up my mind he's not so bad after all. I won't make excuses for the way he treated Lucy Benedict when he found out she was pregnant with his baby, but I won't judge him for the decisions he made either.

It sounds as if he was simply looking out for other people. He wouldn't have been in a particularly good place himself when all this began.

'But what about *after* Lucy got taken? Surely you should have said something to the police?'

'Nearly eight years have passed by now, and, to be honest, I no longer like to think about that part of my life. Everybody is gone. Tess, Katie, Lucia… In my mind, Lucy was and still is John and Jane's daughter. What use would I have been to a child back then?'

Even though I try hard not to, I find my mind wandering to what happened in that garage. I don't think I'll ever be able to scrub it from my memory. As before with Adam Lockwood, I couldn't have been more wrong about Hugh. All along he'd been innocent, whereas Tess Hunter… Oh God, the horror of it is too awful to contemplate.

'I tried to reach Katie,' I blurt without thinking, 'but she melted away before I could help her. I tried, Hugh, honestly, I did.' Seeing the effect my words are having on his ruined face, I wonder how much I should tell him. Making up my mind that no father should have to hear this, I stop. He doesn't deserve it. It's bad enough for me when all I can see is Tess Hunter's hate-filled eyes and her voice chanting the word *bitch* over in my head.

'I don't know how you can stay there,' is all I say to end my tirade, grimacing at the thought of the cottage, the sense of threat and menace that lurked behind the garage door like a dark shadow. 'I'm never going back in there. Never.' I feel myself becoming hysterical again.

'You don't have to, Cindy. Why would you think I'd want you to?'

'I thought you might want me to show you, how your wife...and Katie.'

I feel him shudder. It passes from him to me like an airborne virus. 'I'm not like everybody else. I would never ask you to do that. Besides—' he pauses, and I lose him for a second as his mind wanders back there, to the cottage '—something about the way you say it makes me feel the same. I should never have carried on living there after what happened. But I wanted to be close to Katie. It's where she was born, where she grew up. Sometimes I can feel her there. It's as if she's still with me.'

I want to tell him that it's Tess he can feel, not Katie. It will always be Tess. But I can't get my words out. Some things are too painful to hear and don't need to be said. So instead, I say weakly, 'You need to get out of there. For your own sake.'

'You're right.' He goes along with me, but something in his eyes dies at the thought of abandoning his daughter once again, of going away and never coming back. 'That is exactly what I should do.'

'What happened to her? Lucy Benedict?' I ask, changing the subject.

'I honestly don't know.' He drifts off someplace else, and I will him back again. He returns, chastened, like a dog that has been called too many times. 'Even though Katie, my daughter, was gone by then, I couldn't bring myself to think about Lucia. It seemed disloyal. It was only when I found out she'd left that I gave her or the baby any more thought. The Valentines were shocked when she took off like she did without so much as a thank-you, but I was secretly pleased. I hated having her around. I couldn't see her face, even from a distance, without being reminded of what happened to my family.'

'So, you never spoke again?'

He shakes his head. 'It suited both of us to ignore each other after that. Thank God she didn't stick around after having the baby. Within a few weeks, she was gone. And I was glad. Even though it was my fault, I blamed her for what happened to Katie. I should have been there to protect her. I should have known Tess was on to us and would have been up to no good, plotting some suitable punishment. But I never guessed in a million years...'

After pausing, he picks up where he left off as if determined to finish what he started. 'A day doesn't go by without me regretting every word and decision I made that summer.' He swallows hard, his Adam's apple moving up and down like a contestant in an apple-bobbing competition.

So much pain. So many lies. All in one summer. One village. Only twenty miles away from where I live. It doesn't seem possible. My heart goes out to him. To all of them...

'Tess broke me. She poisoned everyone she touched. And I made the mistake of falling in love with somebody else who wasn't mad and vicious but gentle and kind, or at least that's what I thought at the time, and the people I loved died because of that. I should have been the one, not...'

Voice breaking, Hugh Hunter does something I never thought he'd do. He sobs into his hands, all bravado gone from him. The absence of the rugged masculinity that draws women like me to him sends me into a panic, wondering if he'll ever get it back again. But then I remind myself that I'm not one of the Tess Hunters of this world.

Unlike *her*, I understand that men should be allowed to show emotion, the same as any woman, and not be judged for it. In the three years Skid and I were together, I never once saw him cry, and look how he turned out – a drug-dealing, useless wanker if ever there was one. Only ever one step away from homelessness, prison, or worse.

'Do you think me weak for crying?' Eyes burning with whatever reserves of pride he has left, he surprises the hell out of me with his sudden insight into my head.

'No,' I splutter guiltily. 'Of course not.' I reach out and pat his hand, a gesture he clearly isn't comfortable with, but as with Grace, I can't read him, and I thank God for this. I don't want to delve any further into this poor man's life, nor rip out what's left of his heart.

'Does knowing any of this help Lucy Valentine?' he asks doubtfully, eyes softening back to their normal countryside olive.

'Yes and no. I don't suppose you know a man on a bike who goes around singing hymns, do you?'

He shakes his head at me as if I've lost the plot, and perhaps I have. Lord of the Dance is only in my head. And Grace's. I have yet to see him in the flesh, so he could still be a vision. A memory of someone who once lived, but I still can't shake off the feeling that he's real. A living, breathing man.

'I still think John and Jane are hiding something,' I blurt out, suddenly deciding to trust this man who's lied to everyone, including John and Jane.

'Something to do with Lucia?'

As he says this, I feel him edging away from me until

I'm no longer touching his hand. It disappoints me to know that he's still wary of me. Losing myself in the gap he's created between us, I nod to show I'm listening, but I'm really hovering somewhere above the rooftop of Moon Hollow, staring down on it like a bird of prey, willing it to give up its secrets.

What don't the Valentines want me to know? If Jane still believes John is Lucy's real father, then I can't imagine what it is they're trying to hide.

'Unless Lucia returns to Moon Hollow, and I'd say that's extremely unlikely given the circumstances, we may never find out,' Hugh advises sensibly.

I don't answer straightaway. Instead, I gaze down at Lucy's silver bracelet, which rests heavily against my wrist like a burden I'm not strong enough to carry, and trace the engraved lettering of her name with my fingertips, resolving once again not to let her down.

'But what if she never left?' I ask, speaking aloud the thought that's bothering me most.

On her way to church, Jane sees Cindy and Hugh hiding in the shadowy treehouse, standing too close and whispering to each other like a regular couple. Except they are not and never will be. Jane will make sure of that. She does not know what Cindy or Hugh were talking about, but she intends to find out. Not from Cindy. She is too wily for that, but Hugh is soft and stupid. Jane can easily manipulate him. Besides, he owes them. Contrary to what John thinks, acting as if Hugh has some hold over them, they owe him nothing.

As she lets herself into the cold confines of the church, it dawns on Jane that nobody is on her side anymore. Not one single person. Not John. Not even Hugh, after everything they have done for him. And certainly not Cindy.

It seems to Jane that everyone is colluding with each other and plotting against her. She fully intends to hold this against all of them. Especially Hugh, who should know better. After his monstrous wife and spoilt-rotten child died, they'd had him over for dinner every week. That lasted for a year or more until he gradually started drifting away from them.

John said this should be encouraged, as it meant things were getting back to normal for the poor fellow, but Jane took it personally. She refused to forgive him for giving them the silent treatment as if they did not matter. Instead of coming cap in hand, grateful for their kindness, he would skulk off like an injured dog back to the cottage to lick his wounds.

It still irks Jane that John allows him to live there rent-free. It's not as if they don't need the money. The estate is falling around their ears, and because John does not contribute to their finances, Jane refuses to use her private trust fund to maintain it. She once voiced her opinion on this touchy subject, but John cut her down. Silenced her with one look. Made her feel as small as one of the church mice.

Despite what other people think, Jane does not consider herself a cruel or uncaring person. She prays and carries out charitable acts, donating money to the poor when required. She has sympathy for Hugh, or did, but she also holds something against him, which makes it impossible for her to be reasonable where he is concerned.

She will never get back the nights Hugh stole from her when he and John stayed up late drinking and discussing women. "Man talk" they called it. But the words they used were not written down in any Bible she had ever seen. Unholy, that is what they were. Yet John kept on insisting that they involve Hugh in their lives. At one stage he even wanted him to be Lucy's godparent. A gamekeeper godfather to their child! Like that was ever going to happen.

Nobody would have dared suggest such a thing in her parents' day.

Hugh could leave tomorrow and nobody, other than John, would be sorry to see him go. This is all the impact Hugh has had during his ten years at Moon Hollow, firstly stepping into his father's shoes as a gamekeeper and later as odd-job man.

With his rugged good looks and attractive green eyes, soft as any girl's, he could easily find someone new to settle down with. He could even have another child. There might never be another Katie for him, the same as there will never be another Lucy for her, but he at least is capable of spawning others.

Just in time, Jane lights a new candle and extinguishes the dying, flickering flame of the old one. *What sort of mother am I?* She cannot believe that she nearly let Lucy's candle go out. Hadn't she sworn to keep it going for as long as there was hope?

For once, she does not fall to her knees on the harsh concrete floor. Instead, she slides into the nearest pew and demurely bows her head. If she is to avoid all hell breaking loose, then she must pray harder than she has ever prayed in her life.

'Please, God. I beg this of You. Do not let Cindy Martin find out that wicked girl Lucy Benedict changed her mind and decided to keep her baby.'

47

CINDY

I watch Hugh disappear among the trees while I remain in the treehouse a while longer. Tracking his movements brings me a simple pleasure that I couldn't have imagined experiencing a few months back. The old Cindy would've taken the piss out of me for this. But as soon as he's out of sight, I find I want him back again.

There's something reliable about the way he marches, each foot taking measured strides as if competing in a sporting event. His vintage wax jacket, muddy boots, and tweed cap are by now so familiar, I expect everyone to wear them.

Having cadged another fag off Hugh before he left, I strike a match and light it, wondering what Jane thought when she saw us in the treehouse. She didn't say anything. Just stood there staring at us before continuing on to the church. How she knew we were there, I'll never know. Later, she'll demand to know what we were talking about, but I won't say a word about Tess and Katie Hunter. That's Hugh's story to tell. Not mine.

The truth is, coming face-to-face with Jane is the last thing I want to happen right now. She will, no doubt, accuse me of doing nothing to find Lucy. And she'll be right. If I'm lucky, I may avoid bumping into Jane for the rest of the day, but I can't say the same for my daughter. Grace, I'll have to face. There's no putting her off till morning.

Sighing, because I'm coming to dread the few moments we get to spend together, I clamp the roll-up between my teeth and begin the climb back down. By the time I reach the bottom, my eyes are streaming with cigarette smoke. I've cried so many tears today that I decide a few more won't make any difference. They've got to be the last. Surely?

Noticing that Jane's feet have worn a path through the long grass in the graveyard, I follow in her footsteps, wanting to know why she went out of her way to get to the church when she could have taken a more direct route. When I stumble across the Valentine family plot, I think I understand why. I never suspected Jane of being sentimental, but judging by the flattened grass surrounding the chained-off monument, she must come here often.

Here lie her ancestors, her mother and father, perhaps. Or the siblings I saw in the trompe l'oeil painting. There are no flowers. Not even a container to hold any in. I don't know if this is unusual because, so far, I haven't lost anyone close to me. Unless I count my mother, who is as dead to me as the people in the graveyard.

Georgina Valentine. Wife. Mother. Lover.

What an unusual inscription. Lover? Not a word you'd normally associate with a gravestone. She must have been an extraordinary person, this Georgina. As far as I can tell by the dates, this could indeed be Jane's mother. But there's no sign of Mr Valentine.

Taking a quick look around me to check I'm not being watched, I gently place one hand on the inscription and close my eyes. The subtlest throbbing at my temple lets me know I'm in no danger. I'm not about to witness anything awful. Thank God.

Peals of elegant laughter. The clink of champagne flutes. A harassed maid with red cheeks, handing out canapés. Georgina Valentine. *Gorgeous Georgie.* Tall. Beautiful. Waist-long hair teased into blond curls. The woman from the painting. The same evil-eyed, velvety blue hunting dog stands majestically by her side, one eye on the canapés, the other on its adored owner. Three children, all with the same blond hair, looking on in a detached way. Not really a part of their mother's world. One girl. Two boys. Again, like the painting. Then, shouting. A woman's voice, brittle and angry, remonstrating with one of the children.

I spring back and snatch away my hand when I hear a rustling behind me. At first, I think it's Jane returning from the church, and I know a moment's fear, sensing she'll be angry if she finds me here, snooping into her past. But it's not her, so I'm safe, for now, at least.

The sound, more of a buzz than a rustle, is coming from inside a large oak tree that's vaguely familiar, so I make my way over to it and peer inside the hollowed-out part of it. When I see the dried-up remains of a bees' nest with a handful of bees buzzing around it, maintaining a vigil and mourning their missing relatives in a way I haven't seen the Valentines do, I feel an inappropriate sense of loss.

I remember coming across the nest when I first arrived at Moon Hollow and wish now that I'd done something to help. But as usual, I turned a blind eye. Convincing myself, as I have for years, that what I see in my visions is none of my business, that life has got to go on as if they don't exist.

How wrong I've been, I realise. Instead of hating what I am, I should've been helping people. Warning those I love about the terrible things that were going to happen to them. I certainly could've been more supportive of my best friend Kelly, who begged me to tell her who the father of her unborn baby was so she could get an abortion if she needed to.

She'd been having an on-off affair with a hot estate agent while her childhood-sweetheart hubby renovated the beat-up old house they'd bought together. Her dream home, she called it. I could've told her that the baby would be a redhead and prone to freckles, not at all like Kell's husband, but refused to get involved, citing moral grounds.

What a joke coming from me. Worse still, I refused to accept any blame for her divorce three years later, when blood tests revealed the baby's true parentage.

Jesus, Cindy, you've been a proper bitch, haven't you?

Even more of a bitch to myself, I argue back, as if that makes up for what I did to my BFF, who is, unsurprisingly, a bestie no more.

Knowing I can no longer help Kell, no matter how much I'd like to, I focus on my own problems and ask myself this – if I'd known Tess Hunter was going to kill herself and her daughter, would I, knowing what I know now, have warned someone? The answer is yes, without a shadow of a doubt. And I'd have done the same for the Valentines if I'd known their daughter would be taken.

But what about my own situation? If I could've foreseen what was going to happen on the night of the accident, would I have done anything differently? Once again, yes, yes, and fuck yes. For a start, I wouldn't have gone out. Wouldn't have had hot sex in the back of an alley with an unimportant guy called Zak, wouldn't have got stoned and come home in a taxi, not knowing how to direct the driver, getting lost on the way because I couldn't remember what fucking street I lived in.

I'd have stayed at home with my beautiful daughter, drinking pop and ordering in a Domino's pizza. We'd have watched *Frozen*, Grace's all-time favourite movie, in our pj's and slept in the same bed.

Digging my hands in my pockets, as if that's where I keep my shame like small change, I make up my mind to do things differently in future. Starting with Lucy Valentine, I'll do my best to help people from now on. The old, selfish Cindy must be kicked into touch.

As good as that sounds, I'm not ready to make a difference to Jane Valentine's day just yet. So, before she comes out of the church and finds me lurking around outside, I exit the graveyard. But as soon as my boots crunch on gravel, I become aware that somebody's watching me. I can feel their eyes, narrowed to small slits, burning into my skin, willing me to turn around. As a result, I spin around so quickly I feel something in my neck pop.

At the end of the long driveway, close to where the derelict gatehouse stands – I see him.

"Dance, then, wherever you may be, I am the Lord of the Dance, said he."

The freak. The nutter. The weirdo.

He's watching me, and I'm watching him the fuck right back.

Outside the closed gates of Moon Hollow, he straddles his bike in the middle of the road, gripping hold of the handlebars with locked arms and bunched fists. It's a pose he seems comfortable with, as if he rests like this often, surveying the world with an outsider's eyes. Yet his face is turned in my direction, eyes bolted onto mine.

Shit.

A split second. That's all I get to observe him. Trousers tucked into something, socks, perhaps, making them appear like hip-hop pants. Thin arms, almost puny. An old-fashioned straw hat is pulled down over his ears, obscuring his face. He wears sunglasses, or, rather, they wear him, as they're much too big for his face. But there's no little girl, Lucy, tucked into his coat and sitting on the handlebars as there was in Grace's drawing.

He moves a fraction of a second before I do.

'Wait!' I shout, already moving. Already running as I watch him mount the saddle and pedal furiously away. 'Stop! Don't go!'

I run until I can't run anymore. Until I'm red in the face and out of breath. That fucking hymn pounding in my head like an intruder climbing in through the window. An intruder I'd beat half to death, given the chance.

I can't hope to catch him. He's way too fast, so I slow up and bend down to catch my breath, sides heaving in and out like a cow in labour. I never take my eyes off him, though. Nor he me. He looks back over his shoulder so many times his bike begins to wobble beneath him, and, clutching at straws, I hope that he's about to fall off. But

I'm not that lucky. He gets clean away. The bike is now no more than a small black dot in the distance.

Glancing up at the derelict gatehouse, where I've ended up, I feel my heart thump. Thickened branches of dusty ivy crawl over it, invading its glassless windows and peering into rooms I can't see. Once again, I experience a strong sense of being watched, but I know that nobody lives here, so I've got to assume whoever is inside isn't of this world.

48

Trudging wearily, kicking off my damp clothes as I go, I open the bathroom door and peer cautiously inside. I can hear the ominous drip of a leaking tap. The sides of the rolltop bath are so high I wonder how people haven't drowned in it before now. *Perhaps they have, but that isn't something I want to think about right now.* Grabbing my cheap satin wrap off the back of the door, hastily purchased for a hen weekend I never attended, I slip it on, careful not to glance into the bathroom cabinet mirror before closing the door behind me.

Back in the bedroom, I check out the wardrobe doors, relieved to see that they remain closed. The pillows on the bed have been plumped to double their size, and the peacock eiderdown has been folded back as if nobody had ever slept in it. A result of Jane's tidying, no doubt. I don't like her coming in here when I'm not around, but it's her house, after all.

But Jane can wait. I've more important things to worry about. Lord of the Dance, for one thing. Knowing that he's real and not simply a vision dreamt up by me and my daughter fills me with a sickening unease. I need to find Grace so I can find out why she drew him in the picture alongside Lucy. Does she know more than she's letting on?

I've got to make her tell me how many times she's seen him. He could be the key to everything, so the more I know about him, the better. The trouble is, whenever Grace thinks I'm getting any closer to finding the little girl, she clams up on me. It's a hopeless situation.

Where are you, Grace? Hiding to punish me, is that what you're up to? On a sudden hunch, I walk out of the bedroom and continue along the galleried landing until I reach Lucy's bedroom. The door is open, so I walk straight in. There's no sign of my daughter, but I'm struck once again by how tragic and upsetting a child's bedroom it is. I can't imagine Lucy, or any other child, being happy here.

My eyes are drawn to the doll's house, remembering how distressed Jane was when the baby doll in the cot went missing and it turned out Grace had taken it. I peer down at the fake grass, grazing horses, and white geese and shudder, making a promise to myself that when life goes back to normal, I'm throwing out Grace's Sylvanian Families doll's house, felt rabbits and all. I won't care how much she complains.

When I see a pair of unmoving eyes staring straight at me through one of the windows in the doll's house, my knees buckle, and I feel my heart race ahead of me as if it wants out.

'Grace. You made me jump.' I laugh nervously when I get over my shock, not liking the deadpan stare my daughter is giving me. 'I was looking for you.'

Grace comes out from behind the doll's house but

doesn't tire of looking at me. Her eyes, so unlike mine at this moment, brim with disappointment. They're not like a child's eyes at all, I observe sadly. I screwed up her childhood, and now she's more of an adult than I am.

'When were you looking for me, Mummy?' she asks without emotion. As always, she has the aura of someone who's used to being lied to. 'I've been here all day.'

'Well, only just now,' I admit apologetically, although we both know this won't make any difference to how she's feeling. The tenseness in my daughter's eyes reminds me of Tess Hunter before she... I force myself to close my eyes against this unwanted memory, as Grace is demanding my undivided attention. 'I couldn't look for you earlier because I was busy. But I'm always thinking of you, even when I'm not looking for you,' I wheedle.

She doesn't argue with this statement. Rather, seems to accept there's an element of truth to my words, but I can also tell that she's no happier. Then, I notice that she has one of the figures clenched in her hand again. Not the baby this time, but the man on the bike. I can see the wheels poking out of her fingers through her vicelike grip.

She's also humming that fucking awful song. I would recognise it anywhere, with or without words. It's as if she sensed I was thinking about him. Lord of the Fucking Dance. Guessed I was going to ask her about him. Knowing this completely throws me, and I begin to realise that her second sight is more terrifying and even more powerful than mine.

I avoid the obvious conversation I should be having with her – like, *How do you know that song, and why are you carrying that bloody awful man doll around with you? And, more importantly, why did you draw a picture of him on the bike with Lucy?* – and instead say, rather tersely, 'That wasn't nice, what you did just now.' I point in the direction of the doll's house so she'll know exactly what I'm getting at. 'You frightened me.'

'Do I frighten you, Mummy?'

In this rather macabre moment, she appears like one of Lucy Valentine's dolls. Dead behind the eyes. *My God, what is this house – and those people – doing to her?* I want to ask, but of course I don't because I'm the parent, and she's…

Let's face it, I don't know what she is anymore.

I try to study her objectively as if I weren't her mother and she weren't a child I'd pushed out of my womb, but I become consumed with hatred for Jane, for trying to change her and daring to put my daughter's hair into a fancy French plait. Grace's blond hair, yellow as any doll's, isn't as neat as it was this morning, though, I observe with satisfaction.

By now wispy strands of it are escaping. The glossiness I witnessed earlier is gone. This makes me want to claw at it and loosen it some more so Grace resembles my little girl again. But, judging by the way she's looking at me with amused eyes, I begin to doubt this is possible. I haven't seen my daughter act like this before, and I don't know how to react. She stands silent as a statue, while I, on the other hand, am incapable of remaining still.

Do I frighten you, Mummy?

49

JANE

It occurs to Jane that God might be angry with her for involving a clairvoyant in the search for Lucy when she should, as a devoted Christian, be putting all her trust in Him. But the truth is, she does not need to be a psychic or a God-fearing woman to know that there is no escaping her past. Or guilt. A missing child cannot alter that fact. That is why at night, in the house that she grew up in and once hoped to escape from, her feelings of panic intensify.

John does not like her walking these corridors at night. He strongly advises against it. Says it is bad for her mental health. Jane wants to scream that losing her daughter is significantly more damaging. But she chooses instead to keep her nighttime activities a secret.

That is why she is walking barefoot, as silent as a mouse, down the stone steps of the trompe l'oeil staircase, the one that leads up to their suite, which consists of a morning room – where they open their letters, bills mostly, with an ivory letter opener that once belonged to her papa – a large his-and-hers marble bathroom, and a walk-in dressing room for Jane, where forgotten fur coats grace silk hangers and boxes of shoes gather dust.

She no longer wears the furs due to the risk of being ridiculed in public or spat on, and as they no longer get invited to smart dinners, she hasn't worn anything with a pointy heel for years. John has his own dressing room, where he pulls on his clothes in secret, the eyes of dead game birds glaring down at him from the walls along with images of gouty men in shooting gear. John has not loaded a gun in years, but he still has a killer instinct.

Jane does not miss their old life. The one they lived before people found out about them. A whiff of their secret was all it took. Nothing could be proven, but the rumours persisted nonetheless. All Jane remembers from the old days are the sneers behind hands and constant references to what a beauty and natural hostess her mother had been. Jane has never tried to emulate Gorgeous Georgie, as she was known. She's incapable of stepping into her mother's shoes. She simply does not shine the way she did.

Stopping on the stairs, Jane gazes in admiration at the trompe l'oeil painting on the wall. She can hardly believe she painted it herself, over twenty years ago. Who was this other Jane who was so talented and accomplished? Where has she gone? She used to think that she knew herself inside and out, but does she really? Does anyone?

Jane did not attend a university like John; girls of her class were rarely allowed to attend school at all, but she had private tutors who all admired her. Back then, Jane took their flattery for granted. She was a confident person who did not require reassurance. Now, she would kill for some. She still gets pleasure from telling anyone who will listen that she used to "paint a little". But her success fades in comparison to women who can have babies.

Whispers from the past come at her from every direction. She hears voices she has not heard or thought about in years. Her mother and father quarrelling, of course; when didn't they? The groom who tried and failed to teach her to ride. His screams at her to get straight back in the saddle after a fall or risk shaming the family.

Unlike John, who becomes easily bored by such things, she knows every nook and cranny of this old house. It is as familiar to her as her own face. Jane's fingers have slid open every single one of the secret peepholes located throughout its shadowy landings, put there by an eccentric old relative who thought his family was plotting his death. Knowing the Valentine history as well as she does, Jane believes there might have been some truth in this theory.

The Valentines were as much a morally bankrupt family as they were a financial nightmare. Jane has never forgiven her parents for having the castle, her childhood home, demolished in favour of a less-expensive-to-maintain manor house.

While sick and twisted individuals often turned up in their family, they were not to be tolerated. Not then. Not now. Evidence of that was born out in the way Jane's mother would bash the heads of newborn puppies against the wall for not being quite right. Being born too small, the wrong colour, or failing to develop quickly enough meant they paid the ultimate price, as did everyone in the Valentine family, for not fitting in.

Cindy is somebody else who does not fit in. Her clairvoyance sets her apart from most, giving her a completely different outlook on life. Jane knows how that feels. That is why spying on the girl comes naturally to her. She feels no shame in what she is doing. It has become as regular a routine as serving up afternoon tea or changing for dinner.

Watching through the peepholes in the walls, Jane has seen Cindy kick clothes around the room in temper. Watched her defecate on the toilet. Seen her cramp up with period pain. Observed her naked in the shower. Noticed how Cindy gives the rolltop bath a wide birth. She has also watched her bring herself to orgasm under the bedcovers.

When Jane hears the clock chime in the downstairs drawing room, she scurries down the steps two at a time, her floor-length dressing gown hugging her ankles. It is nine o'clock, and she does not know where the day has gone. Moon Hollow has its own sense of time. It does not allow anyone else to take charge. Jane no longer tries. All she knows is she must hurry.

The term "winter is coming" is a phrase Jane grew up with. The Valentines used it to describe a period when the house was shut up and visitors barred. It heralded the return not only of the colder months but of her younger brother, who, like the puppies, was considered not quite right in the head.

His arrival was dreaded because it meant the end of summer. And here it comes again. Jane can feel its quickening in the crisping of the leaves on the trees, the fur thickening on the foals' coats, and the geese growing their winter plumage. Soon the light will fade, and Moon Hollow will be plunged into darkness. Again.

50

CINDY

Knowing that Jane will soon be stealing her way along the unlit landings of Moon Hollow, flitting from one wing to another like a thief in the night, I wait, all the while holding my breath and making as little noise as possible so as not to give myself away.

Although I've never actually witnessed Jane locking me in my bedroom, I know it's her. Who else could it be? I can sense Jane's presence hovering outside the door even when she's not there – breathing, sighing, listening. *Always watching.*

Like a sexual predator, Jane comes each night, punctual as clockwork, at nine p.m. She's never said a word to me about this ritual, nor asked me if I mind. *I do. Shit-loads.* Dreading the moment when Grace and I are locked in keeps me awake most nights. Listening out for the sound of the key turning in the lock at the ungodly hour of six a.m., when Jane returns to free us from our prison, is like experiencing daylight for the first time.

From my hiding place in the walk-in airing cupboard, I

have a clear view of my bedroom door, and I plan to catch Jane in the act. Although I'm holding the door slightly ajar so it doesn't shut on me, I still feel claustrophobic. I don't like the idea of being trapped inside such a small space, surrounded as I am by shelves of folded-up bedding that are no doubt infested with spiders and moths.

The heat from the hot-water tank brings me out in as much of a sweat as my anxiety does. Already, I can feel droplets of perspiration running down my neck and gathering under my armpits. When I hear the swish of footsteps approaching, my heart rate increases. The fear of being discovered causes my body to tense, allowing images of the Valentine children playing hide-and-seek in the church to invade my thoughts like an old black-and-white movie clip. Until Jane comes into view, I can't be certain it *is* her. It could be anybody. Living or dead. I'm not sure who I fear the most. But the one person I don't want to run into is John, intent on creeping into my room so he can finish what he tried to start the other evening when we flirted in the games room.

When I glimpse Jane's elegant shadow on the landing wall, I'm relieved, for once, to see her. Anything is better than a sweaty-faced John. Jane barely makes a sound, but I can smell her expensive perfume and creamy skin. It reminds me of the cosmetic counter at Boots.

I watch Jane put her ear against my bedroom door. She stays like that for a while, listening. To be on the safe side, in case Jane knows more than she lets on, I have bunched up my side of the bed so it looks as if I'm sleeping. It unnerves me that Jane seems to know so much about my movements and personal life.

Sometimes, it feels as if she's in the room with me

even when she isn't – listening to every word I say and watching my every move. It's not a nice feeling. I could call her out on this, of course, but I've put off doing so because I want to turn this around on her so I can do my own sneaking about in the dark. But for that, I need the set of keys Jane's using now to lock my bedroom door.

How fucking dare she lock us in our room? What if there was a fire? What if one of us got sick and needed help? Jane knows I have no phone and no means of contact with the outside world.

I resist punching a hand in the air when I see Jane hiding the bulky set of keys inside an ugly vase that graces one of the tables with turned-out legs that hug Moon Hollow's landings. As soon as she's gone, I burst out of the hot airing cupboard, shake the keys out of the vase into my sweaty hand, willing them to be silent, and then I'm off. Creeping along the corridors and tripping down the stone steps as silently as Jane did.

I decide to go out the back way, as the main doors at the front of the house screech when opened and clunk loudly when they're closed. They're better than any burglar alarm. As I pass by the study door, I'm surprised to see a light glowing under it. The flickering of it touches my toes. Finds me easily, making my skin go cold. Does this mean John is still up?

I thought the Valentines retired to their suite of rooms at eight o'clock each night. That's what Jane told me. I imagine John on the other side of the door, slumped in his chair, staring vacantly at the laptop screen. More Russian girls, no doubt.

Slipping out of the door in the garden room, the pungent aroma of wilted flowers following me, I pull trainers on over my bare feet and tighten the belt on my satin wrap. I don't have a torch, so I make my way through the graveyard in the dark, careful where I tread, not wanting to trip over one of the squawking geese that nest here at night, their bodies curled around the wonky grave-stones. I try not to think about how close I am to the Valen-tine family plot. The thought of running into that blue hunting dog fills me with terror.

As I'm not familiar with the metal skeleton key that's coated in rust and embellished with fancy scrollwork, I struggle at first to unlock the church door. Breathing in a damp wood smell, I try to force it to open, but it resists my touch as if to say, "I don't know you." When I hear rustling in the long grass behind me and an ominous growling, I frantically try again, fearing that Georgina Valentine's ghost dog is about to pounce on me. When I feel the key turn in the lock, I tumble inside the church, quickly closing the door behind me.

Breathing a sigh of relief, I take a look around. I've never been inside a church at night before, but at least there's a candle burning at one end, giving off some light. There's electricity too, but I dare not flick on the lights in case John or Jane should see them from the windows of Moon Hollow. The last thing I want to do is wake the house. Never mind a dead dog.

I'm surprised that Jane has banned me from visiting the church. I would've thought she would have wanted me to see the candle that burns twenty-four hours a day for her missing child. Yet I don't get a sense of the little girl in here. Only Jane. Her majestic presence fills this building in a way that Christ does not. It's almost as if she's eclipsed God. This thought catches me out, making me want to snigger. Like a naughty Sunday schoolgirl, I clap a hand over my mouth to silence it.

When all is said and done, I'm my mother's daughter, and I've grown up around all kinds of superstitions surrounding the church and the Bible. I might not be a believer, but I dare not, *must* not mock Him.

There's a whiff of John in here too, and this surprises me because he never shows any inclination to join Jane in her prayers. He goes out of his way to avoid coming in here at all. I don't blame him. There's something depressing about a church without people. I remember vividly the sounds from my past that I associate with morning worship. The shuffling of feet. Sporadic coughing and sniffling. Somebody in the back blowing their nose. Children being told to be quiet. Children refusing to be silenced. Those who cried too loudly being marched out, the eyes of the congregation following them. People tutting in disapproval.

I was never one of those children. Even my mother said I was good as gold in church. She thought this meant I would become like her. Someone with faith. It would've killed her to know that I didn't sit quietly so I could listen to the morning sermon. The church was the only place where I could escape the terrible visions that dogged my childhood.

This church is much like any other. It has a nave roof with a bell tower above it, and there's a frieze with the type of gargoyles that terrified my childhood self. Over the arched doorway that I came in through, there's a five-light window. A private family pew is accessed through a gate with a sign marked "reserved", and I imagine the monuments inside hold more of the Valentine family.

I wonder if this is where Gorgeous Georgie's husband is buried, but part of me doesn't want to know. It would be too sad to discover that he was buried away from his wife, who was a lover as well as a wife and mother. Instead, I focus on the dusty, unused organ, which has several of its ivory keys missing, reminding me of Grace's gappy-toothed smile when she was younger.

Captivated by the candle that glows for Lucy, and all the hope that has gone into keeping it alight, I slide into one of the pews so I can watch its flickering flame caress the walls. Stretching out my hands, I rest them on the polished wood of the fixed pew in front of me and, closing my eyes, feel the warmth of the flame dancing across my cheeks. I don't know what'll happen if I break my self-imposed rule of never trying to connect with the past – living or dead – in a place of worship, but I'm about to find out. The small part of me that's my mother's daughter hopes I'll be forgiven for this.

Children's laughter immediately bounces off the church walls. At first I think, *hope*, it's Lucy, that I've found her again, but no, it's Jane and her brothers. A game of hide-and-seek. I sense excitement, fear, and something else, a burning desire. A wish stronger than anything I've come across before. A steely determination that won't waver. No matter what. Winter. It's winter. A time that brings them no joy. When the house is closed to guests and they only have each other to play with. Or fall out with as is more often the case.

They spend their days alone and unsupervised. No nanny. No tutor. No schooling. No mother or father to guide them. A natural leader emerges. The girl, of course. She rules over them as if she has every right. Occasionally, a maid takes pity on them and provides them with prohibited treats, biscuits, and lemon drizzle cake. Sometimes, in the absence of any parent, she pretends to admire their pictures.

These pictures are unlike any children's drawings I've seen before. They involve dead animals. Geese lie in pools of feathers and blood on the lawns. A horse with no rear legs drags itself along. A pitiful sight. I don't know what these images mean, but they make me want to recoil in horror. Whoever drew them can't be normal. Not right in the head.

Whispers fill the church like an invisible congregation. There's a shuffling of shoes on the uneven concrete floor. Curls of white breath spill from corners of the church as the children unwittingly give their hiding positions away.

"One. Two. Three. Coming!" the smallest boy shouts.

But no matter how hard he looks, the others are nowhere to be found. He feels betrayed. Left out of their games as usual. They should be punished for the things they say and do. "You are not worthy," their voices ring out spitefully in his head.

Unlike the boy, I have no trouble finding the other two. They're hiding among the church bells, careful not to touch the frayed bits of rope that hang down from the tower, knowing that if they do, the bells will ring out and deafen them, not to mention give them away. The girl's in a flood of tears over something her mother said.

"I am not ugly, am I?" she pleads with her brother.

Then comes the boy's whispered reply. "No. You are perfect just the way you are." Something about the urgency in his voice tells me he wants to be taken seriously.

She looks at him then, blue eyes meeting blue. "Do you really think so?"

The boy nods and puts an arm around his sister's shoulders, wanting to console her. It's such a grown-up, gentlemanly thing to do that an unfamiliar emotion catches in my throat. I can't help thinking that Jane was incredibly lucky to have such a brother. Of course, this gets me thinking about my own sibling, Anthony. Our relationship in comparison was awful. It was always going to be, him being my mother's favourite. I never understood why at the time. But I do now. Her disappointment in me is obvious, as is her fear of me.

I always had my dad, though, and he tried to make up for my mum, calling me his special doll. The older I got, I found it increasingly irritating. I wish I'd been more patient with him. He never meant any harm, and he was the only one to love me, but he was a weak man. Still is. I don't think I've ever forgiven him for not being one of the heroes of this world.

Blinking away tears, I sit upright in my seat as my mother used to insist I do in church and make up my mind that I'll ask Jane about these brothers of hers. She won't like it. But it might help to know more about them. For Lucy's sake, it's got to be worth the effort.

For now, though, the trio of Valentine children have gone back to their forever game of hide-and-seek, of which they can never hope to escape – chased back to the past by my own childhood memories. Perhaps they're hiding in the corners of the church, waiting desperately for someone to come and find them. As little Lucy must be doing.

51

When I let myself out of the church, it's daylight. I know that this is impossible. I was only inside the church an hour, so it should be ten o'clock at night. Yet the sun is shining down on me as if it were midday. This is a new phenomenon. Nothing like this has happened before.

Having no choice but to go along with the illusion for now, I take a few tentative steps in the long grass, worried in case the ghost dog should appear. An eerie silence surrounds me. No birdsong or squawking of geese. No friendly whinnying of horses in the neighbouring parkland. Thankfully, no growling either.

When I see two people standing beside the Valentine plot, barely moving, I guess straightaway who the first figure is – John. Although he's facing away from me, gazing at the monument, I can tell it's him from the floppy blond hair and the polo shirt and chinos he's wearing.

I hear the murmur of their voices. His is loud and arrogant, too sure of himself, keen to impress, and the girl's is quieter, gentler, as if she's of a shy disposition. I recognise the twang of her foreign accent immediately. It's Lucy Benedict.

Longing to catch sight of her again, I close in on them, careful not to make a sound, although I know they can't hear me. They exist in another dimension. Giving them a wide birth, not wanting our paths to cross in case that should make them disappear, I approach them from the other side of the monument. John is younger and more handsome than ever, I notice, but I treat him to a fleeting look. I'm only interested in Lucy Benedict.

This is the first time I've seen her as she once was. A living, breathing girl existing outside of the confines of Moon Hollow and away from the secret room. Her hair is blacker than I remembered, and her skin is as light as almond milk.

Today, there are no dark shadows under her eyes, but a faint look of concern lingers – as if dark thoughts prowl her head. She's a girl with something on her mind. Hugh, I wouldn't mind betting. I can't say I blame her. Whatever it is, she's trying to hide her feelings from John, avoiding his probing questions and sexual innuendo.

He dwarfs her, making her seem younger and more vulnerable. There's an awkwardness about the sagging of her shoulders, as though she wants to hide her body from his prying eyes. Again, I don't blame her. When he nudges her shoulder, laughing at an unfunny joke, she bows her head.

"How come you took Jane's name? That was very modern of you," she says, squirming, like she feels obliged to say something. Anything.

John shrugs as if he's never given this any thought

before. As if it doesn't matter. But when I see his eyes go cloudy with secrecy, I know he's lying.

"That's where the money was." He laughs self-consciously.

I watch Lucy Benedict wrap the edge of her cardigan around her body as if she's cold, although it's a scorching hot day, and subconsciously try to reach out to her. I can't help myself. I'm desperate to know what she knows. I'm certain she can help me find Lucy. Her daughter.

When I see her body stiffen and her hands form fists, I know that she senses my presence. Her eyes widen in alarm, and I can tell that I'm making her feel anxious.

This isn't what I intended, but it can't be helped. I need her to reconnect with me. I'm about to try harder, dig deeper into her psyche, when I see her hand fly agitatedly to her cheek as if to hide the disfiguring birthmark on her face. I get the feeling this is a habit of hers. That she does this whenever she's nervous.

I wish I could explain to her that she has no reason to be afraid of me. All I've ever wanted to do is help her. But when John snatches at her hand, he breaks the link between us. There's little chance of rekindling our connection now. Her eyes are locked. Her mouth is set. She's pushed me from her mind.

I glower angrily at John, not liking the way he's bent over her hand, the one that touched her cheek, kissing the whites of her knuckles. *You're not some fucking knight in shining armour, John. Far from it*, I'm tempted to shout. But I hold back when I see the sun's rays catching on the silver bracelet Lucy Benedict is wearing, making it sparkle.

It's the same bracelet I'm wearing, which I've vowed

not to take off until I solve the mystery of what happened to her. What John says next jerks me back to the here and now.

"I've told you before, you don't have to hide it." John admonishes sternly yet gently, as if he cares for her. "You are perfect just the way you are."

Perfect just the way you are.

These are the same words I heard inside the church. Does this mean anything, or is it a coincidence? Glancing up from the bracelet I'm wearing, my eyes flicker back to the Valentine family plot, and I feel bereft when I see that John and Lucy Benedict have vanished, leaving no trace of themselves behind. Not that I care two figs for John. He could disappear off the face of the earth for all I care, but she's a different matter.

Cindy. Cindy.

I hear her voice then. Lucy Benedict's. Barely a whisper. But there nonetheless. Acting on instinct, I find myself heading in the direction of the treehouse. I can't explain why. I follow what my gut is telling me to do. It's as if Lucy Benedict is willing me to go there.

As soon as I arrive, I notice that something is different. Resting against the trunk of the old tree, whose twisted roots poke greedily out of the ground as if desperate for air, is Lucy Valentine's doll Heidi. The one that got left behind. The one that Grace appropriated for herself, much to the horror of Jane Valentine.

I wonder if what I'm seeing is part of the vision I've stumbled into or if someone put it there on purpose. Grace, perhaps, to throw me off the scent. Unlike before, on my subsequent visits to the treehouse, the grass around the tree is muddied with footprints.

I don't attempt to pick up the doll, knowing it's likely to dissolve in my hands if I try to touch it. Gazing into its beady black eyes, I find myself wishing it could tell me everything it knows. The doll is the last thing Lucy touched. It probably witnessed her kidnapping. Knows who took her. But it refuses to reveal its secrets to me. Like the Valentines.

Suddenly they are there. John and Jane. They bring nightfall with them, and I'm thrust back into the dark. Feeling shivery and faint, I close my eyes to stop my head spinning.

When I open them again, everything is blurry, but in the blackness I can make out the Valentines' indistinct silhouettes. Jane is clawing wildly at her hair, as I've seen her do before, while John is standing still, a familiar pose for him when he doesn't know what to do. Somewhere behind them, the beam of car headlights can be seen, but the vehicle itself is quite far away, closer to the house than here.

"She is not here either. She has gone. Gone!" Jane is screaming. "You have to find her, John. Go after her. What are you waiting for?"

I watch Jane shove her husband in the direction of the headlights. Caught off guard, he stumbles before righting himself but does not immediately obey. His lack of urgency infuriates Jane. When her fingernails flail wildly at his face, he's finally provoked into action. Thrusting her away, he plods despondently in the headlights' direction.

I get a sickening feeling that, for once, they're not talking about Lucy Valentine.

52

JANE

When Jane walks into the morning room, where they drink their coffee and read their newspapers before getting dressed in the morning, and talk over the events of the day last thing at night – or at least that's what they used to do before Lucy went missing – she is alarmed to see John standing straight-backed at the window, hands on hips, gazing intently outside. She is so surprised to see him she almost spills her cup of tea.

'I thought you were…' Jane feels wrong-footed. Why is he standing so still? Like a cardboard cutout.

'Otherwise occupied? Yes, I know you did.' He growls over his shoulder.

'I only made one cup,' Jane explains as though this is something he is unlikely to forgive. 'If I had known you were in here, I would have made another. I can make you one if you like,' she offers as if this is all it will take to erase the thunderous look on her husband's face.

'I do not want a fucking cup of tea.' John explodes, turning around to glare at her.

Jane knows she should be paying closer attention to how her husband is behaving and what he is saying, but instead her mind wanders to the wisteria-patterned wallpaper. Until now she had not noticed how tired and worn it looks. Like her. Like John. Everything about them including Moon Hollow is fading with age. The house has a weary sound to it these days as if its foundations ache with exhaustion like arthritic bones.

'There is no need for language like that,' she remonstrates weakly, wondering what he wants to get off his chest. Best get it out, she is tempted to tell him but wisely refrains.

'Where have you been, Jane?' he demands.

'Nowhere. Why? What are you looking at me like that for?'

'I heard you at the study door, but you weren't the only one creeping about downstairs.'

Jane narrows her eyes in irritation, wishing he would tell her what is bothering him. His eyes remain fixed on her, never once wavering. Anger is etched on his face.

'Come here.' He grunts, indicating that she should join him at the window.

Intrigued to find out why he is acting so oddly, Jane goes to stand beside him. When her shoulder brushes against his, he moves away, as if he cannot bear to be touched by her. His eyes are settled on whatever it is outside that has his attention.

'Look,' he commands.

Jane follows his watery blue gaze. At first, she sees nothing out of the ordinary. It is dark, after all. Then, eyes thinning to mere slits, she peers harder until, at last, she glimpses movement – and the hint of a white face in the blackness. A lump in her throat forms as she tracks the familiar figure walking through the graveyard.

'But it can't be Cindy. I locked her in her room. How could she have got out?'

'Don't you ever learn?' John admonishes harshly. 'We both know what happened before.'

Jane closes her eyes and winces at his words. Nothing hurts like the truth.

'This time will be different,' she wheedles, determined that he should believe her.

'There will be no next time, Jane. I forbid it,' he snarls, thrusting his unshaven face into hers until their noses are almost touching. Jane can sense the surge of adrenalin rushing around his body, caused, no doubt, by the power he thinks he is exerting over her.

'You forbid it!' she sneers, letting him know he has overstepped the mark. A flush of red creeps onto John's broken-veined cheeks as he realises too late that she is back in the driving seat. He should have known better to think he could get one over on her.

What an ugly man he has become, Jane observes cruelly. It is no wonder Cindy does not fancy him. Overweight and smelling of sweat, fat gathers at his jowls. In a rare moment of self-awareness, Jane accepts that he repulses her. For a man as vain as John, he has let himself go in a way she would never have expected.

'We have to let things take their natural course,' he is saying as if trying to regain some control, 'leave Cindy alone so she can get on and do what she came here to do. What you asked her here to do, may I remind you. There's still every chance she might find—' He falters as if saying his daughter's name might choke him. 'Otherwise, you'll end up chasing her away, as you did before with—'

'As I did?' Jane reels in disbelief.

'Look, Jane,' he blusters, 'I only say this to warn you—'

'You warn me. How dare you. How dare you.' Jane pulls herself up to her full height, until she is looking down on the bald spot on top of his head that she knows he is self-conscious of. She will not have her superiority challenged. Not by him. Not by anybody. She is Jane Valentine. The rightful heir to Moon Hollow.

'What? Am I not allowed to speak the truth! Do you think you are so far above everybody else that you cannot be challenged?'

That is exactly what Jane thinks, but now is not the time to admit it. She must pretend to a reasonableness that she does not possess. But before she can open her mouth to assure him otherwise, he interrupts.

'What gives you the right to judge me or anyone else?'

'God gives me that right, John, because I continue to believe in Him, whereas you have turned away, like a Judas.' Jane breaks off momentarily because her voice is wobbling with emotion, and she feels suddenly faint. She cannot remember the last time she ate anything. She must look after herself better. She needs to stay strong for Lucy's sake. 'He gives me the strength to go down on my knees every night and pray for Lucy, for hours on end. Until I bleed. But you are nowhere to be seen. You are never there. For her or me.'

'I would do anything for Lucy. You know that.' Tears collect in his eyes as he says this.

'But you won't pray for her,' Jane persists icily. It is

cold and lonely where she is standing. She feels the chill coming off her own shadow.

'No. I won't do that,' he admits, guiltily refusing to meet her eyes.

'Then that is where you and I are different. Because I truly would do anything for Lucy. Anything.' Jane screams hysterically, waiting for the familiar look of disapproval to surface on his face. The one she has come to dread. Instead, his jaw clenches so tight she hears it click.

'And to hell with anybody else. Is that what you are saying?'

'To hell with anybody else,' Jane agrees triumphantly. Winning has never felt more important. Later, she might reflect on things differently. But right now, seeing the smugness wiped from his face is all that matters.

'At least now I know where I stand.'

'You stand where you have always stood in our relationship,' Jane reminds him coldly.

'What relationship?' he scoffs, hurling a last insult her way. 'You are mad to think there is anything left.'

With that, John marches towards the door, viciously snatching at the handle as if he would like to snap it in two. Jane is thankful for small mercies. It could have been her neck and not the handle in his hands. It would not be the first time they have come to blows.

'That's it. Go back to your whores,' she taunts. 'You can pay them to tell you how wonderful and charming you are, but, as God is my witness, I will not lie to you.'

53

CINDY

A s if by accident, I end up at Hugh's house. But I don't go in. Not yet, anyway. I know I'll knock at the door eventually, but for now, I'm content to watch from the shadows. Until my last visit, I felt at home here. I fit in more at Hugh's than I ever could at Moon Hollow.

I think this is because his back-to-front house reminds me of home. I miss my tiny two-bed semi more than I thought I would. Of course, after what happened in the garage, I can never go inside Hugh's house again, but that doesn't stop me wanting to see him. Wanting to be close to him is fast becoming a habit that I could easily get used to.

When a light comes on in the kitchen and I see Hugh's frame fill the window, I watch him wrestling with the cork of a wine bottle. He appears to be looking straight at me as if he can see me. But I'm plunged in darkness. He can't possibly know I'm here. The smile lighting up his face suggests otherwise. He must be able to see me after all.

Deciding that a few minutes spent in Hugh's kitchen should be fine, I step out of the shadows. Some time spent away from the madness of Moon Hollow is what I need. Providing I don't go anywhere near the garage, I'll be safe from Tess Hunter.

I'm a few feet from the door when I hear his voice. At first, I think he's calling out to me, welcoming me over the threshold, but I'm wrong. He's calling over his shoulder to someone else. I look for a place to hide. Now that I know he's not alone, I can't have him know I was here. That would be too humiliating.

I'm about to make my escape when I see a woman appear behind Hugh. I feel an intense pang of envy as I watch her drape a possessive arm around his neck. I feel my body go numb. I can't feel a thing. All I can do is stare at them through the window.

As if in slow motion, I watch them kiss. The jealousy dies inside me when the woman's eyes open. I know this woman. Those eyes. Full of hatred and jealousy, Tess Hunter's eyes lock onto mine like she knows I'm watching her.

Needing to get away, I head back down the path, making up my mind never to come here again. I was stupid to think it was possible. When I feel someone's hand on my arm, my pulse quickens, and I spin around, ready to claw out Tess Hunter's eyes if I must.

'Cindy? I thought it was you. What are you doing out here? Aren't you going to come inside?'

Dazedly, I look into Hugh Hunter's eyes. They're the same countryside olive they've always been. His smile is warm and trusting, and there's a reassuring crinkling around his eyes that suggests he's amused by my sudden appearance, not annoyed.

'Are you on your own?' I snap without meaning to, still upset by what I saw through the window.

'Of course.' He pulls a face that suggests he never gets any visitors. 'This is the countryside, after all.' He laughs as if that should explain everything.

'For a minute or two, then.' I shrug as if I'm doing him a favour. As soon as I step inside, I feel my body shudder. Memories of what happened flood my mind. I force the lingering dark thoughts away. Thinking that I'm cold, Hugh ushers me into the living room and gestures towards the log fire. Obediently, I sit down beside it on the comfy sofa made for two, my bare legs poking out from under me.

'You're a sight for sore eyes in that,' he jokes with a glint in his eye.

At first, I don't know what he means, but when he nods down at what I'm wearing, I realise I'm still wearing my satin wrap. Feeling suddenly exposed and vulnerable, I almost find myself blushing – until, that is, I remind myself that I'm Cindy Martin, council house and proud and not the sort of girl who gets embarrassed.

'I can't stay long. Just for a few minutes,' I splutter. 'I have to get back for—'

I don't say Grace's name out loud because tonight I'm a woman first, not a mother. Talking about children will spoil things. Besides, it would be unfair of me to mention my daughter after what happened to Hugh's little girl.

'Go whenever you feel like it, Cindy,' he says, pouring me a large glass of wine that we both know will take more than a few minutes to drink. 'I'm no one's jailer,' he adds, making me think of Jane locking me in my room.

I take a sip of my wine, noting that it's a good one.

Tempranillo or a Merlot, I would say. I might be as working-class as they come, but I'm also a wine snob.

'I thought you didn't drink,' I observe.

'No. But you do.'

'You didn't know I was coming.'

He shrugs comically, insinuating that he did know.

'You never said you were psychic,' I tease.

'Actually, I did think you might pop by,' he admits awkwardly, as if he's about to break some bad news to me. 'Because Jane rang to ask if I'd seen you. She sounded concerned.'

'I bet she did.' I almost spit out my mouthful of wine. 'How the bloody hell did she know I would come here?' I ask incredulously.

'Maybe she's psychic too. Maybe we all are,' he jokes again.

I'm not sure I like this new side of Hugh Hunter. I never had him down as a comedian before. I give him the benefit of the doubt for now, as I have more important issues to worry about. Like Jane Valentine. How bloody dare she check up on me as if I were a child, and how could she have possibly known I'd escaped from my room?

Deciding that I'm no closer to solving Moon Hollow's secrets, I feel myself deflate. I may as well give up and go home. But though there's nothing I'd like more than to return to my hometown with Grace, the terms of the court order are clear. If I were to leave here tomorrow, I wouldn't be allowed to take my daughter with me. She'd be returned to social care, or, worse still, Jane could apply for a court order that would allow her and John to keep my daughter. It's a worry I can't shake off, knowing Jane is capable of doing exactly that. She will stop at nothing to get what she wants.

Glancing up from my wine, my eyes roam automatically to the living room door. The doorway to the garage is just through there. I'm sitting a few measly metres away from where it all happened. When I turn to look at Hugh, I notice he's sitting on the edge of his seat and his eyes are wide in alarm.

'What's wrong, Cindy?'

Intuitively, I sense that he's terrified I'm about to mention his wife and child and the circumstances surrounding their ghastly deaths. He must've guessed that I was thinking about them. He doesn't know me well enough yet to understand that I would never reveal the awful truth of what happened that day – how Katie sobbed and begged to be let out of the car or how Tess Hunter cruelly punched their daughter in the face. The blood-splattered window. The grasping hand on the glass.

'Can I talk to you, Hugh? I mean really talk to you.'

He gets to his feet, rubs his hands on his trousers – a habit, I'm guessing – stirs up the fire, and then sits next to me on the sofa. Before I can object, not that I was going to, he takes hold of my hand and folds his own around it. *Whoa*, I think. He must trust me to do that.

'You can say anything you like to me, Cindy.'

Taking him at his word, I dive straight in, desperate to get my thoughts off my chest, where they've been lying heavily for some time. 'I know this sounds crazy, but I feel as if I'm losing myself. It's like I'm the missing person, not Lucy. The symptoms that alert me to the fact I'm going to have one of my visions are either worse or nonexistent. That means something. I know it does. It's not right that I should be spending more time in other worlds than my own. Dipping in and out of other people's lives has never been something I can control. But it's got worse since coming here. I'm trying to help the Valentines and Lucy, but sometimes I feel like screaming, *What about me?*'

'And yet you feel nothing when I touch you,' he states, gazing down at our joined hands. His skin is earthy brown, whereas mine is milky white now that the fake tan has faded.

'I wouldn't say I feel nothing.' I grin to let him know I'm flirting. 'I think I've told you before that I can't see my future, no matter how hard I try, nor can I read those who are closest to me. I've never been able to.'

Even as I say this, I know I'm not telling the complete truth, because sometimes I can read friends. I knew about Kell's pregnancy before she did and who the father was. There's no working out this so-called gift. No hard-and-fast rules. It's always been a case of "learn on the job". All I know is my warm feelings for this man mean I can't get inside his head.

'But we're not as close as we could be, are we?' He removes the glass from my hand and puts it down somewhere safe.

'No, we're not,' I agree, wondering what he's up to. I don't have to wait long to find out. I think he's about to kiss me. Touch me. I won't be able to bear it if he doesn't. I'll have to leave. Do what I promised myself earlier, never come back here again.

When his lips brush against mine, I realise that I'm as much his prisoner, to do with as he wants, as that magpie in the cage was. *Aren't magpies meant to be lucky? Or is it unlucky?*

54

It's morning. The start of a new day. New me. New life, perhaps. I've done my share of sleeping around, but I don't think I've been in love before. Not properly. Not like this. Or what this *could* be, whatever it is right now. Men might be a weakness of mine, but they're attracted to me too. Always ogling me, yet they rarely take it any further, leaving me to do the chasing. I used to put this down to them steering well clear of me because of my psychic abilities. I know from experience that men are more reluctant to be read than women. Too many secrets, that's their trouble.

"It's in the eyes," Skid used to say. "They give you away." I gaze into their green murkiness now, wondering if this is true. I'm sitting at the dressing table, staring at my reflection. The girl in the mirror staring back at me looks like me. Sounds like me. Smells like me. But I've changed. Hugh is only one of the reasons for this change. Mostly it's this house that's having the biggest effect on me.

Nothing could have prepared me for the numbers of

undead who linger at Moon Hollow, a house with the darkest of secrets. Ghosts wander its halls and landings, seeking me out as if I were an old friend they'd lost touch with. I'm never on my own, yet I've never felt so alone, estranged as I am from my daughter and my old life.

The terrifying visions I stumble upon leave me with nowhere to hide. I've never experienced anything like it before. My senses are on high alert all the time, and I grow ever more fearful of who I might run into next. For all I know, John and Jane might be ghosts themselves. They certainly don't behave like normal people. A house of spirits is what this house is, I decide, unsurprising given its history. The fact that it was once a castle and parts of it still exist within these very walls speaks volumes.

There's no getting away from the gruesome fact that it has a graveyard for a back garden where all the Valentine ancestors are buried. And now there's a missing child too. Moon Hollow certainly attracts trouble and tragedy. The same could be said of me, I suppose.

All my life I've been plagued with dreams, visions, apparitions, call them what you will, but until coming here I never imagined how all-consuming they could be. Those who know about my so-called gift are curious to know what it's like to be able to see into the future. I try to explain that it's not like what they see on the TV or read about in books.

The visions I experience are rarely clear. Often, they present me with nothing more than hints and suggestions of what might or might not have happened. They can represent both the past and the future, which means the boundaries aren't always obvious. With all that goes on in my head, it's no wonder I get confused and struggle to find the people I'm meant to, like Lucy.

Here, at Moon Hollow, I'm a different Cindy to the one my friends and family are used to. Back home, I'm loud and opinionated but always up for a laugh, no matter what. A good-time girl, that's me. Remembering that partying is what got me into this mess in the first place brings me to a new all-time low. *Shit! How did I allow my daughter, who I love more than anything, to become a chore, a drag at best to have around?* Only when it was almost too late did I come to understand that she was all I ever needed and wanted. And I would give anything to be the one to put a grin on her face, not Jane bloody Valentine.

I frown at the glass perfume bottle on the dressing table. Something about its hourglass shape bothers me. *Was it Lucy Benedict's? Did it get left behind when she left Moon Hollow?* Picking it up, I turn it over in my hand, expecting to see, smell, or hear something – a flashing image from the past – but nothing springs to mind. All I can see is my face reflected in the glass. Deciding that I need to do something about the breakout of acne that has erupted on my cheeks, I forget about the bottle and rummage in my makeup bag for some foundation.

As I apply it to my skin, I think how nice it would be if I could cover up my other imperfections so easily. Fuck knows there's enough of them. Yet Hugh doesn't appear to see them. He's a true friend, or he could be, the more we get to know each other, as I believe he cares for me too. Yet though he might have helped to lift my spirits, I'm still out of sorts with myself and feel incredibly homesick.

Not only do I miss my old life, I miss me. Cindy Martin, the single parent whose busy life was filled with loud, boisterous people who don't eat their meals in formal dining rooms, armed with silver cutlery, but on a tray in front of the telly. I also miss my dad. Not surprising, considering I've always been a daddy's girl. I was given little choice growing up, now that I come to think about it. As for my mother, I can't think of her without feeling intense anger. I'll never forgive her for not taking me and Grace in when the court agreed I could have my daughter back under supervision, but only if a temporary foster home among family or friends was found. Knowing *why* she refused doesn't ease the heartbreak.

The truth is, I terrify her. Always have. She doesn't like being in the same house as me, let alone the same room. As a result, she couldn't wait for me to move out, which I did at the ripe old age of sixteen. But even then, our relationship didn't improve. Because of my "gift", which is not a gift at all but a curse, my mother couldn't bring herself to love me. I go against everything she believes in – God and her Christian beliefs.

She once told me that she could forgive me being a whore, a thief, or a druggie like Skid, but not for being psychic. The Bible, she claims, condemns the use of clairvoyants, psychics, horoscopes, tarot cards, or any aspect of the occult. As soon as she cottoned on to the fact that I could see things, she rejected me, cruelly labelling me an abomination. I was seven at the time. A year younger than Grace.

Grace, the traitor, is outside playing. I can hear her laughter trickling in through the open windows. I try not to blame her for her thoughtless behaviour. She's only a child when all is said and done. My child. And I want her back. I don't need any more obstacles put in my way. This morning she was up before me, which is so unlike her, and out of the house before I knew it. Jane sent her up with a cup of tea a while ago to make sure I was awake, but Grace didn't stay long, skipping out of the room as soon as she could, so I couldn't even get a single word in with her, let alone finally ask what she knows about the bicycle man.

I should be used to this feeling of rejection by now. There was a time, not so long ago, when I was shunned by almost everyone I knew. After the accident, people quite rightly blamed me, ignored me, spat on me. Most of my closest friends turned against me, but I was determined to pick myself up and reclaim what little life I had left, for Grace's sake. She needs a stable environment to come home to, and I've worked hard to achieve this. Helping the Valentines find Lucy should be bringing me one step closer to achieving that goal. But instead, it feels as if everything, including my daughter, is slipping away from me.

When I think about Tess and Katie Hunter and the unhealthy relationship they shared, I realise I'm not in such a bad place after all. Grace and I still have a future ahead of us, whereas they don't. If I wanted to, I could spend the day playing with my daughter and keeping out of the Valentines' way, winning Grace around and enjoying her smiles and laughter.

But that isn't what I've come here to do. Grace must wait. Lucy cannot.

55

Before entering the drawing room, where Jane and John are waiting, no doubt irritated at having been summoned there by working-class me, I pause to check out my reflection in one of the ornate mirrors gracing the walls of Moon Hollow. I wonder why there are so many. Jane isn't the sort of woman to stare at herself all day, but then I remember that John is extremely vain. I bet he stops at every one to inspect his face for signs of aging. It must be bloody awful growing old, but thankfully I don't need to worry about that just yet.

Happy with what I see now that the spots and oily skin have been covered up, I chuckle inwardly, wondering what the Valentines will make of the new me. This morning they'll meet a different Cindy to the one they've become used to. Sassy Cindy is back.

Throwing what I hope is a sexy smile at my reflection, I hear my dad's encouraging voice in my head – "Looking good, doll." Promising myself that when I return home, I'll stop telling him off for calling me that, I take a deep breath before making my grand entrance.

Immediately I'm met with Jane's icy smile and glassy-eyed expression. 'Nice of you to join us, Cindy,' she says from the cream sofa that perfectly matches her skin tone.

Pretending not to see her glance pointedly at the clock on the mantelpiece, I sit down on the chaise longue opposite her. John remains standing with his hands tucked firmly in his trouser pockets. His hair sticks up in places as if it hasn't been combed properly. I hope for his sake that Jane doesn't notice. She's likely to jump to her feet, spit on a finger, and smooth it down. John is a man and doesn't need mothering. Yet Jane treats him like he's a small boy. Strange that, when she's the least maternal person I know.

'I want to ask you about a couple of things that are bothering me,' I say, carefully choosing my words so as not to alarm them, but I fail anyway.

'Oh my God. It's Lucy. Something has happened to Lucy.' Jane is on her feet, wringing her hands and looking as if she's about to bolt from the room.

'No.' I reach out a hand and place it on her arm. She shrugs me off, but at least she's a little calmer. 'It's not about Lucy. Please sit down, Jane.'

Shakily, Jane does as she's told but grabs hold of a cushion and squeezes it for comfort as though she can't get through this conversation without it. The last thing I want to do is cause her any more upset, but I'm determined to see this thing through.

'I need both of you to tell me the truth for once.'

Jane's shoulders relax like she has nothing to hide, which throws me. John, on the other hand, buries his hands deeper into his pockets and looks at the floor, his face reddening.

'I want to start with your brothers first, Jane—' I pause to watch them slide their lying eyes at each other before coming to rest guardedly on me '—and before you say it's none of my business, I think it is. If I'm to find Lucy, then I must know everything.'

'My brothers.' Jane snorts derisively, abandoning the cushion as if she no longer relies on it. 'What makes you think I have any?'

Could I have got this wrong? I don't think so. She's lying. Has to be. I'm about to challenge her when John throws in his two pennies' worth.

'She means George. That's who she is talking about.' John is also dismissive, making me think that my vision in the church has led me down the wrong path. Again. Neither of them is acting as though there's any mystery that needs solving.

'Are you saying you only have one brother, Jane?' The question must be asked.

'Why are we talking about George after all these years? I don't understand,' Jane queries snootily, not meeting my eye.

John interrupts in a surprisingly bossy way. 'George was Jane's brother, who died many years ago.' It's unusual for him to be doing the talking. It feels wrong.

'I'm sorry to hear that, Jane,' I say, feeling that things aren't quite adding up. 'But I had another vision in the church last night, and I saw two boys. Two ghostly brothers. Are you sure there isn't another brother?'

'Of course she's sure,' John snaps, for once protective of his wife.

'Jane?' I persist in focusing on her rather than John. Eventually, she sighs and gives in.

'If you're saying that you saw two boys – ghosts, rather – in the church, although I don't like to think about that'—Jane pats her heart dramatically as if for effect—'it is quite possible. You see, we had many visitors that stayed with us over the years. Often for weeks at a time. Apart from the winter months, the house was full of guests.'

If the smallest boy was an unwanted houseguest, then that might explain why he was left out of the other two's games. But then I remember that all three were included on the trompe l'oeil wall painting, which is strange. The Valentines are a complex family. I begin to think I'll never come to understand them.

'How come you never mentioned him before?'

John chips in, again. 'A black sheep, by all accounts.'

'Is that right, Jane?' I ask, wondering why she's allowing John to speak for her.

'We rarely speak of him.' Jane sighs as if it pains her to remember. 'He wasn't quite right, you see, in the head. He attended a special school three counties away and was only allowed to come home at certain times of the year.'

I'm surprised to learn that the brother she's referring to is the smaller boy, who, I remember now, looked different from the others. Something about the over-smiley eyes made me suspect he might have learning difficulties. He also had a cruel smile, which caused me to believe he was the one responsible for the drawings of dead animals.

This must mean that the bigger boy was the houseguest and unrelated to Jane. Again, this makes sense when I recall the words he used to her: "You are perfect just the way you are." He obviously had a crush on Jane. My mind wanders back to the smaller boy again – George. Knowing how it feels to be considered an outcast, somebody different from the norm, my sympathy goes to the boy, not the family, who liked to pretend he didn't exist. *These upper classes are a law unto themselves*, I think bitterly. And Jane is no different.

'And when did George die?' I ask, instinctively guessing that I won't find him in the Valentine family plot. He'll be buried elsewhere, ensuring there's no lasting connection between him and his family. No evidence of him having ever lived will survive.

'He was sent abroad as a young man to study so he could not bring any more shame on the family. John is quite right; George *was* a black sheep. We lost touch after that. He never came home again.' Jane is curt. She may as well be talking about a stranger, but her glacial expression doesn't fool me. Raw emotion lurks in the back of her eyes.

'So, he could still be alive?' I blurt without meaning to. A missing relative with a grudge to bear is something I should have been warned about.

56

JANE

'A telegram arrived, informing us that George was dead.' Jane lies brilliantly, coolly dismissing whatever ideas might be leaping into Cindy's head. The girl is getting closer, warmer all the time, but she is still way off the mark. George has nothing to do with any of this. But Jane is not going to tell her that.

Cindy is quite capable of working out everything for herself eventually. Jane is not going to do the hard work for her. 'Papa travelled to France to identify the body. After the funeral, we were told never to speak of him again,' she states as if bored of the whole discussion.

Nothing could be further from the truth. She thinks about George every day. He holds the key to their secret. He cannot be found or dug up. She will not allow it.

John is rattled. She watches him go to the drink cabinet, where the decanter of expensive Macallan whisky is kept. She wants to remind him that it is only meant to be taken out for special occasions, and this is not one of them, but with Cindy present, she does not. When the cabinet door does not immediately open, he turns accusing eyes on Jane.

'Must we lock every precious thing away in this house,' he grumbles, snatching for the key that he suddenly remembers is hidden on a shelf where the glass tumblers are kept.

'What is the other thing you wanted to discuss, Cindy?' Jane says, ignoring John's outburst. 'You said there were a couple of things that were bothering you.' But Cindy is staring beyond her at John, who by now has a glass of gold liquid pressed against his mouth.

'What is it, Cindy?' John and Jane ask at the same time.

'Why are you staring at us as if you have seen a ghost?' Jane continues, unsure if the girl is having another of her visions. Cindy is on her feet, backing away from them, looking at them as though they were monsters. And perhaps they are.

Jane gets to her feet. Something is happening to the girl. Her face is twisted with pain, and she is rubbing furiously at her right eye as if suffering from an unbearable migraine.

'What's wrong, Cindy?' John's concern is like a whip lashing into Jane's flesh.

'Keep out of this, John,' Jane barks, preventing him from going to assist the girl. 'Let me handle this.'

'I don't know why it never occurred to me before, but it's obvious now that I come to think about it,' Cindy garbles.

'What are you talking about?' Jane demands.

'You know very well what I'm talking about. There's no point in denying it. I know what you did…'

I know what you did. There it is. The sentence that has been haunting Jane since day one. It hangs there in front of her, taunting her, like a mad old woman with her fist raised. Five dreaded words that could alter their lives forever. Jane must not fall apart. Not until she discovers what the girl has found out.

'What is it you think we have done, Cindy?' Jane asks as calmly as possible, holding up a shushing hand to John when she hears his intake of breath from somewhere in the room.

'You used to lock Lucy Benedict in her room, didn't you? She wanted to leave, and you wouldn't let her. You're trying to do the same to me.'

Relief floods Jane's heartless veins. Finding time to share a knowing look with John, she sees that he is equally thankful. The squirming has disappeared from his face, and the straightness has gone out of him. *Are they to get off so easily?* God must be on Jane's side if that is the case. *Is that all you have?* Jane wants to torment Cindy with her superior knowledge but decides it is not in her interest to do so. It also occurs to Jane that if that is all the famous psychic has come up with so far, then their chances of finding Lucy are slim.

'That is absurd,' Jane tells her, trying to sound more in control of the situation than she is. Inside, she is a bundle of nerves. A mess. 'Why would we do that?'

'You've been locking me in my room at night ever since I got here.'

Cindy is right to be indignant. Jane is surprised she has kept her temper this long. If their roles were reversed, Jane's screams would have brought the house down around their ears.

'If I locked Lucy Benedict in her room, it was to protect her and her unborn baby,' Jane says quietly, retaking her seat on the sofa now that her worst fears have proven unfounded. 'You know yourself how disruptive this house can be, especially at night.'

'Disruptive! Is that what you call this hellhole?'

Jane presses down the flare of irritation caused by this attack on her family home. Moon Hollow means everything to Jane. She will not have its reputation tarnished by a cheap slut.

'She could have tumbled down the stairs. Anything could have happened to her.' Jane takes a shaky sip of her cold tea.

'Anything did.' Cindy folds her arms, her tone trying to convey that she knows more than she is letting on. It is a ploy Jane does not fall for. Not this time.

If Cindy knew the whole truth, she would not be wasting her time standing here arguing. She would be getting the hell out of this house while she still had the chance. Surmising that all Cindy knows so far is that Lucy Benedict went missing after leaving Moon Hollow, Jane decides that is all any of them need to know. Their Lucy is all that matters.

'You are meant to be looking for my daughter, not worrying about this other Lucy.' Jane cannot keep the annoyance from her voice.

'That other Lucy was the mother of your child. Have you forgotten that?'

'How could I forget?' Jane points out icily, fighting back the urge to slap Cindy and send her flying into the wall. Instead, she turns to glare at John. He is to blame for all this. 'There are reminders everywhere.'

'If what you're saying is true about locking Lucy Benedict in for her own safety because she was pregnant, that doesn't explain why you'd do the same to me.'

'Doesn't it?' Jane asks, appearing genuinely surprised.

'I'm not pregnant,' Cindy protests, growing increasingly frustrated by Jane's evasiveness.

'You could be.' At last, Jane drops the bombshell that she has been saving.

I look from Jane Valentine's crazed eyeballs to John's lowered eyes, wondering why I ever came here. Jane is mad. Completely bonkers. She thinks it's perfectly acceptable to have locked Lucy Benedict in her room. She didn't bat an eyelid when I accused her of doing the same to me. It's as if she feels she has every right to do so.

And now, to suggest I might be pregnant—

'Why would you say that, Jane?' Despite trying to stay calm, I feel myself bristle.

'How do you know you're not?' Jane rallies.

She's on her feet, standing too close, scrutinising my flat stomach as if a child really were growing there. Under her gaze, I feel a trickle of fear run along my spine. I look for a way out and see none. She would catch me and drag me back again before I made it to the door.

'You could already be carrying Hugh Hunter's child, for all you know.'

'What?' The terror growing inside me is also responsible for the thumping of my heart. It beats so loud I begin to imagine it'll explode from my chest. 'You really are mad, Jane. Insane.' I console myself with the fact that she's madder than I gave her credit for, considering I've only slept with Hugh the once, and that was barely a day ago.

I haven't even had a chance to ovulate yet, having just had my period, so there's no fucking way on earth I could be pregnant. Yet my periods have always been erratic. I can bleed at any time during the month, so it's possible that what I had wasn't a real period at all, in which case...

'You have had sex with him,' Jane says, pursuing her point, 'so you cannot rule it out.'

'Even if that were true, I still couldn't be pregnant. I take the contraceptive pill,' I retaliate and recover at the same time, thanking God for the contraceptive pill and all the while wondering how the bloody hell she knows so much.

She persists with glee. 'But can you be sure you didn't miss any?'

I desperately want to punch her in the face, but this only stirs up unwanted memories of Tess Hunter attacking her daughter. Before I can tackle Jane further, I must force these horrifying images from my mind. Once done, I'm ready to pick up where we left off.

'I never miss,' I say with gritted teeth. Having Grace so young meant I missed out on a lot of opportunities, and this made me determined not to go down the same path again, even though many of my so-called friends expected me to pop out a kid every other year after that, as others on my estate were doing. Once was enough for me.

'You might have taken a different pill by accident or

vomited one up…if you drank too much,' Jane suggests innocently. 'Anything is possible.'

What is she up to? What's she trying to get at? Surely, even someone as fucked up as Jane wouldn't mess with somebody's contraception. *What sort of woman would do anything as depraved as that to another? No, I can't believe it of Jane. What possible reason could she have for wanting me to get pregnant?*

The penny drops when I remember how young and unprepared Lucy Benedict was when she found out she was having a baby. Was her pregnancy something to do with Jane? Had Jane interfered with her choice of contraceptive too, as she seems to be implying she did with mine? That, I can't rule out.

Deciding that it's best not to air my suspicions until I'm back in my room, when I can check for myself if my pills have been tampered with, I glare into Jane's goading eyes and see nothing but hatred there. It hits me then that she's indeed capable of such a crime.

'You bitch…' I can think of nothing else I want to say to her, and I'm about to storm out of the room when her next words halt me.

'That is what Hugh used to call that wife of his whenever she caught him cheating. Not just the once, mind, but many times. He never could resist a pretty face. Quite the ladies' man in his day was our Hugh. And still is, by all accounts. Isn't that right, John?'

At this point, Jane and I turn to look at John for confirmation, each competing for his attention, but he's frozen to the spot. His eyes search both our faces, and his mouth opens and closes as if to form words, but he's incapable of speaking.

'It drove her quite mad, you know. His wife. Poor thing. But she refused to give him up. He must be good, that's all I can say, but then I expect you would know that.'

Jane's eyes are locked onto mine as she tries to read my thoughts. But I'm the clairvoyant, not her, and this is one argument I won't let her win.

'Hugh isn't like that. He's a decent man.' *I won't let her get to me. It isn't true. Hugh wouldn't.* But he did with Lucy Benedict. I begin to doubt myself as Jane wants me to. *Why would she say such things if they weren't true?*

'Decent. My, you are smitten, aren't you?' Jane sneers in my ear.

'Tell her, John,' I plead. 'Tell her what you told me, that Hugh is a good sort.' But when I seek out his eyes, I can see they're as downtrodden as the rest of him. 'If you're that frightened of your wife you can't come to the defence of a friend, then you're a bloody coward.'

At that, John's head bounces up, but one look at Jane's snarling face convinces him where his loyalty lies. His days of offering me protection are over. I can see it in his bloodshot eyes.

'Why are you being so cruel, Jane?' I ask because suddenly I want to know. As I watch her eyes go cloudy with sadness, I suspect that the spitefulness she's directing at me is really intended for those who were responsible for hurting her – John and Lucy Benedict. I wonder how she might react if I reach out to her, as one woman to another, but when I see anger flare in her eyes again, I sense she doesn't want or need my pity.

'You could not wait to give yourself to him, could you? You are a whore, Cindy. Just like Lucy Benedict,' Jane says viciously.

'And Lucy isn't yours. She never was,' I shout, evening the score.

58

JANE

'Are you going to tell her, or am I?' Cindy is yelling at John, who looks like a man who's had his jugular ripped open and nothing like the self-serving predator he is.

'Cindy, don't,' he implores, as if that will stop her.

Jane feels hysteria rising inside her, which threatens to bubble over into manic laughter. No, not laughter, exactly, but foul language, terrible thoughts, the dark truth that will expose what she has become. Lately, she has sunk to new depths, taking advantage of her position as a grieving mother to win over the press and police so that they would not suspect them of anything. On that thought, Jane turns furious eyes on John. This is all his fault.

'What does she mean?' Despite wanting to kill him, Jane finds a voice that sounds perfectly calm and reasonable.

'Cindy, please. I'm begging you...' Ignoring Jane, John focuses all his attention on Cindy. His eyes are wide with fear. He looks as if he is about to have a stroke.

Cindy is wavering, Jane can tell. But she will not let that happen. They do not get to decide her fate.

'The Valentines never beg,' Jane says curtly, holding up a protesting hand, warning John to keep quiet. 'Besides, I want to hear what the girl has to say.'

'Lucy wasn't, isn't…' Unable to get her words out, Cindy gives up and hangs her head, her ratty, blood-red-tipped hair partially covering her face. Jane would like nothing more than to grab hold of it and pull handfuls of it from her head.

'Speak up, Cindy,' Jane taunts in a deceptively friendly fashion. And when the girl still refuses to speak, Jane's face twists into a sneer. 'Who is the coward now?'

That does it. Cindy snaps her head up, and her eyes, jam-packed with insolence, lock onto Jane's. John is forgotten about at this moment. They are the only two people in the room.

'John isn't Lucy's father.'

'That's a lie.' Jane scoffs, not believing the girl. But if she thinks laughter and ridicule will chase away this preposterous allegation, she is wrong. Already, it is tunnelling its way inside her, coiling itself around her heart. Refusing to acknowledge the look of pity on Cindy's face, which has turned deathly pale, Jane feels her heart ice over with dread.

'Tell her.' Jane snaps her fingers at John, desperate for him to come out of his horrible stupor. He appears like a man who has given up all hope. She is about to tell him off for this when, like a blind man, he gropes his way over to the sofa and slumps onto it.

'I'm so sorry.' John buries his head in his hands.

'Why would you be sorry? It's obvious she is making

this up. To cover up the fact that she is a terrible psychic. That is what she does.' Jane throws an accusing look Cindy's way as if to prove this, but John will not come out from behind his hands.

Less sure of herself, Jane turns to confront Cindy, but she is distracted by the howling sound coming from the sofa. In Jane's world, men do not cry. Her mother would not have stood for it. Nor should she. But for once, Jane does not know what to do.

'I'm really sorry, Jane, I shouldn't have blurted it out like that.' Cindy is shaking her head in disbelief.

Why is everyone sorry? First John. Now Cindy. Is this a game? Jane should be paying more attention to the two traitors, but her mind is wandering off again. To the piano this time, with the silver-framed photographs of Lucy and Jane's mother on it. Gorgeous Georgie was a talented pianist. She had the voice of an angel too, but it was the devil in their mother they had to watch out for.

Jane was not as gifted a musician as her mother and was often punished for hitting the wrong notes during music lessons. Once, the piano lid had crashed down so severely on her hands, three fingers were broken. After that, she was not asked to play again. Jane can hear the tinkling of the piano keys now and the distinctive rustling of her mother's satin dress as she imagines her sitting down to play her favourite classic, Debussy's "Clair de Lune".

Having removed herself from the scene in the drawing room and the people in it, Jane is brought back to the present by Cindy's whining voice. Jane tries to shut out the amplified sound, but it kills the opening notes of the music, squashing Jane's memory as if it were nothing more than a bothersome housefly. *What lies is the girl coming out with now?*

'Lucy is Hugh Hunter's child. I thought you had the right to know,' Cindy is saying.

The walls crumble away. The furniture slides out of vision. The ticking of the clock ceases. Unaware of what she is doing, Jane staggers over to the sofa and picks up the cushion she was holding earlier but does not sit down next to her husband. Instead, she tears clumps out of the silken duck-egg-blue material, spilling feathers everywhere.

'Jane, stop, please. I didn't mean to—' Cindy, distraught and red-eyed, dares again to put her hands on Jane, but she is shrugged off once more. Violently this time.

'Hugh Hunter?' Jane blinks, letting this news sink in. 'Did you know about this, John?'

One look at John, who has disintegrated in his own misery and shame and is unable to speak coherently, reveals the truth to Jane. It feels like a stake piercing her heart. Next, she turns to stare at Cindy, seeking further clarity. If Jane had any doubts left as to Lucy's real parentage, the girl's crumpled face convinces her otherwise. Cindy is telling the truth. It is there for all to see in the murkiness of her eyes.

Jane recognises that there is pain in Cindy's eyes too. The same look must be reflected in her own. They should have been friends. A comfort to each other. They share a similar story, after all. Both live in constant fear of losing their daughters for good. Instead, they are sworn enemies. They will go to their graves despising each other. Cindy, the slut. Jane, the liar. Hatred is all they have in common.

It is enough of a relationship for them to want to continue it. Anything is better than loss. It is what keeps them both going.

As for John. She will never forgive him for this. The weak, pathetic adulterer that he is. If he has lied to her all these years about not being Lucy's real father, and he must have done, because he showed no surprise when Cindy revealed who the true father was, then what else has he lied about? That is what she would like to know.

Not only has he tricked her into taking on the game-keeper's bastard, a servant's child, no less, but he has also denied her the right to have a child of her own. Lucy Bene-dict was meant to conceive John's baby, not Hugh's. That was the deal. And Jane had made it clear from the start that she would not accept a child who was not a blood relation.

Just because she was unable to conceive did not mean she was willing to take on anybody's child. It had to have John's blood running through its veins. Continuing the family line was of vital importance to Jane, and John knew how much this meant to her.

How could he, of all people, do this to her?

Unable to stop herself, Jane lashes out at John's stricken face, tearing at his hair and raining blows down on his head. He does nothing to stop her.

'You fool. You bloody fool. You let her trick us. How could you?'

59

CINDY

Muttering profanities, Jane staggers from the room, leaving John and me alone. He's slumped on the couch, hands covering his head as if afraid his ordeal isn't over. Jane could come back at any time and renew her attack.

Blood is trickling down John's forehead, dripping onto his shirt collar while strands of blond hair, yanked out by Jane, are scattered on his navy blazer. He doesn't attempt to wipe away the blood or smooth down his hair. He's nothing like the smart, sophisticated John I first met. Gone – forever, I suspect – are the flirty eyes and sharklike smile.

We don't speak, as we've nothing to say to each other, saving our accusations for ourselves. As soon as Jane left, my first thought was, *Oh God, what have I done? How could I have been so cruel?* I never meant it to happen. Didn't mean to say those things, having already decided that Lucy's real parentage was not my secret to tell.

But when Jane called me a whore, I couldn't help

myself. *How fucking dare she?* I can't blame Jane entirely, though. She might have started it, but I had to go and finish it, didn't I? Me and my big gob. I could have, *should* have, ignored her. The truth is, her words touched a nerve. Until meeting Hugh, that's exactly how I saw myself – a cheap slut, a whore, a good-time girl.

I won't be that girl anymore.

When I hear the sofa creaking, I glance up tearfully and see that John has dropped his hands in his lap. They look as limp and useless as the rest of him. Instead of anger, which is what I expect to see in his eyes after my unforgivable outburst, there's only relief. He looks like a man who's had a burden lifted from his shoulders. *But that can't be right. Can it?*

'I just want this to be over,' he says flatly, as if he knows what I'm thinking.

I don't ask him what he's referring to. He's talking about an outcome for his missing daughter. He would rather know, one way or another, what has happened to Lucy than go on in this way. This is understandable. I get that. He's one of the many grievers I've come across in my line of work who needs to see a body. Unlike Jane, whose face drains with blood at any mention of death. Hope is her crutch. God her only friend. She persists with a dogged-ness that would wear anybody else out.

'How long have you known?' I ask John.

'I guessed almost straightaway. Contrary to what Jane thinks, Hugh is a terrible liar.' John smiles for my sake, and I'm tempted to jump out of my chair and hug him. Instead, I say a silent thank-you to him for confirming what I've always known – that Hugh is a good man. As I suspected, Jane made the whole thing up about him being a womaniser. She said those things to hurt me. To get back at me. For being young and beautiful in her eyes, for still having my daughter with me, for a hundred and one other reasons.

'Fair play to Lucy. She never set out to trick anyone, and I did seduce her, so I have to take responsibility for that.' John pulls a face as if it pains him to acknowledge this. 'And Jane was desperate for a child, so I thought, why not? It seemed like a good idea at the time.'

A flawed plan, I can't help thinking. Still, I can see where he's coming from. His intentions weren't exactly honourable, but he meant well. Deciding that the last thing he needs is a lecture from me, I change the subject, sort of. 'Do you think Jane will forgive you?'

He's about to reply when we hear a loud crashing noise reverberating through the house. We both look up at the ceiling and come to the same conclusion. It can only mean one thing: Jane is taking her temper out on something. I spring to my feet, ready to help if I'm needed. I would give anything to be of use to someone right now, but John gestures for me to sit back down, insinuating in that polite way of his that this will not be necessary.

'I have got a better chance than you, put it that way,' he jests, getting unsteadily to his feet. His mind appears to be on his wife at this stage rather than on the conversation we're having. Perhaps he does care for Jane after all.

I can't let him leave without explaining, though. I've never sought John's good opinion, but I find myself wanting it now.

'I never intended to come out with any of that just now. It wasn't planned. Please tell Jane how sorry I am…'

John nods as if he'll give my request some thought,

then distractedly walks towards the door. He's a braver person than I am if he's about to tackle Jane alone.

'I want to help,' I say feebly. 'Please let me try.' I'm like a child. Desperate to make amends. Wanting approval.

It hits me then. What I should do. Making up my mind to follow through on my instinct, something I've always fought against due to my hatred of being psychic, I march over to John as if I'm in charge and snatch up his arm, startling him in the process. His face pales even more as it dawns on him what I'm about to do.

'Oh God,' he says, closing his eyes and grimacing.

Taking John's pearly-white hand in mine, I place it against my chest where my cold, unforgiving heart is. It thuds so loud I imagine the vibration must travel down his arm so he can feel it too. In this moment I don't give a fuck about myself and what may happen to me after today. I've been a selfish bitch. How could I have said those things to Jane? I will myself to try harder than I've ever done before to find Lucy, believing it may be my only chance. Having John next to me, his hand in mine, will help. I'm sure of it. I've always had the impression he was closer to the little girl than Jane, and that always helps.

All the distractions that Moon Hollow heaps on me have made the task of finding the little girl almost bloody impossible, blocking me time and time again. This time, I push those forces fiercely aside, wading through a thousand whispers in my mind so I can concentrate on the one thing that matters—Lucy. Mirroring John, I close my eyes, sensing that his have opened again. I feel him staring at me, willing me to do this. Part of me doesn't want to let him go, but I can't take him with me, so I remove myself from the room. From him. From all thoughts of what a horrible thing I've done to Jane Valentine. A woman who deserves my sympathy, not my venom.

A passageway opens in front of me. It's dark and too confined for my liking. I'm crawling along on my hands and knees. My fingers scrape the sides of the walls, which are soft and earthy, like a grave. Bits of branch and creeper scratch at my face, making me wince.

My old self feels the throbbing pain in my temple, but I brush it aside in a way I've never been able to do before. Having John here, urging me on, makes all the difference. The one scene that's evaded me for so long is within touching distance. I can feel it. I won't let the others who also linger here rob me of it, so I concentrate harder than I've ever had to.

'At last, I have you,' I whisper, unable to contain my relief.

She's here with me.

Lucy Valentine.

I watch her touching things that don't belong to her. Guessing that the kidnapper won't like her meddling with his belongings, I warn her to stop, but she places her hands over her ears, not wanting to connect with me. She's careless. Paper rips. A nib of lead on his pencil snaps. She laughs at that but falls silent when she hears creaking footsteps above her.

We sit together, inches apart, and look up at the same time to where he must be standing, listening. Our knees are drawn up to our chests because there's no room to move. When Lucy turns to look at me, I notice that her face is smudged with dirt, but her dark eyes show no fear. Her shoulder-length hair is matted – I long to brush it – and she wears the same clothes I saw her in on the day she was taken.

I can't be sure if she is really seeing me, but she raises a shushing finger to her mouth and shakes her head, warning me to be silent. It breaks my heart to know that she's worried about me. Pressing her eye up against a piece of rotting wood, which allows the tiniest crack of light to seep through, Lucy concentrates on what's on the other side. After a few seconds, she hitches up, making space for me, and gestures for me to take her place. Lucy wants to show me something. As Tess Hunter did.

Nodding to show that I've understood, I shuffle forwards, fighting back the urge to grab hold of her and take her back with me so I can reunite her with her parents. But if I so much as lay a finger on her, I know that she's likely to vanish completely.

Swallowing nervously, I stare once more at Lucy before pressing my eye to the hole. To start with, I see nothing. The light on the other side is blinding after the dark. Then, indistinct shadows emerge. The black-and-white pencil drawings of Lucy that I saw in an earlier vision are spread out on dusty floorboards. They're creased and crumpled. As tired and worn out as the little girl sitting next to me.

Then – brown leather and lace. Part of a shoe, I think. It doesn't move, so I can't tell if it has anyone's foot inside it. Stomach clenching with fear, I feel a rush of adrenalin surging through my veins when the owner of that shoe moves out of my vision. I hope he can't hear my heart hammering. I don't want to be the one to give away Lucy's hiding place. I'm about to pull away, so I can warn Lucy he's on the move, when the snippet of light disappears and

I'm looking into the blinking black dot of the kidnapper's pupil.

I feel myself drowning in that solitary pool of darkness until I'm thrust headlong into his world. Breathing in his stinking breath. Smelling his sweat on my skin. Seeing what he sees. Feeling what he feels. Darkness. Hatred. Revenge. A lack of empathy for others. A twisted mind. One step into his domain is enough for me. Even Lucy cannot keep me here. Unable to stop myself, I open my mouth to scream.

'Cindy. Are you all right? What happened? Is it Lucy?'

I come around to find myself on the sofa with John sitting beside me, holding my hand. My head has been tipped back, and blood is pouring from my nose. Raising a tear-streaked face, I gaze into John's watery blue eyes, which for once are full of kindness.

They're as close to me now as the kidnapper's were, and because of this, I look away again. I might only have glimpsed the kidnapper's eye for a second or two, but what I saw there terrified me. The man is a monster. Though I dare not say so to John, I suspect Lucy is in more danger than I feared.

'She's alive, John,' I tell him. 'Lucy is alive.'

60

JANE

Dressed all in black and looking like the darkest of widows, Jane perches on the edge of Lucy's bed and surveys the damage in front of her. Destroying the doll's house felt good. Better than good, in fact. But now, she is exhausted from her efforts.

Strewn around the room are the smashed remains – evidence of her meltdown. The conical church spire is the only feature to remain intact, having proved resistant to all of Jane's efforts to crush it. *God truly does work in mysterious ways, just not in the right ways*, Jane had told herself bitterly before finally admitting defeat.

The caving in of the blond John doll's head with the heel of her shoe brought her more pleasure than the living version has done in years. The thought makes Jane chuckle. The more she thinks about it, the funnier it becomes until she is laughing openly when, quite frankly, there is nothing humorous about the situation at all. Still, she laughs. Laughs until the tears are streaming down her face.

'What possible reason can you have for laughing?'

Jane whips her head around to see John watching her from the doorway. He wears the disapproving look on his face she has come to dread. *Oh dear, I must be in trouble*, Jane surmises, allowing another giggle to escape her. *What's wrong with me?*

'What's wrong with you, Jane?'

It further amuses Jane to know that John is wondering the same thing, and this almost sets her off again. But she must not laugh. *Get a grip of yourself, Jane. Show some control.*

Taking in a quick succession of breaths to steady her nerves, Jane critically observes the way John stands in the doorway, like a boy asking his mother's permission to enter the room. Irritated by this, she gestures for him to come inside.

'Shut the door behind you,' she orders.

Once inside, John purposefully picks his way through the debris, careful not to tread on the already broken remains of the doll's house. Battling down the desire to scream at him to hurry up, Jane follows his movements as he comes to stand in front of her. He does not get too close in case she should decide to lash out at him again. He is not as daft as he looks, although his comical hangdog expression suggests otherwise.

'We need to talk,' he tells her.

The tone of his voice implies that he aims to be strong for her sake, and she is tempted to remind him that she has more than enough strength for the two of them. Resilience should have been her middle name, not Dorelle. She has never lived up to the name. John would have preferred a wife that matched the glamourous-sounding title. With his good looks, he could have had anybody he wanted. Yet he chose her. They both know why. If he hadn't, then she would have become the nun she always wanted to be. Jane's life is full of "what-ifs". What if Lucy had never been born? What if they had never heard of Lucy Benedict?

'I suspect deep down I always knew but couldn't face up to the truth that we were duped.' Jane is surprised by the truth of her words, John appearing more so. If Jane is honest with herself, she often wondered why Lucy did not look like John but convinced herself this was because the child took after her mother, inheriting Lucy Benedict's Eastern European origins. In contrast, all of hers and, indeed, John's ancestors all had blond hair and blue eyes. In living history, there has never been a dark-haired, brown-eyed child at Moon Hollow.

'Duped by an ugly little thing like Lucy Benedict, who was dumb and ignorant and who wouldn't say boo to a goose,' Jane cries angrily, getting to her feet and kicking out at the broken pieces of the doll's house that represent her broken home. Broken life. It hurts to know that she has been tricked by somebody as weak and insignificant as their former au pair. Jane no longer trusts her own judgement. Is unsure of herself. It occurs to her that she lost a big part of herself downstairs when Cindy revealed the truth about her daughter.

'Calm down, Jane,' John urges, feeling more in control now that he is playing the hero and Jane the weeping woman about to have a mental breakdown.

But Jane *is* calm. She does not know how she is managing to hold herself together, but she is doing a bloody marvellous job. Inside, she is fighting an inner battle with herself, trying not to give in to the feelings of hatred and rage that are threatening to overwhelm her. But no one would know that to look at her. Certainly not John.

'No brains or talent, yet both you and your so-called friend fell for her,' Jane continues as if John had never spoken. 'She made fools of everyone. You included. And you thought you would get one over on me too, didn't you?'

'Of course not. Why would I think such a thing? You are my everything—'

'Your everything. Ha!' Jane scorns. 'Only when it suits you.'

'Jane, please. I'm trying to explain.'

Jane explodes. 'There is nothing *to* explain! You let me think Lucy was yours, ours, and you lied. You lied for years, John. Years.'

'I know, and I am truly sorry.' Shame gets the better of John, and he lowers his head, unable to meet her eyes, which overflow with tears and suffering.

Knowing John has been brought low is not enough for Jane. Whatever he is feeling right now will never match her own level of anguish and distress. He deserves to feel as she does. If not more so.

'Even though I was never invited to join you, I used to listen to you and Hugh sniggering in the games room late at night. Do you remember how shut out I felt by that?' Jane puts up a protesting hand, preventing John from answering. 'No. I don't suppose you do,' she answers for him. 'I used to think that it was the drinking and tales of whoring that made you laugh so much. Now I know that it was me you were laughing at.'

John attempts to interrupt her again, but this time Jane

shoots him down with just a look. 'Be sure of one thing, John. I will have the last laugh if it kills me. See if I don't.'

'I can't talk to you when you are like this,' he informs her coldly, his patience running out. 'I only came to tell you that Lucy is still alive. I thought it might put your mind at rest.'

'Alive?' Jane's heart opens a fraction.

'Yes. Cindy had another vision. She saw her. Lucy is okay. Our daughter is okay.' John's voice wobbles with emotion as he says this. Before Jane can challenge him on using the word *our*, he is gone, slamming the door behind him.

61

'Lucy is alive. Our daughter is okay.' Jane flops down on the bed, exhausted. There are no tears of relief or joy. She has cried herself dry. As much as Jane tries to tell herself that she must harden her heart where Lucy is concerned, she struggles to do so.

It is too soon to go downstairs and ask Cindy about her vision. Jane does not feel able to face the girl yet, no matter how desperate she is to know how Lucy is doing. John will not have bothered with the detail. Finding out she is alive would have been enough to satisfy him.

He will not have asked if his daughter is being looked after properly or what conditions she is living in. Nor would it have crossed his mind to find out if she cries herself to sleep at night, missing them. Although, if Jane is honest, that does not sound like her Lucy at all. The little girl has inherited Jane's strength and resilience if nothing else.

Nothing else. This reminds Jane once again that there

is nothing of John in Lucy. His blood does not run in the child's veins.

'Lucy is no longer my concern.' Jane has harsh words with herself. 'She is not my, our, daughter.' But in trying to close her heart to the little girl she has invested over seven years in, Jane is aware that she is making a bigger fool of herself than John, Hugh, or Lucy Benedict ever did, because she still feels like someone's mother.

This catches her unawares. She always thought blood meant everything to her. Went along with the whole "blood is thicker than water" philosophy shared by the Valentine family. *But only when it suited them,* she reminds herself.

Take her brother George, for instance. Named after their mother, he was meant to do great things. It always surprised people to know that it was he, and not Jane, who was the eldest and therefore the natural heir. George was a sickly child. Although he was two years older than Jane, she was taller and possessed the confidence of an older child.

As George got older, it became apparent that he suffered from behavioural as well as physical disabilities. The diagnosis meant that Jane's mother could no longer cope, and he was sent away to a special school for difficult boys. His stunted growth and pronounced lisp could no longer be tolerated at Moon Hollow. What would their guests think if George had one of his screaming fits or lashed out at them as he was prone to do? The lies and profanities he used to spout would send their mother scuttling to her room for a lie-down, emerging hours later when her eldest child had been put to bed.

Even if poor George had not been struck down with an incurable disease while abroad, he would never have been allowed to inherit the Valentine estate. By then, he had already been disinherited and Jane installed as the rightful heir.

Jane had never liked her brother. Most of her days were spent avoiding him. He always wanted to tag along, cramping her style, and when Jane refused, he would spy on her with the judgmental eyes of a wise old man – something any teenage girl would object to. She regrets now that she did not show him more compassion. He was her brother, after all. But he could be beastly too and cruel with it, especially where animals were concerned.

An unnatural, puny little thing, he reminded her of the puppies who had their heads bashed against the wall for not being "quite right". How George escaped the same fate at her mother's hands, she will never know.

It unnerves Jane to know that George's ghost walks within the walls of Moon Hollow's church. She does not like to think of him lurking in the corners and spying on her – as he did when he was alive. Even in death, her brother brings her trouble. Jane is glad she did not tell Cindy the whole truth about the circumstances surrounding his demise.

While it is true that the family did receive a telegram informing them that George was dying, Papa, God rest his soul, refused to travel to France to see his firstborn son, nor did he go to identify the body when George eventually died. Deciding that nature should take its course, the Valentines did nothing to assist its black sheep in its hour of need.

Almost a woman by then, Jane, aged nineteen, did not challenge her parents' decision. Still smarting by the horrible truths George had flung at her, accusing her of committing the most grievous of sins, she felt it was better he did not return home to die.

Life went on as normal at Moon Hollow without him. George was neither mourned nor missed. *No wonder his spirit haunts the family church.* Jane shudders at the thought. Now that she is older, it pains her to know that her brother died alone without his family around him. And at such a relatively young age too. Twenty-one is hardly old. That is why she never fails to include him in her daily prayers even though John mocks her for being soft.

Still, George was her brother, and it bothers her that she was as ashamed of his existence as the rest of her family were. This is something she cannot forgive herself for. A secret she shares only with God. What they did to poor George was despicably cruel. Her parents were a cold, thoughtless couple, and Jane did not feel their loss when they died in a car crash ten years later, but she should have been more charitable where George was concerned.

The treatment of her brother is one of the things Jane regrets. It has haunted most of her adult life. The other transgression she is guilty of is a much darker secret. Nobody must ever find out to what extraordinary lengths she went to force Lucy Benedict to go through with the adoption. By the time the bitch decided she wanted to keep her baby, their baby, *Jane's baby*, it was too late. By then, they already thought of little Lucy as theirs.

But the girl reneged on their deal, insisting they hand her back. Against all the odds, she wanted to return their money and start a new life somewhere else with Lucy. John might have considered this an option, but Jane refused to entertain the idea.

"That is never going to happen, John!" she screamed. He could tell straightaway by the fire in her eyes and belly that she meant it. There was no going back. He knew that Jane would kill herself if she had to give Lucy up. They had no choice.

It became Jane's job to get the girl to change her mind. Jane is not proud of the depths she plummeted to, but "Needs must," as her mother would have said while drowning another litter of Queenie's kittens in a bucket. Consoling herself that Lucy Benedict was not a fit mother, Jane set about eroding the girl's confidence in her ability to raise the baby alone.

It was not difficult. The girl already had little belief in herself, so she proved easy to manipulate. But to be on the safe side, in case she tried to run away with the baby when they were not looking, Jane got into the habit of locking her in her room at night. John was not allowed anywhere near the girl in case he caved in. Seeing how emotional and tearful she had become would have been his undoing. He never could resist a damsel in distress.

Aside from themselves, only Hugh knew about their illegal adoption arrangement, but Jane is unsure how much he knew about the girl's imprisonment at Moon Hollow.

Damn and blast Hugh Hunter, Jane seethes angrily. Her Valentine blood, which can be found in the landed gentry section of Burke's Peerage and traced back to the fifteenth century, boils at the thought of his being Lucy's real father. Lucy might not be blood, but, knowing what the child means to her, Jane can find it in her heart to forgive that.

The same does not apply to Lucy's double-crossing biological parents. Lucy Benedict might have disappeared from their lives and is therefore out of Jane's unsympathetic reach, but the same cannot be said for Hugh. Right from the start, he has been a thorn in Jane's side, coming between her and John and then destroying all their plans for John to father a child of his own. Unlike Lucy Benedict, Hugh has proven difficult to get rid of, but Jane will make sure he gets his comeuppance in the end. Isn't that what she promised John?

Furiously punching Hugh's number into the telephone beside the bed, Jane waits to hear his hateful voice. When he picks up, she can tell by the laziness in his greeting that he is not expecting a fight. *Good*, she thinks smugly, glad that she is about to ruin his day, week, year, even, forgetting for the moment that Hugh has already dealt with the worst possible thing that could ever happen to him – the death of his daughter.

62

CINDY

I remain downstairs in the hope that things will eventually blow over or that John or Jane will come down and ask to speak to me so I can apologise properly. In the meantime, I've been trying to get hold of Hugh, but he's proving to be as invisible as the Valentines. Using the kitchen phone because I still haven't had my mobile returned to me, his number is constantly engaged. It doesn't go through to voicemail, so I can't even leave a message.

This leaves me shitting my pants at the thought of what he'll say when he discovers I've betrayed him. That's why I'm desperate to talk to him before anyone else does, so I can explain, or try to. He's going to be so hurt or, worse still, fuming when he finds out. The thought of losing his good opinion of me is unbearable.

Since the bust-up with Jane, I haven't been able to think properly. Guilt over what I've done continues to eat away at me, but the vision of Lucy imprisoned in that small dark space is what fills my head. I can't concentrate on anything else. As a result, I barely give my own daughter a second thought. Sensing this, Grace is on the attack.

'Why can't I go and see Jane?' Grace demands stroppily, folding her arms in a way that reminds me of John. The Valentines' ways are rubbing off on my daughter, I notice.

'Because I said so,' I retort as long-suffering parents are prone to do, picking up the phone one last time in the hope that Hugh will answer.

'Because I said so,' Grace mimics spitefully. Then deliberately drops the cup she's holding onto the floor so it smashes into pieces.

Immediately, I'm reminded of Lucy's miniature tea set. The one that got broken on the day she disappeared. *Where are you, Lucy? Where is he hiding you?*

'Jane is upset. You're to stay away from her,' I say to my daughter, more sharply than I intended, as I bend down to pick up the broken pieces, worried in case she cuts herself.

I love it, Daddy. It's perfect.

Lucy's voice. On the day she saw the tea set for the first time. An early birthday present from John. I look beyond my own daughter at the figures of John and Lucy, who are standing in the kitchen facing each other as Grace and I are doing. Jane is notably absent. I get the impression she felt the gift was an extravagant expense.

The tea set is a replica of the Royal Albert Old Country Roses antique set that graces the shelves of the large dresser in the Valentines' kitchen. Guessing that Lucy wouldn't have been allowed to play with it, I understand why John had the miniature version made. The gift does seem to lift Lucy's mood, and I catch a glimpse of her smile, which I suspect is a rarity for this solemn child. It lights up her face, making her look almost pretty. Sensing that she's aware of my presence, I close my eyes and try to reach her. It may be too soon after the last attempt, but it's worth a try.

'There's nothing to do around here.' Grace stomps her foot, commandeering me back to the present and causing Lucy to slip away, out of reach, as she so often is. I wonder if Grace did it on purpose, guessing that my mind was on the other little girl and not her.

'It's boring. And it's not as if I can go and play with the doll's house.' Grace sneers in such an unpleasant way that I find myself disliking her.

She knows something I don't, I realise. Something to do with the doll's house. And let's not forget about the man on the bike, Lord of the Dance. I still haven't got to the bottom of why she drew him in a picture alongside Lucy. There's probably no point in asking her now, as when Grace is in one of her difficult moods, nothing I do or say is good enough. But to hell with her mood – I can't put this off any longer.

'Grace, give me five more minutes, and I promise I'll come and play with you,' I say, trying to keep the annoyance out of my voice, 'but first I need you to tell me—'

'You never keep your promises,' she scorns, storming towards the French doors that lead onto the garden. Once safely outside, she turns to glare at me. Her eyes are brimming with angry tears. 'You let everybody down,' she sobs before flouncing off.

'Grace. Come back.' Half-heartedly I try to get her back, but it's no use. When Grace makes up her mind to do something, there's no stopping her. *Who does she remind you of?* I ask myself wryly, thinking what a chip off the old block she is.

'Shit and fuck it.' I slam down the phone in frustration when all I can hear on the other end is a busy tone. I don't know who I'm more annoyed at, myself, Grace, or Hugh.

Reaching up to the tall cabinet that houses the Valentines' supposedly secret supply of cooking wine, I take down a bottle of red and glug a generous portion into one of Jane's dainty china cups. It's too early in the day for a drink, even for me, but that doesn't stop me knocking it back. The liquid burns my throat. It tastes disgusting, but it'll have to do. "Needs must," as Jane would say. Then, pulling out a chair from the breakfast table, I sit down and refill my cup. From here, I can see through the French doors into the garden.

Although Grace is gone, I find myself trying to track the path she took in my head, but it's no use – I can't see her. Nothing new there. I didn't mean to snap at her just now; God knows it's the last thing she needs, but I couldn't stop myself. Nor did I mean to blurt out the truth about Lucy's real parentage to Jane Valentine, but that didn't work out as planned either. *What's wrong with me? Once a chav, always a chav, isn't that how the saying goes? Is that what I am? A chav? A blabbermouth. Somebody with a big gob.*

Jane and I are alike in lots of ways. Nothing is as important to us as our daughters. We're both single-minded in that respect. This is how I know how much my words must have hurt her. It was wrong of me. The worst part is knowing that I did it on purpose, wanting revenge for what Jane had said about Hugh. Putting doubts in my head about him was an unkind thing to do, and Jane should take some of the blame for that, but what I did was crueller. I can tell myself all I want to that Jane had a right to know. That it was wrong for her to be lied to and I was doing her a favour by telling her the truth, but I would only be lying to myself.

Determined to make it up to Jane, I decide that I'll set about looking for Lucy in a way I haven't done before, but first I'll finish my drink and then go and find Grace so I can say sorry. Again! But I still can't get the image of Lucy Valentine hiding from the kidnapper out of my head. I keep imagining how I would feel if it were Grace, not Lucy, who was being held captive. After what I did to Jane, this makes me feel worse.

Jane might be the least likeable woman on the planet, but never knowing from one day to the next if her daughter is alive must be terrible. I think it would kill me. As it is killing Jane.

63

Unlike the rest of Moon Hollow, which is cluttered with mirrors, paintings, and fancy tables with turned-out legs, the hallway leading up to John and Jane's suite of rooms is stark in comparison. An echoing void. There's not a stick of furniture to blunt the impact of the cold white walls and glossy tiled floor that is as slippery as ice.

At one end there's a door, which, judging by the excessive amounts of locks and bolts on it, doesn't get opened often. Two shiny interior doors lead off the hallway. One takes you into a grand-looking downstairs toilet, another into a living room that's decorated in soft yellows with a bird-pattern wallpaper. It's a lovely room, far nicer than the drawing room, and I find myself wondering why the Valentines don't use it more. Then, I think perhaps that it's too sunny and cheerful for a couple whose daughter is missing, and I understand why.

Dominating the hallway is the curving stone staircase

with the scrolling iron handrail that guides you up it like an arm around your shoulder. I'd hoped I wouldn't have to come up here again. The last thing I want to do is disturb the Valentines, especially Jane, but I can't find Grace anywhere, so I've got to assume she disobeyed me and went to find Jane anyway.

Knowing that one little girl has already vanished from Moon Hollow keeps my stomach churning. I'm sure Grace is safe. She's got to be. God, if anything happened to her – but I mustn't allow myself to think that way.

As I'm about to climb the stairs, I see someone standing at the top.

Jane.

She wasn't there a second ago. I know that for a fact. She watches me intently as if I'm a curiosity. A freak. When I realise I've unknowingly been whistling the "Lord of the Dance" hymn, I get why. His voice goes off in my head, like an unsupervised explosion.

"Dance, then, wherever you may be, I am the Lord of the Dance, said he."

Ignoring the hateful voice, I concentrate instead on climbing the stone steps to where Jane's waiting. She stands tall and proud, like her arrogant Valentine ancestors who grace the walls of Moon Hollow. I feel myself trembling in her presence, though out of fear or awe, I cannot say. Her cold blue eyes track my progress, and there's a suggestion of an amused smile on her face that has no right to be there, given the circumstances. *Has she always been this way, or did losing her daughter do this to her?*

'Jane. I'm sorry, I didn't mean to disturb you, but I can't find Grace anywhere, and I was wondering if you've seen her?' I stumble on my words but refuse to let my nervousness get in the way of finding my daughter. I need to know she's safe.

'She is with John.' Jane is curt, and I sense she's about to dismiss me and go on her way, but now that she's here, I decide I may as well try to apologise – but first I have to know one thing: 'Are you sure, Jane?'

'Yes, of course,' Jane snaps. 'They're outside feeding the geese. Go and see for yourself if you don't believe me.'

There's no reason why I shouldn't believe Jane, but I find it weird that having looked everywhere, including the gardens, I never once saw any sign of John or my daughter. They could easily have gone out one door while I entered by another, I suppose, missing each other in the process.

Relief floods through me then, and I breathe properly for the first time in over an hour. Grace is safe. That's all that matters. Except that I would rather she didn't spend so much time around John or Jane. They have an unsettling effect on her, but this is a sacrifice I'm forced to make. Looking for Lucy must come first.

'While I've got you, Jane, I wanted to say how sorry I am—'

Jane cuts me off. 'George was an artist too.' She obviously doesn't want to hear my apology. Perhaps she never will. She's not even looking at me. As if I don't matter, she's focusing all her attention on the trompe l'oeil painting that starts and ends on the wall closest to the staircase. Now that I know Grace is okay, I join her.

'He was not as talented as I was, of course,' Jane boasts, finally acknowledging my presence but still refusing to look me in the eye.

It dawns on me then that Jane painted this homage to her family herself and that she wants me to know this. I'm staggered by the discovery but feel she has every right to be proud. For the first time, I see Jane as an individual. A woman in her own right. Self-assured and competent. Stripped of the Valentine empire and her husband's confidence-crushing unfaithfulness, she could have carved a new and successful life for herself. Yet she chose to remain at Moon Hollow when everyone else had abandoned it.

'But he could get by if he had to. And he did have to,' Jane is saying.

'Is that why he went to France, to study art?' I ask, kicking myself for not having asked for this information before. *What an idiot.*

Jane nods, confirming I'm right, but doesn't elaborate further. I tell myself that it doesn't really matter, as Jane's brother couldn't possibly be the kidnapper. Because George is dead. Isn't he? A part of me questions whether I should believe everything I'm being told about him.

Can I be certain he's dead and therefore not a threat to this family? But it wouldn't make sense for Jane to lie. She wants Lucy back more than anything, so she would be the last one to protect her brother if he were still alive. Besides, if I accused everyone who could draw of being Lucy's kidnapper, then Jane would be a suspect too.

'Disowned by his parents, cast out and disinherited, he turned to art and religion and ended up confused by both.' Jane goes all mysterious on me as if an inner battle is going on inside her head. Her eyes are vacant like she's returned to her past.

I hold back from pointing out that nobody uses such words as *cast out* or *disinherited* these days. Christ, it feels

like I'm living in another world. Jane's world. *Been there.
Done that once already*, I remind myself, feeling a cold
shiver run down my spine. The memory of being inside
Jane's head isn't something I would ever want to repeat.

'George used to say that this was the kind of house
where you expect to hear screams, and he was right. I
expect you would know all about that, Cindy.'

I feel her eyes burning into me as she says this. This is
such an abrupt change of topic that I don't know how to
respond. Frantically, I search for the right words. I need
Jane to hear me out. I desperately want to tell her how
sorry I am. I'm about to open my mouth and say something, anything to relieve this tension, when we both hear a
car pull into the driveway. The crunching of the gravel
reminds me of the sound of logs crackling on Hugh's fire.
God, I miss him. I suspect he won't feel the same about me
when he hears what I've done.

'Who's that?' I ask, evidently more surprised at the
arrival of a visitor than the owner of the house is. Jane
remains calm as though this is a normal occurrence, which
we both know isn't the case. The Valentines have no
friends. Nobody ever visits them.

'Someone is coming to take John's car away.' She says
this like I should know. 'It's such a shame because he
loves that car.'

*What is wrong with her? Why is she behaving so
oddly?* I want to grab her by the shoulders and shake her,
but of course, I don't.

'What's wrong with it?' I ask instead, knowing full
well that this is a weird kind of conversation to be having
with all that's going on.

'Oh, there is nothing wrong with *it*.' Again, Jane is

deliberately mysterious, placing special emphasis on the last word as if it should mean something. It doesn't. But I suspect that she's enjoying herself. Knowing more than I do seems to amuse her. *So much for having psychic abilities*, I imagine her thinking.

'Jane, I know you're not ready to hear my apology yet, but I do want to ask you one thing. A favour, really,' I say tentatively.

The way Jane looks at me, never giving anything away, does little for my confidence. I'm terrified of tackling her on this subject in case it upsets her even more. But it needs saying.

'I know that Grace is fond of you and that we've had our differences, but please don't try to turn my daughter against me.' There, I've said it. And whatever reaction I expected from Jane was not of her laughing sarcastically or rolling her eyes.

'Your daughter. Do you think I would be interested in a child of yours?' She scoffs, making me want to punch her in the head. 'You won't have any daughter if you don't find Lucy. I have already been on to Social Services and given them the same notice I am giving you, Cindy. Two days.'

My heart sinks when I realise Jane means it. Our original agreement was for two weeks. Two days doesn't leave me nearly enough time. I'm about to protest, will resort to begging if I must, but one look at her hardened jawline and steely eyes tells me she's made up her mind. There's no point pleading. When her eyes then glaze over as if with boredom, I know that we're done here. I watch her walk away, the bottoms of her wide-legged linen trousers gathering dust from the stone steps.

Before disappearing into her suite of rooms, she looks over her shoulder at me. Her face at this moment is as white as the stone walls and unreadable.

'Nobody crosses me and gets away with it, Cindy,' she snarls. 'Nobody.'

64

My eyes flicker open when I hear a dog growling. Bolting upright, I glance around, terrified in case I'm about to be attacked by Hugh's fucked-up collie or, worse still, Georgina Valentine's ghost dog. Since being badly bitten by a "he won't hurt you" poodle when I was a child, I've never outgrown my fear of dogs. Relieved to find there's nothing there – *It's all in my mind* – I rest back against the trunk of the tree.

The knotted circles in the bark pummel my shoulders like fists. Above me, the treehouse looms, casting its all-knowing shadow over one side of my face. This is the last place Lucy was seen, and that's why I keep coming back to it. I meant to go inside to take another look in case I missed anything on my previous visits, but I fell asleep at the base of the tree, too tired to climb the ladder, the long grass and pollen in the air acting like a sleeping pill.

The other side of my face is warm from the sun, and bugs attach themselves to me, content to sunbathe on my unmoving body – as if I were dead. A fruit fly, glued to the corner of my eye, attempts to suck moisture from my skin. I bat it away but don't hurt it. I must be mellowing if I can no longer bring myself to kill an insect.

The crumpled cigarette I put in my mouth before falling into a dream-crammed sleep is stuck to the edge of my mouth. That cooking wine must've had a powerful punch. I only had a couple of glasses, but it knocked me out. I take a plastic lighter out of my pocket and light the cigarette. Inhaling deeply, I revisit the nightmare. Not the one about Grace and the car, thank God, but the one where Adam Lockwood's tattooed arm was pinning me down.

Absently, I scratch at the mark around my neck. It's a habit I'm unable to break. As usual, the scarring feels ugly to the touch. Some people think I put it there myself. Why anyone would think I would want to damage my body like that is beyond me. I don't hate it as much as I used to, though, as it acts as a reminder of what I did.

The shock that I felt on waking one morning to find it there, only to discover that Adam had strangled himself the same day, is still felt. Most people make mistakes, but mine have the potential to be bigger than anybody else's. I guess that's why I still think about him, admittedly not as much as I should, but nobody else asks me about him anymore.

Typically, my mother never once referred to what she called the "incident" or my part in it, but I know that she used to read the newspaper reports when I wasn't around. The only person who understood the guilt I felt when I learned of Adam's death was his sister, Ruth, who came into court every day during the trial to hear how her brother had been wrongfully arrested on nothing more than the assertion of a girl who was meant to be clairvoyant.

Learning that Adam had mental health issues made me feel even worse, but Ruth went on to explain he was a forgiving person and wouldn't have blamed me. Like many convicted sex offenders and killers, he was a single white male in his thirties. A loner who fit the serial killer mould in every way except one – he was innocent.

Ruth understood that I was only trying to help when I went to the police about her brother. The big black cross on his arm was the same as the killer's tattoo, and God knows that predator had been stalking my head for weeks before Adam was arrested. What the real killer did to those women is something I can never unsee. I might not have been there in person when the victims were butchered, but I came to know them well on repeat.

For that reason, nobody could blame me for wanting him put away as quickly as possible. The visions I had to endure at the time those murders took place were torturing me, which was nothing compared to what his victims went through. But in my haste, I picked the wrong man. As a result, Adam's death will always be on my conscience. The real killer was found a day or two later, and I still can't bring myself to mention his name.

Sighing, because life can be cruel, I try to find something more positive to dwell on that doesn't involve dead men or missing children. My dad is always urging me to look on the bright side of life. "Stop for a minute, Cindy, and appreciate what's around you," he'll say. Taking a leaf out of his book, I try to focus on the clouds rolling above me, which leave behind intermittent patches of faded blue. Unseen birds chirrup, caw, and coo in the trees. Grass with razor-sharp edges nips at my fingertips, and fragments of white stone rise out of the ground like old bones –

remnants, I suspect, of the oldest parts of the castle that used to stand in this spot.

The snap of a twig. A rustling. The parting of the long grass and the sudden absence of sound alerts my senses. Has me sitting upright again, on edge, pulse racing.

"Dance, then, wherever you may be, I am the Lord of the Dance, said he."

Clasping my hands over my ears, I scramble to my feet, wanting only to escape now that my peace has been destroyed by the unknown man on the bicycle, whose song prowls inside my head. *So much for being at one with nature. Sorry, Dad, I tried, but some of us are born to be haunted. For me, there's no peace. You can't fight the dead.*

But you can fight the living, which is why I'm heading in the direction of Hugh's house. The urge to spill the beans is growing stronger. Deciding that everything else must wait, as I won't be able to concentrate on finding Lucy until I can explain myself to him, I wonder what I can say that will lessen the impact of what I've done. The answer is nothing. So, is the risk of getting found out worth it? Grace won't thank me for going AWOL again, and Jane will of course be furious with me for wasting more time, but I still manage to convince myself that the loss of an hour in my search for the little girl is justified.

All the time these thoughts are swirling around in my head, I remember to check around me, regularly glancing over my shoulder to make sure I'm not being followed in case the Lord of the Dance should make an appearance, but no stranger lurks in my field of vision. I speed up, determined to get to Hugh's as fast as possible so we can get this over with. Until we do, it feels as if the blackest of clouds is dogging me.

Except it's not a cloud at all but a real-life dog – in the distance, a shadow at first but gaining on me all the time. Hoping that it's a stray whose intention is to avoid me, I break into a jog, but when I speed up, it gathers pace. Likewise, when I slow down, it crawls almost to a halt, but every time I turn my back on it, somehow it gets closer until we're standing staring at each other, neither one of us moving.

It's Georgina Valentine's dog. I recognise it easily. The velvety blue fur. The whites of its eyes. The proud, almost regal way it's standing. Head up, tail pointing out rigidly behind it like a baton. How can a dead dog be both beautiful and ugly at once? Then, remembering that this is no ordinary dog, I feel my heart sink.

'Why are you following me? What do you want?' I shout.

At the sound of my voice, its cropped ears prick up, and its hackles rise. I already know what it wants. It's doing what any hunting dog would do. It's hunting me.

65

As if an invisible barrier is preventing the dog from following, it refuses to come any further than the lake. Although relieved to have finally shaken it off, I pause to watch it gazing down into the water, not to drink but to stare at its reflection. The lake fascinates me too. Each time I pass it, I imagine I can see a face in the water or a hand visible beneath the surface.

I wouldn't wish to be as close to its murky waters. Sensing that something dangerous lurks there, I recall with a shudder how I almost fell in the day I tumbled down the bank. I'd seen the dog that day too. Had I gone in the water, I'm certain I would've drowned. I'm reminded of the glass bottle I saw bobbing in it, how it caused a ripple effect that spread out towards the middle of the lake, like a pointing finger.

Not being able to solve the mystery of why that memory is important bothers me. What significance does the bottle have? Or the dog, for that matter?

Deciding I can't make sense of any of it, I plod on with

a heavy heart. Alone on the Fen, I become aware of how isolated and irrelevant I am. I could walk five miles in either direction and never see another human being. Unused to silence and stillness, this fact plays on my mind. The closer I get to Hugh's cottage, the more anxious I become. He's unlikely to forgive me for betraying his secret, which leaves me wondering why I'm bothering.

But, unlike the puzzle surrounding the glass bottle and the dog, my motive is clear. I like Hugh, more than like him, and his opinion of me matters. If I can, I aim to put things right.

We meet on the path outside his cottage. He has his head down, hands rammed in pockets, and is striding towards his jeep. When he looks up and sees me, I'm mortified to discover that I'm looking into the eyes of a stranger. The man standing in front of me with guarded eyes and a face full of stubble is not the Hugh I know. Knowing that I'm responsible for this sudden change hurts like hell.

'You told her. I thought we were friends, Cindy, more than friends, and that I could trust you, but as soon as my back was turned, you blurted the whole thing out.'

A waft of whisky cuts through the air, making it obvious he's been drinking. This explains the ruddy-cheeked farmworker complexion. It's no wonder he doesn't drink if this is how it affects him. Some people get morose when they have a drink, and judging by Hugh's bloodshot eyes and crumpled clothing, he falls into this category.

'I didn't mean to, Hugh. Honestly. It's just that some of the things Jane was saying, I couldn't help myself.'

'Couldn't help yourself!' He snorts, balling his hand

into a fist. 'You say it as if you're different to everybody else. Well, let me tell you something.' He stabs a finger in the air as he says this, causing me to take a step back. 'You're not. You did this to get back at Jane. Plain and simple. It had nothing to do with me.'

Not wanting to accept that he's right, I search his face for signs of the man I used to know. The green of his eyes has darkened to a muddiness that matches the black Fenland soil, and his voice is laced with sarcasm. His face crawls with movement, like a restless crowd. *Could Hugh be violent after all? Have I misjudged him? Did Tess have a reason to fear her husband?* Doubts gather as I wonder, not for the first time, if Hugh is as innocent as I thought he was. But on his next breath, he reverts to the old Hugh.

'You used me,' he says brokenly.

'Oh, Hugh. I'm so sorry. Really, I am. Please let me try to—'

He ignores my outstretched hand and digs deep in his pocket for a piece of paper. Flinging it at me, he says, 'She gave me notice. Jane. I have to be out of here in two months.'

My tears drip onto the letter, making the ink bleed. I recognise Jane's personalised stationery with the elaborate *V* for Valentine, soft and rounded and not at all like the woman herself.

'Perhaps it's for the best. It can't be good for you. Living here must be hell after what happened.' Knowing what goes on inside that cottage behind Hugh's back, I genuinely believe that what I'm saying is good advice, but Hugh is shaking his head at me.

'That was my decision to make. Not yours. This is all

your fault, Cindy. Me losing my home. John having his car towed away. When is it your turn?'

I want to tell Hugh that it's always my turn, but now is not the time to feel sorry for myself. I must take what he says on the chin. With a pinch of salt thrown in.

'You should put your own house in order before handing out unwanted advice.' He snatches back the piece of paper and stuffs it in his pocket.

'What's that supposed to mean?' I cut in, an edge to my voice now, but this is mere bravado. Fear of what he's about to say is all I can think about. Facing up to the truth has never felt so terrifying.

'You know what I mean. I might have been an unfaithful husband, but I never neglected my daughter. I would never have left her alone as you did yours.'

Forgetting for the moment that this is exactly what he did as far as Lucy Valentine was concerned, abandoning her while she was still in her mother's womb, I realise that Hugh has revealed how he really feels about me. How long he's been holding on to those thoughts is another matter. Knowing he's no different from the friends and family who turned their backs on me when I needed them the most, something inside me dies. This knowledge tempts me back to the dark place I visited soon after the accident.

'I'm paying the price for that, Hugh.' I dredge the words from somewhere, as it's obvious from his body language that he requires, no, demands an answer.

'But are you really, Cindy? Are you?'

His face is pushed so close to mine I can see the angry red pores on his drinker's nose. I'd like nothing more than to land a punch on him and maybe break it, *fucking bully*, but because of what's going on behind him, I resist.

Tess Hunter is sitting behind the wheel of Hugh's jeep and is revving the engine until white smoke fills the air. Her unhinged eyes burn into mine. A smile tugs at her mouth. She's enjoying this moment. Has been waiting for the fallout to happen. Hugh's dog, sensing Tess's presence, scrambles to get at his former mistress, its claws scratching at the leather seats that separate them. But its excitable barks don't reach Hugh's ears.

'Look, Hugh. I know you hate me right now, and you've every right to, but please listen to what I'm about to say. You need to get out of that house.'

'You're the one who should go. It's you who doesn't belong here. I said so from the start, remember?' he yells, spinning around to find out what my eyes are glued to. Seeing nothing there, he turns puzzled eyes back on me.

'I don't have a choice,' I mumble pathetically, hating myself for sounding so weak. 'I have Grace to think about. If it wasn't for her, then—'

'Who are you trying to kid?' Hugh snarls. 'This is nothing to do with your daughter and all about you. It always has been.'

With no sign of Hugh's temper lessening, I decide to be the better person, the one to walk away. Rather than reverting to type, somebody who lashes out without thinking, I'll be the sensible one for once. Dignity has never cost so much.

'That's it, walk away. Like you did with your daughter!' he shouts cruelly. The next thing I hear is the slamming of the jeep door and ferocious revving of the engine as he fires it up. Then, the screeching and sliding of tyres on grass as it speeds off.

I cling to the hedgerow as he passes me, worried in

case his drunken state causes the jeep to come off the road and hit me. Now, wouldn't that be poetic justice? His words have broken me. The person I thought he was is gone. So, where does that leave me? The girl who thought she could've fallen in love and dared to hope for a happy ending.

Being around Hugh had made me feel like happiness was within my reach. Before meeting him, I never imagined I would want to swap my wild lifestyle for one of contentment and reliability. It occurs to me that I was ready to say goodbye to the good-time girl who's been holding me back my entire life. Without her, I could have been somebody. Had a proper life. A decent job, decent boyfriend. Perhaps a white wedding.

Like most women, I've dreamt of being rescued by a knight in shining armour – or tweed, in Hugh's case – but denied myself any chance of that, choosing instead to rebel against everything and everyone. Until I stop blaming my mother for everything that's happened to me, I can never hope to change. Blame is an unhealthy obsession that I need to snap out of. Accepting that my mother will never love me is the first step to recovery. *Fucking hell, Cindy – only you could pick a moment like this to experience such perception.*

Hugh had every right to speak to me as he did. God knows I fucked up with my daughter, everybody knows that, but I'm trying my best to make amends. I've a lot of making up to do where Grace is concerned. But I owe Dad a few million apologies too. He was the only one to stick up for me, and he was the one I took it out on most. Poor sod.

Making my way back to Moon Hollow, I become

conscious of the fact that I've had to find ways to protect myself the last few months. Lying to myself is one of those safety pockets. I don't dwell on how much I've been through because it was all my own doing. But I'm still a person with feelings the same as anybody else, even if I did do a terrible thing.

Like Hugh, my mental health isn't in a good place. Rather than wallow in self-pity, I make a bargain with myself. If I find Lucy, then good things will happen to all of us. John and Jane will be happy. Hugh will forgive me; Lucy is his little girl, after all, and despite not playing a part in her life, he's bound to have feelings for her. Lastly, and most importantly, Grace and I will live happily ever after, like in a Disney movie.

Looking for Lucy is the key to everything. I've always known this.

66

JANE

As Jane watches the ruby-red blood that flows through her Valentine veins disappear down the plughole, she gathers her thoughts – wishing now that she had not gone into the blue room, Cindy's room, to snoop. But curiosity had got the better of her, and now she is paying the price. A mistake she will not repeat. Once Cindy is gone from Moon Hollow, *and that must be soon*, Jane will have that room locked up for good.

After what happened, she does not know how she made it downstairs in one piece. The trail of blood she left behind will have to be erased before John and Cindy return, but right now Jane has not got the stomach for it. Her nerves are all over the place. She is not sure if this is a result of taking increased amounts of the prescribed seda-tives she keeps for "special occasions" or because of what happened in the room. Both probably, she concedes.

Jane is not dealing with her emotions in the way she has been taught, with a stiff upper lip – the Valentine way of getting through things. But the secret she is keeping is killing her. As things stand, she might have to live with what she did, what *they* did, for another thirty years, possibly more, some of it alone if John should die before her. How will she cope?

Jane feels faint thinking about what happened upstairs. They had thought all traces of Lucy Benedict had been obliterated from this house, but the girl's presence lingers on.

It started with the perfume bottle.

Jane had been rifling through the dressing table drawers – looking for the open packet of contraceptive pills that Cindy usually keeps there, only to find them gone – when she caught sight of its opaque blood-red blackness. The hourglass bottle mirrored her blurred reflection as she peered unwillingly into it, mystified as to how it got there. Jane tried to convince herself that it had always been there, that she simply had not noticed it before or that it belonged to Cindy, but she knew this was not true.

Her pounding heart had caught her out in the lie. She knew Cindy's preferred perfume only too well, and this was not it. Memories came back to haunt Jane of John coming home with a prettily wrapped box that was not intended for her. The bottle of perfume had appeared on Lucy Benedict's dressing table the next day.

Jane had been glad when both the bottle and the girl disappeared. But the bottle had somehow returned. Jane was unable to resist picking it up. Lifting off the gold lid, she inhaled its unforgettable and timeless scent, rich in spices and precious woods. John had once described it as one of the sexiest fragrances ever, yet he had never gifted her a bottle. The memory cut through Jane like a knife.

Before she could decide whether to smash it, throw it,

or burn it, it felt to Jane as if somebody had grabbed hold of her wrist and refused to let go. Was she having a stroke? Her first thought was that this could be some form of paralysis, but when her hand seemed to be deliberately squeezed around the bottle until the glass was about to shatter, Jane understood something more sinister was happening. The more she tried to resist, the firmer the grasp became. Jane could not free her hand.

I know what you did.

A voice. Not hers. Not Cindy's. Not John's. Whispered close to her ear.

Jane swung terrified eyes around the room. 'Who's there? Who's that?'

You didn't look after my baby like you'd promised.

The voice again. Angry this time and coming from directly in front of Jane, a hiss of decaying air blowing across her cheekbone. Eyes bulging with fear, Jane tried once again to wrestle her hand away so she could run, run, run—

You are a beastly mother, Jane.

The thing. Whatever it was. It knew her name. Jane could not go on pretending that she did not know whom that voice belonged to. Lucy Benedict.

'No!' Jane screamed. 'We didn't mean to. It was an accident.'

Jane was about to drop to her knees and beg for forgiveness, confess to everything, when the glass exploded in her hand. Broken shards fell through her fingers onto the pale blue carpet, and her blood soon followed. Sensing that Lucy Benedict's ghost had crawled back to wherever it had come from, the secret room most probably, Jane opened her clenched fingers, exposing multiple cuts in the palm of her hand.

She did not stop to pick out the vicious pieces of glass but bolted from the room, bouncing off walls and knocking expensive vases from tables, pausing only when she was halfway down the stairs to catch her breath. Half expecting to hear the ghostly tread of footsteps giving chase, Jane was relieved to discover that the only thing trailing her was the smell of Lucy Benedict's perfume. It lingered on her clothes and fingers. Jane doubted she would ever rid herself of it. Just as she could not rid Moon Hollow of its ghosts.

Back downstairs, Jane winces with pain as she picks out the last shard of glass from the palm of her hand. Knowing that the perfume bottle was real fills Jane with dread. Like the voice she heard upstairs, it was no illusion. Unlike the blood trickling from her hand into the sink filling with cold, stinging water, the past is not something that can be easily washed away.

With sudden perception, Jane understands that this is what Cindy's life must be like, interacting with the dead as she sometimes does. Going by how Jane felt when she experienced the utter terror of the presence upstairs, a feeling that makes her tremble with fear even now, she ought to feel sorry for the girl, but the more Jane thinks about it, she feels certain that Cindy is to blame. Whether intentional or not, Cindy's psychic abilities have unearthed a secret that was better left untouched.

Lucy Benedict was meant to be gone. But now she is back, resulting in a homecoming of the worst possible kind. And not the one Jane has been praying for.

I know what you did, the girl whispered in the foreign

twang that used to fray Jane's nerves, believing as she did that it was exaggerated to ensnare men. It certainly worked with John. Jane had been right to have her doubts about the au pair, because she turned out to be nothing more than a liar and a fraud. This fact justifies what they did, Jane now considers. But this is a dark thought even for her. It both surprises and frightens her.

While Jane was self-righteously doling out punishment to the lying cowards who had destroyed her life, she had not considered that she was as guilty as they were, more so, in fact. After all, she was the one who had come up with the plan. John was incapable of thinking for himself. Because Jane coveted a baby of her own so much, she had calmly and coolly taken Lucy Benedict's contraceptive pills and popped the next one out of the packet, hoping Lucy would be tricked into thinking she'd already taken that morning's dose.

Naturally, Jane didn't do this every day, otherwise the girl would have become suspicious. It really was as easy as that. Jane had then cleverly gone about coercing John into seducing the girl. That is not to say he did not enjoy it! Far from it. His falling in love with her, however, even for a short time, was not part of Jane's plan.

She wonders what Cindy would think if she knew it was Jane who was responsible for what happened. But in the end Lucy Benedict had fooled everyone. The lying whore had outwitted them all. What does the girl's ghost want from her? The truth? Revenge? But can Jane be sure it *was* her? Somebody could be trying to trick Jane into thinking she's going crazy – like her poor mad ancestor, who had been driven insane so that the rest of his family could get their hands on his money. But who would do that

to Jane? John? Cindy? Hugh? She's wronged them all.
Was it her turn?

Sighing because she cannot remember why she went
into the large walk-in cleaning cupboard, where she finds
herself, Jane goes back into the kitchen. Once there, she
remembers what she was looking for – something for her
cuts. Storming back into the cupboard, she grabs a
bandage from the first-aid box on the wall. Unrolling the
crisp white dressing, she goes back to the kitchen and sits
on one of the comfy sofas facing the large state-of-the-art
TV. Wrapping the bandage around her hand, Jane is
annoyed to find that the TV still has a protective film
covering its screen and has not even been plugged in.

They were meant to sit here as a family, her, John, and
Lucy, so they could watch their favourite movies together.
Belatedly, it occurs to Jane that she does not have any
favourites. She prefers reading to television. Lucy is the
same. Only John likes watching TV. Sport, mostly. And
other late-night programmes that Jane cannot bring herself
to think about. In many ways, she and Lucy are alike.
Funny that. Except, why should it be? Jane used to
imagine there was an invisible bond between John and
Lucy simply because they were father and daughter, a fact
she now finds ironic, considering neither of them is
related.

She also used to believe that not being able to have a
child of their own was God's way of punishing them for
what they did. Now she begins to wonder if it is John's
fault they remain childless. The idea that he might be the
infertile one has never occurred to Jane before, but now
that she knows he never fathered Lucy or spawned any
children with his other women, this puts a different slant

on things. Jane's stomach turns over. Could being with John have cost her the only chance she had of having her own child?

She must stop torturing herself, thinking like this, but the voices she hears that are not her own are making her irrational. Arguments go on inside her head all the time, and nobody, not even Jane, is foolish enough to try to intervene. *None of this is John's fault*, she tells herself. *Or mine.* They will get through this together. They adore each other and always have. She needs John. He needs her. *Where is John?*

Jane wants to tell him that she is sorry about the car. She acted impulsively. She did not mean it. He will understand, and she will buy him a much nicer one. The crestfallen look on his face when the men took his Jaguar away brought her no pleasure in the end. Handing over the key fob had broken him. "Isn't it time we stopped hurting each other?" were his last words to her before leaving the room – and her. He will come back. It is not as if he has left her forever. Where would he go?

Earlier, when he tried yet again to apologise for not telling her about Lucy's real parentage, he sounded as if he meant it. Jane almost yielded, but when John made the mistake of trying to comfort her, she shrugged him off coldly as if he did not matter. Reprimanding him like a child is a habit Jane cannot reverse. Such behaviour is ingrained in her. She's too harsh. Too strict. A result of her own authoritarian childhood.

If she could have Lucy back, she would never scold her or John again. Rather than insisting upon educating the child, Jane should have played with her more, as John did. It is no secret that Lucy favours her father, and who could blame her? Lucy Benedict was right. Jane is a beastly mother. Beastly wife.

And murderer.

There it is. The word that haunts Jane from the minute she wakes up in the morning until the last thing at night before falling asleep. *If* she falls asleep. Clutching at nothing, Jane's fluttering fingers reach for one of the floral cushions that complement the sofa. It smells of Lucy, making Jane want to weep. Making her want to scream. To lash out. Hurt somebody else. Then, sighing, she brings the cushion to her lap and kneads it as a kitten might. This action does not erase the accusation from her memory, but it does bring some comfort.

Seeing her reflection in the black TV screen reminds Jane of the glass bottle. Glancing down at her bandaged hand, now sprinkled with red dots, she grimaces. The cuts feel as sore and angry as she did when she first found out about Lucy. *It is all that girl's fault. Which girl? Cindy or Lucia? Who is Cindy?*

Jane warns herself to stop this. She knows perfectly well who Cindy is. She is being forgetful again. That's all. Having been menopausal for some time, she has been warned about the possibility of memory loss and feelings of confusion and paranoia. Going through the change has affected Jane badly. Fortunately, she has a private doctor who is understanding of her condition. Unlike John.

If he knew what went on inside her head, he would have her sent away "for her own good." And what would happen to Moon Hollow in her absence? Jane shudders to think about what wickedness and debauchery might occur in her ancestral home then. As for Cindy, it might be better to send her packing now rather than later. Before it is too late. An acute coldness seeps into Jane's bones as she realises that it probably is already too late.

Eyes smouldering with grief, Jane wrestles constantly with the same haunting thought. *What will happen if the truth comes out?* It cannot. It must not. She will do everything she can – correction, she will do *anything* to make sure that does not happen.

Deciding that she needs to focus on something less depressing, Jane toys with the idea of planning Lucy's homecoming. This is a much nicer idea to escape to. Convinced that Cindy is close to finding Lucy, Jane is sure that afternoon tea would be an excellent way of celebrating her little girl's return. Lucy would like that. They will have cake and cucumber sandwiches with the crusts cut off and cups of Earl Grey tea poured from a china teapot.

Jane will go one better than her husband on this occasion and serve everything on the Royal Albert Old Country Roses china tea set that Lucy coveted but was never allowed to touch. In the end, to spite Jane, John had a miniature set made especially for Lucy for her birthday. Jane refuses to think about how it got broken on the day her child disappeared. Instead, she thinks what better way to welcome Lucy home than with afternoon tea? It will be like the ones she herself used to have as a child.

For the briefest of moments, Jane is reminded of happier memories. The three Valentine siblings sitting around a table in the upstairs nursery, helping themselves to slices of Victoria sponge, Jane insisting they each had a napkin folded ready in their laps to catch any rogue streaks of jam. She might not have been the eldest, but she was the leader. George, in one of his rarer good moods, would make them laugh by imitating their houseguests. And there were plenty of them. That was before poor George got sent away.

But what about her other brother? The one John does not like her mentioning, not to anyone but especially not to Cindy. Forehead wrinkling, Jane tries to remember what her younger brother looked like at that age, but all she can recall is the shock of yellow hair and blue eyes they were all born with. "Three times trouble" her mother used to call them, as if she were proud of the fact that each of her children was difficult in his or her way.

When a single church bell rings out ominously, Jane believes at first that she imagined it. The church is redundant. The bells are never rung. No one except Jane goes into the church. She is parishioner, churchwarden, and priest all rolled into one. Nobody can access the church without the keys, and they are hidden in a vase upstairs. Could somebody have taken them without her knowing? John knows where they are kept, but he has not stepped foot inside the church since Lucy went missing, not even to pray.

Jane waits on tenterhooks to see if the bell will ring a second time, but it does not. This can only mean one thing. Not normally superstitious, Jane clambers fearfully to her feet. Typically, church bells ring once at funerals to signify the passing of someone. What she has just heard is a death knell. A warning. *Not Lucy. Anybody but Lucy* is all Jane can think.

67

CINDY

Glossy red jam, appearing on the floor like streaks of blood, attracts buzzing flies that bounce off as I approach. Sandwiches and spongy bits of cake are trodden into the gaps between the floorboards, and the smell of boiled egg lingers in the air. Tea stains have spilled onto the tablecloth on the kitchen table, where Lucy sat *alone* for most of her meals. Jane informed me of this early on, stressing how important it was that young children learnt their manners before joining adults at the bigger, more formal breakfast table.

Jane's need for detail allowed me to glimpse the anxiety she tried to hide whenever she explained what was normal for her family. Nobody knows better than me how it feels to be under the microscope. Being judged as a parent is a painful experience.

What the fuck has been going on here? If I didn't know better, I'd think an intruder had broken in and created all this mess, but the sound of Jane's sobs coming from upstairs tells me otherwise. This is her doing. It's the sort of thing she would do in temper. She's a revenge queen if ever there was one – giving Hugh notice, taking away John's prized car, and threatening to send Grace back to social care.

Jane's obviously lost it again. That doesn't explain why the table has been set for three, though. Or why Jane chose to wreck all her efforts when it must have taken ages to bake the cake and set everything out so prettily.

The china plates patterned with roses and edged in gold remain intact, a carefully folded napkin forming a white mountain peak on each one. But the big teapot lies in pieces on the floor, where it has also spat its contents. I imagine John and Jane will be stepping on the smaller shards of broken china for weeks to come.

Ignoring the grotesque Alice in Wonderland tea party scene, I fetch the half-drunk bottle of wine from the kitchen cupboard, not liking to admit how much it's been on my mind, and collapse wearily onto one of the matching sofas that sit directly in front of a widescreen TV. The "cosy corner" Jane calls it, although the sofa is hard and uncomfortable. Not cosy at all. I suspect it's not been sat in enough and needs breaking in, like a horse. As it is, the sofa is as tense as I am.

Realising that the wine is the only reason I came into the kitchen depresses me. I thought I was over this stage. *Once an alcoholic, always an alcoholic.* But the fact is, I use booze as an excuse to beat myself up. Self-hatred is something I carry around with me the same way other people do designer handbags.

Clearing my throat, I cough several times, noticing that the air is dense and full of dust motes. It's as dirty as I feel. My clothes also feel grimy to touch, leaving behind a stickiness on my hands. The skin on my arms is raw and angry from being out in the sun too long, and my hair, damp with sweat, clings to the back of my neck. I long for a shower, but the effort required to go upstairs is too much. Besides, I don't want to bump into Jane.

Drinking straight from the bottle, almost knocking out one of my teeth when the lip knocks against my mouth, a cloud of sadness settles over me. I'm not prone to being maudlin when I have a drink, unlike Hugh, but oblivion is all a girl really needs – not a mum or a man. The row with Hugh, the ability of my daughter to disappear at will, only allowing herself to be found by one or other of the Valentines, John's distance from his wife, Jane's cruelty, and the claustrophobic atmosphere of Moon Hollow is getting me down.

I'm desperate to find Lucy so Grace and I can return home, but every time I think I turn a corner, something happens to prevent me from finding her. I don't know how I'll ever find the missing girl in all this mess. John isn't the man he used to be. Jane has gone mad and is no longer safe to be around. I should take my daughter and run, but if I do, I may lose her altogether. Jane doesn't issue fake warnings. She'll be on the phone to Social Services straightaway, informing them that I've broken the terms of my access.

This bleak bloody house that's never silent, complaining as it does whenever it gets too hot or too cold. Sighing and groaning like an old woman who can't reach her cobwebs. Always wanting to be heard. The atmosphere of Moon Hollow is something I can't wait to leave behind. It festers in me as it does the Valentines and all those who have ever lived here. I should know. I fucking hear them all the time. The house is as stirred up and restless as a sky filled with circling birds, like the murmuration of starlings I saw from the treehouse.

I wish I were at home. Wrapped in a towel, clean and fresh after a long soak in the bath, with coconut-scented hair. I would be putting on my lip gloss, getting ready for a night out with the girls. Tight dress. Pushed-up bra. High heels. Hoping to meet a guy with dark skin and amber eyes. My favourite type – before Hugh. Now all I can think about are his crinkly green eyes. Besides, that's not who I am anymore. These days I would be just as happy staying at home with Grace and getting a takeaway kebab.

My mouth waters at the thought of doner meat or a bucketful of southern fried chicken. I'm not into the avocado and quinoa shit that the Valentines eat. I bet John doesn't like it either. Just pretends for Jane's sake. It's surprising I stay so slim with all the crap I eat, but I've never been one for my five-a-day. The only green thing to find its way down my throat is a mojito on a Saturday night, and the only fruit I've ever knowingly consumed was when a slice of lime, again from a mojito, slipped accidentally out of the glass into my mouth.

Belching loudly, as girls do when they're on their own, I swallow another mouthful of the wine, and it dawns on me that I was lucky not to have walked in on Jane when she was attacking the tea table. The woman is distraught. God knows she has every reason to be, but she scares the hell out of me. Even on a good day. I worry about her erratic behaviour. She's up and down like a yo-yo, a saying of my dad's that suddenly springs to mind.

Sighing, I kick off my boots and put my feet up on the floral footrest. I'll remove them the instant I hear Jane's tread on the stairs. That's if I don't fall asleep first. The truth is, I'm worn out from all the harrowing visions I've been experiencing. They take their toll on me. And right there on the spot, I decide to put off my search for Lucy today and resume it tomorrow with fresh eyes and mind. *Why put off until tomorrow what can be done today?* Another of my dad's sayings pops into my head, and this time I'm bloody annoyed by the reminder. *I'm entitled to a bit of peace, aren't I? Not everything is about Lucy.*

Help me find my daughter, Cindy, please…

Lucy Benedict's voice, appearing from nowhere, startles me, and I jerk upwards, spilling wine down my top. The whispering is like an electric current passing through me, leaving every nerve end jangling. And I think because I'm physically as well as mentally exhausted, I feel intense anger stirring inside me. Towards her. This house. And of course, the Valentines.

'Leave me alone!' I shout, clasping my hands over my ears, determined not to let anyone else in. 'I just want five fucking minutes to myself.'

Silence. It worked.

Hands falling to my sides, my fingers close around a remote control that has fallen into a gap between the cushioned seats of the sofa. I point it at the TV and click furiously in the hope that loud noise will prevent Lucy Benedict's ghost from returning. But the TV does not come on. *Bollocks.* Taking out the batteries, I slide them back in again and try once more. Nothing. That's when I realise the TV isn't plugged in. It still has the film on it that it came in.

'Fake TV. Fake people. Fake lives,' I snap, tossing the remote to the other end of the sofa. I really could have done with vegging out in front of the TV and losing myself in a movie. Anything to shut out the past.

Peering into the bottle, I watch the scarlet liquid rolling around in it and, avoiding the bitter sediments that have sunk to the bottom, take a large gulp. The first sip is always the best. Shame I'm beyond that point. The anticipation of it is better than the drink itself. As soon as I see or smell alcohol, a brawl breaks out in my head, worse than any of the late-night scuffles I've witnessed in town. I don't want to be owned by alcohol, so I fight back, as my dad taught me to do at school. That's what you're meant to do with bullies, isn't it?

The downside is I spend most of my days thinking of valid reasons not to drink, but the rest of the time is devoted to dreaming up excuses to do exactly that. Finding something new to celebrate or commiserate over are all good excuses for opening a bottle. In the past I've sunk low enough to hope my day ends so badly I can convince myself I deserve a drink at the end of it. Grace, on the other hand, doesn't deserve a mother who falls into a drunken stupor with her head inside a toilet bowl full of vomit.

Even my dad disapproves of "Drunken Cindy". I almost laugh at the made-up name, as it reminds me of the old adverts for my namesake, the Sindy doll. "The doll you love to dress" went the slogan, only in my case it was the boys who wanted to undress me. Unlike "Air Hostess Sindy" or "Pony Club Sindy", I'm "Foul-Mouthed, Bad Mum Sindy". Dad would pull a sad face if he could hear the way I describe myself. *Sorry, Dad.* But in the end, I fear he'll give up on me too. I've left him with little choice.

Rightly or wrongly, I feel as if I've been abandoned by everyone. Story of my life, I suppose. First there was Mum. Then my friends. Even my co-workers at the supermarket turned their noses up at me although they were just as bad. Always out getting drunk and sleeping around. The courts and Social Services were the worst offenders of all, and they're supposed to help people like me.

Before I can stop it, my daughter's name pops into my head. *Bugger it*, I think, deciding to include her among the other traitors because, as usual, she's nowhere to be seen, hiding from me, no doubt, *because Mummy's been drinking again.* If I ask Jane if she's seen her, she'll only say that Grace is with John as she always does. But Grace doesn't even like John. I've no idea where my daughter is hiding, but I can guess where John is. Sulking in his study. After the row earlier, he and Jane will avoid each other for the rest of the day, but tomorrow they'll don polite smiles over the breakfast table, where Lucy never got to eat.

I will myself not to gaze across at the tea table for fear of seeing Lucy sitting there all alone, straight-backed with a napkin folded neatly on her lap. I cannot bear for her tiny white neck to turn in my direction or to see her dark eyes pleading with mine to save her. Helped along by the wine, I push all thoughts of the little girl aside and allow the weariness of my mind to carry me away from Moon Hollow. This is the escape I've been craving.

Feeling myself soar like a bird in the sky, I find myself gazing down on the pinnacles of the church tower. The horses in the surrounding field lift their heads as I pass over them, their jaws munching lazily on grass. The sky is the colour of faded roses. I can almost smell their dusty fragrance. A bubble of hot anger surges through me when I see the figure on a bicycle warily circling the gates of Moon Hollow. The man I've come to think of as Lord of the Dance is like a trapped fly buzzing around in my head. I can't shake him off.

"Dance, then, wherever you may be, I am the Lord of the Dance, said he."

68

The whites of Lucy's eyes are visible in the dark as she blinks dust from her eyelashes. The air is cloying and damp, heavy with mildew and rotting wood. The spores of it stroke the back of my throat, making me want to gag. Never too far away is the stench of a man's sweat – worse than any wet-dog smell.

Kneeling by the peephole, where a crack of grey light filters through, Lucy doesn't have her eye pressed up against the bullet-shaped hole this time. Instead, her attention is on me. She wants me to know that she's not been let out in a long time. The drawing phase has ended. Neither of us knows what this means. Only that it's not a good sign if he's bored of her already.

Her limbs are cramped from being in the confined space for so long. The cold deathliness of her skin and her shallow breathing is immediately obvious. She's weak. Exhausted. About to give up. The nipped-in cheeks and shrunken eyes let me know that she feels abandoned. By everyone. At this moment she reminds me of me.

'I want to go home. You said you would find me. You promised. But I'm still here. Waiting. Waiting for you.' She accuses me with the saddest eyes I've ever seen.

Feeling my eyes well with tears, I'm about to reassure her that I haven't given up, that I intend to keep my promise – *I just need to know where she is, where he's keeping her* – when I'm woken sharply from the nightmare by a slap to my face. Someone is tugging at my hair and hitting me repeatedly around the head with a rolled-up ball of paper, sharp in places. Gradually, my daughter's face comes into focus.

'Grace. Stop it. What on earth are you doing?'

Grabbing at her thin arms, I try to restrain her, but she's stronger than any eight-year-old should be, so when she snatches her arms away from me, I'm left feeling stunned.

'What is it? What's wrong?'

'You're wrong,' she states cruelly. 'Everything about you is wrong.'

It was inevitable, I suppose, that I would fall asleep on the sofa, mouth propped open, dribbling red wine onto a cushion. As yet, I'm unable to process things as accurately as I would like, but as I slowly emerge from the drink-addled fog that's more comforting than any of my mother's fake pats on the back, I try to reason with my daughter. But my words give me away by slurring. 'Why did you hit me, Grace? You know that isn't a nice thing to do. Wait a minute, what have they done to your hair?'

Scrambling unsteadily to my feet, I grab hold of her; this time I'm quicker than she is, and I spin her round on the spot so I can inspect the new haircut. I hold her more tightly than I should, ignoring her cries for me to stop.

'Don't touch me. Let me go!' she yells, trying and failing to squirm out of my grip.

'Jane did this, didn't she? She cut your hair so you'd look like Lucy.'

I can see Grace's mouth working, but I can't hear a word she's saying. A red mist of anger is curling itself around me, preventing me from hearing my daughter's pleas. I grab hold of a lock of her hair and let it slip through my fingers. The long yellow mane has gone. All that's left is a short aggressive bob with a savage fringe. Like Lucy Valentine's. This time I will make Jane pay. Even if I have to sleep with her husband, I will get her back for this. How fucking dare she cut off my daughter's lovely long hair. Who does she think she is?

'Stop it. Let me go.'

Realising too late that my fingers are nipping cruelly at Grace's skin, I let go of her more abruptly than I intended, and she crashes to the floor. Instantly, my hands reach out to help her, but she scrambles out of the way, a horrified expression on her face. Only when she's at a safe distance from me does she pick herself up again, dropping the ball of paper she was holding onto the floor. She doesn't attempt to reclaim it, hugging an elbow instead, a clear indication that she hurt herself in the fall, and her eyes glisten with unshed tears. Chin jutting out at a proud angle, she's far too adult at this moment for my liking. She weighs me up as if I were something on the bottom of her shoe. And perhaps I am.

'You're talking rubbish, as always. Nobody did anything to my hair. Nobody.' She screams the last word before storming towards the French doors, her favourite means of escape. Except, while I was asleep, dusk has fallen. This means it's much later than I thought.

The sky is a weak watercolour blue, reminding me of Jane's trompe l'oeil painting. Soon it will be dark. I don't want my daughter roaming the grounds of Moon Hollow at night. It's not safe. A child has already been taken. *How many more will there be if I don't catch the kidnapper? I'm all Lucy has. If I don't find her, then no one will.*

I want to go home.

You said you would find me.

You promised.

But I'm still here.

Waiting.

'Grace. Come back. I'm sorry,' I plead, pushing Lucy's whispers out of my head. The memory of them is like the thump of a fading pulse. *I'm running out of time.*

'You're always sorry.' Grace stomps her foot. 'But you never mean it. And you've been drinking again. I can smell it on your breath. That's why you didn't come and find me.'

'Grace. That's not fair. I looked everywhere for you.' Knowing this isn't strictly true, I reach out an imploring arm, hoping she'll believe me. Hoping she'll come back. But she remains wary and standoffish. I cannot say I blame her. All I can do is stumble like the drunken idiot I am, and by doing so I seal my fate. Straightaway, Grace recognises the movement for what it is. Her scowling gives her away. She's no fool.

'You promised you'd given up drinking, but you lied.'

'It was just a couple of glasses, Grace. To help me sleep.' I hate the wheedling sound of my voice. Will there ever be a time when I don't have to beg for a scrap of affection?

'You say you couldn't find me, but I've been here all along. I'm always here, Mummy, waiting for you,' Grace tells me more calmly, a thread of sadness and mystery to her grown-up voice, but there's no affection in the way she calls me Mummy. She proves this by shaking her head, indicating how disappointed she is in me, then, snatching at the door handle, she disappears into the night without a backward glance.

'Grace. Come back. Don't go out there!' I shout. But my words are stolen by the sudden blast of wind bursting through the door.

When I pick up the abandoned piece of paper from the floor, darkness envelops me. It's Grace's drawing. The one I've been meaning to ask her about. But the bicycle man, Lord of the Dance, has been viciously scribbled out. As has Lucy. A single gravestone takes their place. The words engraved on the stone, *Much-loved daughter*, spelled correctly for once – Grace was never a scholarly child – has me gasping for breath. *What does it mean? Has Grace seen the future? Is she trying to tell me that Lucy is dead?*

Now that she has taken a sedative or two more than is good for her, Jane is feeling much better. Far more rational than earlier. A twenty-minute nap also helped restore her to her former self. Having crept down the stairs, making sure nobody else was around to bother her, Jane has decided to prepare a special meal for this evening. To cheer John up, she is cooking his favourite dish – avocado and quinoa salad. She may even allow him a bottle of Sancerre from the cellar to go with it, served chilled as he likes it in paper-thin glasses.

She hopes Cindy keeps out of their way. If the girl knows what is good for her, she will make herself scarce. She is poisoning this house and John with her lies. Slipping on an apron, Jane dances around the broken bits of china teapot that are dotted around the floor, careful not to cut herself, before finding exactly the right sort of knife needed to slice the avocados.

Fingers closing over the handle, Jane recalls that it will be their anniversary next week. Not that they had a traditional wedding. Few guests would have turned up for a formal ceremony like that. John insists he does not want to mark the occasion, not with Lucy gone, but fifteen years is a huge accomplishment, so they should celebrate somehow. Although she agrees with John that a lavish do would not be appropriate, Jane suspects he is saying that to put her off. He might secretly be planning a trip away.

But then, remembering that Lucy is still missing, she accepts that this will not be possible. Perhaps when they are all together again, they can rent a seaside cottage on the coast. Cornwall or Devon would be nice.

Jane pauses the knife when she recalls that John is in a foul mood over something. She cannot imagine that it is over anything she has said or done. They rarely argue. She is fond of telling people this – her doctor and hairdresser, mostly, and the woman at the charity shop. The one who greedily sorted through Lucy Benedict's clothing, which got left behind when the girl went away. Preferring not to think about that, Jane ponders on the fact that after fifteen years together she and John are as happy as ever. No matter what others might say, and people say the cruellest things when they are jealous, they are devoted to one another.

One day John will tire of his womanising. That day cannot come soon enough for Jane. Living with a ladies' man has not been easy, not by any stretch of the imagination. Jane would not wish it on her worst enemy. Except, perhaps she might. Turning a blind eye has been extremely difficult. When John is old and grey, he will be grateful to her for standing by him. But it is what her own parents did, although in their case it was her mother who was the adulterer, not her father. Poor Papa simply had to "put up and shut up", a term Jane's mother used to giggle about with her friends. She was part of a glamorous crowd that looked down on old money, even if she had tied herself to it by marrying Jane's father.

Jane will never know if her father deliberately set out to kill himself and his wife that night. He was already quite drunk by the time they left the house for some cocktail party or other. Not that her mother would have noticed. Nobody ever looked Jane's father's way when he was stood next to Gorgeous Georgie. She outshone everybody. But by then he was fed up with the affairs and had tried to put his foot down.

Jane can remember idling outside their bedroom door, *her* bedroom door now, listening to her mother laughing at the absurdity of her short, fat, and rather square husband's demands. Her mother had breezed past Jane on her way out, as if she did not exist. This was perfectly normal for her, so Jane did not mind. Following her mother downstairs, Jane watched her snapping her fingers at a servant, telling him to hurry up and fetch her fur stole before slipping gracefully into the back of the waiting car, her slim stockinged legs disappearing under her in a polished finishing-school way.

Papa had lingered in the hallway, which was unusual for him. He was not one for words, but that night he spoke to Jane as if she were not invisible. As a rule, the Valentines did not fuss over their children, not wanting them to become spoiled. Jane could have told them there was little chance of that happening in their loveless household.

'Be a good girl, Jane. Look after the place in our absence,' he said, because Jane was a young woman by then and heir to Moon Hollow, George having died ten years earlier. The girl who wanted to be a nun was now a wealthy heiress.

A sudden hot flush causes Jane to break out in a sweat, and her hands and neck begin to itch like mad. These are symptoms she is all too familiar with. And absolutely nothing to worry about, or so her doctor keeps informing her. As if growing old was not something she should be concerned by.

Why must she accept that nature must take its course? It is her ravaged body. Nobody else's. Night sweats. Morning sweats. A thickening waistline. They are all commonplace now. As well as a feeling of being invisible. Perhaps that is why her mind keeps drifting back to the past when she was young if not exactly carefree. Jane hardly had a happy childhood. Her memories are not worth taking another look at.

Going back to chopping up the avocados, Jane enjoys the feel of the soft ripe flesh oozing out of their skins onto her fingers. It helps relieve her desire to crush something.

70

CINDY

A roar of thunder followed by a sliver of lightning illuminates the sloping lawns of Moon Hollow that dip down to the lake in the distance. The storm that's been brewing with its threats of downpours and dark skies now rages overhead like an angry god, but the moon keeps one blue eye open, doubling the already ominous size of the lake with its reflection.

Rain lashes down, hindering my search for my daughter, but I know she came this way. Now and then I manage to catch a glimpse of her, appearing like a pale ghost with yellow hair. Like me, she's running with her head down and is soaked to the skin. As I stumble after her, I'm reminded of the two shadows I saw out on the lake chasing each other, as we're doing now, and wonder what significance that vision had. *Was it a warning? An omen?*

'Grace! Grace! Come back!' I tip my head back and shout, but my voice is drowned out by another rumble of thunder.

By now it's properly dark, and I can no longer see her,

but I can hear her. The squelching, panicked steps, the slipping and sliding on wet grass. Big intakes of wet air. Spluttering and ragged breathing.

'Grace! Please! Come back. It's dangerous out here.'

Still, no response. It's as if my daughter has vanished.

Closing my eyes, I try to imagine what direction she might have taken, but it's no good. I can't read her. So, I head in the direction I would've taken if I were her. I can only hope that my instinct is correct. Heading to the high bank that surrounds the lake, I think I hear someone fall. A sudden yelp. Followed by a scuffle.

When I hear a giant splash and a muffled scream, I know that Grace has plunged into the water, and I feel my heart race faster.

'Grace! Oh my God, Grace. Call to me, baby. Let me know where you are.'

'Mummy!'

The voice is faint and far-away sounding. But it definitely belongs to my daughter.

'I'm coming. Hang on!' I yell, running as fast as I can towards the edge of the high bank that I know plummets a good ten metres to the lake below. *She must have tripped and fallen, as I did. Only, she's gone into the water, I'm sure of it.*

'Mummy! Help me!'

Grace's voice is all the compass I need. As soon as my feet hit the soggy grass bank, I throw myself lengthways down it, shielding my head with both hands as I slide. The descent seems to take forever, but I manage to steady myself at the bottom so I don't end up falling in too. If I'm to save my daughter, I need to keep my wits about me and establish exactly whereabouts in the lake she is. I must stay alive for her sake.

'Where are you, Grace?' I call from the water's edge. Mist comes off its glossy, unruffled surface like a hand hovering above a poisonous fog. A cold, deathly silence is all that greets me. For a second, I start to hope that I'm wrong, that Grace didn't go into the water after all. It's the night playing tricks on my mind. But then—

'Mummy.'

Her voice comes out as a strangled gargle. She must be taking in water. Knowing that she won't be able to stay afloat for long – *Please, God don't let her die, anything but that* – I launch myself into the ice-cold water, pushing aside the creeping weed as I go.

'Keep making a noise so I can find you.' My teeth chatter as I shout this. I've never felt so cold. I'm sure my heart is about to freeze over. Keeping my mouth above water for now, although it's already up to my chin, I know that soon it will be too deep, and I'll have to swim. I refuse to think about how many people have died in open water such as this. Grace can swim a little, but she's by no means a strong swimmer.

'So cold.' Grace's voice is fainter than ever, and I sense, with a sinking heart, that she's giving up. *I must not lose my daughter. Not again.*

'I'm here, Grace. I'm right here.'

'Where are you, Mummy? I can't see you.'

I'm swimming now, fighting the current that's trying to pull me in the opposite direction to my daughter. I hear her hands thrashing about in the water as she tries to search for me. Sensing how desperate she is, I spread out my own hands, clutching at nothing in the blackness. I must be close. I can hear her. Just. Although it's stopped raining by now, the water around me feels too calm. Eerily so. And reflects the moon many times over. I see glimpses of it whichever way I turn, but I can't see her.

'Grace.' I sob, knowing that I don't want to live if I've lost her. *It's not fair. Why would God let me have her back only to take her away again? Why? Why?* In desperation, I blame a deity I don't believe in. I dare say I'm not unique in this in my hour of need.

I don't know if I say those words out loud, because a thick dampness suddenly creeps over me that stills my mind and body. Even takes my mind off Grace. *How is that possible?* Blind terror has frozen me. Turned me into one of the crumbling statues in Moon Hollow's church-yard. I suspect that I'm suffering from hypothermia and don't fight it. I'm ready.

There's no time to look around for Grace's body, face-down in the water with her yellow hair fanned out around her, because I'm already slipping away. Under the water. The lake is my destiny. It has both fascinated and terrified me since first arriving at Moon Hollow. *Now I know why. It's about to give up its secrets at last.*

Not wanting to miss a thing, I keep my eyes open. My vision is blurry, as if in slow motion, but the murky water becomes clearer the deeper I sink. Imagining that this is what it must be like to throw yourself off a tall building, I concentrate on what will be my final scene. Everybody has one. For Tess Hunter, it was her daughter's blood-spattered face. For Adam Lockwood, a shit-stained toilet. For some-body who's about to die, I feel calmer than I should. *I don't care. Without Grace there is nothing.*

Cindy. Cindy.

I hear her. Smell her. Feel her. Lucy Benedict.

My subconscious has always known where to find her. She's tried to show me, many times, but I refused to listen. There were enough clues. The perfume bottle was hers. I saw it here in the lake and back at the house. The smell of damp, dirty water that's accompanied every vision I've ever had of her should have pointed me in the direction of the lake. I knew she was trying to tell me something, but I was unable to figure it out. My search for Lucy, for myself, for Grace all got in the way.

She appears in front of me. No longer an apparition but real. A dead girl with skin as green as a mermaid's. Her eyes, like mine, bulge in the flow of the water, but hers are cloudy and empty, flimsy with death. Although her gaze is settled on me, her eyes look past me as if I were the one who didn't exist. Her long black hair floats around her like an eerie crown, partially covering the disfiguring birthmark on her face. Bubbles spout from her nose and mouth, reminding me that the ghost of this girl continues to live. In my visions, at least.

I'm incapable of moving. Only my eyes flicker from side to side, tracking her every move as she drifts closer. As I go down, deeper and deeper, her fluttering hands reach out for me. She touches my face. Oh God, she's touching me. Looking into my eyes.

Cindy. You must find my daughter.

They took her from me. Made me give her up.

I tried to run. I took Lucy with me. But they would not let me leave.

I understand at last what she wants me to know. She changed her mind about keeping her baby, but the Valentines forced her to go through with the adoption. Did they murder her too? The knowledge comes too late.

What about my daughter? I want to sob. *We matter too.*

My tears join the green murky water that's the same colour as my eyes, and I watch Lucy Benedict recoil in horror as I shake my head at her. She must know that my heart bleeds for her. That I understand what she went through was terrible, unimaginable. As a mother myself, how could I not? But she must also realise that I cannot help her now. Grief for my daughter, and for myself, is all I can feel. There's no room for anything else.

She's here, Cindy. Your daughter has always been here. Like me. Waiting for you.

What she's saying doesn't make any sense. *Or does it?*

Deciding that I would rather live than hear her next words, I thrust her away from me, and, kicking out my feet behind me, I aim for the surface. Whatever is waiting for me at the top has got to be better than what lurks beneath. Lungs burning for lack of air, I feel myself weaken before I get far. The black pool above me that forms the swirling surface of the water grows ever more distant. I would give anything to see the angry, balled-up fist of the dark sky again, but it's getting further away.

When I feel Lucy Benedict's hands clutching at my clothing and pulling me back down, I try to scream but end up swallowing more water. Choking and arms flailing, I struggle against her, but she's stronger than me. Never taking her eyes off me, she takes hold of my wrist in a vicelike grip and unfastens the silver bracelet that has her name on it before slipping it onto her own wrist, where it belongs. It is of course a perfect fit.

Her eyes switch to the bracelet, and she strokes it for a

second or two, remembering happier times, I think, but when our eyes next meet, I see a different young woman to the one I'm used to. A much darker side of her confronts me now. Her fury terrifies me. Makes me wonder if she intends to keep me down here with her. Forever. Her eyes smoulder with hatred and a desire for revenge, reminding me of Jane Valentine and Tess Hunter.

I decide I don't blame her. Not after what they did to her. But I've seen more than enough hatred lately to last me a lifetime. Lucy Benedict never had a proper funeral or a grave with her name carved into it. There's no epitaph to remind the world that a girl like her ever existed, a young mother who died alone, without family or friends.

Thrust into a house among people she was supposed to trust, she'd faced the ultimate betrayal. Her family in Romania will never know what happened to her. They might continue to believe that one day she'll come home. But this is her home now.

Help me, Cindy. Help me look for Lucy.

71

JANE

J ane's mind dashes from one subject to another until she hardly knows where she is. One minute she is thinking about John and their forthcoming anniversary, the next the past and her unhappy childhood before finally settling back on Lucy, the only place her mind likes being, if she is completely honest.

Thinking about Lucy is unbearably painful, which is why Jane takes the sedatives the doctor prescribed for her, but it is the only way of keeping her daughter alive. By now, Jane has given up on the idea of having another child. Had she really thought Cindy would be a suitable surrogate? What a joke.

Everyone else, the police and the press included, even her husband and the clairvoyant she brought in to help find her daughter, have all given up on Lucy, but Jane refuses to. She remembers the advice she was given when her daughter first went missing. The detective who supplied her with all the relevant information sounded like he was reading from a script, without any empathy. Jane later found out that he did not have any children of his own. That made sense to Jane, and she was able to forgive him for this. Only a parent would understand what she was going through.

The first thing the police did was search the house and grounds. The treehouse, which was the last place Lucy was seen, became their focal point. Apart from the doll, Heidi, which Jane knew Lucy would never deliberately leave behind, they found nothing. So many weak, sugary cups of tea and requests to "sit down and rest" had Jane's nerves stretched to breaking point during that time. Jane wanted to scream at anybody who was not Lucy.

Apparently, ninety-four percent of missing children are recovered within seventy-two hours, but, more impressively, forty-seven percent are found within three. *The detective loved his statistics.* He didn't say so, but he implied that the unlucky ones were usually dead shortly after being abducted.

Because of his reluctance to say any more on the subject, Jane had gone to a library to look up more of those unsettling statistics for herself. What she learned terrified her. After seventy-two hours, the police are really searching for a body, not a living child, although nobody, of course, had suggested such a thing to her. Another discovery that filled her with a cold, numbing dread was the fact that seventy-four percent of missing children who are ultimately murdered are usually dead within three hours of being abducted.

As Jane had not raised the alarm until four hours after Lucy went missing, the odds were already stacked against them. Moon Hollow was a large property with lots of land

and outbuildings, so they had carried out their own search first. Not wanting to involve the outside world unless they had to, Jane had even allowed Hugh to help them.

But, because they had delayed calling the police until they were sure Lucy wasn't just hiding from them, as she sometimes did, this meant her daughter was potentially one of the unlucky ones in the seventy-four percent club. But that was before Cindy got involved and claimed to have seen their daughter alive.

As much as Jane detests Cindy, she clings on to the hope that the girl is right *this time*. It's all Jane has. The police were next to useless. They insisted on searching the lake, of course. Reports of late-night dives taking place well into dawn the next day had Jane's skin crawling with fear, but, thankfully, they came across nothing but weed. Jane could not bear the thought of Lucy having drowned. That would have been too cruel a trick by anyone's standards. Even the land and air searches and door-to-door inquiries revealed nothing. Nothing. How could a child vanish without once being spotted? It was inconceivable.

Right from the start, John and Jane's relationship with the police and press had been strained. Refusing to take part in a television appeal, they became the closest thing to a suspect they had. Both Jane and John felt the TV appearance was an unnecessary diversion and an infringement of their privacy. As if forced tears from them and grainy footage of their child would ever bring Lucy back. The police should be out looking for their daughter, not concentrating on them, their relationship, lack of friends, the fact they homeschooled their daughter, or that she was hardly seen outside of Moon Hollow.

John and Jane had perfectly good reasons for keeping

Lucy away from the rest of the world, but they could not risk their secrets becoming public, even if it meant reducing their chances of finding Lucy alive. If anyone found out about the illegal adoption, not to mention what they did, there was every chance Lucy would not be allowed to return to them.

As a result, they did not come across well in public. Jane remembered too well the case of that poor little girl who went missing abroad – Madeleine McCann – and how her parents were treated throughout the investigation into her disappearance. Both were condemned as guilty simply because the mother, Kate, did not show enough emotion. If Jane had not been careful, the same could have been said of her.

Instead, she tried to win the press over. Baking them cakes, taking out trayfuls of tea; she had bought the mugs especially. Always asking them how their own children were doing. It worked. They thawed. Towards her, at least, but they remained suspicious of John, who would bark at them as if he were still "Lord of the Manor". He was so like his father in that respect.

In the early days, when Lucy's sad little face was plastered all over the newspapers, the press had, with permission, parked on Moon Hollow's lawns. But after they printed a photo of John with his arm around an exotic beauty weeks after his daughter had gone missing, they were instructed, in a fit of temper, to move back beyond the gates. "Get off my land," or words to that effect, John had said. The fool.

The search dogs who returned whimpering each day, unrewarded for their failed efforts to find Lucy, were eventually retired, put back in their caged police vans, where they quickly forgot about a missing girl whose scent eluded them. The day the police finally packed up and left, shutting the door behind them with a click so final it nearly killed Jane, is something she will never forget.

In the absence of any reassuring police presence and unable to rely on her husband, who had withdrawn into himself, adrenaline became Jane's trusted friend. It was the only thing keeping her from saying too much and giving herself away. She could not afford to slip up. John was already saying too much. Making too many demands. Calling in favours he wasn't owed. All in a bid to uncover the body of his missing child.

Unlike Jane, John talked of bodies and burials, not hope and the future. When Jane told him that she would know it in her bones if their child was dead, a mother knew such things, he walked away from her in disgust. He might not have said out loud the words "But you are not her mother, are you, Jane?" but she felt them nonetheless.

Becoming aware of a persistent knocking, Jane frowns and turns her head in the direction of the French doors. For the last couple of hours, a fierce summer rain had been lashing at the side of the house, causing the glass in the frames to vibrate. Although it has since stopped, the rain reminded her of the warm nights and long days of her childhood.

Looking at her reflection in the glass, longing to see a glimpse of her younger self standing outside, looking in, all Jane sees is a matronly looking older woman with a thick waist, dull hair, and lined skin. Had her mother lived to be Jane's age, she would still have been beautiful. Jane is sure of it. Thinking of her mother, Jane realises that her precious "Lady of the Lake" roses have been battered in the storm. Their delicate petals have been ripped from the bare-looking bushes and carried away by the wind.

In the distance, lightning punches the earth. Jane feels the menace of it. Thunder growls above too, like the not-so-friendly purr of a sleepy tomcat who has one eye open – the kind that wouldn't be stroked and lived out in the stables of her childhood home, back when it was a castle. When the Valentines were a family to be admired, looked up to.

Jane had grown up in an era when working men would doff their cap at her father, who was everybody's landlord as well as employer in those days. That was before the Valentines were sunk low and had to demolish the expensive-to-maintain castle and sell off their lands. The respect they had been shown by their community seemed to vanish along with their money. A fact that hurt Jane more than anything. Turned her against the villagers.

The last thing she wanted when Lucy went missing was for them to show up on their doorstep, feeding the police lies about the Valentines. Thankfully, most of them had moved on by then. The youngsters could no longer afford to live in the villages they were brought up in, which meant John and Jane's secret was safe. *For now. Always, for now.*

Thump. Thump. Thump.

The intrusive knocking blunts the sharp edge of Jane's vision. Realising that the sound is coming from elsewhere, the front doors, in fact, Jane slips off her apron and walks cautiously into the hallway. Stopping in front of the oak double entrance doors, she wonders if the knocking is real. After all, nobody ever visits Moon Hollow. No one.

Thump. Thump. Thump.

Hanging on to the stair bannister that ends in a generous walnut whip swirl, Jane takes several deep breaths, hating the fact that she feels intimidated in her own home.

'Who is it? What do you want?' she demands, trying to keep the tremor of fear from her voice. She is alone. There is no John to save her. *Nobody ever visits Moon Hollow. No one. Why won't they go away? What can they mean by coming at this late hour? Where is John?*

Thump. Thump. Thump.

It occurs to Jane that the visitor might be bringing news of Lucy, which would make sense. If she had been found, the police wouldn't announce this from the other side of a door. The shock would be too much. They would want to break the news face-to-face.

Ignoring the quickening of her pulse that warns Jane something bad is about to happen, she makes up her mind that, whoever is on the other side of the door, they are not going to go away by themselves. Left with no choice, she slowly slides open both top and bottom bolts. They shriek in protest, as if warning her she is making a mistake, but she is determined not to feel threatened by a stranger without manners.

Why must they knock so loudly? The apologetic clicking of the doors opening seems to imply they don't want to be held responsible for what happens next. They did warn her.

Afterwards, Jane will always remember that she walked into this situation with her eyes open. They open even wider when she sees the washed out, trampish-looking figure standing on the steps in front of her. As if he has every right to be there, challenging her, he does not automatically take a step back from her. His face is older and more ravaged than it used to be, but Jane recognises him instantly. How could she not?

'You!' Jane gasps, her voice edged with glass.

I look around, frightened in case what John is telling me is the truth. But it can't be. I would know it. Feel it if this were the case. Surely to God, a mother knows these things.

'Grace.' I call out pathetically, searching for an upturned face, a splay of hands, a mound in the middle of the lake resembling a small child in a big bed with cold feet. I remember now that my daughter was always ice-cold. Distant and different. But still somehow Grace.

'Grace!' I shout against John's ear, pummelling his chest once again as he insists on carrying me towards the bank, strong thighs wading through the surge of water and suffocating reeds as if they were nothing. In the darkness, his white teeth are on show, reminding me of the ghost dog in the graveyard. Although numb with grief and disbelief, I'm surprised to feel a sharp stab of pain when John drops me onto the ground. I expect to feel nothing. Absolutely nothing after what he's just told me.

Having rescued me from drowning by pulling me to

the surface by my hair and then dragging me to the side of the lake, John falls exhausted into the long grass beside me. He's shivering as much as I am. Staring at the great expanse of the lake in front of us, we lie side by side, chests rising and hands almost touching as if we were friends. As if we were lovers.

On that thought, I pull myself up, still noticeably winded. Coughing up a blade of green grass, I fight all attempts by John to help me get it up by thumping me on the spine. Intent on going straight back in the water, I shrug him off and scramble to my feet.

'Get off. Leave me alone.' I sob when John grabs hold of me again and refuses to let go. His arms are locked around my chest, where they have always wanted to be, crushing me. 'I have to go back in,' I plead. 'I must find her. I can't leave her there. She might still be alive.'

'She's dead, Cindy. Grace has been dead for a long time.'

I punch him then. Hard. On the mouth. The lying bastard. Realising that I've always wanted to do this to one or other of the Valentines, I pick on the weaker one of the two and hit him again. With a right hook this time. Blood spurts from his mouth, reminding me of the horrific image of Tess Hunter's daughter before she died.

'Oh God.' I whimper, bending over and hawking up green phlegm. This time, John doesn't try to help me, although I think I might choke to death. I watch him wipe his mouth on a wet, crumbling tissue that he tugs out of his pocket and wonder why I can see so much now, when out on the lake when I'd been looking for Grace, it had been inky black. That's when I notice there are car headlights turned on us from the other side of the lake. The ghostly shape of a volcanic-orange bonnet reveals a glimpse of Jane's MINI Clubman, which John must've driven here.

The thought of coming face-to-face with Jane fills me with dread, and I panic even more. Pushing John out of my way, I drag myself towards the lake, but he hauls me back by my wet clothing. Once more, I struggle against him and lash out with my feet, aiming painful blows against his shins that must hurt like hell. At last, I sense him tiring, giving up. *Why does he care so much? Why is he bothering to save me?*

'God help me, Cindy, if you insist on going back in there and killing yourself, then I won't stop you.' He releases me as he says this, and I feel my lower half sink into the water. It's as freezing as I remember. Nobody could survive longer than a few minutes in it.

'But I am telling the truth. As God is my witness, your daughter is as dead as my own probably is right now.'

Even though the truth shines from John's exhausted-looking eyes, I remind myself that he's not a man of God. Because my world is crashing down on me, I don't tell him that I believe his daughter is alive. I'll save this information for later in case I need it. I don't owe him anything after all the lies he's told. About Lucy Benedict. About everything.

'How do you know Grace is dead? She could still be alive, clinging on to a rock or something,' I argue, teeth chattering like mad due to the cold.

Before freezing to death, I accept John's extended hand and use it to pull myself out of the foul-smelling water. Although he has saved me again, I'm convinced he's up to no good, and so I keep my distance. If I can get past him, I may be able to reach my daughter before it's too late.

'Your daughter isn't in the lake. She isn't at Moon Hollow. I have never met her,' he tells me, face twisting with several different emotions at once, none of which I can read.

'What are you talking about?' I yell, thinking I must be going mad. That the Valentines have finally pushed me to the point of no return. 'She's been here all the time. It was part of the agreement. I look for Lucy while you take care of Grace. That was the deal.'

'We were wrong to take advantage of you in the state you were in. I should never have agreed to it. Jane knew how delusional you were, but she wouldn't listen. She said if we went along with it, you might help us.'

'Went along with what?' I ask, terrified of what he's about to say next.

Mindful of what Lucy Benedict whispered to me under the water – *Your daughter has always been here. Like me. Waiting for you* – I begin to wonder if what John's saying is the truth after all. They both can't be wrong, can they?

'If Grace isn't in the lake, where is she?' I demand as if everything is John's fault.

'Your daughter died six weeks ago in a terrible car accident.' The words fall out of John's mouth with a finality that makes me want to vomit.

A chilling stillness descends on me as I shut out John's voice, which intends to be kind. I drift away from the lake. From Moon Hollow. Mostly, I drift away from Lucy Benedict. And step closer towards the truth.

'That's not possible.' I hold back, not quite ready yet to face the horrific night that ambushed my life. Terrified of returning to the dark place I visited soon after the accident, part of me wonders why I'm arguing with this man when my daughter could still be alive.

What sort of mother stands by doing nothing when her child's in danger? A distraught one. A grieving one. A delusional one. A mother who hasn't been able to accept the truth. Grace wasn't killed by a drunk driver. She wasn't abducted as Lucy Valentine was. She wasn't blown up in a terror attack. Nor did she drown in a lake that she's never seen. The truth, when it comes, arrives too soon. Before I'm ready. *I will never be ready.*

John has helped me to get there as gently as he could, but the truth still catches me unawares. Devastated, I drop to my knees and say a last silent prayer – *Please, God, don't let it be true* – all the while knowing that for once John isn't lying.

'She died because of me, didn't she? I'm to blame for what happened. Nobody else.'

73

John shrugs as if he can't help me. As if he doesn't have much of a clue when it comes to such things. I dare say I believe that Jane put him up to his part in the deception. He wouldn't have acted alone.

'So, I could have left at any time?'

'I'm sorry, Cindy,' John admits. 'We should never have put you through this. But we had a good reason.'

'Lucy,' I say. *The daughter who's still alive.* As if he knows what I'm thinking, John bows his head, unable to witness the hell he must see reflected in my eyes. Later I'll have to face the consequences of what I did to my child. But not now. Not in front of a Valentine.

'Are you going to hurt me? Drown me, like you did Lucy Benedict?' I ask, too tired for anything other than a straight answer.

John's head bounces up when he hears this. 'Why on earth would you say something like that? That's a terrible thing to say.'

I watch him squirm. This time he's lying. I know this

without a shadow of a doubt. I'm probably in more danger than I know, but I don't care. In the worst way possible, this man's responsible for taking Lucy Benedict's body, her child, her freedom, and her life. Hatred for him and Jane, but mostly against God for taking Grace away, rages inside me.

'What did you do to her?' I knock him backward, taking him by surprise, and he stumbles, falls onto his elbows and backside. 'I know you hurt her. Tell me.' I advance on him again. When he doesn't retaliate, it dawns on me that he wants this. His need to be punished, in the hope of exoneration, is clear to see.

It tumbles out of him then, as it did the night he confessed to the affair with Lucy Benedict. *If there ever was an affair*; he might have raped her. John is used to taking what he wants regardless of the circumstances. Sitting among the long grass, wet and shrunken, he buries his head in his hands and howls. Emotions gush out of him. All restraint is gone. Hugh wouldn't have given up like this. He would've fought back, refused to take the punishment I'm handing out. Because of this, I despise John more than I ever have. Anyone would think he's lost a child. *She's dead. Grace. My lovely daughter. Dead.*

'It was an accident. I swear it. Lucy was trying to run away with our daughter after all Jane had done, *we* had done, for her. She was going to leave me, us, with nothing. As soon as we realised she was missing, we looked for her, but we couldn't find her anywhere. You can imagine how worried we were.'

'I can imagine how frightened Lucy Benedict must've been,' I bark sarcastically, resisting the urge to kick him in the ribs and really hurt him. John nods as if to show that he's aware of how she must have felt, but I doubt that. He and Jane only ever thought of themselves and their desire for a baby that wasn't theirs to keep.

'Jane remembered that Lucy always took her walks by the lake, so she told me to go there and look. She would go back to the house in case she turned up there. So, that's what I did. When I saw Lucy running with the baby in her arms, I chased after her and shouted for her to stop. That's when she fell down the bank and dropped the baby. Or at least I think that's what happened.' Stopping for a breather, John licks his lips and swallows several times. The terrible memories of that night play out in his down-cast eyes.

'Anyway, I could hear Lucy in the water, screaming for help, but God forgive me, I went to find the baby first. I could hear her crying close by, and she was so tiny and helpless, I felt I had to. Stupidly I thought Lucy would be all right for a few minutes. I genuinely thought I could save them both, but time wasn't on my side.'

'But you didn't save her, did you, John? Perhaps you never intended to. Her death would've been more than convenient, given the circumstances. Not only did you get to keep the baby, but you didn't have to stump up any of Jane's precious inheritance either.'

Momentarily, John looks as if he might be about to argue back but, having second thoughts, sticks faithfully to his story.

'I would never have hurt a hair on that girl's head. I adored her,' he splutters.

For all I know he's telling the truth, yet I'd still like to dump his body in the lake and watch him sink to the bottom. But then I remember that John didn't have to save me from drowning. He could have stood by and watched me die. Another loose end nicely tied up.

'I didn't know what to do, where to go, who to save, but little Lucy was, well, my daughter, or at least that's what I thought at the time. Even when I knew for certain that she wasn't, that didn't stop me loving her as my own. And Lucy would have wanted me to save the baby, wouldn't she? At least that's what I told myself. But then Hugh showed up, and I thought all my prayers were about to be answered.'

'Hugh was there.' I feel my face whiten with shock. *Hugh was there the night Lucy Benedict died, and he never told me.* That's all I can think. Grace has so quickly gotten away from me. *How can I be thinking of Hugh after what I've found out about my daughter? What sort of mother am I?* Then I remember that Grace has been dead weeks. I've had time to adapt. *Except I haven't, have I? That's the whole point of denial.*

Time doesn't lessen pain. It's a myth. A lie. A slap in the face. How can one day more make life bearable for someone like me? I've stopped listening to John's whining voice. Stopped caring about anything else. True to form, John doesn't notice.

'Don't ask me where he came from at that time of night or why. I didn't care then, nor do I now. I was just grateful to have someone with me. I'd left Jane back at the treehouse screaming at me to go "do something for once. Be a man," she had said. "Take some responsibility." And that's what I did. I didn't want to be the failure she thought I was.'

'What happened when Hugh showed up?' I ask impatiently, putting on a brave front for John's benefit. I must convince him to tell me everything. Prove he can trust me, though inside, I'm back in the water, drowning. *There's no air. I can't breathe.*

'I sent him into the water to find Lucy. He did his best. God knows he tried. I could hear them in the dark, floundering. Hugh was shouting at her to keep her head above water, to doggy paddle, to try to grab hold of something until he could reach her. But she couldn't swim that well, and she must have—' John shudders at the memory of that awful night almost eight years ago. 'She stopped making a noise soon after that, and despite doing his best, Hugh was unable to save her. But we had the baby. Little Lucy was alive and well, thank God. Eventually, Hugh gave up and came to join me on the bank, and we sat there for what felt like ages, staring at the lake, just as you and I are doing now.'

'Does Jane know?' I ask, holding my breath.

'Of course Jane knows. I tell her everything.' John rallies somewhat, seeming both annoyed and offended that I should feel the need to ask him this. It's as if he somehow wants, even now, to keep up the pretence that their marriage is alive. Normal, even.

I start to think that John is remarkably like Jane. Why didn't I spot this before? Although they appear to dislike each other, they're fiercely loyal when it counts. Both are capable of great deception. Of plotting to destroy other people's lives. Up until today, I would've said they're mismatched, completely wrong for each other, but now I begin to wonder.

I notice for the first time that John doesn't wear a wedding ring. Nor is there a faded white band on his finger indicating he's recently taken one off. Now that I come to think of it, I can't remember seeing Jane wearing one ether. Strange that, considering they're quite the traditional couple, except for the missing-child, adoption-gone-wrong, dead-au-pair business.

'You mustn't blame Jane for this.' John is insisting as if old-fashioned chivalry is alive and kicking at Moon Hollow. 'It was a terrible accident for which I take full responsibility.'

'Full responsibility would have meant going to the police,' I point out curtly. *Selfish bastards. Arrogant, uncaring, selfish bastards.*

'I can assure you I thought about it. But we had little Lucy to consider. Our name. Everything. And Jane was not well. She could not have handled it. You must know, Cindy, that none of this was Jane's fault. She is completely innocent.'

'A woman died,' I remind him. 'Nobody who knew about this is innocent.'

74

JANE

E yes staring with a shocked glassiness, Jane watches the MINI Clubman pull onto the drive and dim its lights. There are two darkened silhouettes inside. They appear not to be speaking to each other, just sitting deep in thought. The clunk of the door opening and closing at last alerts Jane to the fact that John and Cindy will soon become aware of her presence. How could they not? She is sitting on the concrete steps of her ancestral home covered in someone else's blood.

What a shock she will give them. The thought makes her chuckle. In her mind, she can see John's mortified face already. Imagine the scene unfolding in front of her. Cindy's shock and horror. The girl is meant to be clairvoyant, but she doesn't see anything that matters. *Lucy, for instance.*

John is coming towards her. At first, he doesn't see her. She is not surprised because she has been invisible for so long where he is concerned. He cannot help but pay attention to her when he realises what she has done. For him.

For them. She has done what nobody else, John included, could do. She has made sure nobody can ever hurt them again.

'Jane, my God. What's happened?'

He comes towards her, but, annoyingly, he is still not looking at her. Only at the body, which is sprawled out on the stone steps below her, a pool of dark liquid surrounding it.

'What have you done, Jane? Jane?'

Laughter is a funny thing. It catches Jane out when she least expects it. The same thing happened when her parents died. She could not stop laughing. Even at the funeral. Causing people to tut and throw her the same critical look that John is treating her to. Is she odd? Is she one of the mad Valentines she grew up hearing about? *Does it matter?* Not really. All that matters is that John is finally looking at her. Paying her the attention she deserves.

'It wasn't much of a homecoming for poor George, was it?' Jane sniggers, enjoying the shock and surprise on John's face as he goes to inspect the body. Somewhere in the background, she feels Cindy watching them. Without looking in her direction, Jane can tell that the girl's hands are clasped over her mouth as if stifling a scream. Jane wants to tell her to *scream away, as nobody will hear her*, but she refrains, thinking it beneath her.

But Cindy seems more interested in the bicycle that has been abandoned at the bottom of the steps than the dead man who lies at an odd angle, twisted and bent like one of the figurines from the doll's house. Perhaps Cindy cannot bring herself to look. Some people are squeamish about such things. There is rather a lot of blood when all is said and done. Death is not for everybody. But then again, it is. Eventually. The thought makes Jane want to laugh again, but this time she beats the temptation into submission.

'Is it really him?' John is saying now that he has rolled the dead man's body over. Now that he is staring into the face of a man they both know.

'I did it for you, John. For us. He can't tell anybody about us if he is dead.' Ignoring the look of revulsion on his face, Jane gestures towards the body, who stares up at the moon with unblinking eyes.

'What does she mean?' Somebody else's voice chips in. Cindy's, of course. Both Jane and John ignore the outsider. This has nothing to do with her. Nothing to do with Lucy.

'You killed him?' John's shoulders have slumped. His arms are hanging limply by his sides.

'Well, he certainly did not get like that by himself.' Jane is curt, surprised at his stupidity. She refrains from telling him that their brother bled out like a stuck pig when she stabbed him repeatedly.

'Why, Jane. Why now?'

Is he really that daft? Does Jane have to spell it out for him? Obviously, she does.

'He threatened to talk, John. To expose us. He came back from the dead to punish us, and if the police discovered our secret, they would suspect us even more than they did before. They would find out what you did,' Jane points out.

'What I did?' John seems taken aback. Acts as if Jane has somehow wronged him when all she has done is protect him, saved him from himself. What's wrong with him? She is about to tell him to man up and take responsibility for what he did, when—

'You think I killed her, don't you? You think I drowned Lucy Benedict. On purpose.'

'Didn't you?' Jane murmurs, starting to doubt her own judgement. Isn't that what happened? She has suspected that this was the case for so long that in her mind it has become the absolute truth. She could not be wrong, could she? John murdered the girl out of loyalty to her and Lucy. In doing so, his love for her was proven, and if that was not the case, if John did not kill Lucy Benedict, then where does that leave her?

'I loved that girl. I would never have harmed her.' John's eyes, full of hatred, lock onto Jane's. Where is the gratitude she had expected to see? The thanks.

'That is not true, John. You love me. You always—'

'If she had said the word, I would have left you for her.'

'Nonsense.' Jane snorts, refusing to accept what John is telling her. 'You would have forgotten that girl as you have all the others. There was nothing special about Lucy Benedict. Nothing.'

When John hangs his head and weeps openly, Jane knows she is right. It is now her job, as it has always been, to comfort him. No one else can do this for him. Only her.

All men are cruel, Jane decides, clambering unsteadily to her feet. Her clothes are streaked with congealing blood. The stench of it invades her nostrils. Curls around her nasal hairs. She will never rid herself of the smell. She does not look at her brother's body as she steps around it. Her eyes do not stretch in its direction. Not once. He has been dead for too long for her to have any remorse now. He was meant to have died twenty-seven years ago.

It is a shame he ever came back. Jane is not a gambling woman, but she would like to bet that he wishes he had not. How dare he threaten her. Them. She has been the rightful heir to Moon Hollow for most of her life, and she is not going to relinquish it now.

'We Valentines are all the same, aren't we, John?' Jane smiles inappropriately, not noticing that John is gawping at her as if he does not know her. 'Always coveting what other people have. Like Hugh's magpies,' she adds for Cindy's benefit, knowing the girl's ears will prick up at the sound of his name. Jane was not lying when she told Cindy he had been unfaithful before. Hasn't the girl learned yet that no man is to be trusted? Not Hugh. Not John. And most of all, not George, Jane's brother who could not even stay dead.

'What does she mean by that? What's going on, John?' Cindy is tugging at John's arm as if trying to rouse him out of a trance. Her eyes never leave George's body. They flit from it to the bicycle and back again, as if she cannot make up her mind which is more important.

'You mean you have not guessed our secret yet, Cindy?' Jane taunts scathingly, her pent-up hatred and jealousy of this girl rising to the surface once again. 'I really did hit rock bottom when I chose you to be our psychic. What a joke that was.'

Ignoring Jane as if she does not exist, as if she were invisible once more, Cindy spins John around and forcefully grabs hold of his blood-crusted chin, making him face her.

'John. If you don't tell me what Jane means right now,

then I'm going to go straight to the police, and I'll tell them everything.'

'She means that Jane and I are not married,' John says, finally snapping out of his stupor. 'Never have been. We are, in fact—'

Jane finishes her husband's sentence for him. 'Brother and sister.'

75

CINDY

The night is still and warm. The air hums with the sound of insects stirred up by the rain, and the scent of roses and wisteria cling to my clothes. The storm has raged and gone, like a passing tantrum. The puddles, glistening under the moonlight, are already drying up. "God's tears" my dad used to call them.

A bird's nest dislodged by the rain lies a few feet away from where we're standing. There are three broken eggs inside it. The mother will never know what happened to her babies. The thought makes me want to sob as if I care about the bird. But I don't. I doubt I'll care for anything or anyone ever again now that Grace has gone. *Grace has gone*. Lucy Benedict and her daughter have gone. Only the bad people, me, Jane, and John, remain.

Out of the three of us, I suspect Jane cares more than anybody else. It's a revelation that takes me by surprise, as I thought I was the only good one among us. But I was wrong. I let my daughter die. Jane is still desperately struggling to keep hold of hers. She's a better woman than I.

But she cares only about three things: John. Lucy. And God.

The words that the Valentines spoke shot through me like an electric shock. I felt my body stiffen then, and it remains like that now. Tense and on edge. Face darkened by shadow, the whites of Jane's eyes are fixed on me, waiting for a reaction. A light behind her, coming from the open door, gives her hair an ethereal glow.

Yet the glossy shine I usually associate with her has gone. Her mouth twitches, forming silent words, and a fresh wave of hatred slices through me. But a niggling fear keeps at me, which means I dare not take my eyes off the gates, in case I need to escape. Perhaps I shouldn't have warned them of my intention to go to the police. Lying about their relationship is one thing, but murder is quite another. I could end up in the lake myself if I'm not careful. One glimpse at John's caved-in face convinces me that he won't protect me this time. But there's more they need to know…more that I need to know first, in case I'm right.

'So, you're a Valentine too.' Keeping my voice neutral, I address John, the less dangerous of the two, in my opinion, who, looking sheepish, chews at the corner of his mouth.

'The youngest,' he admits as if we're being introduced for the first time. I half expect him to offer me his hand to shake. *What a wanker.*

'George said that Lucy was a child born out of the greatest of sin.' Jane interrupts, clearly wanting the attention back on herself. Her eyes fill with indignant tears, but her posture remains arrogant and proud. 'He called us an abomination and demanded that we repent by giving her up, as if we had not done that already.'

An abomination. The word my mother used to describe me. But Jane and I aren't the same, and I refuse to feel sorry for her. Not after what she's done.

'But she wasn't born out of that kind of sin, was she, Jane? It was another kind of sin that brought Lucy into this world. A crime,' I point out, thinking of Lucy Benedict's imprisonment, the illegal adoption, and her subsequent death.

Jane flinches at my words, and her eyes widen with fear. Her fingers, bony and white and without any sign of a wedding ring, are crusted with blood. 'George didn't know that Lucy wasn't ours,' she concedes. 'Nobody did until you came along. Least of all me.'

Again, I won't be moved to sympathy for her. 'All this time I've been looking for Lucy, you've been lying to me. Withholding vital information.' I spit out my words, observing John exchanging shifty glances with Jane as if seeking permission to speak. She obviously doesn't give it, because he remains silent.

Face all cloudy, Jane folds her arms and juts out her chin. Her defiance is impressive. But I'm seething with rage, and this gives me the courage I need to stand up to her. How bloody dare they keep all this from me? Why would they jeopardise their chances of finding Lucy? Anybody would think they didn't want their daughter found. All along they've been difficult and secretive, but I would never have suspected them of this.

They played me right from the start. Not only did they pretend that Grace was alive so that I would agree to help them, but they lied about everything else. What an idiot I've been. I was completely taken in by them. Even when I began to have my doubts, I continued to believe them though their story never quite added up.

They were damaged, broken people grieving for their lost child, and I knew all about how that felt, didn't I? My grief and subsequent denial allowed me to be deceived by them.

But not anymore.

Jane has thrown her arm around John's shoulders and looks like she's about to lead him away. She glowers triumphantly at me as if she's won some sort of battle. John, on the other hand, is behaving exactly as I would expect him to. He's withdrawn into himself. Under Jane's wing, he's more of a helpless boy than ever. I sense that he's given up. Jane can pick fault with Hugh Hunter all she likes, but he wouldn't have folded like this.

I'm unsure of what to say to Jane. There's no telling what she might do. Clearly, she's capable of murder. This I've witnessed for myself. Her own brother! Stabbed multiple times, judging by the wounds on his body. But where has George been all these years, and did he really come back to expose them for being brother and sister? If so, why now? How long had he known about Lucy? And why did everyone think he was dead? Unless that's what he wanted people to believe. If I were related to the Valentines, I wouldn't want people to know either.

As for John and Jane being brother and sister. I can hardly believe it. Her being so religious and everything. Yet they do look alike. I noticed this from the beginning but didn't think too much of it. People are often attracted to each other because of family similarities. Aren't girls meant to favour men who remind them of their fathers? Isn't that how it goes?

I exchange wary glances with Jane, trying to sum her up, but she's more interested in patting John on the shoulder and whispering assurances in his ear.

'Jane. You can't walk away from this. Not this time. Even you can't hush something like this up,' I tell her, convinced that she's about to take John into the drawing room for a nice cup of tea for the shock. 'You don't realise what you've done.'

'I believe I am fully aware,' Jane says dismissively, pointing vaguely in the direction of her brother's body. 'You must do what you need to do, Cindy. As I had to. He was never quite right in the head, you see. He was like one of Monty's puppies. He had to be put down. That's what Mama would have done, isn't it, John?' Jane glances fondly at her brother as if she's expecting a response, but he offers none.

Mad and deluded. And now walking in the direction of the house. But we're not finished here yet.

'What if he did know?' I wonder out loud, summoning the nerve to finally confirm what I dread. 'About Lucy. That she wasn't yours. Would it have made a difference?'

'What? Made a difference to what?' A sensor light hidden behind the wisteria lights up Jane's face as she pauses to look back at me, making her appear ghostlike. Her face is grave and drained of colour. A puppet beside her, John remains immobile and silent, like the doll from Lucy's doll's house before Jane ripped its head off.

Ignoring her, I go over to the body and, careful not to let the ends of my hair dangle in what's left of it, lean over it. I can see the family resemblance. It's there in the aristo-cratic nose and prominent cheekbones. It really is George. John and Jane's eldest brother.

For a second, I imagine he moves, and fear grips hold of me. What if he isn't dead? The sharp kitchen knife that Jane used, the kind you use to chop up vegetables, has been left beside the body. Jane's sticky fingerprints must be crawling all over it. What if he's still alive and makes a grab for it? Should I check for a pulse?

But no. He's dead. His eyes are a creamy white, and his pupils are dilated. The stubbly jaw, slack and open, exposing rotten teeth is a sure-fire giveaway. The way he's sprawled out on the steps with one hand tucked behind his back and the other raised above his head suggests that he tried to minimise the impact of his fall while defending himself from Jane's frenzied attack.

Reaching for his free arm, I flip it over, gasping when I see the extent of his injuries. Puncture wounds are dotted along the sleeve of his shirt like extra buttons. The forearm has many cuts in it, as does his neck and chest. Jane wasn't messing around. She aimed for the lungs and heart. If this didn't terrify me quite so much, I'd be impressed by the sheer ruthlessness of her.

All that pales into insignificance when I uncurl his blood-splattered hand, revealing what I hoped not to see. Gnarled grey flesh. Dirty fingernails. Sparse black hair sprouting from white knuckles. Scanning down his body, I spot the trouser leg tucked into a metal clip shaped like an angel's wing.

Jane and John creep closer, dread etched onto their matching faces.

'What is it, Cindy? What do you see?' Jane insists on knowing. Her hands are curled into fists, which John has hold of. As before, nothing this couple does surprises me.

One minute they hate each other, and the next…but never mind that now.

Nodding at Jane, I do what I've come here to do. I grasp the dead man's hand in my own, and I reach out. A throbbing behind my right temple is all it takes. Within seconds, I'm gone from Moon Hollow – and I'm on the other side of its gates, looking in.

76

JANE

When Cindy vomits up green bile alongside George's body, Jane realises she has been holding her breath for too long and is almost ready to pass out through lack of oxygen. Beside her, John seems as frozen with fear as she is. Her clenched hands are crushed inside his, but she doesn't feel any pain. Her mind is as numb as her body.

They could not have been watching Cindy tremble and cry out for more than a few minutes, but the wait to get her back again felt endless. As soon as Jane realised Cindy was about to have one of her visions, her stomach hit the floor, where it remains still. Her eyes never moved from Cindy when she went to inspect the body, watching her pay special attention to George's once artistic hands.

When Cindy took hold of his hand, she was thrown backward as if she had received an electric shock. For a minute, Jane thought Cindy was having a heart attack. But now she is back, thank God.

Jane's mouth won't open. She cannot talk. *What is it, Cindy? What do you see?* It certainly appears as if she has seen something, but the girl's furrowed brow suggests that an inner battle is going on inside her head.

When Cindy finally turns to face them, Jane reels from that all-knowing stare, which screams of defiance, pity, acceptance, and revenge. *Oh my God.* She imagines what the girl is thinking: *You've got yours coming. After what you did, this is so deserved.*

'Tell us, Cindy,' John implores. 'No matter how bad it is, tell us.'

'He had her. He took her.' Cindy speaks in the same muted, almost disinterested tone she uses whenever she comes out of one of her visions. Jane does not know if Cindy is aware that she does this, but it hardly matters now.

'Who took her? Who?' Jane glares at John until she sees in his eyes that they are thinking the same thing. 'She means Lucy. She's talking about our daughter, John.'

'Oh God.' John groans, agitatedly running a hand through his hair.

'George took Lucy to punish you,' Cindy tells them in her normal voice, which is now weighted with bitterness. Blood drips from the girl's nostrils onto her clothes, but she doesn't attempt to wipe it away. Perhaps she is not even aware it is there.

'What? That's not possible,' Jane protests, but when she turns back to John, seeking reassurance, she can see that he does believe it.

'That's why he took her. He was going to return her if you promised to give her up for good. Have her adopted or put in care or something, anywhere away from you. But he never got the chance to explain. You never let him, Jane,' Cindy accuses.

Jane shakes her head. 'No,' she whispers as it occurs to her that, if Cindy is right, Jane is to blame for this. She has brought this on herself. 'No,' she wails, pulling wildly at her hair as if that will bring Lucy back. As if anything will. 'No.'

'What have you done, Jane? What have you done?' John demands.

The blow he aims across the back of Jane's head sends her reeling. The sound of knuckles against bone cuts through the air, reverberating around them. Reeling from shock, Jane fights off the swell of dizziness that threatens to bring her to her knees, then offers her face up for more of the same. It is not as if she doesn't deserve it.

A fine spray of blood fountains from her mouth when John hits her again, this time in the face. But he is tiring; that one felt more like a slap than a punch. Jane should be grateful for small mercies, but she is not. Who makes up such ridiculous sayings? That is what she would like to know.

'How could you? How could you?' John repeats on autopilot, fussing with his hair like he does whenever he is distressed. Jane has no words. She is in denial. As Cindy was over her daughter, who died. Jane felt no pity for the girl when she found out about that and feels none for herself now. She is not a hypocrite. Jane is aware that she is not a kind woman. The Valentines are not nice people. For Lucy's sake, they pretended. But without her, John and Jane will go back to being bad.

'You have ruined any chance of getting Lucy back.' John is ruthless when he is on the attack. It does not happen often, but Jane cannot help thinking that this is as good a time as any. Laughter continues to bubble away inside her. If she is not careful, it will erupt.

'Now we will never know where he was hiding her,' John states coldly.

Then, as if they are one person, they turn to stare at Cindy, looking to her for the answer. But she is shaking her head and crying uncontrollably. It is not the sign Jane hoped for. The girl is on the retreat, walking backwards and not looking where she is going. As if she cannot face them with whatever dreadful news she is keeping from them.

'What?' they say as one.

'Please, Cindy,' John begs. 'I know we were wrong to pretend that Grace was alive, but at least it gave you some hope. Can't you do the same for me now?'

Jane notices that John uses the term *me* and not *us*, which means he has already cut her out of his life. Once a rat, always a rat. This is hardly surprising. He has done so many times before, but she will win him around again. She always does.

What does intrigue her is that Cindy must finally have woken up to the fact that her precious daughter is dead. Briefly, Jane wonders when and how that happened. She is only sorry she did not get to see the look on Cindy's face when it did. So much for being psychic, Jane thinks again, aware of how cruel she is being but not caring.

'I want my daughter back, Cindy. As I am sure you do yours.' Jane plays on this connection, hoping it will do the trick, but Cindy is no fool. She recoils at the idea.

'But she wasn't your daughter, was she?' The hatred Cindy levels Jane's way is justified. She will not hold it against the girl. But what does bring Jane to her knees, fearing the worst, is the fact that Cindy is using the past tense where her daughter is concerned. *But she wasn't your daughter, was she?*

'She has gone, hasn't she? She's not coming back.' Jane sobs, clutching at her heart and wanting to curl up and die. But Cindy is not looking at her. She is shaking her head at John, confirming what they have been dreading all along – that their daughter has indeed gone. Cindy must have seen this in her vision when she grabbed hold of George's hand.

Cindy's gaze softens when her eyes land on John as if she believes he is the only one capable of feeling grief.

'But if George came here to expose us, to get us to give Lucy up, why would he hurt her?' John's desperation makes Jane want to turn on him and snipe while he's vulnerable. But at least they agree for once. She also wants to know why George would blackmail them if he meant to kill the child. After all, he intended to punish them, not Lucy. What Cindy is saying does not make any sense.

'He didn't mean to, but he forgot about her for too long, and then it was too late.'

Oh God. Oh God. Their daughter is dead. Jane watches John stagger backwards, hands outstretched and grasping at nothing, but she does not go to him. Unable to move, she wishes she were lying in a grave next to her daughter. Earth covering their faces. Rose petals fluttering down on them. The sky growing ever distant. Blackness is not her colour. It does not suit Jane's paleness. But that is all she wishes for now.

After today, she and John will remain in mourning for the rest of their miserable lives, if she decides that living is a more suitable punishment than death. The curtains of Moon Hollow will be pulled closed. The doors never unbolted again. The striped lawns will grow long and wild. The geese will die, one by one, until they are no more. The church will decompose like a rotting body.

The Valentines will live in silence, roaming the hallways and landings like ghosts, never speaking. John is dumbstruck even now. He will not ask how Lucy died. He will already have guessed, as Jane has done, that their daughter starved to death, alone and uncared for in whatever black hole George was keeping her in. Their eldest brother was not capable of caring for a child.

He was bad. Not right in the head. Like them.

It occurs to Jane that although George might not have intended to kill Lucy, in doing so, however inadvertently, he has finally taken his revenge on them. He got his wish in the end. His not knowing is the only comfort Jane can take from that fact.

When Jane next hears Cindy speaking, her mind clears momentarily, allowing the outside world to creep back in like a poisonous fog that destroys everyone in its path.

'Your name was on Lucy's lips, John. Her last thoughts were of you.' Cindy gently breaks the news to John as if he were a friend, but when her eyes land on Jane, her tone is harsh. 'The day she went missing, she saw something. Heard something.' Cindy pauses as if trying to remember what it was.

Jane is as confused as Cindy appears to be. It is hard to be certain of anything when all she can think about are the girl's words: *Her last thoughts were of you.* Why John?

Why not Jane? She has been the one doing all the praying. To a god who never listened. But Jane must stop this. Now is not the time to examine her relationship with Christ. Cindy is about to say something else. Perhaps, out of kindness, she will mention a fond memory Lucy might have had about Jane before she—

'It was you, Jane. You were calling for her, but Lucy was too far away to respond. She wanted to. Oh yes, she wanted to. But you'd told her off that morning and slapped her. You slapped her hard, didn't you, Jane? But you never told John about this.'

'That is not true. That's an outrageous lie. Don't listen to her, John.' Jane bristles with indignation. Locking eyes with John, she is desperate for him to be on her side, but when he sneers down at her in disbelief, she clasps bloodied hands to her face. She wants to run. Hide. Bury her head in a pillow. Suffocate herself. Pull out her hair. Gouge out her eyes. Shut out Cindy's hateful words. Bile stings the back of her throat. She is slowly dying.

'She'd been spying on you and John in the church, and you found out,' Cindy continues relentlessly, singling out Jane again. 'It was dark inside, but she could see that you were both naked. Doing things you shouldn't be doing. Strange things that frightened her, causing her to run away and hide in the treehouse.' Cindy's voice fades to an echo.

Armed only with snatches of stolen light, Jane dares a glance at John, whose face is partially hidden by shadow, and wishes she had not. All she can see is hatred in his eyes. Any love he had for her has been sucked out of him. There is nothing left. No comfort to be had. He is already dead. To her, at least. Finally, he has done what she has always feared. He has left her. Lover and child gone in one sentence. And still, Cindy is attacking them. *Her.*

'He promised her he would let her go if she was a good girl and didn't cry, but, like you, Jane, and like you, John, he lied.'

77

CINDY

C onsumed with grief, they allow me to walk away, towards the gates of Moon Hollow. Finally, I'm safe from Jane but not from myself. No wonder I went mad for a time. How long can a person keep going around in circles of fear and heartache?

All along it was me blocking myself from finding Lucy. Not Grace, obviously, nor Lucy Benedict, and not John or Jane either. Just me. Finding Lucy would've meant the end of my time at Moon Hollow, and all I'd have been left with then is the knowledge of what I've been denying all these weeks. The fact that Grace is gone and she's never coming back. Just like Lucy Benedict.

There was no court order. No refusal on my mum's part to take me and my daughter in. Just me. Who is as good as dead to her now too.

When Jane came to see me that first time, she knew she was asking me to do the impossible: search for her daughter, knowing I had lost my own. But when I informed her that Grace wasn't dead but had been placed in care – how could I allow a woman like Jane, who'd looked down at me from the very start, believe I was responsible for killing my own child – I don't know who was more surprised, her or me.

Jane, being Jane, latched onto the idea straightaway. She was, after all, as desperate as I was. How she convinced John to go along with it, I'll never know. But anything is possible, I suppose. Who'd have thought I was capable of using Jane as much as she was using me?

My denial, in the end, cost more than time lost looking for Lucy. It cost human life, which makes what I've done doubly hard to stomach. In my defence, I didn't realise how delusional I'd become.

But Jane did. It was obvious she disliked me from the start, hated me, even. She's unlike anybody I've ever met before, and I lived in fear of her in that house. But now it's over. The Valentines are as broken as they should be and are still arguing, even now, as I stumble along in the dark. Finding my own way is something I'll have to get used to from now on. Now that I don't have Grace.

Gravel crunches underfoot, and I know I'll never forget the sound it makes. Like old bones that have been ground down over the years. I try to block out the Valentines' raised voices, but I can't. Bad habits are hard to break. A glance over my shoulder confirms what I already know. Neither of them is looking in my direction. I'm of no consequence to them now.

John is yelling. 'I will never forgive you for this, Jane!'

Even in the dark, I can picture his grotesque expression. Lips snarling, spit flying, he'll be hell-bent on making this all Jane's fault. He's a weak man. I can't believe I once thought him attractive. I think I might've even admired him at one stage, but the thought of him now makes my skin crawl. Jane was mental to think I would've looked twice at her husband.

'She is lying, John. I know she is.' Jane sounds desperate. And so she should be. 'I can feel Lucy in here. She's not dead,' she insists.

I imagine Jane clutching at her heart as she says this and find myself amused, though I have no right to be.

'And I never hit Lucy. Not once. Cindy lied about that too. I swear.' Jane can swear it all she likes, but one thing I know about liars is that they always get found out in the end, and then everybody stops believing them even when they're telling the truth. As Jane is now, admittedly, but John will never know I made that bit up.

'Shut up, Jane!' John roars, slapping her again. He can lash out at his wife and kill her for all I care. They deserve each other and nothing more. Not Lucy, that's for sure.

But Jane is right about another thing.

I lied when I told them their daughter is dead.

I wouldn't have imagined I'm capable of such dishonesty, but after what they've done, all the lies they've told and the lives they've ruined, this is the least I can do for Lucy. How could I let that poor child return to those monsters? Lucy Benedict's death might have been a tragic accident, but Jane killed her own brother. Not in self-defence either.

When I touched George's hand, everything about him, including Lucy's secret hiding place, was revealed to me. The dead man showed me everything I needed to know. Ironically, his body also took me back to the time he thought he was dying, alone and impoverished in France after his family had disowned him. Afterwards, he vowed revenge on the Valentines.

As a boy, he had witnessed John and Jane doing things that a brother and sister shouldn't do and told tales on them. His parents either didn't believe their troublesome son or didn't care, choosing instead to look the other way. But in a village the size of Hollow Fen, the rumours had spread like wildfire. When Jane got wind of this, she plotted revenge against her brother, who dared to speak of the terrible sin she and John were committing.

Jane wanted both God and John in her life and refused to be blackmailed. She couldn't have been happier when George got sent away and was later reported as having died. But as puny and sickly as he was, George had survived. And had gone on surviving. When he eventually received the news that he had an inoperable brain tumour, however, and had only months left to live, he decided to return to the family home and make John and Jane repent.

It became his dying wish to see them separate. When he learned that they had a child, the magnitude of their sin consumed him, and he began twisting every word ever printed in the Bible to suit his own desires.

I'm on my way to Lucy's hiding place now. It was one of the first places the police searched. But George was crafty and moved the little girl many times so as not to be detected. Always at night and always on the handlebars of his bike, tucked up out of sight under his coat. Among other places, Lucy has been kept in the church bell tower and an underground icehouse. The kind that was popular for big houses in the last century.

Since the police vacated Moon Hollow, he'd grown braver and eventually brought her here, right under our noses, so he could keep an eye on us. The bastard. I swear, if he's hurt a hair on that little girl's head, I'll set fire to his body myself. All I can hope for him is that he's on his way to hell by now. *Once a Sunday schoolgirl, always a Sunday schoolgirl.* I might have disowned God, but it would appear He hasn't abandoned me. I often find myself calling on Him or quoting from the Bible. Like my mother.

Like Jane. Like George. I shudder at the thought of them.

And here I am. Staring up at the old gatehouse that has always bothered me. Much like the lake. How couldn't I have known that Lucy was here? It seems obvious to me now. Whenever I passed the derelict building, it felt as if I was being watched. In there somewhere is the same hiding place I visited in my vision, where Lucy was being kept under the floorboards. A dingy, dark, squalid place that wasn't fit for a dog.

In the daytime, the main house is visible from here. It would kill the Valentines to know that Lucy has been so close all this time. When I first agreed to come to Moon Hollow to look for the little girl, I reluctantly struck a deal with Jane. I would give them Grace while I looked for Lucy. In a roundabout way that's exactly what I've done. I have left the memory of my daughter at Moon Hollow, and I've found Lucy.

Soon the little girl will accept that John and Jane are dead and that I'm going to be her new mother from now on. She's better off with me, I think. You might think me cruel for telling the Valentines that their daughter is dead, but it's Lucy I feel sorry for, and Grace too, of course. That goes without saying.

The Valentines left Lucy Benedict's body in the lake,

and just like that, with a snap of Jane's upper-class fingers, they thought she was gone. As if she didn't matter. But they were wrong. They sent me to look for one Lucy, their Lucy, and instead I found another. That's the one thing they hadn't banked on.

78

The cemetery reminds me too much of Moon Hollow's churchyard, but this is where my daughter Grace is buried, so I come anyway. Admittedly, not every week. In truth, I don't venture out much at all. Things are difficult right now. And they're only going to get worse.

I've been ill recently, and some days I can barely drag myself out of bed. The sickness I keep experiencing is, I'm sure, a result of grief and guilt. It can rear up from nowhere at any time, leaving me scared to leave the flat. I'm poorer than I've ever been, surviving rather than thriving, and this means the future is uncertain in so many ways. As life and death are.

Sometimes, I imagine I can see Lucy Benedict flitting in and out of the gravestones. But if she does, I sense that she's at peace now. I kept my promise. I found her daughter as she asked me to, and I have her with me still. Only, she calls *me* Mummy now.

I'm reminded of the magpie in the cage. Hugh's magpie. He once told me that they're notorious for preying on other birds' nests and taking young that do not belong to them. That's exactly what the Valentines did with Lucy, and I could argue that this is what I'm doing now. But what I'm doing is different, isn't it?

My mother still refuses to have anything to do with me, but that suits me. I rarely see my father either. He knows that I've moved away, but I won't tell him where. As I said, things are difficult. I've been back only once to Hollow Fen. To see Hugh. He was distant, on edge, not his usual self, but that was understandable, as I'd caught him out in a lie.

Not once had he mentioned being there on the night Lucy Benedict died, and I couldn't forgive him for that. We both knew it was over between us, before anything even had a chance to start, but I was surprised to discover that he intended to stay in the cottage. Jane, or, more likely, John, had a change of heart and was allowing it. I'll never know what they did with George's body. I didn't go to the police as I'd threatened to. How could I? That would have meant giving Lucy up, and after all she'd been through, I wasn't prepared to do that. I suspect that Hugh helped them cover everything up as he did with Lucy Benedict.

I only went back to warn him about Tess. I thought he deserved to know. But he was adamant about staying on although I warned him it wasn't safe, that Tess was watching him all the time. Even as I spoke, I could see her shadow in an upstairs window, her eyes burning into mine. Hugh didn't seem surprised nor taken aback by what I was suggesting. He knew. Said he'd got used to it over the years. This made me wonder if his marriage to his wife was alive after all. Even if she was not.

I still have the same nightmares about Grace. Every night. Waking in a sweat, confused, and terrified every single time. I still can't remember her funeral. The day had passed by in a blur, leaving me with snatches of black clothes and grim faces. The scent of flowers. Shuffling of feet on a church floor. People crying. Making small talk. The uncomfortable kind that's meant to lessen the awkwardness of the situation but doesn't.

I'm told that the sun was shining that day, and I vaguely remember pretending that I was attending someone else's funeral, not my own child's, and that helped a little. And then it helped a lot. The more I pretended, the easier it got. If Grace were still alive, then how could I be responsible for her death?

Grace Martin. Much-loved daughter and granddaughter. Taken away too soon. Aged eight. Nowhere on the white marble headstone shaped in a heart does it mention she was killed by her own mother. I'm coming to terms with the past and my part in it, but Grace was not a child to forgive easily, and this makes it harder. An unwanted memory of another gravestone tugs at my conscience. Gorgeous Georgie, wife, mother, and lover. Moon Hollow and the Valentines will remain a part of my life whether I like it or not. As Lucy Benedict and little Lucy are. As my daughter is.

Sometimes I talk out loud to Grace, and when I do Lucy throws me curious looks. I'm not sure how much she knows, but she's only a child, and I protect her from the truth where I can. I'll never reveal to her what an evil woman Jane Valentine was. Lucy only remembers being happy with them. John called her Lulu for short, which she liked, but she won't let me do the same. She's here now, playing with an imaginary tea set and passing invisible cups to dead-eyed, made-up dolls. This is something she likes to do.

I've washed the bird shit off Grace's headstone with bleach and a wet cloth and put buttery yellow daffodils in a stone vase. She was too young to have a favourite flower, but I like them, so I'm sure Grace would have too. Whenever I come here, I'm scared I might run into my dad. I know he comes here sometimes to say hello to Grace. I miss him more than words can say, but if I'm to have a new life with Lucy, then I must cut him out of it. He doesn't understand. And this makes me sad. But I have no choice.

'How did you know it was me in the car that night?' I ask my daughter, as I do on every visit.

'Silly Mummy.' Grace giggles, offering up the same reply each time. 'When I woke up in the dark, all alone, and found you were gone, I was scared at first, but then something told me you were on your way home, so I got out of bed and went to meet you. When I saw the car coming down the road, I knew you were inside.'

'But how did you know, Grace?'

'I could see you. I've always been able to see you, Mummy. No matter where you are. I don't know why. I just can. That's all. I asked Granny once if she was the same, but she said I was bad and shouldn't let on to you or Grandpa, so I didn't.' Grace is matter-of-fact about all of this as if she's told me this story a hundred times. And perhaps she has.

The last memory I have of my daughter is of her standing in the middle of the road, mouth stretched wide in a frozen cry as she realised too late that the car was not going to stop. The driver couldn't see her. He was too busy gawping at the drunken woman in the back of his cab with her knickers on show. Me. This last image I have of her is like a torn-up photograph that won't burn no matter how hard I try.

Feeling my eyes prickle with tears, I wipe them away with my sleeve, then get to my feet. It's time to go. I don't like being out in the open too long, certainly not in broad daylight. Lucy's hair is starting to grow again, and I'm thinking of dying it blond to match my own, in case people recognise her from the picture that was once on the front page of every newspaper, but so far she's resisted all my attempts to do so.

Her stubbornness reminds me of Jane. Lucy isn't at all like my Grace. She's a serious child and remains wary of me. Even now. She rarely lets me touch her, except to comb her hair. I can't know if this is how she's always been. We'll never get to know each other's complete pasts.

'Grace. It's time to go,' I call softly, panicking when I can't see her. But it's all right because there she is, coming out from behind one of the old gravestones where she's been hiding. She's a bugger for that. Worries me half to death, she does. Since she last tried to run away, I don't let her out of my sight if I can help it.

Sulkily, she ambles over, not hopping or skipping as Grace would have done. She's a clever girl, though, much smarter than my own daughter, and because of this, she understands why we must pretend that her name is Grace and that I'm her real mother. She knows there will be consequences if she doesn't obey me. For that I praise her. And she thanks me as if I were a stranger.

She looks so much like her real parents that I sometimes have to catch my breath. The unruly hair is all Hugh's, but the brown eyes are Lucy Benedict's. Lucy will never be pretty like her mother, but she makes up for it in spirit. I'm not left to wonder where her sense of superiority comes from.

She spent almost eight years with the Valentines, and some of their snobbery is bound to have rubbed off. I sense it now in the way Lucy is looking down on me as I rummage in my worn bag for the sweets I promised her if she was a good girl. But when I pass them to her, our hands accidentally clash, and I'm catapulted straight back to Moon Hollow and the lake.

Something is wrong. Hugh and Lucy Benedict are in the water. But he's not trying to save her. He's forcing her head down. Holding her under the inky black water. Struggling against him, her hands come out of the water to claw at him, but she can't breathe. There's no air.

'You bitch,' he hisses. 'You told Tess about the baby. You stupid cow, did you really think that would make a difference? That I would leave my wife and child for you.'

I watch him let her up for air, and she comes up gasping and choking, unable to get any words out. I think it's all over. That he was intent on punishing her, not killing her. But I'm wrong. He wants only to stare into her terrified eyes to remind her of one thing. 'You killed them. You.' And then he's holding her under again and shouting something back to John about not being able to find her.

All the while, Lucy Benedict struggles, arms flailing. Bubbles rise to the surface until they don't, and then I know she's gone. Only then does he let her go, and I see her long black hair floating on the surface of the water, drifting away from him.

I can't stop my tears from falling, not caring if Lucy sees. I allow them to run down my cheeks unchecked and into my unzipped bag. I've been a fool. An utter idiot. Lucy Benedict's death was no accident. Hugh was the killer all along. How could I have not known this? What's the point of being psychic when I can't see anything that matters?

He played me too, as the Valentines did. I let him in as he wanted me to, knowing that the closer I got to him, the less likely I was to see anything about him. He never felt anything for me. It was all pretence. Everything comes down to that in the end.

As much as I'd like to see Hugh punished for what he did to Lucy Benedict, I can't go to the police. They would take Lucy away, and I've already lost one daughter. I dread to think what Hugh would do if he found out I knew his secret or that I have his daughter. Any thoughts I had of one day coming out of hiding are destroyed. Hugh would hunt me down and kill me, given the chance. And if the Valentines ever find out Lucy is alive, there's no telling what they'd do. They would all come looking for Lucy then.

When my stomach suddenly clenches, I find myself vomiting down my daughter's headstone, leaving behind a trail of stinking brown-and-grey gravy that is far worse than the bird shit. I kid myself that this has nothing at all to do with the half bottle of gin I secretly consumed last night. I think I've mentioned before that all a girl really needs is oblivion.

LUCY

My name is Lucy Valentine, and I have been missing for 331 days. I can dress myself and count backward, and I will be nine on my next birthday. I know all the days of the week, and I can tell the time, although I sometimes wish I couldn't, because every day is the same. At first, I liked it here. But things have changed since my new mother had the baby.

Most days she forgets my name and calls me Grace. I do not mind that so much, as it is a pretty name. But since Heidi came along, my new mother is too busy to home-school me or take me to the park. Although I have not been given any sweets in ages, she says I am lucky to have her as a mummy because she has kept her promise to somebody called Lucy Benedict, who I do not know. I know now that all mummies are wrong. I am not lucky at all.

Heidi's hair and eyes are brown, like mine. We look like sisters, and I wish we were, but we can't be, can we? My new mother warns me against mentioning this. She will be cross with me if I do, and that makes me sad. Most days she is nice. Except on Saturdays, when she drinks. When this happens, I take Heidi into the bedroom and cuddle her in the bed that all three of us share. Sometimes the way my new mother looks at Heidi as if she has done something wrong scares me. Even I know babies are never bad.

I hardly remember my old mummy and daddy now or Moon Hollow. I am told that my parents are dead and that this is my forever home now, but it is just a small flat on the third floor of an ugly building. There is no garden to play in and no treehouse either. Under no circumstances am I to have a doll's house of any kind, but I am being allowed to grow my hair long again. It hurts when my new mother takes a comb to it, but it reminds me of home. This is when she likes to call me Grace.

The man who took me told me he was my uncle and that I was a child born out of the greatest sin who deserved to be punished. He looked so much like my daddy that I believed him. My new mother tells me that my mummy and daddy were not my real mummy and daddy at all and did not deserve me. That is why I must live with her. Although I do not say so, I do not believe that any adult is to be trusted. They tell lies all the time.

Heidi is my best and only friend, but I am not allowed to pick her up when she cries, except on Saturdays.

My name is Lucy Valentine, and I have been missing for 331 days. I can dress myself, and I am nine on my next birthday. I would very much like to go home now.

Wherever home is.

ACKNOWLEDGEMENTS

I've worked with some of the nicest, kindest and most professional people during the publishing process of writing of this book. Editor Colleen Wagner was an absolute pleasure to work with. She was just what I needed during a very trying and exhausting period. Huge thanks also to fellow authors Ross Greenwood (author of the DI Barton series) and Shani Struthers (queen of Gothic) for beta reading during the book's early stages. They provided me with the kind of constructive and intuitive feedback that money can't buy.

As for that fabulous book cover, I have Elena Karoumpali of L1 Graphics to thank for this. She captured the heart of everything I wanted it to be in an instant. Finally, it wouldn't feel right not to mention my wonderful all-action-hero hubby, Darren. As ever, I couldn't have done it without you.

When Madeleine McCann went missing in 2007, one week before her fourth birthday, the plight of her parents,

Kate and Jerry, resonated deeply with me. I have always believed that Kate and Jerry McCann were innocent of all the ugly charges that were thrown at them and desperately hoped that their little girl would be returned to them. Sadly, this has not yet happened. But, like them, I have never given up hope that Maddie will one day walk back through their door.

This is not Maddie's story, but I have always known that I would one day write a book about a missing child. As this is an extremely popular genre, though, I knew that I would have to make it unique enough to stand out—hence Cindy, the reluctant, foul-mouthed, boozy psychic, who is also missing a child. Cindy is a character who has lived in my head (and heart) for fifteen years, and I couldn't wait to introduce her to my readers. I had lots of fun writing her character. But as for my namesake Jane! Even I fear her.

As many of you know, I love setting my books against atmospheric backgrounds, especially old, creepy houses. Moon Hollow (not its real name) is a house I know well, and just like in *Looking For Lucy*, it was once a castle. But that's another story…

As for setting Cindy's hometown in Stamford, Lincolnshire, England, I did this for a particularly good reason, as I moved to this area two years ago. Love it, by the way.

If you are not from the UK, then please excuse the English spelling. Oopsy daisy, it's just the way we do things across the pond. Apologies also for the swearing, but this is entirely Cindy's fault, not mine. As is the blaspheming.

Now for the best bit where I get to thank my lovely readers for all their support, especially my ARC reading group. You know who you are!

Your loyalty and friendship mean everything. As do your reviews.

ABOUT THE AUTHOR

Best-selling author Jane E James creates chilling reads that appeal to fans of psychological thrillers, mysteries and dark fiction.

Jane loves to weave tense and haunting tales that stay in the reader's mind. She is especially fond of unreliable narrators who never let truth get in the way of a good story. All Jane's books are standalone novels.

Her second novel, *The Crying Boy* (a compelling suspense thriller inspired by actual events) became an overnight best seller on Amazon, knocking both Stephen King and Dean Koontz off the top suspense spot. Her third novel, *The Butcher's Daughter*, is a tense and haunting psychological thriller; also available in audible.

Jane enjoys living 'the good life' in the countryside in a small village near the olde world town of Stamford, Lincolnshire in the UK and when she isn't out walking in the fields and woods near her home she can be found with her head in a book or writing at her desk.

Look out for Jane's next novel, *Not My Child* - due to be released in 2022. It's one you won't want to miss.

Learn more at www.JaneEJames.com

ALSO BY JANE E JAMES

The Butcher's Daughter

The Crying Boy

The Long Weekend